Brothers in Gray

Book II
of
The Alternative History
Trilogy

by

11-25-86

R.W. RICHARDS

~

~ Publisher's Note ~

This book is a work of historical fiction. Names of characters, places, and incidents are either the product of the author's imagination or are used fictitiously, and any resemblance to actual persons, living or dead, events, or locales is entirely coincidental.

Also by R.W. Richards: *A Southern Yarn* The first novel of The Alternative History Trilogy.

ISBN# 0-9625502-0-5
LC# 89-092811

Library of Congress Cataloging - in - Publication Data

Richards, Ronald, 1947
Brothers in Gray, by Ronald W. Richards

ISBN 0-9625502-1-3

Brothers in Gray is published in the United States by ROKARN PUBLICATIONS, P.O. Box 195, Nokesville, Virginia, 22123.

First Printing, October, 1993
Printed in the United States of America

The Spring of 1862 was a dark moment in the history of the Confederate States of America. The Civil War had been raging for less than a year and already vast stretches of the Confederacy were either occuppied or cut off from the rest. General George McClellan, with a huge army of Federals, was moving steadily up the James River peninsula toward Richmond intent on administering a final coup de grace to the fledgling Confederacy. Only from the Shenandoah Valley of Virginia was there news of an optimistic nature. Here Stonewall Jackson was fast becoming a living legend taking the measure of three Union armies. Then came word from Richmond, General Joseph Johnston had been seriously wounded. The Army of Northern Virginia was without a commander. One man would answer his country's call and step forward to take the helm. His name was Robert E. Lee ...

My sincerest thanks to the following individuals who contributed so much time, energy, and talent to the production of this book:

Stuart and Winnie Bowcock who typed the original manuscript

John F. Cummings III of Southern Heritage Magazine, who painted the cover illustration

Richard Chiarizia of Silver Sky Publishing Company, who typeset the manuscript

Skydance MacMahon for the illustration of the maps, which are based on those found in Shelby Foote's *The Civil War*

Jeffry R. Bogart, the editor of RoKarn Publications

My thanks to **Randy Covington**...He'll know why.

My special thanks to **Ivory**...He'll know why as well.

The author would like to extend his gratitude once again to **Shelby Foote** whose *Civil War, A Narrative,* provided the actual history for this alternative history.

This book is dedicated to the people of the South,
both White and Black, who stood shoulder to shoulder
to defend their homes through four terrible years.

For **Shane Wesley Richards,** my fourth child
and youngest son. How you have blessed us all!

~ INDEX OF THE MAPS ~

~ Chapter One ~
1843

The afternoon sun stood high in a stunningly blue October sky. It seemed uncommonly warm that day, but the temperature came as no surprise to anyone. It was Indian Summer in the Shenandoah Valley.

Two men were working their way across a seemingly endless rolling field of gold, threshing and binding a bountiful harvest of wheat. The white man, Tom Covington, was nearing his thirty-seventh birthday. He was a big man, not especially tall mind you, just big; broad shoulders he had and sturdy big-boned legs. He had a wide face which was home to a thick sandy brown beard. Tom Covington was right fond of his beard which grew in stark contrast to the thin wispy strands of hair which barely covered his head. The black man was nearly ten years older than Covington, and he stood an inch or two taller than the man he called "Marse Tom." He'd been born a slave of the Covington family as had his father and his grandfather before him.

Both men were growing weary. Since dawn they'd been working on the harvest pausing rarely to rest. They were sweating heavily and their muscles ached with fatigue.

Moses Henry took a moment to pause from his labor. He placed the handle of his scythe against the ground and leaned against it for perhaps a minute or two. As his master worked ahead of him Henry placed his right hand into the small of his own aching back and stretched with a groan. "Marse Tom," he said in a deep clear voice, "I'm gettin' powerful tired, suh. Do you suppose we might rest a spell?"

Covington took one more swing with his own scythe and stood back to gauge what they'd already cut against the work which still awaited them. What he saw was a cause for satisfaction. The two of them had already accomplished a great deal that day. A short rest had certainly been earned. Besides, there was a matter he wished to discuss with his slave, Moses Henry. "You're right, Moses," he replied, "it's time for a break. Let's walk on up to the orchard and sit for awhile."

"Yassuh," Moses nodded with a pleased though somewhat weary smile, "those words are music to my ears."

Side by side the two men climbed the lengthy knoll atop which grew a small orchard of apple trees. When they reached the crest it became necessary to climb through a bulging formation of rocks in order to reach the shade of .he trees. Covington climbed up first then extended an arm back to help Henry through.

"These legs of mine, they must be gettin' old, Marse Tom."

"Nonsense," grinned the white man. "You're as strong as an ox! I'll bet you live another fifty years!"

"Go on, suh!" Henry chuckled aloud. "You sho' wouldn't want to be feedin' ol' Moses for that long!"

Covington returned the smile as he removed the food pouch and water bag from his shoulders. The food he let drop, intent on quenching his thirst before anything else. He uncorked the goatskin bag and took a long drink, spilling quite a bit as he pulled it away from his mouth. With the sleeve of his shirt he wiped the water from his beard as he handed the bag to Henry. The black man quickly downed three deep gulps.

"I swear, Marse Tom, that water tastes like a slice of Heaven itself!"

Covington reached down and grabbed the food pouch. "C'mon up here!" he beckoned. He led the way through the apple trees to another large rock formation which jutted out from the knoll. Once again he reached back and helped Henry to the top. Here they found enough room for both of them to sit in reasonable comfort and share an afternoon meal. Moreover, the rock afforded them a commanding view of the rolling hills on which they had spent their lives together. Many times they had shared this view together, the master and the slave, enjoying a quick meal while their eyes drank in the beauty of the Shenandoah Valley.

"Speaking of Heaven," said Covington as he fumbled through the food pouch, "I'll betcha God had his own backyard in mind when he put this valley together."

"Yessuh, I do believe that's so. It does so fill my heart with peace to look out over this farm."

Understandable. The Covington farm was situated in the heart of the valley, some fifteen miles southeast of Staunton, Virginia. Considering there were but two men to work it, it was a sizeable spread. Four hundred fifty-nine acres in all, including more than two miles of frontage on the Shenandoah River. A more peaceful place could scarcely be imagined.

Covington smiled as he examined the contents of the food pouch. There were four thick slices of ham wrapped in cloth, along with several freshly baked corn muffins, a tiny jar of honey, and two apples, which had been recently picked from the trees which shaded the two men. All of this had been prepared by his wife, Mary Ann early that morning. He removed half of each item for himself and handed the pouch to Henry.

"You and I have known each other for a long time, Moses," he said as he took a bite of ham.

"Yessuh. I reckon I been knowin' you all your life. I remember when you was born, suh. I warn't but ten years old myself! Your mother and father, they was so happy! Had themselves a son! I'll never forget your father, Marse Tom. He taught me to read. He opened up a whole new world for me."

"Did you ever read the Declaration of Independence?"

"No, suh. I don't remember that one."

"Thomas Jefferson wrote it."

"I know about Mr. Jefferson. My own father said he was a great man."

"He was one of Virginia's finest. In the Declaration of Independence he wrote that all men were created equal."

"Well, suh, I don't know about all that. I suppose in God's eyes we're all equal."

"Do you know you're the first friend I ever had?"

"Well, suh, you was always gettin' into mischief. Your folks told me to look after you."

"You did a right smart job."

"Thank you, suh. I reckon I was always kind of fond of you, but I gotta tell you, Marse Tom, you was an ugly baby!"

Covington laughed merrily. "So I've been told!" he grinned. He started to say something else but stopped, as though his thoughts weren't properly ordered and the words wouldn't come.

Henry knew there was something his master wished to talk about, something he was finding it difficult to approach. There were things he wished to say as well, but he decided to hold his tongue.

For several moments neither man spoke. Each was lost in his own thoughts as he munched pensively on his share of the meal. Covington was thinking of his wife, Mary Ann. Ten years they had been married and from the very beginning they had wanted children. For so long this was the one thing God had denied them. Two pregnancies had ended in miscarriages. A third culminated in a stillbirth. Their efforts to have a child seemed doomed to tragedy. Now she was pregnant again. Five months had passed without incident. So far so good.

Henry was also dwelling on an approaching birth. His wife of twelve years was but a month away from the delivery of their first child. Sarah Henry was a strong robust woman who radiated the happiness she experienced each time she felt the baby move within her womb.

Each man stared out at the fields of the farm on which they had both been born and raised. Each was picturing two young children scampering playfully across those fields. Were these memories of their own childhood, or visions of the future?

Just beyond the river rose the gentle, sloping peaks of the Blue Ridge Mountains alive with the colors of Autumn. Looking down from the higher elevations it would appear as though someone had laid a giant quilt of bright yellow and blazing orange across the earth. To describe this scene as breathtaking would be a definite understatement.

"Marse Tom?"

Covington shifted his gaze away from the spellbinding mountains to meet the eyes of the slave who had been his first friend.

"I don't mean to pry, suh, but is there a reason you was telling me about the Declaration of Independence?"

Covington pondered this question momentarily then decided the time had come: "there was Moses. Do you remember what we were talkin' about two weeks ago when we were deliverin' that calf?"

"Yessuh. You was tellin' me you'd been doin' a lot of thinkin' 'bout slavery."

"I reckon I've made up my mind, Moses."

"Well, suh, just what is it you're tryin' to say?"

"I've been prayin' a lot Moses. Been askin' God to show me the right way."

"Has he showed you, Marse Tom?"

"Reckon so. He's told me I shouldn't be ownin' a fellow human bein'."

For the longest time Henry could say nothing as the two men sat there staring at one another. At last he spoke. "Marse Tom, I reckon I've done a bit of thinkin' 'bout slavery myself. I've had me a whole lifetime to think about it. On balance, suh, me and Sarah don't have it too bad. You and Miss Mary have always treated us good. We've had a happy life here, not like some of them poor souls on the big plantations. But I've got to tell you, Marse Tom, no matter how good a life I've lived with you folks, my heart yearns to be free, suh. It does so yearn to be free."

"Of that I have no doubt," mused Covington. "What would you do? I mean if I do free you? Would you leave? Would you go North?"

"I don't rightly know, Marse Tom. I ain't never been in the North. Don't know that I'd like it much up there. This land here...." he paused a moment to ponder his words, "this land is my home, Marse Tom. I was born here. So was my pappy and grandpappy. It ain't that I want to leave, suh. I just want freedom... that's all. Freedom."

"I was hopin' you'd say somethin' like that, Moses."

"I'm speakin' from my heart, Marse Tom."

"So am I. I'm ridin' in to the county seat tomorrow, Moses. I may be gone a day or two. When I return I'll have manumission papers for you and Sarah. You'll have your freedom...both of you."

Tears came to the black man's eyes as the impact of

those words dawned on him. "That's music to my ears, Marse Tom, music to these old ears."

"Do you remember when the surveyors were here last week?"

"Yes, suh. I was wonderin' 'bout that. I thought maybe you was plannin' on sellin' off some land."

"Not exactly. This land has been home to both our families for much too long to part with it. Freedom comes with responsibility, Moses. You have to support yourself and your family. I want to make sure you're never destitute. You've worked this land all of your life, some of it should be yours. You see down there?" he pointed toward the northeastern corner of the farm. "They measured forty-two acres. When I return I'll have a deed from the courthouse. That forty-two acres will be yours, your own farm, my friend. I figure the two of us can help each other work our respective farms, except when you work on mine you'll be earning salary as well, not a lot mind you, we'll have to work somethin' out, probably a percentage of each year's harvest."

By this time Henry was making no effort to control the tears which flowed down his cheeks. "Marse Tom," he stammered, unable to find the right words, "I just don't know what to say, suh."

"Covington offered his right hand which Henry clasped with a warm firm grip. "Say nothin'," said the white man, "I have freed myself as well. I'll be proud to call you my neighbor and my friend."

"God bless you, Marse Tom. I pray for God to bless ya."

"I hope he will," smiled Covington, "in the meantime we've got about two hours of daylight left and an awful lot of wheat to cut. You ready to get back to it?"

"Sho' nuff, Marse Tom! The way I feel right now

I could cut another ten acres by my lonesome!"

"Careful," grinned Covington, "I may hold you to that!"

The two started down the knoll side by side, but they had taken only a few steps when Henry stopped and turned to Covington.

"Marse Tom, does this mean my child will be born free?"

"It does indeed, old friend. Your child will never know slavery."

*   *   *   *   *   *   *   *   *

By late February Tom Covington was on the edge of anguish. Mary Ann had carried the baby for nine months and should have delivered. She was overdue by nearly two weeks. There was no longer the fear of miscarriage, but every day without contractions in her womb constituted a threat to the health of both mother and child.

Winter in the Shenandoah was harsh that year, and the stoves were kept burning throughout each day in the Covington household. Sarah Henry was never far from Mary Ann's side, despite the demands her own baby boy made on her time. Levi Henry came into the world several weeks before the completion of his parents' new home on their farm just north of the Covington spread along the river. Sarah laughingly claimed he had the appetite of three babies not one.

On the twenty-fifth of the month with a good two hours before dawn Tom Covington was awakened by a sharp cry of pain from Mary Ann.

"Tom!" she shrieked, "oh, Tom! It's time! Oh, God! It's time! Get Sarah!"

Fortunately, Sarah wasn't far away. For the last week she and Levi had been staying the night in the front room of the Covington house. Covington left his bedroom and charged down the stairs, trying to pull a robe over his longjohns. He nearly bowled Sarah over as she was climbing those same stairs, having been awakened by the intensity of Mary Ann's scream. "Sarah! Did you hear?"

"They done heard her in the next county, Marse Tom! You best be fetchin' the doctor! I'll stay with Miss Mary. You go on!"

"But..."

"Don't you be arguin' with me, Marse Tom! On your way out the door load some wood in the stove, and put that kettle on to boil!"

"Wood in the stove...water on top!" stammered the soon-to-be father as he moved past her on the stairway. He reached the bottom but stopped there as another horrific shriek echoed through the house. This one woke Levi who released a demanding cry of his own. Covington paused and cast a worried glance in Sarah's direction.

"Go on now, Marse Tom! Let me take care of things here!" For weeks he'd been telling the Henrys they didn't need to call him "Marse Tom" anymore, but these were the customs of a lifetime, and they would be slow to change.

Within ten minutes he was galloping toward the home of Doctor Emanual Meyers, some seven miles southwest of the Covington place.

Two hours passed before he and the physician made it back to the farm. Covington was numbed by the intense cold, his fingers all but frozen on the horse's reins. With the doctor right on his heels he charged up to the front door and into the house. Moses was there to greet him with baby Levi in his arms.

"Marse Tom!" he greeted, "you look near froze to death, suh! Come here by the stove and thaw yourself out."

"That you, Marse Tom?" Sarah emerged at the top of the stairway, "is the doctor with you?"

"I'm here, Sarah!" called Meyers.

"Well come on up here!" she ordered. "Miss Mary's been needin' you!"

"On my way," the physician took only a few seconds to climb the stairway.

Covington shifted his eyes to meet Sarah's. Something he saw there sent a shiver up his spine. He started toward the stairway but she stopped him with a gesture. "You go on over by the stove and warm yourself up, Marse Tom," she urged.

"Sarah... is she holding up?"

"She's havin' a hard time with this one, Marse Tom. She's tired, suh. It's worn her down."

"What can I do?" A feeling of helplessness rose up in his throat.

"You can pray, suh. You can sho' nuff pray."

Covington had to wilfully repress the urge to sob. "Sarah," he tried to sound brave, "put your arms around her. Hold her for me. Tell her I'm near. Tell her I love her."

She seemed to be the picture of resolute strength as she stared back at him from the top of the stairway. "I'll be with her, Marse Tom. I'll be with her." She turned and disappeared.

He staggered over to the woodstove as if in a daze. Moses stepped up behind him and placed a hand on Tom's shoulder. "We'll all be prayin' for her, suh."

At that point Mary Ann Covington had been in labor for only three hours. Nine hours later it appeared as if she might indeed be ready for the delivery of the child. Her head was cradled in the lap of Sarah Henry. The black woman held her gently, occasionally brushing matted hair from Mary Ann's temples and forehead. From time to time she whispered Tom's message and Mary Ann would manage a weak smile. She had grown far too weak to attempt a verbal reply.

"Hold on, Mary Ann!" urged Meyers, "push as hard as you can!. There's a baby on the way; I see its head!"

Minutes later the baby, a boy, was in Doctor Meyer's arms. He severed the umbilical cord, cleaned the little boy as much as possible, wrapped him in cloth and laid him in Mary Ann's arms.

She herself had but moments to live. In those moments, she experienced the most fulfilling emotions she had ever known as she gazed upon her newborn son. She shifted her head to gaze up at Sarah, who was able to see the happiness and contentment in her eyes. Mary Ann smiled just at that moment, a smile which spoke volumes. In that same moment life passed from her eyes. The Lord had summoned Mary Ann Covington.

Several minutes passed before her husband glanced up at the sound of the bedroom door opening. He saw Sarah approach the stairway with a small bundle in her arms, but he was too afraid to move toward her.

With her eyes brimming with tears Sarah Henry descended the stairs and handed Covington his infant son.

No one spoke.

A flood of mixed emotions raced through Covington's heart as he held the baby. Pride and love, fear and sorrow, elation and despair, all were present. Unable to put it off any longer, he looked at Sarah and asked the question. "Mary Ann?"

BROTHERS IN GRAY

Tears were streaming down the black woman's face. Words failed her at that moment. All she could do was shake her head.

As the truth sank in, Covington's knees began to weaken. He handed the child to Sarah and sought a chair. The sob he had repressed all through the day finally escaped, followed by another and another.

Sarah handed the baby to Moses, who found himself cradling an infant in each arm. She moved quickly to Covington's side and leaned down to embrace him. "The Good Lord must have wanted her more than we did, Marse Tom. We did everything we could, me and the doctor. She just wasn't strong enough. But I got to tell you, suh, she died a happy woman. I saw her face! She looked into my eyes, Marse Tom, and she was smilin'. She loved this baby and she loved you. She was content, and she's with the Lord now."

Covington nodded and clasped Sarah's arms tightly, but he was lost in his grief.

"Marse Tom, don't you worry about this child. I got more than enough milk for both these boys. I'll nurse him and I'll love him like my own."

On that cold and dreary February day in 1843 a life began and a life ended. Between two families, one black, the other white, a bond was forged through the sharing of these experiences. It would not easily be broken.

~ Chapter Two ~
1862

The 19th of April, 1861, was a fateful day in the lives of all Virginians. Newspapers all over the state had reported on her decision to secede from the United States. She would join ranks with her sister states in the South in the formation of the Confederate States of America. Virginia would quickly become the heart of this new nation and would soon house its government in Richmond.

Tom Covington received the news with mixed emotions. Like most people in the South he did not have passionate feelings one way or the other concerning slavery. As a younger man he had reached a personal conviction concerning his own participation in the continuance of the peculiar institution. He had given the Henrys their freedom and land of their own to farm.

Secession was another question which generated ambivalence in Covington's breast. Did such a right exist? He thought the courts offered the most logical forum for such a question to be resolved, but it was painfully obvious no solution would be forthcoming from any legal venue. Fort Sumter had been fired upon. The die had been cast. The clash of arms would prove the only arbitor of secession.

On one issue alone did he have strong convictions. He was a Virginian from a long line of Virginians. He would not turn his back on his state. If Virginia chose to join the Confederate States of America, so be it. He now considered himself a citizen of the new nation.

At fifty-five years of age he did not think of himself as soldier material. Yet he knew he could make a substantial contribution. The Shenandoah Valley was already shaping up as a strategic piece of geography: by itself it was capable of providing grain to most of the Confederacy.

The men who were quickly filling the ranks of newly forming Southern armies would need to eat. Covington would do his small part to feed them.

There was but one misgiving which gnawed at Covington's heart: what of his son, Wil?. The boy was eighteen years old now. He was soldier material. How long could he keep his only son away from the army? All over the valley young men were forming regiments. Wil had already asked for permission to enlist. Permission had been denied.

The Henrys also had mixed emotions regarding the situation in which they found themselves. Regarding slavery there was no question. They desired its abolition. However, as did many white people in the South, they believed slavery would end eventually regardless of what anybody did or said. They viewed themselves as proof of this assertion. They were among 60,000 free blacks within Virginia alone. In fact there were over 150,000 free blacks in the Confederacy prior to the first shedding of blood. The Henrys also thought of themselves as Virginians. They owned a small herd of cattle which grazed on twenty acres of land. They cultivated fifteen acres of wheat and another five of corn. This says nothing of the produce which came from their half-acre vegetable garden. This family would also make a contribution to the fledgling Confederacy.

By the Spring of 1862 the war had made itself felt on the people of the Shenandoah Valley regardless of their race. Most of the news was ominous. Northern Arkansas and Missouri were lost to the Confederacy. Much of Tennessee and Kentucky felt the oppressive weight of Union boots. Western Virginia had been shorn from the rest of the state. Richmond itself faced the possibility of evacuation in the face of 100,000 federal soldiers moving up the peninsula from Fortress Monroe under the leader-ship of George McClellan.

From one theater alone came news of an optimistic nature. The Valley campaign of Stonewall Jackson consis-tently generated good news, the kind which made south-ern hearts soar with renewed hope. Kernstown, Cross Keys, Front Royal and Winchester were but insignificant dots on a map prior to the outbreak of war. By early June of 1862 the tiny valley army of Stonewall Jackson had blazed these names into the annals of history forever. Stonewall himself had become a hero in the South, and the mention of his name caused many a northerner to glance fearfully toward the mouth of the Shenandoah Valley. Would this demon burst out of the valley to descend in a rush upon Washington? Was he about to lay waste to Pennsylvania?

It was the tenth of June. Perhaps two hours remained till sunset. Tom Covington and Moses Henry had just finished tending to the draft animals and were walking out of the barn anxious for supper after a long day's work. Each man had cause for satisfaction. Both of their farms were prosperous. The spring planting had been successful. The rains had been good of late, giving the promise of a bumper crop at summer's end.

The fine details of the valley campaign hadn't been lost on these two men or their sons. After all the campaign had literally been fought at their doorstep. Both men had provided food and shelter for Turner Ashby's cavalry and Jackson's foot-sore infantry. They had become used to the sight of Union soldiers trying to corner the elusive Jackson somewhere in the valley. The news of each battle reached their ears long before it found its way into any of the newspapers. They knew that another fight was brewing somewhere near Port Republic some twenty-five miles north of their farms. On this particular day they had allowed their sons to have half a day off. The boys had been gone since noon.

"You reckon Sarah's got that ham ready, Marse Tom?"

"Hope so, Moses. I'm about famished."

"Me too." For a man in his mid-sixties, Moses Henry was still the picture of health. Only his hair and beard betrayed his age. Both had turned snow white. His voice was as deep and resolute as ever, and he walked with a steady gait without the slightest hint of a stoop.

"Moses, look there," gestured Tom, "here come the boys."

He had pointed down the dirt lane which led from the road to the Covington house. Levi Henry and Wil Covington had just turned off of the road and were ascending the lane at a dead run.

"Wonder what set them on fire?" pondered Moses.

"Reckon we're about to find out."

"Ol' Jack did it again!" exclaimed Wil. He was still trying to regain his breath, so the words seemed to stumble from his mouth. "He whipped the Yankees at Port Republic! He sent Shields packin' and left Fremont swingin' at air!"

"That so?" Tom cast a dubious glance at his son.

"Yessuh!" Levi volunteered. "We were over at the Ellison place. They had a newspaper from Staunton and we read it for ourselves!"

"You did, eh?"

"Yessuh! And that ain't all! You tell him, Wil!"

"Tell me what?"

"News from Richmond!" gasped Wil, "Johnston was wounded pretty bad. Davis put Lee in charge of the army!"

"Lee?" asked Moses, "Robert E. Lee?"

"Sho' nuff!" nodded Wil, "he'll stop McClellan square in his tracks!"

"I don't know about that," differed the elder Covington. "He didn't do so well out in the mountains."

"He'll stop 'em, Pa. I can feel it!"

"Maybe so, I reckon we'll know soon enough."

Covington paused to regard the two boys who stood before him. What he saw was a source of immense pride. Wil had grown to a fine young man. He was tall and lean with a head full of sandy blond hair. His blue eyes tended to sparkle when he laughed, and he seemed just a little too proud of the faint beginnings of a moustache peeking out above his upper lip.

Levi Henry had also grown into a handsome young man. Older than Wil by several months, he was decidedly bigger than the Covington boy. The difference was not so much height as it was size. Levi took after his father in that respect. It took but a casual glance to detect the power within his chest and arms. His smooth skin was a deep brown color. He had a round face with deep-set pensive eyes. He sported a moustache Wil could never hope to match.

"I'm more concerned about what's goin' on out here in the valley," continued the elder Covington, "Jackson has surely worked wonders. Are the Yanks clearin' out?"

"Don't know, Pa. Rumors are flyin' right now. Some folks are sayin' Lincoln's gettin' worried about Washington. They say he's gonna pull his troops north. We may not see too many Yankees for awhile."

"That'll suit me fine," said Moses.

"Me too," agreed Tom.

"Pa, there's something I gotta tell you." The

change in Wil's tone sent a shiver of fear up his father's spine.

"Can it wait till after supper?"

"No, suh."

"Sounds serious."

"I can't sit around watchin' it any longer, Pa. I'm joinin' up."

"I'm goin' with him," added Levi before either of the older men had a chance to absorb Wil's words.

Tom and Moses looked at one another, neither knowing how to respond. Both had been stunned speechless.

"Did you hear me, Pa?" pressed Wil after several moments of uneasy silence had lapsed.

"I heard you, son."

"I talked with the recruiter this afternoon."

"I see."

Again there was silence. None of the four could find the right words. Both of the older men were grappling with their own emotions. It was Tom Covington who finally broke the quiet. "If you two leave who will help with the harvest?"

"We're not leaving forever, Pa. Maybe in the fall I can get a furlough and come home to help."

This reply was no more persuasive than the question itself. Covington knew the argument wouldn't carry much weight. It had been a half-hearted attempt to dissuade Wil without revealing his true feelings on the matter. Still struggling with emotion he looked away, and his eyes fell upon the tombstone which marked Mary Ann's grave some twenty yards from the house.

"You're all I have," he stammered as his tear-filled eyes focused again on his son, "I can't bear the thought of losing you."

"I know, Pa. I understand. I'm hopin' you'll understand why I have to go. Everyone I know has joined. People are lookin' at me with questions in their eyes. Two of my friends have already been killed. Several have been wounded. It's my duty, Pa. I can't shirk it any longer."

Again silence. The two fathers were drifting through images of the past, of two young boys running carefree over the hills and fields of the Shenandoah, back and forth from the Covington farm to the Henry Farm. They were thinking of the daily wrestling matches and of school lessons. Moses was thinking of how he and Tom had taught Levi to read and write. So much time, energy, and love had been invested in these two young men! Each had shared the other's bumps and bruises as they grew up. They thought of hot summer days during the boys' thirteenth year, the year they discovered the rope swing and swimming hole on the river five miles upstream from the Covington farm. And now this war...this cursed war.

As if reading the minds of the older men, Wil cleared his throat and resumed the argument. "The war's not going to end soon, Pa. The Yankees won't take Richmond now that Lee's in charge. The people who thought it would all be over after one battle were proved wrong at Manassas. The people who think the South's about to fold are also wrong. The Yankees want our land, Pa. They'll do anything to get it. This war's gonna get vicious. They'll aim at civilians. You know it as well as I. Farms like this feed our armies. The Federals won't stop until all these farms are destroyed. Our friends and neighbors are out there facin' death to protect our land from the invaders. How can you expect me to stand by and let other people do what I should be doin'? It goes against everything you ever taught me!"

"I suppose it does," sighed his father after a brief

pause, "still, can you understand how hard it is for me to let you go? You're all I have, Wil. Everything I"ve worked for all my life is here on this land. I want it to be yours. I want you to continue the legacy our family has started here."

"I know, Pa. For that to happen there has to be a farm here when the war ends. If the Yankees get their way it'll all be ashes. I know how hard it is for you to let me go, but it's no harder than what any other family in the South is facing right now. A lot of folks are saying good-bye to people they love. It has to be."

To this Tom Covington had no reply. He had come to the realization that further argument was useless. Wil's mind was set. There would be no changing it.

Moses Henry was less inclined to let the matter drop. He looked his son straight in the eye and made his feelings known. "This is not a black man's war. There ain't no need for you to be goin' anywhere!"

"There's a lot of blacks with Jackson's army!" replied Levi hotly. "I've seen 'em!"

"So have I and they're mostly slaves gone to take care of their masters. You're free, Levi. You was born free! There's no call for you to go off to no damn war!"

"If I'm free, Pa, I can make my own decisions! Wil's the closest thing to a brother I've ever had! I'm not lettin' him go off to war by himself! I'm goin' with him! My mind's made up! I ain't changin' it! Besides, Wil's right about this war. It'll go on for a long time. The Yankees have already started against civilians. These farms feed the Confederate armies. They'll destroy these farms if they get a chance. Do you think they'll spare ours 'cause we happen to be black? You know better than that, Pa! They'll burn it all if they get half a chance. I'm gonna go and do my part to protect this land."

"They're not likely to let you fight."

"That ain't entirely true from what I've been hearin' but even so, I can carry water and ammo. I can help the wounded."

"And you can get killed same as a white boy!"

"If that's what the good Lord wants. Let's pray it isn't. Someday me and Wil will both be comin' home"

"I'm an old man, son. Don't know how much time I got left in this world. I don't want you to go but I reckon I ain't got the means to force you to stay. Since this is your decision, you be the one to tell your mother. This will break her heart, and that's somethin' I won't be a party to."

"Me and Wil already talked about this. We'll both be tellin' her what we're gonna do."

"Well you go on ahead and tell her. She's over to the big house gettin' supper ready."

The two boys glanced at one another for assurance, then started for the house.

Moses looked over at the elder Covington who was idly scratching the chin hairs of his beard as he gazed aimlessly toward the mountains. "What's it all comin' to, Marse Tom?"

"I don't rightly know, old friend," came the reply after a brief pause, "don't seem like a whole lot of things make sense anymore. I suppose Wil may be right about one thing though. The Yankees won't be happy till they've wrecked everything. All them bankers up in New York; they want it all."

It was a somber group which gathered at the top of the lane the next morning. Sarah Henry could not control her tears. All through the night she had done her utmost to dissuade the two young men from going off to war. Try as she might, she could not get them to change their minds. Thus did she find herself saying good-bye to the two boys she had raised.

With tears rolling freely down her rounded cheeks she stood with her right arm around Levi, her left clutching Wil. "My boys!" she cried aloud. "My babies! Why you takin' them from me, Lord?"

"Ma, please!" Levi protested, but she responded by pulling him even closer.

"Watch over 'em, Lord! Please keep them safe and bring 'em home to me!"

"Sarah," mumbled Wil, "if you don't loosen your hold on me I do believe I'll expire before I get a chance to take the first step!"

She released both boys and used her apron to dry the tears on her face.

Wil stepped right in front of her and put one hand on each of her shoulders. With his irrepressible smile he tried to bring cheer back to her eyes, but all he could see in those eyes were the tattered edges of a breaking heart. "Sarah," he said, "I love you dearly. You're the only mother I've ever known." His arms slipped around her back and he hugged her close.

"It won't last forever," he soothed, "pray for us every day, and we'll come home when it's over."

"I'll be prayin' young-un," she stammered, "I'll sure be prayin'." She released Wil and took Levi in her arms. "Good-bye, son," her words were barely audible, "I don't know why you have to do this, but I reckon it's your choice to make. Don't you be doin' anything stupid, hear?"

"I hear you, Ma. You know how much I love you and Pa. I'll be comin' home again. Watch for me."

"I will. And make sure you bring Wil home with ya."

"Yes'm."

Both boys turned then to their fathers, until there was no more time for hugs, and no one could find the right words to speak. Wil and Levi shouldered the small bundles which contained their personal belongings, then turned away, taking the first steps toward horrors the likes of which they had never dreamed.

Sarah Henry stood alone watching after them long after they had disappeared from view. Finally, Moses walked up behind her and took hold of her elbow. "Come home now, Sarah," he suggested gently.

She turned to him with eyes still glistening with tears. "Don't make no sense, Moses, no sense at all."

After they had gone, Tom Covington walked to the grave of his wife. He lowered himself to his knees by the side of her grave and prayed quietly for several minutes. Finishing his prayer, he rose and started toward the house. For the first time since the birth of his son he felt alone, and this feeling of solitude weighed on his shoulders like a ton of bricks. He shut himself inside his home and stared aimlessly out of the windows. He remained thus secluded for the next three days.

Wil and Levi, though aware of the emotional burdens borne by their families walked toward Staunton with light hearts. Most of the time they walked in silence, but here and there they engaged in conversation. It was late afternoon, still two hours from their destination, when Levi asked his companion what he thought it was going to be like.

"What do you mean?" Wil asked for clarification.

"War. What's it gonna be like?"

"I'm not real sure to be honest with you. I suppose if I had joined last spring before Manassas I would have had some of the same romantic notions as Eric Helms and

BROTHERS IN GRAY

Bob Smith. You remember?"

"Yep," Levi nodded, thinking back to younger days and two of the local boys with whom they shared the rope swing and swimming hole. "They talked a tall line those two."

"Sure did. When I listened to them I thought war was just a game. They filled my head with talk of glory and honor, fancy uniforms, girls just-a-swoonin' all over 'em. I got chills just listenin' to 'em!"

"I remember," Levi smiled. "So what do you think now?"

"Not quite sure what to think. Don't see much glory in it. The Yankees killed Eric at Manassas and Bob took a minie-ball in the brain at Kernstown . Nothin' left of those two but memories, and I don't see no girls swoonin' over their gravestones.

In the last year I've seen what war can do. It ain't pretty. I don't have no fancy dreams in my head about what it's gonna be like. I suppose there's some adventure waitin' for us, but I reckon you and I are takin' on about the hardest job we ever tried. Lord knows how it'll all come out."

"You think I'll be able to get near the fightin'?"

"Maybe. I reckon it'll depend on where the fightin' is. I heard tell there's been some Blacks up close to it side by side with their masters."

"Yeah, but I'm a free man. They may not even let me stay."

"I doubt if they'll much care. We can tell 'em my Pa sent you along to look after me. That should work."

"I suppose."

By early evening they were in Staunton. They reported directly to the recruiting office where both of them were mustered into the Confederate army no questions asked. From here they were ushered over to the quartermaster's headquarters where they each received part of a uniform, the tunic, along with a haversack, musket and bayonet. They were then assigned to a regiment, the 5th Virginia. Then they were told to report to a training camp just outside of town. They did so, gear in hand, and began their lives as soldiers of the Confederacy.

Camp life proved to be an interesting experience for Wil and Levi as well. For three weeks the recruits drilled every day. As the regiment was composed primarily of Shenandoah farm boys, most of its' members were already considerably adept with a musket. However, they knew little of marching or fighting in formation, and to this end they trained incessantly.

While Wil learned to march and shoot Levi found himself in a support role. Sometimes he served as a teamster. More often he fetched ammunition and water to the recruits. By no means was he the only Black to be found at the camp. His race was represented in substantial numbers, though the majority far and away were slaves. He set up a tent for himself just behind Wil's, and the two of them were able to share at least some of their free time together. Sometimes they would sample the wares of various sutlers who had set up their operations just beyond the camp perimeter. There was no shortage of food, so they managed to stay well fed, but the times they enjoyed most were the nights, when men of both races would gather around camp fires and spin yarns, or sing their hearts out to the music of a harmonica or fiddle. Army life was beginning to seem like a breeze, but at the same time Wil was becoming edgy. He had joined to fight Yankees and as the summer wore on he began to yearn for action, a sentiment he expressed in several of the letters he sent home.

The time was soon coming which would see his wish fulfilled. Robert E. Lee did more than stop McClellan outside of Richmond. In a series of confrontations he maneuvered and fought the Union army down the peninsula to the James River. The campaign ended with a bloody confederate repulse at Malvern Hill, but even this setback, costly though it was, failed to dampen the enthusiasm many felt at the elevation of Lee to the command of the army. Richmond had been delivered. Certain defeat had been transformed into victory.

The Southern press offered a variety of opinions concerning the seven days battles. Many were harshly critical of Lee's failure to destroy the entire Union army when he had the opportunity. Much was said about Jackson, strangely lethargic during the campaign, who consistently failed to be where he was supposed to be on schedule.

"How can they say this stuff about Jackson?" asked Wil as he lifted his eyes from the Richmond newspaper recently delivered to the camp. "Lord knows he's been fightin' steady for the last three months! The man was exhausted! Anyone can see that!"

"If you say so," smiled Levi, "my but you do go on!"

"Well think about it, Levi, if it hadn't been for Lee and Jackson the Yanks would probably have taken Richmond. These newspaper fellas would have been out of business. They should be thankin' their lucky stars! Instead they're bellyachin' cause Lee didn't bag the whole Yankee army!"

"I don't know much about Lee," nodded Levi. "But Ol' Jack, he does know what he's about!"

"I reckon!" Echoed Wil as he turned to the next page of the newspaper.

The leisure time to browse through newspapers disappeared abruptly on the 13th of July. Word came that Lee had ordered Jackson and Ewell north on the 12th. Already they were taking up positions outside Gordonsville in the eastern foothills of the Blue Ridge. From the regimental commander came one order: "Boys, be ready to march at the tap of a drum."

That night as they downed their rations Wil and Levi listened attentively to Corporal Henry Gilbert, a veteran of both Manassas and the valley campaign. "Pope's in Culpeper with close to fifty thousand men. If McClellan joins him it'll triple that number. Lee's in a pickle, he got to do somethin' to knock Pope off balance and keep him at bay. I think he'll tell Jackson to pitch into him. If ol' Jack decides to take a swipe at Pope he'll need all the help he can get. We'll be headin' for the other side of the mountains. You young boys are goin' to find out what war's about."

Wil thought he'd be thrilled at the prospect of imminent battle. Yet something in Gilbert's voice sent a chill of fear creeping up his spine. He stuffed a final bite of cornbread into his mouth and tried to switch his mind to a different train of thought. Images of his home and father quickly came into focus.

This newly raised troop of Shenandoah farm boys was ready even anxious to march, but the anticipated tap of the drum seemed an eternity away. July passed into August, but no orders came. From Richmond, however, troops were still moving north. A.P. Hill's light division had joined Jackson at Gordonsville.

On the 7th of August, Jackson received a letter from Lee strongly suggesting that he lash out at Pope.

The Federal forces in Culpeper were also thinking in terms of an offensive punch. Nathanial Banks, derisively nicknamed "Commissary Banks" by Jackson's foot cavalry, marched out of Culpeper with the intent of taking the fight to Jackson. Eight miles or so out of Culpeper Banks came under long range artillery fire, and the opening shots of the Battle of Cedar Mountain.

The next morning orders arrived at regimental headquarters outside of Staunton. The orders were brief and to the point: join Jackson.

Colonel B. F. Reynolds immediately called assembly to announce the news himself. "Boys!" he called out loudly. "Strike your tents! We go to the side of Stonewall Jackson!"

Wild cheers greeted this news. Action at last! Hearts were beating a little faster as the tents came down and wagons were loaded. Within the hour they were marching east on a dusty dirt road toward the Blue Ridge. To the untrained eye they didn't look particularly impressive. They were a motley looking collection of teenaged boys and bearded young men. One would have had to search diligently among their ranks to find anything that might appear to be a complete uniform.

As the column reached the stout wooden bridge which spanned the Shenandoah River Wil fell out to rest his legs. Levi had been walking beside one of the wagons. When he spied Wil sitting on a fallen tree he moved quickly to join him.

"Howdy, soldier," volunteered the young black man.

"Afternoon, Levi." Wil looked up from the ground. "You countin' the twigs down there?"

"Nah, just thinkin'."

"About what?" Levi sat down next to Wil.

"Nothin' special, just stuff."

"Another hour and we'll be half way over them

mountains."

"I know. Do you realize we left home more than a month go?"

"Don't seem like it."

"Sure don't. In all that time we ain't been more than a half-day's walk from home. Now look where we are! Our swimmin' hole's only a couple miles upriver. Hell, we're so close to home we could almost be there for supper! Wouldn't that be somethin'? I can almost taste your Ma's fried chicken!"

"We can't be goin' home Wil. Leastways, you can't. If you decide to walk home, I don't reckon Colonel Reynolds would take too kindly to the idea."

"Reckon not," grinned Wil. "You think he'd stand me up in front of a wall?"

"Could happen. Seems like he pays close attention to the rules."

"He's a professional. V.M.I. graduate, back in '51 or so they say."

"I don't know about all that," observed Levi, "but I reckon you'd be smart not to land on his bad side."

"I suppose you're right," Wil rose to his feet and stretched his lanky arms. "So much for your Ma's fried chicken. Time to start walkin' again."

"Marchin'," corrected Levi. "We're soldiers now. We don't walk, we march."

"Don't remind me," said Wil as the two of them rejoined the column.

By nightfall they had crested the Blue Ridge and there they set up camp for the night. Corporal Gilbert was none too pleased at the pace they had set that day.

"You puppies don't know what a hard march is!" he scolded. "Wait'll Ol' Blue-Light gets a hold of ya! He'll teach ya what marchin's about!"

"What the hell's he crowin' about?" wondered Wil after the Corporal moved to the next campfire, "I know we covered better than twenty miles today!"

"Closer to thirty," noted Levi, "but the word is Jackson's soldiers can march fifty in a day."

"You think we'll get that good?"

"I think Jackson will see to that, just like the Corporal said."

"Me too," groaned Wil as he sprawled on his back next to the fire, his aching limbs numbed by fatigue.

Absorbed by the rigors of their day long march, particularly by the long climb up into the Blue Ridge, these foot soldiers hadn't noticed the steady traffic in couriers to and from the column. If they had been privy to the information carried by these messengers they would have known that a battle had already been fought at Cedar Mountain, and that they had missed it. Jackson had held his ground against the Federals and remained in control of the battlefield itself.

By late afternoon of the next day their regiment joined Jackson's troops in the vicinity of Cedar Mountain. To many of Colonel Reynold's green farm boys this moment would be remembered as one of the highlights of their lives. At last they were part of a real army! Their hearts beat loudly and they held their heads high as they filed past the critical eyes of Jackson's veterans to a position in reserve supporting the right side of the Confederate line.

That evening Wil, Levi and several others were gathered about a small fire sharing their evening rations when three figures emerged ghostlike out of the darkness. Tall and lean each of them was, and dressed in tattered homemade clothes. One of them stepped close to the fire so that his face was illuminated in its glow. He had a clean-

shaven face, unlike his companions, and a pale complex-
ion. The fire seemed to spark a twinkle in his bright blue
eyes, and his bushy blond eyebrows gave him the appearance of a merry elf.

"Howdy, boys!" he greeted as he stepped close.

"Evenin'!" returned the corporal. "Y'all hungry?"

"A bit," nodded the stranger. "We're lookin for a
Corporal Henry Gilbert."

"You just found him," said Gilbert, "What can I do
for ya?"

"I reckon we belong with you from here on out,"
came the reply, "Name's Turner, Miles Turner. Me and
my buddies are from down around Suffolk. We joined up
in time to fight at Cold Harbor. There was nine of us then.
There was still seven of us before Malvern Hill. We were
all in the charge. The three of us is all that's left. This
here's Tommie Murphy," he gestured to his right, "and
behind me is Jeb Green."

"Glad to know ya," replied Gilbert, "what brings
you our way?"

"Like I said, we just sort of wandered in and started
fightin'. We got no permanent unit as such. About an
hour ago we got orders from A.P. Hill's headquarters to
report to Colonel Reynolds. We did, and he assigned us
to you."

"So you finally found yourselves a home, eh?"

"Looks that way."

"Sit down and makes yourselves comfortable," gestured Gilbert, who then addressed himself to Levi. "Levi,
how about rustlin' up some grub for these boys?"

"Sho 'nuff Corporal."

Once their bellies were full they sat back to relax
and get to know the newcomers. Turner quickly realized
he had landed among a batch of raw recruits who had yet

to see their first shot fired in anger.

"Lemme get this straight," he smiled after downing several gulps of water from his canteen, "you boys are all neophytes!"

"Neo...what?" gasped Lonnie Andrews, an eighteen year old from outside of Waynesboro.

"Neophytes, boy!" laughed Turner, "ain't you got no schoolin'?"

"Never heard of that word," Andrews replied apologetically.

"Means you're a like a babe in the woods. You're brand new...untried."

"Sorta like you before Cold Harbor," interjected Wil.

"Sorta," Turner glanced over at Wil with a grin.

In Wil's mind Miles Turner was shaping up as an amiable entirely likeable fellow.

"Anyway," Lonnie Andrews spoke again. "We're not all new...." he paused; trying to figure out the word Turner had used.

"Neophytes," whispered Wil a bit loudly.

"Yeah!" Lonnie nodded, "we're not all brand new at this. Corporal Gilbert here is a veteran of Manassas, and he fought with Stonewall up and down the Valley all through Spring!"

"That a fact?" Turner glanced over at the Corporal.

Gilbert took a sip of coffee from the mug he was cradling in his palm. "Yep," he said calmly.

"Then I reckon there's some things you could be teachin' me and my buddies, eh?"

"I reckon."

"Did you say you were at Malvern Hill?" Wil seemed more than a little eager to hear every story this

"Can you tell us about it?" We've heard it was a grand charge!"

Turner's expression changed visibly as the memories of that fateful day welled up inside of him. He sat up, leaned close to the fire, which cast an orange glow across his face. "I don't know that there's much about Malvern Hill to tell," he said in a voice tinged with bitterness, "I heard one of our officers say it wasn't war, it was murder. I think he about summed it up. Grand charge? Grand slaughter would be more appropriate! We attacked straight up the hill, right into the teeth of those Yankee guns. They chewed us up right proper." He glanced over at his friend, Murphy. "We left Tommie's brother on Malvern Hill. He got real close to the crest, but a Yankee put a bullet right between his eyes. He never knew what hit him."

He paused again, and sighed audibly as he collected his thoughts. "A lot of possibilities awaited the outcome of Malvern Hill. If we had carried the day, we might have bottled up the whole Army of the Potomac, every Mother's son of them. We would have trapped them with their backs on the river. Sad to say, it wasn't meant to be. Let me tell you something, I've got a lot of respect for Robert E. Lee. He's a smart one, no doubt about it. He'll make his mark before this war's over, but Malvern Hill won't be remembered as one of his wiser decisions."

"Everyone makes mistakes," defended Wil.

"No one knows that better'n me," agreed Turner, "I've made a passel of 'em in my time."

"And I'd say Lee's already made his mark," noted Wil. "He saved Richmond. The city would have fallen if he hadn't done what he did!"

"You'll get no argument with me on that score," nodded the newcomer from Suffolk. " You wanted to know about Malvern Hill. I told ya."

nodded the newcomer from Suffolk. " You wanted to know about Malvern Hill. I told ya."

"How about yesterday's battle?" pressed Wil, "What was it like?"

The question brought a mischievous smile to Turner's face, "Interesting to say the least," he replied, "did you know Jackson was sleepin' during the first phase of the fight?"

"He was?"

"I'll swear it on a stack of Bibles." Turner let his eyes roam among the group of curious young faces which peered up at him from around the campfire, including that of Levi Moses who seemed most eager to hear the story. "Hey, boy!" he addressed himself to Levi, "what do you know about Jackson?"

"Me?" For a moment Levi shrank back from the fire.

"Yep. Tell me."

"Well, suh, I've got a right high opinion of General Jackson. He done showed them Yankees a thing or two in the Valley. I think he's a fine officer. Besides, suh, ol' Jack's been known to donate money to Negro Sunday schools,and he's taught in some too. I reckon I appreciate his concern."

"That a fact? Well you should've seen him yesterday! Like I said, before the battle started he was asleep. He went up on the front porch of a farmhouse and dozed off."

"It's no wonder!" Wil interrupted, "look how much he's done in the last three months! The man's got to be exhausted!"

"Don't get me wrong!" enjoined Turner, "I ain't criticizin'. I know he's got to be tired. We've been marchin' with him since Cold Harbor. You just keep your shirt on, boy, and let me finish my story! Okay. Like I

said, Ol' Jack was just a-snoozin' away when all of a sudden
all hell break's loose! Yankees are everywhere and they're
chargin' right at us with blood in their eyes! We gave way
cause there was just too many of 'em, and they was comin'
on hard!" He paused to peer round the fire, making sure
he had everyone's attention, "I confess we might have
been routed. We were sure close to it. I gotta tell ya, I was
plenty scared! Thought sure the game was up. Then we
got word from A.P. Hill. He's close at hand and gettin'
ready to pitch in. Suddenly....there was Jackson! All that
noise must've woke him up, and I guarantee he woke up
on the wrong side of whatever he was sleepin' on! Yessuh!
He was spoilin' for a fight! Seemed like he came out of
nowhere! He was mounted on his horse standin' tall over
everybody! Had that old Kepi pulled down so far on his
nose it was a wonder he could see at all! He charged among
us, wavin' his sword over his head, just a shoutin' out
orders like there was no tomorrow. We couldn't retreat
another step! He'd have shamed us all!" He stopped
speaking and took a sip of water from his canteen.

"So what happened?" demanded young Andrews.

"What happened?" echoed Turner. "Well I reckon
we turned around and stopped them Yankees cold in
their tracks! A.P. Hill came up and helped us drive 'em
back!"

"That's it?" gasped Wil.

"In a nutshell," nodded Turner, "we thought they
might come at us again today, but they must've thought
better of it. We're still holdin' the field of battle, so we
reckon we can call it a victory."

"I reckon!" Levi spoke up with a wide grin from
outside the circle.

Turner glanced over at the young black man. "So
tell me, boy, which one of these baby-faced aristocrats do

you belong to?"

Just a tinge of anger rose in Levi's cheeks, but he knew better than to yield to it. "Don't belong to no one, suh. I'm nobody's slave."

"You're not a slave? What the hell are you doin' here?"

Levi gestured toward Wil: "His pappy freed my pappy before we were born." he explained. "We grew up together. When Wil said he was goin' to fight the Yankees, I said I'd go with him."

"If that don't beat all!" chuckled Turner.

"I don't mean no disrespect, suh, but what makes you think I'd like Yankees any more than you do?"

"Don't get all riled," Turner replied good-naturedly, "I just find it curious, that's all. Besides, I'm of the opinion that we ought to free more of you people, and let you stand against the Yankees same as us."

"That's not a real popular opinion these days," noted the Corporal.

"True enough, but that seems strange too, in view of all the Blacks I see in this army since I joined up."

"They're slaves," said Gilbert, "at least most of them," he added with a deferential nod in Levi's direction.

"They may be slaves," agreed Turner, "but some of 'em are fighting alongside their masters. With my own eyes I've seen black men servicing some of our guns."

"So have I," agreed Gilbert, "but the official line is that they're slaves and they are here in non-combatant roles."

"I don't see where we need no Blackies to help fight this war!" There was venom in Tommie Murphy's voice. "We can lick the Yanks without 'em."

"Time'll tell," sighed Turner, he rose to his feet, stretched and yawned, "reckon it's time to find me a place to bed down for the night. I'll see you fellers in the mornin'."

Corporal Gilbert glanced over at Levi, "I saw you target shootin' when we were back at Staunton'" he said, "you look like you know what to do with a musket."

"Been huntin' since I was a young-un," came the reply.

"How do you feel about bein' close to the fightin' when the shootin' starts?"

Levi's heart began to beat a little faster. Were these white men about to accept him as a real soldier? "I ain't afraid," he said with as much calm as he could muster.

"I may want you close to us," continued Gilbert, "to load muskets for the men."

It was easy to read the disappointment in Levi's face as the impact of Gilbert's words sank in. "I'll obey your orders, Corporal," he said.

"Hope so," noted Gilbert, "Army has to work together like a team."

The next morning this same group of soldiers were gathered about the breakfast fire when Turner spied a familiar face. "Hey, Ivory!" he called out to a sturdily built black man whose head was a bald as a new-born's butt. "C'mon over here, boy!"

Ivory dutifully appeared before the group of infantrymen, his arms and shoulders burdened by a load of cooking utensils and harnessing gear. "What you want, Marse Turner?" The black man grinned broadly and Wil immediately saw how he got the name Ivory, "you knows I gots work to do."

"Hell," laughed Miles, "don't worry about your chores, Ivory! They'll get done soon enough! Take a load off your shoulders! Sit on down here a spell and tell these boys that story about ol' Jeb!"

"Which story?"

"You know which one! The one you told me yesterday about his hat and plume!"

"Oh, yeah!" a smile spread across Ivory's face followed quickly by a look of consternation, "you mean these boys haven't heard about Stuart's plume? Where they been?"

"Babes in the woods, Ivory. They just got here."

"Ah see!" Ivory's smile returned.

"Sit on down!" gestured Miles, "and don't you be callin' me marse, hear? You ain't my slave."

Ivory dropped his armload of gear and joined the circle.

"Boys," continued Miles, "this here's Ivory. He ain't got no last name. He's from down in South Carolina... whereabouts?" Turner glanced at the black man.

"Outside of Greenville," explained Ivory.

"Greenville," repeated Turner with a nod, "anyway, Ol' Ivory here's got a very patriotic master. Ain't that right, Ivory?"

"Yessuh! That would be Marse Giles. He done hired me out to the Confederate army. Told me I could keep whatever money I earned, he did."

"This boy can drive a team of mules like there's no tomorrow," explained Miles, "and he's a right mean cook to boot!"

"Excuse me," ventured Wil, "I thought you wanted him to tell us a story about Jeb Stuart."

"I do!" maintained Miles.

"Well let him tell it!" grinned the young volunteer from the valley.

"Oops!" Turner's histrionics drew chuckles from those gathered about the morning fire. "Go on, Ivory. Tell 'em about the plume."

"Well now," started Ivory, "it all started a week ago. Yessuh, it was last Sunday. Ol' Jeb was waitin' for Fitz Lee at Clark's Mountain. Did y'all know Fitz Lee is the general's nephew?"

"We know that," replied Wil a little impatiently.

"Of course you do!" Ivory slapped his own thigh with an open hand. "you fellas is Virginia boys. I forgot about that! Anyway, Marse Robert planned to use cavalry to hit the railroad bridge up to Rappahannock station, and Stuart, he was gonna use Fitz to take out that bridge, but Fitz didn't show!"

"Where was he?" wondered Andrews.

"He was supposed to come up from Hanover Junction, but he was runnin' a tad late," explained Ivory. "Late that night Stuart got tired of waitin', so he gets his staff together and they rides out to find Fitz Lee. Around midnight they ain't seen no sign of him, so they stop to get some sleep on the front porch of a house by the side of the road. Long about dawn they hears hoofbeats, so two of Stuart's officers mount up and ride out to meet Fitz, only it ain't Fitz. It's Yankees!"

Ivory paused at this point and let his eyes travel around the circle. Satisfied that he had everyone's attention he continued. "For once the Yankees done turned the tables on Jeb. He and his boys barely got out of there alive, but he left so fast he didn't even have time to grab his hat...you know, the one with the plume? Lost his cape and haversack too! Word is the Yankees had themselves a good time with that stuff. As for Stuart, he was one upset general, I'll tell you true!"

Finding the whole thing rather humorous, the group of infantrymen broke into smiles and grins and turned to make small talk with one another. A couple even stood as if to leave.

"Hold on a minute!" demanded Miles, "he ain't finished yet!"

"There's more?" Levi wondered aloud.

"Sure is! Y'all ain't heard the best part yet!"

"Wait a minute," said Wil, "you said Ivory was a teamster. How's he know all this stuff?"

"He's also a cook! Sometimes he cooks for people in high places. Besides, I ain't never seen a man with an ear for stories like Ivory's got! He hears 'em all, and remembers everything. It's downright uncanny!"

"Marse Turner," smiled Ivory, "you do go on! Truth is I got friends what cook for some of Stuart's officers. They heard the story and passed it on to me."

"Well now," huffed Turner, "I reckon I like my explanation a sight better. Anyway, you best be finishin' this story. These boys are actin' like they got ants in their pants."

"Okay," nodded the burly slave, "I'll tell you fellas how Stuart got even."

Once again the small assembly of foot soldiers settled into their circle and gave their undivided attention to the black man with the bald head.

"Y'all may be new to this army," declared Ivory, "but I'm sure you know that Lee's plans for Rapahannock station didn't pan out. If they had we wouldn't be in this line with the Yankees on the other side of the river. So the general came up with another idea. He sent Stuart on a raid up behind Pope's army. Y'all must know about that 'cause they just got back the other day."

Most of the men nodded. They knew at least that Stuart had left and returned.

"You know the details?" Ivory had no desire to tell a story which had already been told.

"Just that they were supposed to burn a railroad

bridge but the rain interfered." offered Wil.

"No suh! I mean the real details!"

"I reckon that's what you're about to tell us," replied Covington a little sheepishly.

"And you best get on with it!" added Levi with a grin, "else we'll be eatin' lunch fo' you're finished!"

"Well all right!" laughed Ivory, "Ol' Jeb he rode out of here on the twenty-second. Took fifteen hundred troopers and a couple of guns. You already knows what they was aimin' to do, so I won't get into that. I'll tell you one thing, Jeb was some kind a itchin' to turn the tables on them Yankees after they rode off with his plume and hat. Long about noon they reached Warrenton. Word is Stuart was in the company of a young lady up there. She told him 'bout a bet she made with a federal officer...a quartermaster. He said he'd be in Richmond within thirty days. She bet him a bottle of wine he wouldn't."

"What's this got to do with Stuart's hat?" interjected Andrews.

"Why, young marse, you sho' is impatient! Just be keepin' those britches on, hear? I'll get there!
Anyway, Stuart made sure to get he name of that Yankee officer before he set out from Warrenton. Well now, they had just about reached Catlett when the rain hit 'em..."

"Wait a second," Andrews again, "you said you were from South Carolina, right? How is it you know so much about this part of Virginia?"

"Lonnie, will you just let him talk?" shot Wil Covington in a thoroughly exasperated tone.

"Now, now," soothed Ivory, "don't you boys get to arguin' hear? There's plenty of Yankees out there for y'all to argue with. To answer the young man's question: I was part of this army last summer at Manassas. Been with 'em ever since. Had plenty of time to learn the lay of this land.

"Back to Stuart. The sky was dark as night filled with thunder and lightnin'! Lo and behold they captures themselves a prisoner!"

"An officer?" asked Wil.

"Not hardly, young-un. T'was a slave, an escaped slave! He'd been workin as an orderly in the headquarters of general Pope hisself!"

"You're kiddin!"

"No suh! I'm dead serious! 'Cept he decided he didn't like workin' for the Yankees no mo' so he took off. Says he's so happy 'bout bein' with his own people again he offers to guide Stuart right to Pope's personal quarters!"

"Headquarters of the whole Yankee army?"

"Yes, suh, I swear it's true!"

"Well go on! Tell us what happened!"

"Ol Jeb," grinned Ivory, "he kinda liked that idea. He orders a thousand troopers into the saddle and off they go! They found the Union camp and charged in like there was no tomorrow! Bugles was blowin' and men was just a yellin' like wild animals! I heard it was awful spooky, what with the storm and all. Thunder was crackin' and every flash of lightnin' lit up the camp! Yankees was runnin' in all directions!" He started laughing, threw his head back and slapped his thigh, "Lord!" he cried, "that must of been some sight to see!"

"I reckon!" Wil was finding Ivory's laugh infectious. "So what happened?" he demanded, his own sense of mirth fast on the rise.

"Well now, I suppose you could say our boys had themselves a good ol' time! They grabbed a whole bunch of horses and took a couple of hundred prisoners includin' some of Pope's staff!"

"What about Pope?"

"Must've been his lucky night. He weren't nowhere to be found! But they got the next best thing - all of his personal baggage, and a bunch of Yankee money!"

"Yankee money! Yeah!" laughed Andrews. "I'll take some of that!"

"Tell 'em the best part!" urged Turner, who hadn't stopped smiling for several minutes.

"I thought this was the best part!" chuckled Wil. "what could be better than Stuart scatterin' Pope's head-quarters all over the Piedmont!"

"You just listen!" laughed Turner. "Go ahead, Ivory!"

"The best part is what they took out of there," grinned the teamster. "Y'all remember the Yankee officer I told ya about? The one what made that bet with the lady in Warrenton? He was a quartermaster, and he was one of the prisoners!"

"Really?" Corporal Gilbert shed his composure for the first time, "they nabbed him?"

"You best believe it!"

"Too good to be true," the corporal shook his head with a laugh.

"Even better!" beamed Ivory, "Jeb, he done took this Union quartermaster right to the young lady who made the bet!"

"The bottle of wine?" questioned Wil.

"The same," nodded Ivory, "Stuart tells her she lost the bet and to pay up! Says this Yankee will be in Richmond in thirty days - in a prisoncamp!"

Most of those gathered about the breakfast fire found themselves convulsed in laughter as Ivory finished his story. Wil and Levi were laughing so hard tears were streaming down their faces. They found it entirely fitting that the Federal officer's boast should come back to haunt him so soon after it was uttered.

"Word is Stuart sent a note over to Pope," declared Ivory, "offered to exchange Pope's dress uniform coat for his hat an plume!"

"Really?" Corporal Gilbert flashed a wry grin in Ivory's direction. "What came of that? Did Pope respond?"

"Not yet. General Pope must not see the humor in it."

"I can understand that," Wil wiped tears from his eyes with the sleeve of his tunic. "Ol' Jeb just embarrassed him in front of the whole world! I love it!"

For the foot soldiers gathered around early morning fires Stuart's raid provided more than it's share of humorous stories. For Robert E. Lee the raid produced intelligence of a more somber nature. One of the raid's prizes was a dispatch book from Pope's headquarters which spelled out the Union build-up on the north bank of the Rappahannock in considerable detail. The first units of McClellan's army were not even a day's march away. Already Pope had grown too strong to risk engaging him head-on.

Having such intimate knowledge of the enemy's plans and strength did nothing to ease the southern commander's mind. Lee was obviously facing a dilemma. He could not remain in place along the Rappahannock. To do so would be to invite disaster as he would soon be facing the combined strength of Pope and McClellan. Nor could he retreat. Such a choice would merely invite a renewed assault on the Confederate capital. It didn't take long for Lee to come to a decision. In point of fact he had no choice. A way had to be found to maneuver Pope out of his position, preferably in a direction which would increase the distance between his own troops and those of McClellan.

1862

The Orange and Alexandria railroad appeared to offer the best opportunity to accomplish Lee's objectives. It served as Pope's line of supply, extending in a northeastern direction back through the depot-town of Manassas. Twice in recent days Lee had attempted to sever this line with Stuart's cavalry. Neither operation was successful. A stronger blow would have to be landed somewhere in Pope's rear.

Here Robert E. Lee made one of the boldest decisions of his career, one born of necessity, not desire. One of the most basic principles of warfare tells commanders they must not divide their forces in the face of a superior enemy. Lee was about to ignore this axiom on no uncertain terms.

Twice he had tried cavalry to no avail. This time the task would fall to the infantry. Not a handful mind you; it was not a mere raid which Lee had in mind. A full corps would be given the job; Jackson's men. They occupied the extreme left of the Confederate line, which gave them the best jump off position. Moreover, they would be asked to undertake an assignment which fit their reputation quite nicely. They were aptly known as Jackson's "foot cavalry" because they could march farther and faster than anybody in either army.

On Sunday the 24th of August, Lee made the short trip to Jackson's headquarters near Jeffersonton, a couple of miles south of the Rappahannock. The two men conferred during the early hours of afternoon and the older of the two explained what he had in mind to hasten the undoing of General Pope. He asked Jackson to take his entire Corps and loop around Pope's right, marching north along the western slopes of the Bull Run Mountains which hopefully would mask his movements. Once he was well to the rear of Pope's army he was to turn and strike at the Union supply line. If Pope could be made to fear for the security of his supply base he might be forced to withdraw from his positions along the Rappahannock and retire toward Manassas. If all went well the two wings of the Confederate army could reunite near that strategic depot and inflict some serious damage on the man Lee referred to as "that miscreant." The Rebel commander brought the meeting to a close with a word of caution. Jackson was not to trigger a general engagement. The objectives which had been spelled out could be readily accomplished simply by posing a serious threat to Pope's base of supply at Manassas.

Jackson wasted little time in getting ready. As soon as Lee departed Stonewall sent for his topographical engineer and sent him on ahead to find the best route through the hills which would hide his movements. Word spread quickly through the camps: we march at first light. All through the day his camps resembled a collection of beehives humming with activity. The men weren't told where they were going, only that they would carry nothing but their weapons. One wagon train would accompany the march. It would include ambulances for the wounded as well as ordinance. A small herd of cattle would be available for food and there was plenty of corn growing on farms all along the route.

Late that afternoon as Wil and Levi were walking across camp to draw ammunition they spied Ivory who was hard at work replacing a wheel on the back axle of his wagon.

"Hey, Ivory!" called Wil, "what happened?"

The black man paused in his labors to glance over his shoulder. Recognizing the two boys he gave them a nod and a smile. "Spoke's busted," he explained.

"We're movin' out. Did ya hear?"

"Sho' nuff. I'm goin' with ya."

"No kiddin'?"

"Now why would I kid about somethin' like that? Someone's got to drive this wagon, and someone's got to cook for you boys. Who else but me?"

"I suppose," nodded Wil, "you heard anythin' about where we might be goin'?"

"Not a word," Ivory groaned out loud as he strained to lift the wagon just a little higher in order to place the new wheel into position. "Whew!" he sighed as he slumped down with his back to the wheel. Wiping sweat from his face and shiny bald head he glanced up at Wil and Levi. "Reckon I might be gettin' too old to be liftin' that big a load."

"Speak up next time," scolded Levi. "We're here. We could of helped ya."

"I'll remember that next time," he smiled. "As for where we're goin' don't count on Ol' Jack to say. That's just not the way he does things. He keeps his plans to hisself by and large. One thing for sure though, if Marse Robert is sendin' Stonewall to do a job, there's gonna be a fight somewhere down the line. Count on that."

This comment sparked excitement inside Wil. "I shore hope so!" he beamed. "We've been in this army for nigh on two months and haven't seen one minute of action yet!"

"That so?" Ivory stood straight, placed his hands on the small of his back and leaned backwards. "My back hurts," he explained. "Anyway, young-un, don't be in too big of a hurry to start shootin'. There won't be any fun in it and we may end up leavin' you in the ground."

"Ain't afraid of dyin'," returned Wil making it a point to thrust his chest out a little further."

"Maybe not now but there'll come a time."

BROTHERS IN GRAY

Wil found it difficult to sleep that night. This could partly be explained by the commotion made by the caissons and horses as Jackson's artillery was withdrawn and replaced by Longstreet's guns. Noise however could only partially explain his insomnia. He hadn't been able to chase Ivory's words from his mind. If this aging slave was correct there would soon be a battle. No one seemed to know where or how it would happen but everyone believed a fight was brewing. Would he measure up? Despite his brash words he wasn't sure. Talk of courage was just that; bravado...little else. Wil Covington knew this as well as anyone. All the night through he was plagued by self-doubt. Long about three in the morning he rolled over and nudged Levi's ribs. "You awake?" he asked.

"Am now." came the sleepy reply several moments later.

"I can't sleep."

" I noticed. What's botherin' ya?"

"What Ivory said. You think I'll end up a coward?"

"Aw c'mon, Will! It's the middle of the night! Can't we talk about this in the mornin'?"

"I'm worried, Levi! Can't help it! Who else am I gonna talk to? You're the best friend I got. If I can't tell you I can't tell no one. I'm afraid I might run when the shootin' starts."

Levi sighed wearily and sat up, throwing off the thin bed roll under which he had been peacefully sleeping. "I ain't never known you to run from a fight, Wil."

"Those was school yard brawls. Nothin' like this."

"You're no coward. Stop tryin' to talk yourself into believin' otherwise."

"You afraid?"

"Ain't had much time to think about it. Anyhow, you white boys will be doin' all the fightin'."

"Yeah, but you'll be right behind us loadin' guns."

"I'll try not to be noticed," Levi flashed a cocky grin. "Go on back to sleep, Wil. Lord knows we may not have a chance to sleep a whole night again for a while." He returned to a prone position and pulled the thin blanket over his body.

"Wish I could," sighed Wil several moments later.

The sun had yet to make its first appearance of the morning of August 25th when Jackson's men were roused from sleep and formed into a double line of march. Jackson himself was riding up and down the line to keep the men on the move, "Close up, men," he was heard to say, "Close up." The first steps in Lee's bold strategy had been taken.

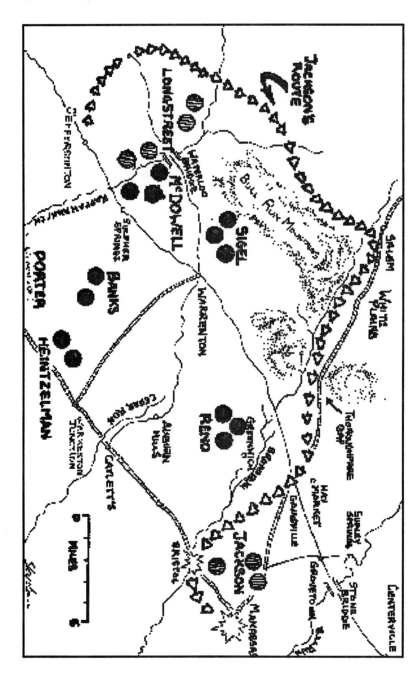

~ Chapter Three ~
Second Manassas

"**I** can't go on another step!" groaned Wil as his legs finally gave out on him. He dropped to his knees tried to right himself, but found it impossible. His mind was willing but his legs refused to pay attention. He ended up stumbling and half crawling to the trunk of a huge oak tree seeking refuge from the blistering August heat in the shade of its majestic boughs. Levi, Miles Turner and Corporal Gilbert were quickly at his side.

"We gotta keep movin', boy," explained Gilbert.

"Can't," gasped Wil. "Legs have never hurt this much in my life. I heard the foot cavalry marched fast, but I never dreamed it would be like this!"

It was three o'clock in the afternoon and they had paused infrequently to rest. The village of Orlean was now well behind them but Jackson showed no signs of either halting the march or revealing its destination. Straggling was becoming a problem as more and more of his soldiers dropped out of the line of march.

"Go on ahead, Corporal," said Turner. "I'll stay with the boy."

The corporal glanced over at Turner and nodded his head. Truth be told, he too was exhausted and would have preferred to drop to the ground beneath that tree himself. He removed his ragged kepi and wiped the sweat from his forehead with the sleeve of his tunic. "Twenty minutes," he said at last. "Then get him on his feet and catch up."

"Levi," continued Turner. "Look out on the hill yonder." He pointed toward a grassy knoll well to his right. "You reckon that's an apple tree?"

"Levi trained his eyes on the tree in question. "You got yourself some keen eyes fo' sho', Private Turner," he affirmed. "Looks like an apple tree to me!"

"How about fetchin' an armful," suggested Turner. "Might do this boy some good."

"Might at that," nodded Levi. "Sit tight, Wil," he suggested. "I'll be back 'fore you know I'm gone."

"I shore ain't goin' no place," Wil managed a weak smile.

True to his word Levi was back in no time at all with a blanket stuffed full of green apples. "They ain't ripe, but I reckon it beats goin' hungry."

"That it do," grinned Turner as he tossed one apple to Wil and bit eagerly into another.

Several men in the passing column called out for apples as well and Levi obliged them by throwing pieces of fruit toward outstretched hands.

The twenty minutes specified by Corporal Gilbert had just about elapsed when Turner spied a small group of foot soldiers dropping out of the column.

"I've about had it, Professor!" cried one. "Got to sit for a spell!"

"Me too," replied the bearded man with the stripes on his sleeve. "We'll take a break. Let's join those fellows under that oak. There'll be shade if nothing else."

Moments later the first trio of exhausted soldiers were joined by another dozen or so.

"Afternoon," the tall, dark-haired sergeant tipped his kepi in the direction of the three soldiers seated with their backs to the tree."Mind if we join you?"

"Our pleasure," Turner rose to his feet. "Name's Turner, Miles Turner," he extended his right hand.

"Seth Reilly," the Sergeant took the outstretched hand with a firm grip and gave it a hearty shake.

"That there's Wil," pointed Turner. "And the darkie's called Levi."

Reilly nodded at the two and felt obligated to

continue introductions. He began to point out the men as he named them. "This is my corporal, Whitt Simmons. That fella we call Ox. I think you can see why. That's Al Watkins, Buck Randall, Hal Saunders..." he paused, realizing there were simply too many to name. "Well," he mused with a warm smile, "These are my boys."

Greetings were exchanged and the group of infantrymen soon sprawled on the ground finding some relief from the blazing heat in the shade of that rambling oak tree. Reilly's men had some corn they had picked along the way as well as a few stale biscuits to share with Turner, Wil and Levi.

"Did I hear someone call you Professor?" Wil addressed himself to Reilly.

"Just a nickname the boys gave me," Reilly grinned sheepishly. "I was a teacher before the war."

"Whereabouts?" quizzed Turner.

"The college down in Williamsburg."

"William and Mary?"

"Yep."

"Really?" Wil's face brightened considerably as his strength slowly returned. "My Pa would like me to go there someday."

"Do you plan to apply?"

"Don't know. Reckon the war's got to come first for the time bein'."

"Reckon so," replied Reilly with more than a trace of sadness in his voice.

"You're from Williamsburg, eh?" offered Turner.

"Sure am," nodded Reilly. "And not a day goes by that I don't wish I was back there."

"I reckon that almost makes us neighbors," returned Miles. "I come up from Suffolk."

The conversation continued along these lines until

Turner suddenly realized he had completely forgotten about the time. Quickly he turned to Wil. "Did Gilbert say twenty minutes?"

"Sure did," a twinge of fear snaked down Wil's back.

"Jesus!" cursed Miles. "We been here an hour!"

"Reckon you'd best get movin'," suggested Reilly.

"Reckon so!" Miles jumped to his feet, followed quickly by Levi.

"You ready to march, boy?" Miles looked down at Wil with an expression that was supposed to reflect sternness.

Wil climbed to his feet and stretched, "I do feel a sight better," he said, "but if you're tryin' to look like you're mad you'd best do somethin' about those eyebrows!"

"I ought to bend you over my knee, boy!"

"Later," grinned Wil. "We've got some catchin' up to do."

As the three walked off to rejoin the column Reilly called out to them, "If you need someone to vouch for you let me know, hear?"

"Much obliged!" waved Miles as they disappeared from view.

The hour spent in rest was most beneficial to Wil Covington. While he hadn't recouped all his strength he did manage to match the pace set by Miles and Levi as they moved briskly to link once more with the rest of the column. The sun was turning red as it prepared to set beyond the mountains when they finally rejoined their comrades. The column was filing into Salem, Virginia, a tiny hamlet which served as one of the stations along the Manassas Gap Railroad. Here it was that the two young farm boys from the Shenandoah Valley caught their first glimpse of the famed Stonewall Jackson. He was bare-headed standing on a large rock by the side of the road, his stare fixed on the setting sun which so beautifully high-lighted the rounded peaks and steep slopes of the Blue Ridge mountains.

"Look there, boys!" urged Miles. "It's Stonewall himself!"

As if in response to a signal, weary foot soldiers forgot how tired they were. Never mind the twenty-five grueling miles they had just put behind them. Here was Stonewall! One man let out a cheer followed quickly by several more. In a matter of seconds, hundreds of men were cheering wildly for their beloved commander. Wil and Levi were caught up in the excitement and competed with one another to see who could yell the loudest.

Though he was truly touched by their devotion, Jackson's first reaction was one of alarm. Quickly he gestured for quiet then turned to an officer standing nearby, "Get down there," he ordered, "and explain to them why they must refrain from making such a racket. Too much noise may reveal our position to the Federals!"

Just as quickly as it began, the cheering stopped, but the men would not be denied this opportunity to salute the general they held so dear. As they filed quietly past they turned their faces to him and lifted their hats in salute.

Genuinely moved by this simple yet eloquent act of devotion Jackson turned to another of his staff officers, "Who could not conquer with such troops as these?" he asked, his face beaming with pride for the ragtag soldiers who continued the silent salute as they moved past him.

Their destination was a source of much speculation among these same soldiers as they bedded down that night. Many seemed to think they were about to swing west and drop into the Shenandoah; perhaps for a strike into Maryland or Pennsylvania. Some argued that Washington D.C. was their target, while others maintained the whole march was merely a feint designed to strike fear into Lincoln's heart. They reasoned that if Lincoln feared for the security of his capital he might draw troops away from either McClellan or Pope, thus easing the pressure on Lee. Not until morning would the answer to these questions be known.

Jackson's men weren't the only ones wondering about the intentions of their tight-lipped commander. Early on in their march their movement had been spotted by Union lookouts positioned in the hills. Pope had been informed that a closely formed column of Rebel infantry had moved passed his right flank and was snaking north through the foothills. Was the legendary Stonewall off for another fling through the Shenandoah Valley? Or had Lee plotted something more sinister? No matter. Upon taking command of the army, Pope had made it a point to boast of his intentions. Perhaps he was hoping to bolster morale which had been on the wane among his troops. "Let us look before us," he announced, "and not behind. Lines of retreat," he asserted, "could be left to take care of themselves." Having framed himself as a bold aggressive leader he could hardly allow himself to be publicly concerned about any possible threat to his rear. He retired that night outwardly confident that events would take care of themselves. They would, but not in a fashion John Pope would find palatable.

"Seems like I just fell asleep," groaned Wil as he shouldered his bedroll and joined his comrades who were forming into a line of march. As for where they were heading, all speculation was quickly laid to rest. To the east they turned, moving parallel with the railroad toward the crimson sunrise.

Spirits began to rise at once. Many sensed it was Pope's supply base at Manassas they were after and the thought of this made many of them giddy with anticipation.

Only one obstacle posed a threat to total surprise: Thoroughfare Gap, a narrow defile which sliced through the southern slopes of Bull Run Mountain. If Pope had displayed any foresight whatsoever there would be Union troops holding that gap and this would force Jackson to fight his way through. The element of surprise would thus be lost.

Throats tightened as they neared the crest. Wil's stomach was doing flip flops and his hands grew so sweaty he was afraid he might drop his musket if he was called upon to use it. Would this be his first action?

Foresight apparently wasn't one of John Pope's higher suits. Not a bluecoat was to be found anywhere. Jackson and his troops marched through unopposed and undetected. Pope had been heard to say that only "disaster and shame lurk in the rear." With regard to the former his words were to prove all too prophetic.

With the gap behind them they continued east to Haymarket. There they swung slightly south into Gainesville. Joined now by Stuart and his cavalry they pushed across country toward Bristoe Station where the railroad, Pope's life line as it were, crossed a meandering creek known as Broad Run. Close to their goal they were, but many were dropping exhausted by the wayside. Fifty miles in two days they had marched and the strain of such a herculean effort was beginning to tell. Jackson seemed to be everywhere. Up and down the column he rode. "Push on men!" he would cry. "Push on!" Push on they did. By sunset the lead elements of the column reached

BROTHERS IN GRAY

Bristoe. Whooping and cheering they found within themselves the strength for one more charge and quickly overwhelmed the federal guards who had been assigned to the bridge. Pope's line of supply was about to be severed.

No sooner had the bridge fallen into Rebel hands than the noise of a train approaching from the south reached their ears. By this time Wil's regiment had arrived in Bristoe and worn out though they were, eagerly joined in the effort to tear up the tracks. There wasn't the time. Before they could unbolt a rail, the engine roared through forcing them all to leap for safety.

"Reckon they'll be spreadin' the word," lamented Corporal Gilbert as he pulled himself from the ground and brushed the dirt from his already ragged uniform.

"Get busy, boys!" Colonel Reynolds arrived on horseback and spoke with a definite sense of urgency. "One of the prisoners has been most co-operative. There'll be several more empty supply trains coming this way from Pope's forward depots near Warrenton. They're headin' for Manassas and Alexandria to load back up."

To work they went, wasting not another second. Several sections of track were soon removed. Whereupon the troops fanned out on either side of the tracks and prepared a warm reception for the next train. They didn't have long to wait.

They heard the whistle first, then spied the pale gleam of the lanterns on the engine in the distance. As the train approached it was struck first by a volley of rifle fire before it hit the section of missing track and crashed with an incredible roar down the embankment followed by at least half of its cars. Red hot coals exploded skyward to the delight of the rebel onlookers and thick clouds of steam billowed in all directions.

Soldiers rushed forward to gawk at the wreck, finding it particularly pleasing to stare at the bullet riddled portrait of Abraham Lincoln attached to the dome of the engine. Ironically the engine was named The President. Soldiers were chatting and laughing it up like a collection of chipmunks when suddenly there came the whistle of a third train.

"Get out of the way, boys!" warned Turner. "He's comin' on fast!"

Too fast as it turned out. The train hurled into those cars from the first wreck which were still on the tracks. Splintered wood and twisted iron flew in all directions as the engine crushed several cars in front of it before leaving the tracks. No sooner had the smoke and debris settled than still another whistle sounded away in the distance.

"Here we go again!" laughed Wil as he grabbed his musket and started for cover.

It was not to be. The glow of burning coal and wood from the previous wrecks was seen by the engineer in plenty of time. Reacting at once he applied the brakes and this fourth train ground to a screeching halt well shy of the waiting rebels. Quickly the engineer reversed the direction of his train which huffed and puffed its way south again - out of harm's way.

Looks like the word's gonna be out in both direc- tions," mused Turner with a stoic expression on his face.

There was little time to bemoan the loss of an opportunity to wreck yet another train. Much work remained to be done. The bridge over Broad Run had to be destroyed and a number of men applied themselves at once to the task. Several fires were built to illuminate the area while Jackson's men sifted through the wreckage and assisted the injured. Jackson himself sat down by one of these fires and turned his attention to the interrogation of one of the captive engineers.

For Wil Covington one of the spoils of this tiny victory over Federalism was a fairly recent copy of Harpers magazine which he plucked from the inside of one of the overturned cars. He, Levi and several others stole away to the opposite side of the fire from Stonewall to page through the magazine to see how the Yankees were viewing the war.

Nearby lay a civilian, an older man perhaps fifty years of age. He had sustained a broken leg in the wreck and had been carried to this place by several Rebels, who then returned to the train itself. The poor fellow was in some degree of pain and found it difficult to lie still. Glancing in the direction of Wil and his companions he called out, "Whose men are you?"

It was Miles Turner who provided his answer, "Why, suh, we're Jackson's men!"

"Jackson? Do you mean Stonewall Jackson?"

"The same," nodded Turner.

"Is he among you?"

This time it was Wil who spoke. Stepping out of the shadows he pointed across the fire and did his best to sound like a grizzled veteran, though he had yet to fire his first shot in anger, "Yonder's Jackson," he pronounced in his deepest voice.

The injured man tried to raise himself so that he could see the man whose name struck fear and awe in northern hearts but the effort was too much for his fractured limb to bear. Once again he turned toward Wil. "I must see him!" he groaned through clenched teeth. "Please...Please, would you lift me?"

"Gimme a hand, boys!" gestured Miles as he moved to assist the man. He was followed at once by Wil and Levi.

Together the three of them propped the injured fellow up so he could gaze through the leaping flames at Jackson on the other side.

Lord knows what he anticipated seeing. Whatever it was Jackson surely failed to fulfill his expectations. His shoulders were slouched. His boots were far too big. His uniform seemed to match quite well the color of the roads on which his men marched. His nearly shapeless cadet cap was pulled so far down over his forehead one could barely discern the presence of a bearded face beneath it. For roughly thirty seconds the civilian stared across the fire.

"That is Stonewall Jackson?" he demanded in a tone which fairly oozed disbelief.

"The same," answered Miles.

"It can't be," He turned and found himself staring at the black face of Levi Henry.

"It is," affirmed Levi.

"Oh my God! Lay me down!" he cried, thoroughly repulsed at the spectacle across the fire.

The Rebels obliged at once. However dozens of them had been on hand when he uttered those last words and they seized upon that final statement as a source of much merriment.

The words "Oh my God! Lay me down!" along with their story spread through the ranks like some sort of wildfire, embellished a little more as it passed from unit to unit. From that point forward Jackson's men would be repeating those words in almost every conceivable situation.

About all this, Jackson himself was thoroughly unaware. He had more weighty matters on his mind. The interrogation of various prisoners had produced valuable information. Only four miles up the tracks lay Manassas, Pope's primary source of resupply. Consistent with the

BROTHERS IN GRAY

Union general's philosophy of allowing the rear to take care of itself the base was lightly guarded. However, the warning of a rebel presence had been sounded both north and south of Bristoe. From one direction or the other reinforcements would no doubt be enroute to Manassas. Jackson wasn't about to allow this prize to elude him. He summoned General Ewell at once who reported to his commander along with a brigadier general by the name of Isaac Trimble.

"The base at Manassas must be secured," explained Jackson.

"In the morning?"

"That would probably be too late. It must be done tonight before it is reinforced."

"The men have been marching for two solid days, suh. They're exhausted."

"Tonight," repeated Stonewall.

"I will do it," announced Trimble, "if your information is correct I should be able to take the depot with two regiments."

"Very well," nodded Jackson. "March at once."

Trimble and Ewell started away but the wheels in Jackson's mind were still turning. What if the information was false? What if the prisoners were attempting a ruse and the depot was in fact strongly held? Quickly he came to another decision. Stuart had joined the column that afternoon with his cavalry at about the same time the infantry had reached Gainesville. "General Trimble," he called.

Trimble stopped and turned around.

"I shall dispatch the cavalry as well."

"As you wish," Trimble saluted his commander and returned to the two weary regiments which were about to take Manassas.

The next morning Jackson along with the bulk of his infantry joined Trimble in Manassas. He reached the depot before his troops and immediately knew there would be problems. Over a square mile of land was stacked high with every kind of provision imaginable. Not just the necessities of war mind you, there were luxuries sitting there which Jackson's ragtag warriors never allowed themselves to dream of: fresh coffee, canned peaches, the finest in European wines, canned lobster, just to name a few. Over a hundred boxcars were sitting on spur tracks loaded to capacity. Sutler wagons were everywhere, though their owners had seen fit to hightail it in the face of Jackson's horde. Stonewall anticipated havoc, and he attempted to forestall it by assigning Trimble's regiments the dubious honor of keeping their comrades at bay.

It wasn't to be. The two-day forced march had left them lean and hungry. No power on earth could have stopped them from ravishing those federal stocks, least of all Trimble's poor fellows. The party was on and what a party it was! Half-starved Rebels gorged themselves with Union finery. During the early morning hours of August 27, 1862, Jackson's foot cavalry were in heaven.

The time for light hearted plunder passed all too quickly so far as Wil was concerned. He and Levi were seated on the ground enjoying peaches and some sort of bread that looked more like cake. Another soldier sat down nearby with a bottle of wine cradled in his arm. He was older than Wil by three or four years. He was using his bayonet to pry open a can of lobster meat.

"Wil Covington," for some reason Wil felt the need to introduce himself.

"Lemuel Vaughn," came the reply. "Folks call me Lem."

"What's that you got there?"

Vaughn finally got the can open and pulled out a chunk of white meat still dripping juices.

"Lobster. You want some?"

"Ain't never tried lobster before."

"It's good. Go ahead, have a bite," he held the can out first to Wil then to Levi.

Both boys tore off chunks with their fingers. Wil took a small tentative bite followed quickly by another. "That stuff's good!"

"Here," suggested Vaughn, "wash it down with this." He uncorked the bottle of German wine.

Wil took two long sips doing his best to hide his lack of experience. "What do the Yankees do with all this stuff?" he wondered aloud.

"Spoil themselves I reckon. They dress better than we do. They shore do eat a sight better than the likes of us. Still the same, I don't see where it makes 'em better soldiers than us."

"Me neither," Wil shook his head in bewilderment at the sheer quantity of material stockpiled for Pope's soldiers.

It was the sound of musket fire which drew the attention of all three men away from their unexpected treat.

The shrill notes of bugles pierced the air and orders were shouted by startled commanders. A threat had materialized from the north.

"Looks like I gotta go," said Lem as he watched his regiment forming hastily into ranks. "You boys finish this stuff. Don't let it go to waste, hear?" As if to emphasize this point he scooped out another chunk of lobster meat and stuffed it into his mouth. One more deep gulp of wine and he was gone.

The threat itself came in the form of a brigade of

New Jersey infantry under the command of Brigadier General George W. Taylor. He and his men had been sent down by rail from Alexandria with orders to secure the railroad bridge across Bull Run. Taylor was under the impression - the wrong one as it turned out - that the mischief in Manassas was the work of raiders and that a determined push would scatter them. Therefore he took it upon himself to exceed his orders and move on to secure the Manassas depot itself. He formed his four regiments into lines of battle and advanced in gallant fashion with the colors flying proudly every step of the way.

To blunt this thrust Jackson employed A.P. Hill's division, quite possibly the best fighters in Lee's army. Artillery opened fire first though the range was still a bit distant. Perhaps Jackson was using the cannons to send a message to his opponent, to make him realize it was no lightly armed raiding party he was attacking. Taylor didn't get the message.

On they came, as though they were the very pride of New Jersey. Heedless of their long range losses they surged forward into the sights of Hill's riflemen waiting patiently to take their turn at these bluecoats.

At this point, Jackson did something neither side expected. He openly admired the courage of these Union soldiers and he knew they had no chance against Hill's infantry. Later, he was to describe this charge as having been made with "great spirit and determination and under a leader worthy of a better cause."

In any event, he called out for a cease fire and as the guns fell silent the legendary Stonewall Jackson himself rode out in front of the lines waving a white handkerchief. Several times he yelled out to the Federals to surrender to avoid being cut to pieces. They paid him no mind. In fact one Union soldier went so far as to take deliberate aim at the Rebel general and fired away. The bullet barely missed Jackson. In fact it came so close as to dismiss any further thoughts he may have been entertaining about mercy. Quickly he spurred his mount back behind the lines, "Return fire!" he ordered in a justifiably angry tone.

The effect was instant: 335 of them were killed, wounded or captured. The rest turned and fled for their lives, ignoring their dying commander's desperate pleas to rally and avoid another Bull Run.

Wil and Levi were but spectators to all this and Wil complained openly to Corporal Gilbert that he might never have an opportunity to fight the Yankees.

The Corporal looked down at Wil with a tinge of sadness in his eyes, "Your time'll come, boy," he observed. "Probably a lot sooner than any of us think."

Sooner indeed. Word had come from Ewell's men at the Broad Run bridge. They were being pressed from the south. No doubt more Federals would soon be heading down from Alexandria. The time had come to leave Manassas.

As for the cornucopia of Federal supplies, Jackson loaded as much as possible into his own wagons, particularly the medical stores. He allowed his men a few more precious minutes of looting then ordered the whole mess put to the torch. The resulting explosion of munitions was heard and felt for miles in all directions. Flames towered in the air and thick columns of black smoke curled skyward. At the Union headquarters in the city of Washington they knew something had gone desperately wrong.

With his command reunited, Jackson wasted no more time. Away they marched. However this was not to be one of the better executed marches in the history of Jackson's foot cavalry. The men simply weren't in a frame of mind for a fast-paced move. For one thing their bellies were too full. Add to this factor the weight of their Yankee loot and you have the ingredients for a general's nightmare. Men fell out of the column by the hundreds to sleep off the morning's excesses. Orders were misunderstood. Ewell marched in one direction, Hill in another. The corps was fragmented and seemingly spread all over the landscape. In truth if Pope had been able to find them they may well have all been destroyed piecemeal.

Pope wasn't able to find them, but it wasn't for lack of trying. He was aware of the massive explosion in the vicinity of Manassas. He knew his supplies were gone but to him this was no source of dismay. Quite to the contrary, the question of Jackson's destination had now been answered, albeit a little loudly. Pope was quick to realize the opportunity which had just fallen into his lap. Lee's army was divided in two with the numerically superior Union army squarely in the middle of the widely separated halves. John Pope was ecstatic. In his mind, Lee had just committed the worst possible tactical blunder. He was determined to take quick advantage of it.

Already he had dispatched Hooker's division in the direction of Bristoe Station. With the thick clouds of smoke billowing up from the Manassas depot, Pope rushed to join Hooker to glean the latest news. By nightfall he was at Hooker's side and learned that the Rebels had retreated across Broad Run in the direction of Manassas. According to Hooker, the Rebels had been soundly thrashed. Hooker's report only served to enhance the optimism which now guided Pope's every decision. At once he dispatched a wire to General Phil Kearny who commanded a division of Federal infantry at Warrenton Junction. The telegraph message read as follows: "At the very earliest blush of dawn push forward...with all speed to this place...Jackson, A.P.Hill, and Ewell are in front of us... I want you here at daybreak, if possible, and we shall bag the whole crowd. Be prompt and expeditious, and never mind wagon trains or roads till this affair is over." General Reno with two divisions in nearby Greenwich as well as General McDowell with three divisions along the Rappahannock received orders worded in similar fashion.

The next morning Pope crossed Broad Run and marched unopposed into Manassas to find a scene of such total destruction even he was amazed. Nothing but charred remains, scattered equipment, and food as far as the eye could see in any direction. Of those who had perpetrated this colossal vandalism there was no sign.

"Looks like they did a right thorough job," remarked one staff officer as Pope surveyed the scene with an expression of pure amazement.

"Had themselves one hell of a party," remarked another.

"Forget this stuff," said Pope laconically. "We have but one purpose now, to find and destroy Jackson. To that end we must all set our minds."

Survivors of the New Jersey regiments began to filter back toward the ruined depot as did some of the original guards and the horde of sutlers who bemoaned the loss of their goods. All were questioned as to the direction the Rebels had taken. All of them seemed to have different answers. Did the Rebels scatter along every point of the compass? Had they gone to ground like so many chipmunks?

"This is beginning to sound a bit absurd," complained Pope after hearing still another version as to the direction of the butternut withdrawal. As Reno, Kearny and McDowell converged on emptiness they found their commander trying to sift through an impossible amount of conflicting intelligence.

"Centerville," mused Pope standing with one foot on a stump, tapping the map which he had spread across his knee. "They must be at Centerville. We have to get there fast, gentlemen! This day will still be ours."

By sunset he reached Centerville with twelve divisions of infantry. Once again they converged on a virtual vacuum. No sign was there of Rebels though quite a few civilians admitted to having seen them.

So far as Pope's men were concerned the whole affair was beginning to sour. Most of them had been marched for fourteen long hours along hot dusty roads. They were exhausted and hungry, most of their rations having been pilfered or destroyed in Manassas. They disliked the region itself as it offered nothing but bad memories of last year's fiasco along Bull Run. As each hour passed and no sign of Jackson was to be found they began to believe they were chasing ghosts. Whatever faith they may have had in their commanders was fast on the ebb. Toward some of these officers, McDowell for example, many of the foot-soldiers exhibited outward suspicion and hostility.

With the sun setting it seemed as though Pope's spirits were moving in the same direction. He found himself struggling to avoid the feeling of despair which was creeping gradually through his body. Where was that damned Jackson!

As for the elusive Stonewall it could be argued his luck was in. Even the chaotic nature of his march out of Manassas worked to his advantage, contributing to the host of conflicting reports as to his whereabouts which in turn left Pope chasing after ghosts. As the Union commander groped blindly about the countryside Jackson managed to reunite the bulk of his command by early afternoon.

BROTHERS IN GRAY

Old Blue Light, as Stonewall was known by many of his foot soldiers, had chosen his position with great care. In the woods of Groveton, just above the Warrenton Turnpike somewhat to the west of the fields on which the two armies had grappled just over a year ago, he knew of a low-lying ridge beyond which he could conceal his troops. There being no particular sense of urgency pending they were allowed to stack arms and relax beneath the shade of the trees.

Not counting those who had yet to filter in, they numbered roughly 23,000, and Jackson packed them into this position in very crowded circumstances. Orders were given for the bands to remain silent but the men found plenty of things to do as they lounged comfortably in the woods. They continued to treat themselves to the delicacies lifted from Pope's store. Card games were underway all up and down the line as men from different units intermingled, talking, laughing, swapping yarns. One could almost think of these few hours as the lull before the storm. For many of these men the day would be their last on God's green earth.

Wil and Levi had joined into a card game with Miles Turner and three of the fellows they had met from the Stonewall Brigade. By and by others stopped in to join. Lem Vaughn was there, having survived the rather one-sided affair with the Jerseymen at the depot. Out of the woods stepped another soldier tall and dark with the look of a cajun about him. "Afternoon," he nodded at the Virginians engaged with their cards. The buttons on his tunic identified his regiment as being from Louisiana. "Y'all got room fer one more?"

"Shore!" beckoned Miles. "Pull yourself up a chair and join in!" Turner flashed the cajun a friendly grin. "Hope you got some coins in them pockets."

"Reckon I can ante up a little," he joined the circle and sat crosslegged on the ground next to Wil.

"You one of them Tiger fellas?" asked Wil.

"You got it. Louisiana Tiger, that's me."

"Well now," ventured Miles, "You must have a name. Folks don't call you tiger do they? Might make the rest of the tigers jealous!"

"Course I got a name!" he laughed. "I go by the name of Armelin Linscombe."

"Damned if that ain't a mouthful!" Ox laughed so hard his belly rolled like waves in the ocean.

"What unit?" wondered Wil.

"Company K, 10th Louisiana infantry."

"What do you think we ought to call him?" ventured Miles.

"We could call him Armi," Levi flashed a broad grin.

"Nah," gestured Miles. "Hell, boy, we're in the army! That wouldn't work a'tall!"

"You could call me Private Linscombe. That is after all my name."

"Much too formal," Miles shook his head.

"How about tiger?" offered Wil. "After all he's one of 'em."

"Good idea," Miles nodded approvingly. "Tiger it is," He finished shuffling the deck and handed it to Linscombe, "Here you go, Private Tiger! Deal away! You name the game!"

"Five card draw," said the soldier from Louisiana. "Deuces wild." With the speed and dexterity of someone who had obviously seen a deck of cards before he began to deal.

Of all this Jackson himself was quite unaware. He remained on horseback pacing his mount back and forth along the crest of the ridge where he could maintain a clear watch over the Warrenton Turnpike. Though his position afforded his troops an open avenue of retreat if necessary, he had no intention of exercising that option. Truth be known, he was spoiling for a fight. So tense was he that no one, not even his own staff officers dared intrude upon his thoughts. It was not for defense that he had positioned his infantry. He was aching to take a swipe at one of the blueclad columns engaged in the searched for Rebels.

When a report came in to the effect that a Union column was coming up the pike from Gainesville he reacted at once moving both Ewell and Taliaferro into position to spring an ambush. All this to no avail as the Federals moved off the pike in the direction of Manassas.

Frustrated, but refusing to yield to his own impatience, Jackson held his ground and continued to pace the ridge. Despite Lee's admonition against a general engagement, he had come to believe it necessary to pitch into Pope before the arrival of McClellan's forces made him too strong. Jackson knew Lee and Longstreet were enroute but time was definitely becoming a critical factor. In point of fact Jackson was fervently praying that Pope would find him...the sooner the better.

The day was very nearly over when an answer to his prayers appeared in the form of a substantial column of Union infantry coming up the turnpike. Jackson himself trotted down the ridge to make sure he wasn't dreaming. Showing utter disregard for his own safety he moved to within easy musket range of the Yankee infantry.

"He must be crazy," muttered one of his staff officers watching in horror from the security of the ridge, "them Yanks could drop him without battin' an eyelash."

In truth they could have, but they didn't. Dressed

as he was he appeared to those federal troops as little more than a lone Rebel cavalryman, hardly worth the effort of breaking their stride. They paid him no mind.

For a minute or two, he maintained a brisk pace back and forth parallel to their line of march. Convinced these bluecoats represented the solution to his problems he wheeled his horse about and urged him back toward the ridge at a gallop.

"Here he comes, by God!" shouted one of those who awaited his return.

Jackson reached the crest of the ridge and reined in sharply. Displaying no emotion whatsoever he tipped his tattered kepi and said, "bring your men up, gentle-men."

Down in the woods where the men waited someone looked up from the card game and saw several officers of general rank rushing toward them, "Somethin's up," he said.

Linscombe looked up from the card game and knew at once what it meant. "Time to fight," he said simply as he gathered his winnings and stuffed them into his pockets, "got to get back to my regiment!"

"Me too!" Vaughn rose and turned away.

"Wait a minute, Tiger!" yelled Miles, "You gotta promise me another poker game! I need to win some of my money back!"

"Whenever you'd like!" Linscombe disappeared through the trees.

"That's one lucky son of a bitch!" growled Turner as he grabbed for his musket.

"Don't seem like luck had much to do with it," said Corporal Gilbert, who had the sense to stay out of the game, "seems like the boy knows what to do with a deck of cards in his hand."

"We'll see about that," Miles turned to join ranks as the regiment hastily stumbled into formation.

For a moment, Wil and Levi just stood there unsure as to what to do. Wil's heart was pounding wildly and his knees started to shake.

"You comin', boy?" It was Corporal Gilbert who drew his attention. "You said you was itchin' for action. Reckon the time's come."

"Yes, suh," stammered Wil trying to steady his nerves as he shouldered his musket.

"What should I do?" asked Levi. "You want me to load guns?"

"Not this time. The surgeons are already settin' up shop yonder through those trees. You'd best get over there and stay handy."

"Yes, suh!"

By now the mood of Jackson's soldiers matched that of their commander. The woods which minutes before had seemed so peaceful now resounded with the roar of men eager to fight.

Three batteries of artillery were wheeled out of the woods to open the engagement. Within minutes they were slamming shells into the closely packed column of Federals. Then came the Rebel infantry, Taliaferro's division to be exact.

Down the ridge they stormed, the wild rebel yell echoing up and down their line. Included in this division was the famed Stonewall brigade which led the charge with its colors flying proudly in the glow of twilight.

Perhaps these wildly cheering Rebels were expecting their opponents to break and flee in panic. Such would not be the case. The Union brigade was comprised of four regiments which had been raised from states of the old Northwest territory. They fought under the command of a man by the name of John Gibbon. They were relatively new to this thing called war. In fact, this was their first major engagement. Gibbon wanted his men to appear different from the average Union infantryman. They didn't wear blue kepis. He outfitted each of them with a black felt hat. Not only was their appearance distinctive but also their courage and their skill with muskets. These were the men who were soon to be known as the Iron Brigade. They were not about to break.

Gibbon's troops faced about at once and formed by regiment to meet Taliaferro's attack. Firing one volley upon another they stood shoulder to shoulder. They stopped the Rebels cold. Presently they were reinforced by two regiments from Abner Doubleday's brigade and with this added strength they withstood the best the Southerners could offer.

Not content with the stalemate which seemed to be shaping up Jackson advised Ewell to add two brigades to those of Taliaferro, hoping the additional numbers would bring the affair to a more hasty conclusion.

"That's us, boys," said Gilbert. "Close up and look smart..you hear? Let's show 'em what Stonewall's boys are all about!"

Down the ridge they marched moving briskly into position beside their brothers in the Stonewall Brigade. Wil stood with Tommie Murphy to his left and Lonnie Andrews on his right.

"Wil?" There was a trace of raw fear in young Andrew's voice.

"Yeah?"

"You scared?"

"Ain't never been so scared in all my life!"

Their voices were barely audible amid the roar of musketry. Black powder smoke stung their eyes and clung to their nostrils.

"Me too! I feel like I'm about to mess my pants!"

Already men were crying out as they were hit by the hail of minie balls from the Union line along the pike.

"I wish to God I was home!" cried Andrews.

"Quiet there!" demanded Gilbert, "stand firm!"

"Load!" came the order.

Almost as one, the men of this regiment reached for their cartridge pouches. In moments they were primed and ready.

"Aim!"

Again, they reacted together almost as if they were a single organism.

"Fire!"

Sheets of flame and smoke spat from their muskets as a wall of Southern lead sped toward the Union ranks.

So it went. For two solid hours the opposing forces, over five thousand Rebels against twenty-eight hundred Yankees, stood in parade formation and slammed away at one another. Casualties on both sides were dreadful. Tommie Murphy died instantly, without so much as a whimper, as a minie ball hit him right between the eyes. One second he was standing. The next, as Wil turned to say something, he was on the ground dead. The fluttering in Wil's stomach seemed beyond any hope of control and he felt sure he was about to die as well.

Just as the sun dropped beyond the western horizon, Lonnie Andrews took a bullet in the stomach. "Oh my God!" he cried in anguish, clutching his abdomen with one hand as he dropped to his knees, leaning heavily on his rifle butt for support.

"Covington!" Corporal Gilbert's voice rang out over the din. "Get him back to the surgeons! Be quick!"

Wil squeezed off the shot he'd already loaded,

cradled his musket then reached down with one arm to haul Andrews up to his feet. "C'mon, Lonnie, I'll get you out of here!"

"Oh my God, Wil! I'm gonna die!"

"No, You ain't! Now hold on!"

Back toward the ridge moved Wil, half-dragging half-carrying his stricken companion. His ears were still ringing with the roar of battle and the thick low-lying pall of smoke made it difficult to see in the fading light. Back into the woods they went where only a little while ago they had been laughing and joking as they were losing their money to Armelin Linscombe.

"Lonnie? Lonnie,can you hear me?"

"Gettin' weak, Wil" There seemed precious little life in Andrew's voice, "can't keep my feet."

To Wil,he seemed as though he were trying to carry a full grown mule,when in fact young Andrews weighed barely one hundred ten pounds.

"Oh Ma!" muttered Andrews,"Ma!"

"Hold on, Lonnie! We're almost there!"

Wil spotted the surgeon's tents and saw Ivory's bald head as he stepped out of one, "Ivory!" he cried, "Ivory! Gimme a hand here! It's Lonnie! I can't hold him much longer!"

The older black man moved as quickly as he could to Wil's side and took hold of Andrews as he was collapsing toward the ground. Ivory was a veteran. He had seen hundreds of wounded men and could recognize immediately those who had a chance of survival and those who didn't. He knew at once that Andrews was dying: that he had but moments left. The poor boy's tunic was stained crimson from the upper stomach on down. The crotch and upper thigh areas of his trousers were similarly soiled. Gently he laid the dying boy on the ground cradling his

BROTHERS IN GRAY

head in one hand as Wil looked on helplessly.

"Ma! Oh, God! Ma!" A fierce frenzied expression took hold of the lad's face as his hand crept up Ivory's arm to grasp desperately at his shoulder, "Ma! Help me!"

"I'm here, boy, I'm right here." Ivory took hold of the hand on his shoulder and clasped it tightly in his own.

"Hurts! Hurts so bad! Please help me!"

"Make peace with the Lawd, son. Make your peace."

A vacant look began to fill the boy's eyes. He tried to speak again but the sounds were incoherent.

Ivory slowly removed his hand from under Andrew's head and gently stroked the boy's blondish hair from his face, "Mama loves her boy," he said softly, "she loves him so."

Lonnie's last breath escaped with a gasp, as if the boy was struggling to hold on to it. Then he was gone.

Ivory gently closed the dead boy's eyes and glanced up toward Wil, who could make out the tears glistening in the black man's eyes. "This is what I hates." His voice was filled with bitterness. "You tell me what business this skinny little white boy had dyin' in anybody's war! Lawd Almighty, this is what I hates! Don't mind cookin' for ya, don't mind drivin' yo' wagons and tellin' stories by the fire! But I hates watchin' y'all die and I don't much care for havin' to put ya in the ground!"

Wil stood there dumbfounded in a state bordering on shock. He had no reply to make. He had just watched one of his oldest friends die in the arms of a slave from South Carolina. His own uniform was soaked with Lonnie's blood. Across the way, wounded men were screaming in agony as surgeons separated mangled limbs from otherwise healthy bodies. In one tent, he thought he saw Levi holding down a man who was about to lose his arm.

"Gotta go," he mumbled. "Gotta get back." He picked up his musket and started walking backwards.

"You do that," said Ivory. Then as though from an afterthought he called out, "Wil! You be careful, son! Don't wanna be diggin'no holes for you!"

Wil nodded and turned around, his mind still wavering on the brink of shock. He took several steps and nearly collided with a group of infantrymen carrying a man toward the surgeons.

"Outta the way, boy!" shouted one.

Wil quickly jumped from their path and recoiled in horror as he recognized his own divisional commander in the arms of those soldiers. It was "Old Bald Head," General Ewell. He was unconscious, one leg battered beyond hope, destined for amputation.

A wave of dizziness and nausea swept over Wil as he stumbled through the woods. As he started up the western face of the ridge he spied several men working to bind the wounds of yet another general. Was it Taliaferro? Wil had to step closer to be sure of the man's identity because it was very nearly dark. Dear God! It was Taliaferro! Wil's thoughts were a maelstrom of confusion. Have we been defeated? Are we lost? The wave of nausea was building. He took a few more steps but could contain it no longer. Stopping to brace himself against a tree he leaned well over and wretched violently, vomiting the contents of his stomach into the leaves on the ground. As he was trying to regain his breath and composure,he heard a familiar voice behind him.

"You okay, kid?"

Wil turned to gaze into the understanding eyes of Armelin Linscombe. He was assisting another soldier from Louisiana to the rear for medical attention. The man did not appear to have a serious wound.

Seeing the blood still glistening all over Wil's clothing Linscombe repeated his query, "Are you shot?"

"What's that?"

"Have you been shot?" Armelin gestured with his
free hand toward Wil's side.

Wil looked down at himself and shook his head,
"No,"he muttered, "No, I'm alright. It's Lonnie's blood.
I had to carry him back."

Armelin nodded.

"Have we lost?"

"Can't really tell," replied the tiger from Lake
Charles.

"Gotta get back,"stammered Covington as he
moved away from the trees on legs which were shaky at
best.

"No need to rush, boy. Mother nature's settled this
one. It's too damn dark to see who the hell you're shootin'
at."

It was true. Now that he was regaining a little of his
senses Wil realized that the firing had stopped, all but a
sporadic shot from time to time. The fall of night had
brought the whole affair to a close. The two sides simply
had no choice but to disengage.

"Still the same," said Wil, "I should rejoin my
regiment."

"And I need to get Deveraux here back to the
physicians. If that feller, Turner, is still alive,tell him I'm
eagerly anticipating our next round of poker."

"I'll do that."

At best,this initial bloodletting in the battle which
would come to be known as Second Manassas could be
called a draw. Both sides inflicted about as much damage
as they endured from the other. On the Confederate side
the losses were considerable. Though both would eventu-

ally recover, generals Ewell and Taliaferro were temporarily out of the war. The Stonewall Brigade itself saw over 200 of its fine men shot down, either killed or wounded. One of its regiments, the 27th Virginia, had been reduced to a mere 24 men as the fight ended. Stonewall Jackson was now forced to rely upon untried officers to replace the fallen Ewell and Taliaferro, men like William Starke of New Orleans who had never carried arms professionally prior to the outbreak of the war, and Ewell's successor, Alexander R. Lawton whose abilities left question marks in Jackson's mind.

On the opposing side those who would soon style themselves the Iron Brigade emerged from this engagement every bit as mauled as their Southern counterparts. The 2nd Wisconsin, for example, started the firing with 500 men. Only 202 were still standing when the last shot was fired, establishing a grisly record for these northwestern farm boys.

Pulling back from the pike the two Union brigade commanders were unsure as to their next move. Their divisional commander, Rufus King, was ill and confined to an ambulance. Their corps commander was nowhere to be found. He had managed to stray from the Pike itself and wound up totally lost in the woods. Thus would he remain till dawn brought the light of a new day. Their orders from Pope had been to march on Centerville. In view of the carnage they had just experienced, they deemed it wise to abandon that objective. After a brief conference with General King they decided to divert the whole column toward the Manassas depot. Runners were dispatched to find General Pope and apprise him of the change in circumstance.

As for Jackson, one might have thought he'd have been perturbed at the loss of his two best divisional commanders. Perhaps he was but whatever his feelings he kept them to himself. Though his losses were serious he was satisfied with the results. Tired of waiting for the clumsy Pope to find him, he had simply reached out and slapped the Union commander in the hindside as if to say: "I'm here, dear sir, come and get me." In this he was taking a huge gamble. Would Lee and Longstreet arrive with the rest of the army in time to rescue him from certain destruction? Jackson went to sleep that night assuming the next day would provide the answer.

Pope and Lee were to learn of the events in Groveton in widely disparate fashion. The Federal commander received his news first by way of couriers from Gibbon. The dispatch sent his mood soaring. To describe him as drowning in optimism would be no exaggeration. At last he had found Jackson! Not only had he found him but according to the reports he had done him serious damage as well. Moreover, he had received word that the rest of Lee's army had attempted and failed to force their way through Thoroughfare Gap. Assuming Lee could be held at bay west of the Gap, Jackson would remain isolated, pinned to the anvil. Quickly he revised his orders once again that he might rapidly assemble a mighty hammer of blue to pound the wounded Jackson to submission. Then he penned a note to General Halleck back in Washington informing his superior of the day's events and whetting his appetite for the crushing victory he anticipated on the morrow. As he retired for the night, he could almost sense the war's end within his grasp.

Of all this Lee knew nothing. From the first day of Jackson's departure he had kept up a ruse along the Rappahannock through the liberal use of artillery. He had sent President Davis an urgent request for more men. Might the defenses of Richmond be stripped a little more if such a move could help effect the total suppression of Pope?

Long about noon of the 26th of August, better than 24 hours following Jackson's departure, there appeared signs that the Federals were beginning to pull back from the river. Had they spotted Jackson? Were they preparing to move against him? After a brief conference with Longstreet a decision was made. The two wings of the Army of Northern Virginia must be reunited as quickly as feasible. Lee left the choice of routes to Longstreet who chose to follow essentially in Jackson's footsteps through the hills toward Orlean. Leaving Lee with but one division of infantry under the command of R. H. Anderson to hold the line south of the Rappahannock, Longstreet started north with 32,000 soldiers. By midday on the 27th his column reached Salem matching the pace of Stonewall's foot cavalry over the same ground.

Lee himself soon followed and as he made camp that night near White Plains two messages reached him, both with gratifying news. First from Jackson came word of the actions at Bristoe and Manassas. Even more welcome was the message from Richmond. President Davis decided to take his chance with those of faint heart and had granted Lee's request for reinforcements from the city's defenses. A brigade of cavalry under Wade Hampton and ten brigades of infantry, a force totaling more than 17,000 men were enroute to join him. In all, once the entire army was reunited, he would have roughly 72,000 men with which to face the combined forces of Pope and McClellan which would number about 150,000. Outnumbered 2 to 1 he would surely be but he found these odds far preferable to those he would have if forced to confront the Northern juggernaut without the reinforcements from Richmond.

BROTHERS IN GRAY

Early on the 28th another of Jackson's couriers came through Thoroughfare Gap with word that Stonewall had chosen to concentrate his forces at Groveton astride the Warrenton Turnpike. This too was good news. The distance between the two wings of Lee's army was now shorter by three miles.

Now only one obstacle to Lee's designs remained: Thoroughfare Gap. If it were held, precious time would be lost in forcing the issue. The gray commander tried to remain optimistic. After all, was not Jackson sending a steady stream of couriers through from the east?

By mid afternoon the first of Longstreet's divisions climbed to within sight of the gap itself. So far so good. Moving rapidly into the gap it seemed as though fortune was surely smiling upon them. Then came the sound Lee, who was far back in the column, least wanted to hear. The echoes of gunfire reverberated out of the gap literally bouncing from hill to hill. Yankees, Lee's heart sank.

Presently he received word from the front. Union troops held the pass itself and had even established a reserve line on a more dominant ridge just to the east. Lee's first reaction was dark indeed. He assumed that Pope must have outwitted him that his vastly superior force now stood directly between the two wings of the Confederate army. If so, the Federals were in a position to crush either wing at their leisure.

It was Longstreet, the very epitome of calmness who came forward to steady the older man's nerves. Assume not the worst, he suggested. Better might it be to test the mettle of those bluecoats up in the gorge. Lee concurred and left the details of such a test to the man he called, "My old warhorse."

Longstreet wasted no time. Two divisions, those of Jones and Kemper, were ordered to pressure the Federals from the west. Hood with his Texans was given the job of locating a way through on the Union flank. Wilcox with his division was sent north to explore the possibility of penetrating Hopewell Gap.

All of this consumed quite a bit of time. It was toward sunset during a lull in the shooting when Lee heard yet another sound he would have preferred not to hear. Off in the distance well to the east came the muted sounds of muskets and artillery. A battle was in progress that was for sure.

There was no time to dwell on whatever might be happening with Jackson. The contest at Thoroughfare Gap was approaching a climax. Hood's men had done their job well. Led by the highly popular "Howdy" Martin, a major in Company K of the 4th Texas infantry, they had discovered a narrow defile through the steep slopes of the mountain and emerged directly on the flank of the Yankee defenders, who quickly realized their position had become untenable. They abandoned the gap and their reserve line as well. Jones and Kemper poured through and joined the Texans. One of the first persons General Kemper encountered as he exited the gap on the far side was the previously mentioned Major Martin sitting cross-legged on a rock watching the gray column as it passed. The major spied the General and greeted him with a wave of his arm, "Howdy!" he smiled.

"Don't you ever salute?" Kemper seemed a little miffed by so casual a greeting by a junior officer.

"Not if I can help it." Martin flashed an affable grin which even Kemper found difficult to resist. Besides, had not the Texans just solved the immediate problem at hand?

Later that evening after the troops had bedded down for the night Kemper and Hood sat by a campfire sharing a small flask of Kentucky bourbon.

"General Hood," said Kemper in a somewhat light-hearted tone, "I must inform you that one of your officers has a most irreverent attitude."

"How so?" Hood arched one eyebrow and took a sip from the flask.

"The fellow seems to have some sort of aversion to saluting his superior officers."

"Ah!" Hood chuckled in humor and nodded his head. "That would be Howdy ... Major Martin. He's in the 4th Texas."

"I believe that's the man. How did he ever acquire a name like that?"

"Oh, it wasn't hard. Seems like whenever Major Martin encounters officers of higher rank he greets them with a wave and a 'Howdy!' His soldiers gave him the nickname and it seems to have stuck. I hope his casual ways haven't caused you offense."

"I admit to having been a little put out when he offered his 'Howdy' as we came through the gap, but I quickly forgot it. He does seem a much likeable man."

"His men think the world of him, and they are splendid fighters, indeed!"

"A point I'd be foolish to argue after today," admitted Kemper as he rose, stretched, and bid the Texan general a good night.

The victory at Thoroughfare Gap proved one thing to Lee: Pope had not outwitted him. The Union forces which had been chased from their defenses had comprised but one division. Their presence in the gap was due more to an afterthought on the part of McDowell, himself lost in the woods near Groveton, than to any strategic maneuver on the part of Pope.

More concern to Lee at the moment was the sound

of battle coming from Groveton itself. Was Jackson still alive? Did his wing of the army still exist? From his position atop the mountain in the black of night Lee had no way of knowing the answers to these questions. Therefore a courier was dispatched to ride through the night. His task was to find Jackson if Jackson was anywhere to be found, and to inform him of the course of events at the Gap. The army could be reunited by tomorrow if all went well.

As for Jackson, he and his corps were still very much intact and delighted to learn that their comrades were so close at hand. Stonewall decided to pull back from his line along the turnpike, to an unfinished railroad embankment sitting a half-mile back from the pike. This comprised a ready made defensive position in which to meet the attack he knew would be coming. His troops reached the place quickly and just as quickly were ordered to dig in. By early morning on Friday, the 29th of August, they were ready.

As he was helping to prepare the earthworks Wil turned and saw Levi for the first time since the previous night's fight. Levi saw at once the dried blood on Wil's uniform.

"Were you hit?" he asked immediately.

"No," Wil paused to look upon himself. "It's Lonnie's blood. It was me who carried him back after he was shot. He died in Ivory's arms."

"I know. I found him after I was finished in the saw-bones tent. I was prayin' I wouldn't find you like that. Poor Lonnie. Who's gonna tell his folks?"

"I imagine Colonel Reynolds takes care of that sort of thing. Look at yourself, Levi. You look like you got shot up same as me."

Levi glanced at his own clothing, soiled every bit as

thoroughly as Wils. "White soldier's blood," he explained. "A whole bunch of soldiers. I had to hold 'em while they lost arms and legs. It was terrible, Wil! I never in my life dreamed I'd see anythin' like that. Man after man, one after the other. Most of 'em conscious, screamin,' beggin' me to stop the surgeons, beggin' to keep their limbs. I was there when they took General Ewell's leg."

"I saw 'em carryin' him back."

"I don't even feel like the same person anymore, Wil, feel like I died everytime I saw a leg or an arm come off. Made my stomach so sick I had to vomit."

"Me too. Reckon I feel the same way. I reckon we're soldiers now, Levi."

"I reckon. Don't know that I much care for the feel of it."

"Know what you mean. We was so anxious to see action. Now I just don't know what to think. I feel numb inside, Levi, just numb. I may have killed a man yesterday. I fired my musket fifteen or twenty times at least. I musta hit somebody. I should feel glad 'cause they're the enemy, but it just makes me feel empty inside."

"You boys finished jawin?" Miles Turner interjected himself at this point. "I sure as hell hope so, another word outta the two of you and I'll bust all into tears! What was you expectin'? A Sunday afternoon picnic? I hate to disillusion you boys but this here is a war. A Goddamn dirty war! That's what you've landed yourselves in the middle of! That and nothing more! You say you're numb, Wil? Stay that way! That's the only way a man can endure all this! We lost Tommie Murphy yesterday. That leaves just me and Jeb Green from the bunch what come up from Suffolk. It's a sad business we're caught up in...a sad business."

"Everything okay over here?" Corporal Gilbert's

voice had an impatient authoritative tone to it.

"Just fine, Corporal," said Miles. "Just fine."

"Less talk and a little more work might be in order. We'll be having company soon. We'd best be ready."

"You bet! C'mon boys," gestured Miles. "Gimme a hand with this log!"

"Wil," Gilbert's voice had lost none of its sternness. "You said you wanted action. You got a dose of it last night. There's a full helpin' on the way today."

"I understand, Corporal."

"Levi, stay close to us this time. Load muskets as fast as you can and keep passing them up to the boys on the line."

"Yessuh"

With that Gilbert moved on to check preparations further down on the embankment.

The entrenchment was still continuing when the word began to spread up and down the line: Longstreet's on hand!

It was true. Longstreet's men had started at the crack of dawn on Friday, August 29th, and Hood's Texans led the way. They set so quick a pace that Longstreet on three occasions had to send orders up the column for Hood to halt so the rest of the army could remain within supporting distance. The sound of gunfire in the distance proved to them that Jackson's boys were still very much alive and Hood's Texans hastened to be first at their side. Through Haymarket they marched then southwest to Gainesville. Here they picked up the Warrenton Turnpike and by 10:a.m. they had established a link with Stonewall's far right. The new arrivals were covered with a thick coat of dust - testimony both to the rigors and the pace of their march. One mounted trooper was to remark of them, "That all looked as if they had been painted one color." Jackson's men rose and cheered them despite the continuous shelling which hadn't let up since the first rays of dawn. The army was one again.

Pursuant to Lee's instructions, Longstreet deployed his troops in a line extending southward from Jackson's right flank across the pike and into the woods toward the Manassas Gap Railroad. They settled into position, and as far as they could determine the Union troops who were pounding Jackson were quite oblivious to their presence.

As for Pope, his notion of this whole chain of events was about as mistaken as it could possibly be. In his mind Lee was still being kept at bay beyond Thoroughfare Gap. He was also clinging steadfastly to the belief that Jackson was trying to escape his clutches when in fact Old Blue Light was quite content to stay exactly where he was.

Pope rose from his bunk that Friday morning in ill humor. His plans for a simultaneous strike at both of Jackson's flanks had already been thwarted. Porter's corps never arrived due to the fall of darkness the previous night. As for McDowell, two of his divisions he'd already retired in the direction of Manassas after their encounter with Jackson at Groveton the previous evening. "God damn McDowell!" Pope was heard to say. "He's never where I want him."

Nevertheless he had three full corps of infantry on hand, those of General's Sigel, Reno, and Heintzelman. These he decided to hurl forward, confident they would put an end to this fellow called Stonewall. All the morning long he had been pounding the Rebel line with artillery. At last he ordered the bombardment stopped and as the guns fell silent the long rows of blueclad infantry emerged from their positions and started forward. All the while Pope remained ignorant of Longstreet's arrival.

All along the unfinished railroad embankment,

Jackson's men prepared to receive the charge. Wil Covington found himself clutching at his stomach trying to stop his insides from jumping so much. He would glance out at the Yankees approaching in the distance still in perfect formation. Then he would look back at Levi crouched on the rear side of the embankment with several loaded muskets at his side. He found support in his friend's black face even though he knew Levi was trying to control his own case of jitters. Glancing to his left down the line a piece he spied Sergeant Reilly and his squad of veterans from the Stonewall brigade. He found it a source of comfort to see so many familiar faces dug in next to his own regiment, more so because of the welcome rest they had shared together on the march north.

All of these distractions soothing though they may have been were quickly shattered by the roar of Confederate guns as Jackson's artillery began to take the measure of the Union assault.

"Wil!" It was Gilbert shouting at him. "Get a bayonet on that thing, boy! What the hell's the matter with you?"

Wil complied at once though his nervous hands were clumsy and dropped the bayonet once before he was able to properly affix it to the business end of his musket.

Taking their losses and closing their ranks the Federal infantry charged undaunted toward Jackson's waiting masses, so that very quickly they surged to within musket range.

"Open Fire!" came the order and the response was instant.

The roar was deafening along every inch of the line. Yankee soldiers fell in droves but the survivors pressed on. Another volley, more of them fell. Levi suddenly found himself scrambling to reload muskets and pass them up to his white comrades. The first wave reached the base of the embankment and rushed toward the bayonets which awaited them.

Suddenly Wil's jitters were gone. Suddenly he realized how close to death he and the others were. The basic survival instinct inside of him triggered a rush of adrenalin. He fired his musket then thrust it left in time to bayonet a northerner at the crest of the embankment. With the butt of his musket he slammed another man in the stomach, bringing him to his knees. With one hand he reached out and grabbed the fellow by the collar, hauling him over the line where he became a prisoner at once.

Hand to hand fighting ensued on a grand scale as bluecoats swarmed up the embankment. All was confusion and mayhem. The integrity of individual units dissolved as soldiers shifted in all directions to repel the attackers. Wil was knocked to the ground by one man but before the northerner could finish the job he was felled by a bullet fired by Levi Henry. Wil scrambled back to his feet, nodded his thanks to Levi and leapt back into the fray.

He soon found himself separated from his own unit fighting side by side with some of the Stonewall brigade. To his left he spied Sergeant Reilly. He was on one knee taking aim at an approaching bluecoat. He fired but didn't see the Federal officer, a captain by all appearances, approaching from a different angle with his saber upraised. Reilly turned and tried to meet the attack but he was too late. Down came the saber. Instinctively the Rebel veteran fell backwards to avoid the swing. Good thing he did, for if he hadn't the saber surely would have sliced his head down the middle. As it was the forward edge of the weapon raked his face inflicting a deep gash from his forehead down into his beard. Reilly ended up on his back one hand clutching his face as he squirmed along the ground to avoid the follow-up swing he knew would be coming. The Yankee captain kept pace and raised the saber a second time. It was the last movement this northerner would ever make of his own volition. Seeing Reilly's plight Wil reacted at once slamming his bayonet between the officer's ribs and piercing his lung; With a loud wail the man toppled to the ground gasping out his last breaths.

Reilly's men were quick to gather around their stricken sergeant. Ox placed his bulky frame between Reilly and the Yankees. Al Watkins grabbed the sergeant under both armpits and dragged him down the embankment to the cover of trees. They looked to find Wil but already he had disappeared in the thick smoke and confusion. So it went.

At last this first charge exhausted itself much as an ocean wave might bash itself against a seawall. Stonewall's battered veterans had bent in several places but nowhere did they break.

Wil found his way back to his own regiment and took up the same position he'd held prior to the Union charge.

"Here they come again!" Someone yelled.

"Oh my God, Lay me down!" growled Turner as he took a loaded musket from Levi and prepared to meet the next onslaught shaping up out on the plain.

All the day long the Yankees hurled themselves against Jackson's line and all the day long they failed to break it. There was one place where they had opportunity for success. The extreme left of the line was held by A.P. Hill's division. At the very end of the line a brigade of South Carolinians under General Maxcy Gregg anchored the flank. They were struck fiercely by Phil Kearny's division of infantry. After a savage fight the Federals managed to establish themselves on the embankment squarely astride Jackson's left flank. Now they were in a position to roll the entire Rebel line up like an old rug.

Here on this rocky knoll the fate of Jackson's position swung to and fro like an unhinged gate in a stiff breeze. Rifle butts and bayonets would finally decide the issue. General Gregg moved all over the place trying to rally his men. Brandishing an ancient scimitar of Revolutionary War vintage he seemed a relic of a bygone era. "Let us die here my men!" he would cry. "Let us die here!" Quite a number of them did, but their sacrifice was not in vain. The knoll was held. It was Kearny's men who finally chose to break off contact.

As the Yankees pulled back A.P. Hill made a quick assessment of the situation and sent immediate word to Jackson, informing his commander that he didn't think his men could withstand another attack of such strength.

Jackson glared angrily at the courier as if he himself had compiled the message. "Tell this to General Hill," he said in a tone which allowed no room for discussion. "Tell him if they attack him again he must beat them!"

"Yessuh!" The fellow saluted and galloped off.

A. P. Hill listened to this reply, took off his hat and scratched his head through his thick red hair. "Stonewall just don't understand what's goin' on over here." Quickly he mounted and rode to confer with Jackson himself. He hadn't gone far when he came across Stonewall who was coming to see for himself what all the ruckus was about.

"General," Jackson spoke before Hill could open his mouth. "Your men have done nobly. If you are attacked again, you will beat the enemy back."

Hill desperately wanted to plea for reinforcements but as he opened his mouth to speak the crackling of musketry broke out again through the woods on the left.

Both men focused their attention in that direction: "Here it comes," said Hill in a tone heavy with strain. He jerked hard on his horses's reins, swinging the animal around, spurring him back toward the renewed fighting.

"I'll expect you to beat them!" shouted Stonewall as Hill disappeared into the smoke of battle. He then pulled back a ways from the line, his attention still riveted on that one critical sector. Would Hill's men endure the Union pressure? Minutes elapsed. The roar of the battle along the left rose to a crescendo then fell off.

Out of the smoke-filled woods galloped a second messenger, his uniform in tatters, his face streaked with the grime of combat. He reached Jackson pulled his mount to a halt and saluted sharply, "General Hill presents his respects and says the attack of the enemy was repulsed."

From Jackson came an audible sigh of relief and a tight-lipped smile. "Tell him I knew he would do it," he said.

Thus did the battle rage all through that long hot dusty afternoon. The Yankees would charge, only to be repelled. After each attack the wounded and dying men cried out for water and called for loved ones hundreds of miles away. After each charge Jackson's weary survivors would slump to the ground yearning for whatever rest a brief respite would allow. Wil Covington lay on his back staring straight up at the blue August sky. Beside him lay Miles Turner whose face was so covered with dust and grime as to make him nearly unrecognizable. He was staring in the general direction of the blazing afternoon sun which seemed to be resisting any idea of setting. "Lord," said Miles. "You know I ain't much for prayin'. Can't think of too many things I've asked for in this life, but I'm askin' now...Please make that ol' sun go down. Bring this day to an end, Lord. Please end it."

"So you found religion, eh, Turner?" Gilbert managed a weak laugh.

"Just want it to end, Corporal. That's all. Just want it to end."

"You ain't the only one!" grumbled Jeb Green, Turner's last compatriot from Suffolk. "Where in the hell's Longstreet? They told us he was up! How come he ain't pitched in to them Yanks? What's he waitin' for? Cold weather?"

'That'll be enough of that!" snapped Gilbert.

"Boy's got a point, Corporal. Seems like the other half of our army is sittin' on their thumbs."

"They're formin' out there!" came the alarm. "Jesus, God! They're comin' again!"

Robert E. Lee was hardly ignorant of the situation. He'd been a witness to the horrendous pounding endured by Jackson's men all through the day. Longstreet's line, by comparison, had been virtually ignored. From the point where they were linked to Jackson's, Old Pete's veterans extended in a line to the east - southeast. Lee met with Longstreet and suggested that he swing his line forward and snare the Federals in the jaws of a trap.

"Not yet," said Longstreet.

Lee did his best to remain patient. "May I ask why?"

Longstreet, by nature, was a rather organized individual, a meticulous planner who was not inclined to lunge haphazardly into battle. "Several reasons," he explained. "I haven't really had time to study the ground as thoroughly as I would like. Anderson has yet to arrive from the Rappahannock. I've also received a report from Stuart which merits closer study. Apparently a sizeable force of Federals is coming up from the south. Were I to move forward now I would expose my flank and rear to those troops. That wouldn't be wise." Longstreet departed briefly verifying Stuart's report upon his return.

Then Jackson appeared, a forlorn looking figure if ever there was one, layered from head to toe in dust. Longstreet and Lee both extended their greetings to the legendary Stonewall, and for the next several minutes three of the most important men in the Confederacy sat their mounts side by side.

"General," Jackson addressed himself to Lee. "My men are particularly hard pressed. What possibility is there of relief?"

By way of reply Lee turned to Longstreet, "Hadn't we better move our line forward?"

"I think not," came the reply. "We had better wait until we hear more from Stuart about the force he has reported moving against us from Manassas."

Just then the sounds of battle erupted again well to the left. Jackson turned his head quickly in that direction then back to his fellow officers. "I must return to my men," he said simply as he turned his horse and rode off in the direction of the firing.

With less than an hour of daylight remaining Lee approached Longstreet suggesting for the third time that an attack on his part might be in order. For the third time Longstreet had to disagree. "Stuart's given me a positive identification of the Federals on my right," he explained. "It's Porter with two full divisions. The movement you suggest exposes us to the same risks we discussed earlier. Besides, the day is very nearly over. Even if we we're successful, darkness would shut us off before we could accomplish anything of a decisive nature."

"I fully appreciate the value of your arguments," sighed Lee, "Yet I find myself increasingly reluctant to allow Jackson's brave men to remain unsupported through such constant punishment. Except for a few batteries of guns, your men have yet to be engaged."

"General," said Longstreet, "your concern for Stonewall's troops does not exceed my own. By all accounts they have conducted their defense quite well throughout the day. Tell me, sir, do you not find it strange that Pope has virtually ignored this half of the army?"

"I do indeed," nodded the gray commander. "I'm at a loss for a logical explanation."

"Could it be he doesn't know we're here?"

"I don't see how that could be possible, but if it's so we're holding rather a strong trump card."

"My thoughts exactly. I think we should wait to see what the morrow brings."

"Then once more I will defer to your judgment."

"At dusk we'll make a reconnaissance by force. I'll send Hood's Texans. Should they detect an opening, I'll move expeditiously to exploit it at sun-up."

"Very well, General," nodded Lee. "I'm returning to my headquarters. You will of course keep me informed as the situation develops."

"Yes, sir," Longstreet saluted as Lee turned Traveller about and started away.

True to his word, Longstreet ordered Hood to advance. Moving forward in the failing light, the Texans bumped squarely into Rufus King's division of Union infantry, many of the same men who had dueled with the Stonewall Brigade the night before in Groveton. Coming up from Manassas, they were just now rejoining Pope. The fight which ensued was sharp, brief, and highlighted by confusion. One Union major shouting to rally his men became a prisoner when he found out "his men" were the 2nd Mississippi infantry.

Hood held his own but sent word back to Longstreet that the Federal line was too strong to break with his present strength. He also requested permission of Lee to fall back to his original position rather than remain exposed. His request was granted. In the process of making his return Hood encountered Anderson's troops who had finally arrived from the Rappahannock. This was fortunate. Had not this chance meeting taken place Anderson would have blundered through the darkness straight into the Union lines.

Night finally brought an end to it. Thousands of dead and wounded Yankee soldiers lay where they fell in the fields and on the face of Jackson's embankment. For the wounded darkness brought no end to the agony. Desperate were their cries for just a sip of water, just a little to sooth parched throats.

At Jackson's headquarters the chief surgeon had just delivered the final report on the day's heavy casualties. As he was preparing to leave he glanced over his shoulder at the worn lean face of his Commander. "General," he said, "this day has been won by nothing but stark and stern fighting."

Stonewall replied with a shake of his head, "No. It has been won by nothing but the blessing and protection of Providence."

That night Jackson decided to offer the bulk of his survivors some badly needed rest. Leaving but a skeletal force to hold the embankment he allowed the rest to pull back some distance into the woods. Wil and his comrades were gathered about a small fire in a stand of sweet smelling pines. They were the last group of men to be served portions of a savory stew Ivory had put together with beef and fresh vegetables donated by several of the local farmers.

BROTHERS IN GRAY

"Damn but you have a way with food, Ivory," beamed Miles. "This is one pleasin' meal!"

"Why thank you, Massa Turner! It's good to know someone appreciates ol' Ivory."

"Stop callin me Massa, Ivory! I done told you 'bout that a half dozen times!"

"We appreciate you, Ivory," said Gilbert. "C'mon and sit a spell. You've earned it same as the rest of us."

"Why, thank you Corporal. I do believe I'll take you up on that. These ol' legs are 'bout worn out. Dug too many graves today."

"They beat up on us pretty bad, that's for sure." said Miles.

"We hurt them worse...far worse." replied Gilbert.

"Ivory," said Wil as he cleaned his bowl with grimy fingers. "You got any more in that pot?"

"Few more helpin's."

Instantly several hands extended empty bowls for refills. "Don't you be tellin' them other boys I gave you seconds!" cautioned Ivory. "Liable to get me in a heap of trouble!"

"We won't say a word," assured Gilbert.

As Wil greedily gulped down his second helping, he cast a sideways glance in Ivory's direction, "Ivory," he said. "I want you to know how much it meant to me...what you did for Lonnie yesterday."

"No need to make a lot of it, young-un, done the same for a lot of you boys."

"Still the same, if I make it home I'll be sure to tell his folks what you did for him."

"Son," Ivory sighed deeply, "you just do your best to make it home. I don't ever want to be hearin' you cryin' out for yo' mama while you's gaspin' your last breaths."

"Never knew my mother," said Wil.

"What's that?"

"Never knew her. She died givin' me birth. I suppose if I'm callin' out to anybody, it'll be Sarah. That's Levi's Ma. She raised me. Reckon she's the only mother I ever knew."

"That right?" Ivory glanced over at Levi.

"Sure is. Me and Wil grew up together."

"Kinda like brothers," mused Ivory.

"You could say that."

"Hey, Levi," said Miles. "Hear you killed yourself a Yankee today."

"He was gonna kill Wil."

"How you feel 'bout that?"

"Can't say. Wasn't somethin' I enjoyed doin'. Just had to be done."

"Reckon you're a soldier now," interjected the Corporal. "You and Wil both. All you new boys, what's left of ya."

"Hey, Levi," laughed Wil. "We're veterans!"

"Sho'nuff," chuckled the young black man.

Just then a figure emerged from the shadows, a tall man with a dark beard, a white blood-stained bandage wrapped about his forehead, and the stripes of a sergeant on his sleeves.

Turner noticed him first. "Hey" he grinned. "It's the professor, himself! How ya doin', Sergeant?"

"Still kickin'," came the reply. He stepped into the pale glow of the fire and the others could see the thick scab which ran down the length of his face into his beard. "Where's Wil Covington?" he asked.

"Right here, suh," Wil started to rise.

"No, no," gestured Reilly. "No need to stand up. I understand I owe you a debt of gratitude. Seems you're the man who saved my life."

Wil blushed a little, not used to being singled out for attention. "Lots of folks were savin' other folks today, Professor. Levi here saved my skin just a minute or so before you took that saber cut."

"Then I reckon I'm obliged to the both of you. I just want you to know I won't soon forget it."

"It wasn't nothin'," demurred Wil.

"It was something to me," countered Reilly as he stepped around the fire and put one hand on Wil's shoulder, the other on Levi's. "My thanks," he said. "My thanks to the both of you."

"Sergeant," Gilbert spoke up. "Would you care to share the fire with us for awhile?"

"It would be my pleasure," Reilly sat on the ground between Wil and Levi.

"Ivory," continued the Corporal, "anything left in that bucket?"

Ivory peered down into the stew and grimaced, "I might could scrape out one more ladle full."

"You hungry, Professor?"

"Ivory's already fed me once tonight, but I swear if there's a better cook in this man's army I haven't met him yet."

"Why thank you, suh!" Ivory beamed happily.

"If you can scrape anymore out of there I'll take proper care of it."

"You go right ahead." chuckled Ivory as he scraped out a small portion of the stew and plopped it into Turner's bowl, who promptly handed it to Reilly.

"Bon appetit!" said Turner with a grin. "Hey! That reminds me! Anyone seen that frenchie fella? Private Tiger? He didn't get himself killed did he?"

"Saw him last night," said Wil. "He was okay then."

"That boy owes me a chance to win my money back!

He'd better be alive!"

"All due respect, Miles," laughed Wil. "But if he gives you that chance you're liable to lose the shirt off your back!"

Laughter greeted this remark and even Turner himself found reason to join in. "I suppose," he admitted with a nod of his head.

They fell silent after that. Each man was more or less immersed in his own thoughts. For the longest time they seemed content to listen to the crackling of the flames and the sounds of cicadas high up in the trees. It was a pleasant interlude for them all, more so since they could only barely hear those of the Federal wounded who were still calling for help out in the field.

"Ivory," Jeb Green spoke up. "Word is you're right handy with a mouth organ."

"Been known to play a tune or two," came the response.

"Miles here has somethin' of a surprise for ya."

"What's that?" The black man's eyes widened in anticipation.

"Well it was a surprise!" complained Miles. "I was savin' it for a special occasion!"

"Hell, Miles," came Gilbert. "We might all be dead by this time tomorrow. What could be more special than tonight?"

"You got a point there, Corporal. Hold on a sec, Ivory," he began fishing through his bedroll. "I got it in here someplace...ah! Here it is!" He withdrew a brand new harmonica. "I lifted it from one of those sutler wagons back there in Manassas. Seemed to me the thing had your name written all over it." With no further ado he reached across the fire and handed it to Ivory.

"Massa Turner," he handled the instrument gingerly, turning it over several times in his hands, his eyes aglow with admiration. "Reckon you've got me all speechless."

"Lord, Ivory! Weren't lookin for no speech! I wanna hear you play the damn thing!"

"Well now, I suppose I could manage that."

"Good! Good! But hold on a minute! Jeb, you still got your fiddle rolled up in your haversack?"

"Yep. Can't guarantee there ain't a Yankee minie ball in it though."

"Well fetch it, boy! Let's liven this place up a mite!"

It took Jeb and Ivory a few minutes to get used to one another before they could establish any sort of harmony, but by and by the black man with the harmonica and the white man with the fiddle produced music sweet to everyone's ears. Several songs did the two of them play but there was one in particular which never failed to bring a tear to even the most hardened eye. Written for the Union soldiers it had quickly become a favorite among the men of both armies. It was called, "Weeping Sad and Lonely." Most of those gathered by the fire joined in to sing the words as Ivory and Jeb played the melody.

> *Dearest love, do you remember*
> *how you told me that you loved me*
> *weeping at my feet? Oh how proud*
> *you stood before me in your suit of*
> *gray...*
>
> *Weeping sad and lonely, hopes and fears*
> *have all faded. When this cruel war is over*
> *prayin' that we meet again.*
>
> *Oft in dreams I see thee lyin' on the*

battle plain. Lonely, wounded, even dyin',
callin', but in vain...

Weeping sad and lonely....

Wil stopped singing and looked away, his mind filled with visions of home and family. He could see Sarah so vividly he almost cried out to her.

When this cruel war is over...

The sorrowful words and melody of the last song drifted through the woods almost like a gentle breeze. They reached the ears of one man who lay on his cot inside his tent, his body at rest his mind awake. Stonewall's normal inclination might have been to send an officer to suggest the soldiers pick another song, one more inclined to boost their morale. Not so this night. He knew they'd all lost friends during the long Friday ordeal. He thought it best to allow them to express their grief if only through the words of "Weeping Sad and Lonely."

It seemed as though they had played for hours, though in truth it wasn't more than thirty or forty minutes. As the last notes died away in the air, Ivory put the harmonica in his lap and let an audible sigh escape from his lips.

"That song sho' do make me homesick," he said. "Lawd, I miss South Carolina." He glanced over at Wil and Levi. "It's beautiful down there," he continued. "You know what I miss most? Spanish moss. You boys ever seen Spanish moss?"

Both Wil and Levi shook their heads.

"It hangs from the branches of the oak trees. Feels kinda like Mother Nature's lace when you holds it in your hands. Why I've seen some trees where the moss was so thick it was like molasses drippin' off a spoon!"

BROTHERS IN GRAY

"What color is it?" Asked Levi trying to visualize the stuff in his mind.

"Color...lemme see now...picture the palest green that you can. Sometimes it's almost gray like our uniforms. It just hangs there like a woman's braids around her shoulders. I sho' do miss bein' home. You boys ever been to South Carolina?"

"Ain't never been out of the Shenandoah before now." answered Levi.

"I went to Charlottesville once," said Wil, "to see the University Thomas Jefferson built. I been to Roanoke a couple of times...and Winchester."

"But you ain't never been to South Carolina."

"Reckon not."

"I have," Sergeant Reilly spoke up.

"Really, suh?" Ivory's face came alive with pleasure. "Whereabouts?"

"Charleston. Three or four years before the war. I was asked to give a symposium on the Aeneid at the Citadel."

"The What?" Wil gave Reilly a look of pure astonishment.

"The Aeneid. It's an Epic poem written by Virgil. The ancient Romans prized it highly because many of them believe it tells the story of the founding of Rome by survivors from Troy."

"What's he talkin' 'bout?" Ivory leaned over and whispered to Corporal Gilbert.

"I don't have the slightest idea."

"Latin is one of the subjects I teach at the college in Williamsburg," explained Reilly. "The Aeneid was written in Latin. Some folks down at the Citadel asked me to come down and talk about it. That's all. Anyway, Ivory's right. South Carolina is a beautiful place, especially down there along the coast of the Atlantic. I found Charleston to be a fascinating city."

"Sho' is!" Ivory slapped his thigh with a grin.

"Well, it's gettin' a bit late," said Reilly as he rose and stretched the tightness from his limbs. "Reckon I ought to be gettin' back to my own boys."

"G'night, Professor," said Wil.

"Same to ya...and Wil, my thanks to you again."

"Weren't nothin'. Maybe someday you can tell me more about that knee-id thing."

"Maybe," Reilly's face broke out in a friendly smile, which made him wince because of the long scab. "You boys sleep well. We may be in for another long one tomorrow."

Morning found John Pope making some of the most extraordinary miscalculations of his career. In his mind, as he stood on a knoll astride the Sudley Springs Road gazing west, the events of yesterday had confirmed everything he believed: Jackson had been trying to escape, but had failed. He had been brought to bay much as a pack of hounds might tree a coon. Satisfied that Jackson would soon be in his back pocket, he fired off a telegram to General Halleck in Washington City, "We fought a terrific battle here yesterday...which lasted with continuous fury from daybreak until dark, by which time the enemy was driven from the field which we now occupy. Our troops are too much exhausted yet to push matters, but I shall do so in the course of the morning... The enemy is still in our front, but badly used up. We have lost not less than 8000 men killed and wounded, but from the appearance of the field the enemy lost at least two to one. He stood strictly on the defensive, and every assault was made by ourselves. Our troops behaved splendidly. The battle was fought on the identical battlefield of Bull Run, which greatly in-

creased the enthusiasm of our men. The news just reaches
me from the front that the enemy is retreating toward the
mountains. I go forward at once to see."

Actually the news he'd received seemed to indicate
nothing but a rearguard remaining on the Rebel embankment. Pope only advanced far enough to ascertain this for
himself which served only to strengthen his conviction
that Jackson had been badly mauled and was now attempting to limp away. Immediately he began formulating
plans for the pursuit.

So far as the previous day's fighting was concerned
Pope's biggest disappointment was blamed on General
Porter who repeatedly declined the suggestion that he use
his Corps to assail Jackson's right flank. Porter insisted
such a move would be folly as Longstreet was to his front
in considerable strength. Pope dismissed his protests
altogether, preferring to believe the Confederate army
was still divided. The news of Hood's appearance and
subsequent withdrawal from the field was merely additional evidence that Friday had left the rebels battered and
in disarray. As for Porter, his Corps was subsequently
shifted from the far left into the main line so as to take an
active role in the pursuit.

As Pope designed it, the final chapter in the legend
of Stonewall Jackson would be written in the following
manner. A two-pronged advance would initiate the chase
with McDowell in overall charge, assuming he could avoid
becoming lost again. Porter's corps with two of McDowell's
divisions were to advance directly down the Warrenton
Turnpike. Heintzelman's corps with McDowell's remaining division were to head down the Hay Market road.
Stonewall's beleaguered Rebels would thus be hemmed in
and soon finished off. The orders having been dispatched,
the principal officers returned to their respective com-

mands to begin the logistical organization necessary for their execution.

It can certainly be said that Pope and his adversary in Gray were operating on widely disparate conceptions of their respective status that Saturday morning. Lee's avowed intention from the outset of the campaign had been - to use his term - the suppression of John Pope, whom he disdainfully referred to as "that miscreant." That morning he wrote a letter to President Davis detailing the tactical situation as it stood. He noted his satisfaction in having relieved the region around the Rappahannock of enemy occupation, but expressed concern that Pope might still avoid the degree of punishment he wished to inflict. He had been hoping that Pope would renew the attacks of yesterday but as the morning waned with no signs of a Federal advance he began to doubt that Pope would take such an initiative.

Finishing his letter Lee turned his attention to the maps. If Pope would not oblige him by attacking then a way would have to be found to maneuver the Federals out of position.

As for Longstreet, whose presence on the field Pope still chose to ignore, he was astounded to see Porter's corps of Union infantry shifted away from his flank to join their comrades directly in front of him. "This is almost too good to be true," he muttered to no one in particular as he lowered his spyglass. "Now if only they can be persuaded to try Jackson's boys one more time."

It was near midday when red-bearded Jeb Stuart presented himself at Lee's headquarters.

"Ah, General Stuart," Lee offered a warm smile to the man he thought of almost as a son. "No doubt you came bearing news. May I dare to guess it might be news of some importance? Otherwise I think you may have

BROTHERS IN GRAY

been more inclined to dispatch a rider."

"A rather accurate deduction, Suh." The expression on Stuart's face was anything but lighthearted. "I believe Jackson may be in grave danger."

"Explain," Lee's smile vanished.

"A short while ago I sent one of my best climbers way up into a large walnut tree, a position which afforded him a thorough view of the Yankee ranks opposite Jackson's line."

"And?"

"The Yankees are massing, General, three full lines of them, thick as flies from what my scout told me."

"Has Jackson been informed?"

"No, suh. I came directly here."

Lee glanced over at his staff officer, Colonel Taylor. "Send couriers to Jackson at once. Alert him to the danger at his front."

"Straight away," nodded Taylor.

Jackson received the news in stoic fashion. In point of fact he had been observing the Union buildup for some time. He alerted his troops back in the woods but told them to stay exactly where they were. Perhaps Pope had been deceived. If so, it might be advantageous to carry the deception a little further. He even commented to the Colonel who commanded the Stonewall Brigade that it didn't appear as if there would be a fight today.

The early afternoon passed somewhat peacefully aside from sporadic sniper fire. By mid-afternoon Stonewall's earlier prediction came roaring back into his face with a vengeance. Three distant waves of blue-clad infantry thrust toward the thinly held embankment without so much as a single artillery shot to serve as warning.

"Oh my God!" cried one young bugler on the line as he placed his instrument to his mouth and sounded the first of many warnings which echoed up and down the line.

"What the hell is that?" mumbled Miles through a mouthful of biscuit.

"Whatever it is we ain't got time to be discussin' it!" shouted Gilbert. "Grab your muskets, boys! Get back on that line! Step quick now! Step quick!"

All through the woods gray clad soldiers snatched up their weapons and dashed pell mell for the embankment. With astonishing speed they were back in position on the line preparing to deliver the first volley. Corporal Gilbert glanced back at Levi who crouched several paces behind the main line with several loaded muskets at his side. "Levi," he growled. "What the hell you doin' down there, boy?"

Levi looked up at the corporal with a startled expression on his face. "I'm doin' what you told me to do, suh! I'm loadin' these guns."

"Forget that! We need every musket we've got up here! Get up on the line! Squeeze in between Wil and Miles! And shoot straight, boy! Shoot straight!"

"Yes suh!" Levi's face flushed with pride as he took up a musket and moved into position with the others.

"I wouldn't be lookin' so Goddamn happy!" said Miles with a sardonic laugh, "we probably got about five minutes to live! That is if we're lucky!"

Onward came the blue wave, confident they were about to overwhelm a mere rearguard as the pursuit of the supposedly fleeing Jackson, finally got underway.

"Open fire!" came the order and Jackson's entire corps greeted the first wave with a wall of lead.

Northerners fell in droves but the survivors came on with a vengeance, shocked to find their "pursuit" snapped off so abruptly. They were quick to realize there would be no chase of Jackson. They were going to have to dislodge him from the embankment. They would have to succeed where yesterday they had failed. Buoyed by their overwhelming strength in numbers they applied themselves to this task with incredible fury.

At Jackson's headquarters, the calls for help started pouring in almost as soon as the attack was underway. Every inch of the two- mile front was under the most intense pressure imaginable. A.P. Hill's men were driven back in several places but each time they were able to regroup and hurl the Yankees from the embankment. Shortages of ammunition began to occur up and down the line. Officers were being felled at an alarming rate. Majors, even captains found themselves in command of entire brigades, which themselves were but a fraction of their normal strength.

One after another came the desperate pleas for reinforcements. Unfortunately Jackson had long since committed his last reserves. Doing his best to keep a steady hand on a storm shaken tiller Jackson barely heard the panic stricken officer who rode up next to him.

"General!" he cried, "Our brigade commander has been shot. The men are badly rattled, sir! We must have help!"

"What brigade, sir?" said Jackson calmly.

"The Stonewall Brigade."

Jackson reflected upon this but a moment. These men were the same who had cemented the Confederate victory on this very battlefield a little more than a year ago. "Go back," Jackson told the man. "Give my compliments to them, and tell the Stonewall Brigade to maintain her reputation."

"Yes, suh!" The fellow saluted and spurred his mount back toward the line.

Unfortunately Stonewall's supportive words weren't sufficient to maintain the line itself. What his men needed was ammunition and lots of it. Where Reilly's regiment linked with that of Wil and Levi the situation was especially critical. The latter unit in particular was experiencing the heaviest fighting since its inception. Years later both Wil and Levi would recall that afternoon as the most desperately contested moment they faced during the entire war.

Miles Turner squeezed off a shot and reached into his pouch for another bullet. He found nothing. "Ammo!" he cried. "I got no ammo!"

Wil groped through his own pouch with the same result. The whole regiment seemed to be running out simultaneously and the cry for more ammunition sang out from hundreds of throats.

The first line of Union Troops had advanced to within yards of the embankment.

"What the hell!" growled Turner. "If I can't shoot lead I can at least throw rocks!" He gabbed up a rock and hurled it, followed immediately by another then a third. Around him his comrades did likewise picking up whatever stones they could find and throwing them at the Yankees.

Bullets opposing stones is an unequal contest in anybody's war. Within seconds Union troops crested the embankment where the issue would be decided hand to hand. Men from Sergeant Reilly's regiment became mixed with those of Wil's as they fought desperately to maintain the line. Very quickly the weight of numbers began to tell. The two regiments, both badly lacking ammunition began to give way. The crest of the hill was lost and the fiercely pressed Rebels found themselves defending the back side of the slope with their own backs to the woods. The sequence of events which followed next took place in the space of no more than sixty seconds, though to those involved it seemed like hours. Wil used the butt of his rifle to force a Yankee soldier back to the crest and over the other side. As he turned back to call for his comrades to rally he was struck by a northern rifle butt across the right side of his face. The blow landed with such force that it knocked out two of his teeth and left him unconscious on the ground.

Levi saw him hit the ground and started toward his side. At the same time the rest of the men fell back from the slope into the woods. The flag bearer from Reilly's unit was shot in the throat. As he fell dying another man grabbed the flag but he too was hit, once in the leg and a second time in the head, though neither wound was mortal. The fellow spun around once and dropped to the ground losing his grip on the battle flag.

Levi had but seconds to react and for those few seconds he honestly didn't know what to do. As if by instinct, he reached out and grabbed the flag before any of its folds touched the ground. Should he fall back and join the others who even now were being rallied by officers in the woods? Bullets bounced all around him, one tore a small piece of flesh from his right forearm. He glanced up at Wil still lying motionless at the top of the hill. He thought of both their fathers on their farms in the valley. Would they be able to forgive him if he turned his back and left Wil to die or become a prisoner? Indecision kept him frozen in place holding the regimental battle standard over his left shoulder.

Up came another line of Union troops but these were hit simultaneously from the right and left as the Confederates attempted to choke off this assault and seal the breech in their line. Levi spied a musket on the ground and recognized it as one of those he'd loaded prior to their first volley. The hammer was cocked and the percussion cap was still in place. The weapon had yet to be discharged. Down he leaned and up he came rifle in hand confidant that he had at least that one shot available to him.

Over the crest came a Union captain, sword upraised in his right hand, revolver in the left.

"Stay with me, Lord!" Levi prayed out loud as he pointed the musket toward the officer and squeezed the trigger. The weapon fired with a sharp report and a puff of white smoke.

The Federal captain convulsed as the bullet struck his belly and he bowled forward onto the ground. Both his sword and revolver ended up at Levi's feet. At once he retrieved the revolver, noting right away that it was still fully loaded. Behind him he heard the rebel yell as his comrades came rushing out of the woods with empty muskets, but with their bayonets gleaming in the sun. From the opposite direction two more Union soldiers topped the embankment. Levi levelled the revolver and fired striking one man in the thigh. He aimed at the second man, "Surrender!" he demanded.

The soldier dropped his musket and raised his hands.

More of them appeared but they crested the ridge just in time to be driven back. The gap had been closed. The line was restored just as it had been all along its length. Levi's two prisoners along with several others were led toward the rear, the wounded man helped along by two others.

Levi became conscious of the presence of a horse next to him. He looked up into the eyes of a Confederate officer, Colonel Reynolds to be exact, a dark haired man with a stern gaze who wore a kepi not unlike that of Stonewall himself. Without saying a word he raised his right hand to the brim of his cap in salute to the black soldier who stood before him. Levi automatically returned the salute and watched awe-struck as the Colonel trotted off to check on another critical sector of the line.

"Hey, Levi," Turner's words brought him quickly back to reality. "Them boys over in the Stonewall Brigade would kind of like their colors back."

"Oh! Oh yeah!" Levi handed the flag over to one of Reilly's men and his thoughts went immediately to Wil. He glanced up toward the crest of the line and saw Reilly and Gilbert pulling Wil out of harm's way.

"Stand ready!" shouted Reilly with a glance back over his shoulder. "They're forming again!"

By this time Wil was regaining consciousness helped along by a canteen full of water poured over his head. He sat up slowly and when his vision finally cleared the first face he saw was Levi's.

"You gonna live?"

By way of reply, Wil turned to one side and spat out two bloody teeth, "Think they might have busted my cheek some," he grunted.

"Is that all?" chided Miles

"You'll live," smiled Levi, gripping both of Wil's shoulders.

"What happened after I got hit?"

"Not a whole lot," replied the Professor. "Most of us fell back into the woods, all except our standard-bearer, Private Thompson, and Levi here. Thompson got wounded. Levi saved him and the flag, shot himself a Yankee Captain and took two prisoners."

"You did all that?"

"I guess so."

"By your lonesome?"

"Well, the rest of the men was chargin' back at the

same time. It all happened real quick like. Don't see the point in makin' a big to-do over it."

"A genuine hero!" Wil tried to smile but his fractured cheekbone pained him badly.

"Are you going to be all right, Wil?" It was Reilly expressing his concern. "Should you be heading back for the rear?"

Those words reminded Wil instantly of Lonnie Andrews whose dried blood remained caked to Wil's clothing. "No," he said immediately as he shook a few more of the cobwebs from his head. "I'm stayin'."

"Levi," said Gilbert "These oughta be yours." He handed the holster and saber from the dead Union captain to the black man.

"What am I gonna do with all this?"

"Strap the holster on. That revolver will come in handy. Send the sword home. Should make a decent souvenir. Somethin' you can tell your grandchildren about down the road apiece."

"I reckon," Levi still appeared a bit bewildered by the whole thing.

"Here they come again!" Turner had assembled another pile of rocks to hurl at the Yankees as they approached. "Where in the hell is the ammo? What in God's name is Longstreet doin' out there? Are they gonna leave us out here alone to die all day long?"

On came the next rush of Union Infantry. Federal bullets began ripping through bark, dirt and flesh. Along that sector of the line those few graybacks, lucky enough to have a few shots left answered the Federal volleys.

Suddenly a deep, loud voice boomed from the woods behind them, "Here 'tis, Boys! Come an' git it!" It was Ivory, and for all the world it sounded as if he was serving an early supper.

"What's that fool up to?" Turner glanced back toward the trees. He saw Ivory's shiny bald head emerge from the woods. Within each arm he cradled a long wooden box. "Ammo!" cried Miles, "Ivory's got ammo!"

With such considerable weight beneath his arms Ivory found it difficult to make much headway, but he lumbered toward the line as fast as his sturdy legs could carry him. He was perhaps fifteen yards away when a Yankee bullet tore a chunk of flesh from his left shoulder.

"Ivory!" yelled Turner as he saw the blood spurt from the top of the black man's arm.

Ivory winced noticeably but kept coming albeit at a decidedly slower pace.

Turner left his place on the line and rushed to Ivory's side. "What in the hell do you think you're doin' old man? You tryin' to get yourself killed?" He relieved the wounded man of his twin burdens, getting the boxes down and bashing in the lids with the butt of his musket. "Ammo!" he shouted and waved for his comrades on the embankment.

Within seconds dozens of hands were reaching into the boxes. Ammo pouches were filled and men rushed back up to the crest to deliver a volley into the Federal ranks.

For the moment Miles stayed by Ivory's side. "You're a crazy old man, you know that?" He pulled out his knife and began cutting away a strip of blue cloth from the trousers of a dead Union soldier.

"Marse Robert sent up a wagon of ammunition. Someone had to bring it up!"

'That someone didn't have to be you! People are gettin' killed up here!"

"I can see that, Massa Turner."

"Stop callin me, Massa! Who'd be fillin' my belly if

you get yourself killed? Tell me that!" Miles fashioned a crude bandage and tied it about Ivory's shoulder in an effort to stop the bleeding.

"Well now, Massa Turner. Dey's plenty of cooks in this here army."

"None like you, now you get yourself back to them Docs and tell 'em ol' Miles said to patch you up good! You hear?"

"You hurt bad, Ivory?" It was Corporal Gilbert who knelt beside the wounded teamster as he stuffed his ammo pouch.

"No, suh," Ivory shook his head. "Corporal, back there through the woods, maybe forty yards...They's a whole wagon of this stuff. Couldn't get it through the trees."

The Corporal clasped Ivory's uninjured shoulder, "We'll take care of it. You get the hell outta here while you still can! That Yankee line's gettin' closer."

Miles helped Ivory to his feet and sent him on his way before returning to the line with a pouch full of brand new bullets. His musket roared with those of his comrades greeting the Union advance with a wall of lead.

Still they came. From Jackson's perspective the story was one of crisis all along his thinly held line. Calls for help never stopped coming until at last he had no help to offer. All of his reserves had been committed. Any shifting of forces from one segment of the line to another had been done. There were no more options. There were no reinforcements for him to send.

It was at this point that Jackson's exasperation began to show. He grabbed the courier with the fastest horse and spelled out his message with a sense of urgency no one could fail to understand. "Ride at once to General Lee," he ordered. "Tell him I must have help immediately! Make him aware of the odds we're facing on this line. We are outnumbered three to one at the very least. Tell him we've lost several brigadiers and the absence of those officers is making itself felt in most unpleasant ways! We need both reinforcements and ammunition, and these needs are critical! Do you understand?"

"Yes, suh! Perfectly."

"Go then, and for God's sake ride fast!"

Minutes later Robert E. Lee was giving instructions to a courier of his own. Having received Jackson's desperate plea he sent a request for one division of Longstreet's troops, still largely idle in this the second full day of fighting.

Longstreet however was well aware of Jackson's predicament. Standing on a ridge near the juncture of his line with that of Stonewall, he had been watching the attack from the moment the first shot had been fired. His prayers had been answered. It seemed as if the entire Union army was charging across his front to hammer Jackson's embankment. The Federals were still acting as though they were oblivious to Longstreet's presence. Soon they would know he was there - but not too soon. Better to wait...patience was vital. Before long Pope would commit his last reserves, then would the blow fall. Old Pete had already stationed eighteen pieces of artillery in a position to decimate the long undulating waves of blue which rolled relentlessly toward Jackson's line.

Then came the message from Lee. The rider didn't bother to dismount. After a hasty salute he handed a crumpled piece of paper to General Longstreet. With the fingers of one hand Old Pete twirled the hair of his thick curly beard as he quickly scanned Lee's request. The moment had arrived and he was finding it difficult to suppress the mounting excitement which had been growing inside of him for nearly an hour. With a stoic expression which belied his true feelings he glanced up at the courier and said, "Certainly, but before the division can reach him the attack will be broken by artillery."

Which was exactly how it turned out. Longstreet turned to his gunners and gave the long awaited signal. Within seconds, eighteen guns were spewing flame and shot into the long waves of blue which were rolling perpendicular to their position. Huge gaping holes were torn out of the Federal lines at once. Shocked and bewildered Union infantrymen were stopped in their tracks by this totally unexpected blow from their left. The second and third lines lost all sense of cohesion. Soldiers stumbled about aimlessly for several moments then began retreating in a state akin to panic. Those in the first line were quick to realize their support was evaporating behind them. They too relinquished any thoughts about taking Jackson's line and began to fall back.

Some distance from the fighting itself Robert E. Lee had been watching a line of wagons making its way toward the front. To a member of his staff he turned and said, "I observe that some of those mules are without shoes. I wish you would see to it that all of the animals are shod at once." Before the last word left his mouth the roar of Longstreet's guns reached his ears. He realized at once what was happening. Immediately he dispatched another messenger to Longstreet to say that if he saw a better way to relieve the pressure on Jackson than sending troops to make use of it, which was exactly what Old Pete was up to. Using signal flags Lee's headquarters contacted Jackson and posed this question: "Do you still want reinforcements?" A reply wasn't long in coming, "No, the enemy are giving way." Lee knew at once the opportunity to suppress Pope was at hand. Orders were sent at once to

BROTHERS IN GRAY

Longstreet and Jackson to attack at once with all their strength.

The Old Gray Fox probably could have saved himself the trouble of sending orders. Longstreet knew an opportunity when he saw one. Led by Hood's Texans, his entire line stormed out of the woods into the faces of a thoroughly demoralized enemy. Nor did Jackson hesitate for the slightest moment. As soon as he saw Longstreet's men emerge from cover, he ordered his own line forward.

Caught between the two jaws of a rapidly closing trap, intimidated by the wild rebel yell echoing from thousands of southern throats, the Union army turned tail in disarray. Once more they had been out-generaled. Once again thousands of them were dying to no good end. Escape became their only thought.

On a little knoll just below the Warrenton Turnpike stood two regiments of New Yorkers. They were there due to the foresight of General Porter who had warned Pope several times about the presence of Longstreet. These men of New York were all that stood between the Army of the Potomac and utter disaster. One of these regiments was overrun almost immediately. The second was a Zouave regiment in full regalia including baggy red trousers and short blue jackets. Along with a battery of six guns they held the knoll heroically, and long enough for the bulk of Pope's army to escape destruction. The cost to these Zouaves in blood was heavy indeed. More than three quarters of the nearly five hundred present for duty were killed or wounded before the survivors retired. The next day one of Hood's Texans was to remark how homesick the sight of all those brightly attired dead New Yorkers made him feel. To him, the knoll on which they fell had "the appearance of a Texas hillside when carpeted in the spring by wild flowers of many hues and tints."

Precious little daylight remained when Longstreet launched his infantry into the bewildered Union columns. It was very nearly dark by the time the Confederate advance reached the base of Henry Hill, which they themselves had defended a year ago. Here and there pockets of resistance were formed to stem the Rebel tide. One of these was commanded by Gibbon whose Iron Brigade became the backbone of Pope's rearguard. The instructions given to him by McDowell were to hold as long as possible then blow up the bridge across Bull Run as soon as his troops had safely traversed it.

Not long after McDowell's departure, Phil Kearny reined in his horse by Gibbon's side. The expression on his face gave stark testimony to the anger which seethed inside of him. "I suppose you appreciate the condition of affairs here, sir." Kearny was shouting at Gibbon so that he could be heard over the sound of musketry. "It's another Bull Run, sir! It's another Bull Run!"

"Well, General," came Gibbon's reply. "I would hope it's not as bad as you say."

"Perhaps not," Kearny's words sounded much like a growl. "Reno is keeping up the fight. He is not stampeded; I am not stampeded, you are not stampeded. That is about all, sir. My God, that's about all!"

Indeed it was. Aside from those involved in rearguard action the bulk of the Army of the Potomac was in full retreat toward the relative safety of the defenses of Washington. The suppression of John Pope had been accomplished. At the Second Battle of Manassas the Confederates suffered more than nine thousand casualties while inflicting more than fifteen thousand on their counterparts in blue.

The true significance of Lee's victory could be seen in a quick glance at the change which had taken place within the overall strategic situation in the East. Lee had been in command of the Army for three months. When Lee took command McClellan was literally knocking on the gates of Richmond. Pope with another army was south of Culpeper and able to move as he pleased. Stonewall Jackson was still playing a game of hide and seek with three sizeable Union armies in the Shenandoah Valley. Suffice it to say the prospects for the Confederacy at the time were bleak at best. In the space of three short months Lee had completely altered the course of the war. Aside from their coastal fortifications Union forces had been driven from Virginia. The war had been taken from the gates of Richmond to the outskirts of Washington.

The fighting in this campaign ended on the first of September. On that day, a Monday, Jackson once again attempted to gain the enemy rear. This time by marching north to pick up the Little River Turnpike, then turning south toward the town of Fairfax roughly eight miles behind Pope's position in Centerville.

Pope was quick to learn of this threat and reacted at once, sending Generals Phil Kearny and I.I. Stevens to intercept and do battle with the Rebels. The Battle of Chantilly, as it came to be known, was fought in the middle of a tremendous thunderstorm. Both Kearny and Stevens were killed and their troops were forced to withdraw. Jackson made no attempt to pursue. The weather was simply too severe to allow such an option.

War tends to bring out both the best and the worst of human nature. Sometimes it merely brings out behavior that most would deem odd...perhaps bizarre. Wil and Levi had become soldiers. For the better part of four days they had witnessed death on a scale they never dreamed imaginable. As the action at Chantilly drew to a close, Wil Covington took leave of his senses for a short while. In the midst of a driving rain he walked away from the lines and sat down alone in an open field. He peeled off his tunic and trousers and sat down in the mud. Grabbing a nearby stone he began scraping the blood stains on his clothing.

"What are you doing?" Levi's words rang out over a particularly sharp peal of thunder.

Wil looked up at his friend who stood before him soaking wet, his face barely visible behind the water which flowed from the brim of his floppy hat. "Can't stand it anymore!" he shouted. "Lonnie's blood has been on these clothes for ..." he paused to reflect for a moment. "How long has it been?" he asked, his voice quivering with emotion.

"Couple of days I reckon," said Levi.

"Can't stand it. Gotta get it off." Wil returned to his task with a vengeance.

Levi said nothing as he sat in the mud opposite Wil.

"We'll never be the same!" Wil glanced up from his labors. "You know that don't ya? Even if we live through this we'll never be the same!" he started to scrape again but quickly realized he was scraping the ground. He had already reduced his uniform to tatters. At last he could control his emotions no longer. He buried his face in his hands and began to sob.

Levi rose to his feet. Reaching down he clasped Wil's shoulder in one hand, gripping it tightly for just a moment. Then he released it and started back to camp without saying a word.

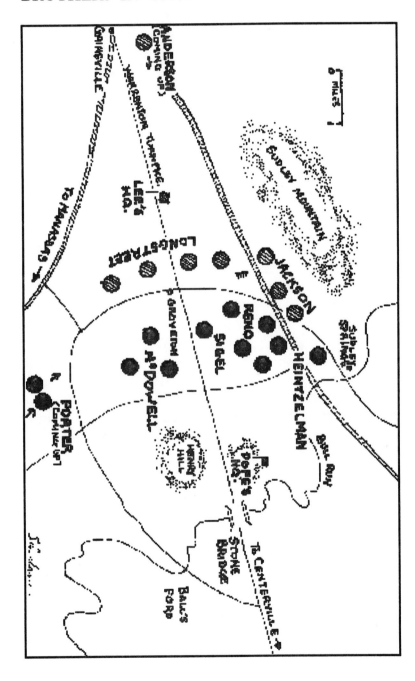

~ Chapter Four ~
"Maryland, My Maryland!"

"**G**eneral," the tone of his voice indicated some impatience on the part of Lee's personal physician, Dr. Gwathmey. "If you expect me to set the wrist properly you must stop fidgeting. I'm afraid I must insist that you remain perfectly still."

Lee glanced up at the doctor and sighed wearily. "As you wish, dear Gwathmey, as you wish."

Earlier that day Lee had suffered injuries which made it impossible for him to ride a horse. While wearing his bulky rain gear he had been standing beside Traveller when the horse was startled. He reached to grab the reins but tripped and fell forward. He broke the fall by landing on his hands, leaving one wrist with a broken bone the other with a serious sprain. Both required splints.

"This is most embarrassing," lamented Lee. "People have come to congratulate us on our victory and I cannot even offer the courtesy of shaking their hands."

"I'm sure they understand," said Gwathmey as he made the final adjustment on the splint which immobilized Lee's broken wrist.

"How long must I wear these contraptions?"

"Hard to say. You must realize you're not a young man anymore. Your bones and muscles will take longer to heal than those of a young man."

"Of that I'm all too aware, doctor, but the question stands. How long?"

"The sprain should heal in a week to ten days. The broken bone will take longer to mend, perhaps three to four weeks."

"Hardly the news I'd like to hear," groaned Lee.

"I could have lied, but that wouldn't change the facts. A broken bone takes time to heal. It's as simple as that."

"I suppose," Lee nodded and glanced out of the open tent flap at the blue September sky.

Colonel Taylor, Lee's chief of staff, was standing close by and caught the inquisitive gleam in his commander's eye. "General," he said, "If you'll pardon my intrusion into your thoughts, I've seen that expression on your face before, especially when you're designing a plan of battle. Might I inquire as to your intentions? Pope's army seems to have been thoroughly thrashed. It would appear we have an opportunity."

"So it would," agreed the General.

"Have you studied the options?"

"My dear Colonel, I've done little else in the last couple of days."

"Have you come to a decision?"

"Almost. In that regard perhaps you and the doctor can be of some assistance."

"At your service," Taylor flashed a smile and bowed his head.

"Let's examine our options. Spell them out for me, Colonel, one by one."

"One by one?" Taylor folded his arms across his chest and cupped his chin with one hand. "Well...I suppose we could start with the most obvious. We could attack Washington itself."

"If only we had the strength," countered Lee. "Unfortunately such a choice could quickly prove calamitous. The city is strongly fortified. The entire army of the Potomac is there along with the normal garrison. McClellan is back in charge, and I understand this move was heartily welcomed by the soldiers themselves. Moreover, if my information is correct there are another 60,000 troops enroute to the city. As much as we'd all love to capture Washington, I'm afraid it's just not possible."

"Very well," Taylor nodded his agreement and posed the next option. "We could stay right here."

"We could," mused Lee, "but for how long? This part of Virginia has been marched over and fought over for the last fifteen months. There's precious little to be gleaned from the ground itself, either for ourselves or for our animals. We don't even have enough wagons to send off for grain. I don't think we can just sit out here and wait for the enemy to come for us. Eventually we would find ourselves overwhelmed."

"Probably...then I suppose we'll have to yield this

ground and fall back to the Rappahannock."

"I think that should be our last resort. To retreat now would be to give up all that we have gained in the last three months. The enemy would quickly re-occupy the region and resume pressure on the Virginia Central railroad, not to mention Richmond. This is a choice I am loathe to make."

"Well now, General, it appears we've run out of options."

"Not quite," returned Lee with a tone which left little room for argument. "We can move north."

"Move north?" Taylor seemed more than a little astonished at this prospect. "Invade? You wish to invade the North?"

"I was thinking more in terms of Maryland, a sister of the Southern States. If things go well I can think of several targets up in Pennsylvania."

"General," Taylor had serious reservations about this idea. "Please don't think me insubordinate, however I am compelled to ask if your vision has perhaps exceeded your reach?"

"Perhaps. We won't know until we reach."

"General, do not the reasons you listed against remaining here apply to the possibility of invading Maryland? If we haven't enough food to remain here how can we entertain the idea of moving further north?"

"It would be a gamble I admit," said Lee. "But consider this: the people of Maryland are known to have strong secessionist sympathies. Did not Jackson use the 1st Maryland to spark his victory at Front Royal?"

"He did indeed, but you must also be aware they were deployed against their Union counterparts. The sympathies of Maryland are quite evenly divided."

"I understand your point," nodded Lee as he held both splinted hands up for inspection. "Yet I am inclined to believe the people of Maryland would be happy to throw off the yoke of Federal oppression if only they had the opportunity."

"Perhaps." Taylor seemed reluctant to buy into his

commander's argument. "but I don't think this part of Maryland contains a lot of secessionists, Southern Maryland probably does, the Eastern Shore as well, but the regions closest to Washington could hardly be called hotbeds of secession."

"Either way I see this as our only choice. In Maryland we'll find much of what we currently lack, forage for the animals, provisions for our men. The farms on the other side of the Potomac have not been ravaged by this war. We can buy whatever we need as we move through."

"With Confederate money?"

"Of course."

"Don't you think you're being a trifle optimistic?"

"Time will tell," Lee sighed wearily. "At this point I have to believe our cause will be best served by a move into Maryland. If nothing else we can keep the war out of Northern Virginia for a time, time enough perhaps for the fall harvest to come in."

"It seems as if you've already made up your mind, General."

"I may have...yes, but to me the choice is dictated by the circumstances in which we find ourselves." Lee paused to ponder his thoughts, then turned his attention to his physician who was packing his bag preparing to leave, "Tell me, Doctor, do you think it's a good idea?"

Gwathmey put the last of his instruments away and closed the bag, fastening each of the clasps before making his reply. "Hard to say," he observed softly as he turned to meet his patient's eyes. "I am not one who is normally given to the assessment of tactics and strategy, and I know you well enough to be certain you're aware of the condition of this army. The men are considerably worn. They've been asked to march long distances in short periods of time. They haven't been fed well and our rations are still woefully inadequate. Illness, particularly diarrhea, has become an acute problem."

"Ah, yes," said Taylor with a lighthearted chuckle. "The Confederate disease."

"Too many of the men have eaten nothing but green corn during the last week. Such a diet can't help but wreak havoc with the intestinal system."

"It's become something of a joke among the men," smiled Taylor. "Some of them claim the ability to hit a dime at seven yards."

Even the normally stoic Lee had to laugh when he heard this, a response which didn't mask the concern he felt for his solders. "If we cross the river we can procure better rations," he argued.

"At least a quarter of our men have no shoes." added Gwathmey.

"We'd be better able to remedy that problem on the northern side of the Potomac," countered Lee. "But I must add this: if we choose to move north the procurement of shoes won't be our objective. Colonel, would you unfold that map we were studying earlier?"

"Certainly," replied Taylor, who moved at once to comply with the request.

Moments later, the three of them stood around a small table studying a map of the mid-Atlantic states. "Keep this in mind," said Lee, "since spring we've conducted three successful campaigns in Virginia. Jackson's Valley Campaign," he pointed toward the Shenandoah. "The seven days in which we drove McClellan down the Peninsula to the water and the campaign we just concluded at Manassas."

"Fair enough," observed Gwathmey.

"Would it not be fair to say that in the process we've earned the admiration of the western world?"

"Their admiration perhaps," replied Taylor. "But the admiration of Europeans will not serve as ammunition for our guns, nor food for our bellies, nor clothes for our backs."

"Well put," noted Lee. "Admiration will not suffice. It is recognition we so desperately need... Diplomatic recognition, particularly by Great Britain, could be the key to the success of our cause, could it not?"

"It could indeed," mused Gwathmey.

"As I see it," argued Lee, "The key to diplomatic recognition lies in the North. If we can mount another successful campaign this time in Maryland, perhaps even Pennsylvania, we might be taking a huge step toward obtaining diplomatic recognition."

"It's a long shot," countered Taylor. "Especially when you consider the size and condition of this army."

"We've taken long shots before, Walter. It's not as though this would be the first."

"True, but this one makes me nervous. How far into the North do you envision us advancing?"

"Harrisburg, Pennsylvania," Lee announced matter-of-factly as he tapped that location on the map.

Both Taylor and Gwathmey raised their eyebrows in surprise. "Harrisburg?" posed Taylor.

"Is there any strategic significance to Harrisburg?" wondered the doctor.

"Indeed there is, "replied Lee. "If we destroy the railroad bridge over the Susquehanna, we can sever the Federal West from the East. It would buy us time to maneuver at will through central and eastern Pennsylvania. We could threaten New York. Baltimore could fall into our hands. Should we win one more battle the recognition we seek could be ours. We could bring this war to an end on satisfactory terms."

"A long shot indeed," remarked Gwathmey.

By the third of September, lee's mind was made up. The army would move at once into Maryland. By way of formalizing the decision he dictated a letter explaining his intentions to President Davis. His words read as follows.

"The army is not properly equipped for an invasion of an enemy's territory. It lacks much of the material of war, is feeble in transportation, the animals b e i n g much reduced, and the men are poorly provided with clothes, and in thousands of instances are destitute of shoes...What occasions me the most concern is the fear of getting out of ammunition."

This message he sent to Richmond but he chose not to wait for a reply. His mind was set. Maryland would be the next stop for the Army of Northern Virginia.

Inside the city of Washington, lamps burned late into the night during the first few days following Pope's defeat. The whole populace was up in arms at the prospect of a Rebel attack upon the capital itself. Government clerks were mobilized and armed to share in the defense of the city. The less stouthearted among the civilian population simply packed their bags and left. Others made plans to evacuate and stood ready to bolt at a moment's notice.

The Army of the Potomac had been thoroughly beaten. The line of straggling demoralized Union soldiers stretched for more than ten miles from the Potomac into Fairfax County. Most of their supplies had been either destroyed or captured. Pope himself had sunk to mood levels bordering on despair. Time and again he complained about the straggling, particularly on the part of those troops who had recently been under the command of McClellan down on the peninsula. Several messages from Pope expressed his fear that the entire army was melting away and only a drastic move by Lincoln could prevent this dissipation and restore cohesion and a sense of integrity to the troops.

Lincoln heard all of this. Moreover he listened. On his own initiative and without seeking any approval from his cabinet he summoned McClellan. He informed the "Young Napoleon" that he was being restored to the command of the Army of the Potomac, and that he was being charged with the safety of Washington. To McClellan was also given the task of informing John Pope of the change in circumstances.

Lincoln's cabinet reacted to this news in shocked dismay. They regarded Lincoln's appointment of McClellan as nothing less than a national calamity. Lincoln paid them no mind. "It is my responsibility," he said, "and mine alone." He was quick to see how much the condition of the army had deteriorated and even quicker to take steps to remedy it. About McClellan he simply said, "If he can't fight himself he excels in making others ready."

BROTHERS IN GRAY

McClellan wasted no time taking over command of the army. Mounted upon his white charger he rode with his staff into Virginia continuing south then west until he came upon Pope and McDowell heading toward Washington. Little Mac promptly informed General Pope of Lincoln's most recent order relieving the latter of command. If Pope was shocked at his sudden dismissal he gave no indication of it. Trying to appear calm he relinquished command to McClellan.

All of this was witnessed by a certain John P. Hatch, who was now in command of Rufus King's division, and who held a particularly strong disdain for John Pope. Making sure he was within Pope's hearing range, General Hatch proceeded to shout the news out to the passing column, "McClellan's back in charge!" he yelled. "Three cheers for Mac!"

This news was received by the soldiers in absolute joy. The cheer was echoed all up and down the ten- mile column. The feeling of despair which had taken so tight a grip on the Army of the Potomac evaporated. Smiles beamed forth from faces which only minutes before had been locked in frowns. Loads suddenly felt lighter. Backs and shoulders straightened. As if the recipient of a miracle, this mob of bluecoats suddenly regained the appearance of an army again. Many of these troops suddenly found themselves savoring the prospect of another clash with Lee and his minions. As for Pope, his ears still ringing with the cheers his men had for McClellan, he had plenty of time to ponder his next assignment...fighting the Sioux.

With its commanding general somewhat incapacitated and riding in an ambulance the Army of Northern Virginia crossed the Potomac river into Maryland on September 6th and 7th, 1862. Lee's hopes and aspirations were set adrift almost from the outset. For starters, the size of the army changed radically from one side of the river to the next. Lee had 66,000 men when he made his decision to invade Maryland. Of these only 50,000 were on hand when the army entered the "Old line state." Why? Old-fashioned straggling accounted for much of the depletion, but not all. No few of Lee's soldiers had serious reservations about invading someone else's country and simply refused to participate. As one soldier put it, "None but the heroes remained."

It was late in the day by the time Wil, Levi, and their companions approached the Potomac. The sky was a vivid shade of blue. The steadily flowing waters of the river itself reflected the bright light of the early evening sun and seemed almost gold in color. A variety of scents from the environs of the Potomac filled the nostrils of these southern soldiers as they approached the water's edge. Some of those with boots or shoes paused briefly to remove them and waded gingerly into the river.

The Potomac seemed awfully cold to Wil as he stepped off the bank and started across. In fact the chilly temperatures of the water as it swirled past his knees and hips made his gums throb in the places where he used to have teeth. "Seems a bit on the cold side," he remarked as he raised his Enfield higher and laid it across his upper back and shoulders.

"Been gettin' chilly at night," explained levi following close behind. "Sure did cool the water down some."

The Maryland shore lay some fifty to sixty yards away. Wil glanced back over his shoulder at his black companion. "We're headin' into a foreign country!" he grinned.

Suddenly, a rock hurled from the bank landed just to the right of the two young men splashing both of them rather liberally. Wil wiped the water from his face with one sleeve and stepped out of the column. "Who threw that?" he demanded with a grin, though his voice could barely be heard over the endless chatter and laughing which echoed all through the column.

"Little ol' me!" laughed Miles as he charged into the river. Within moments he and Wil were locked in a wrestling hold as each tried to dunk the other. Levi stood to one side holding all the weapons and such as the other two grappled in fake fury while the army marched past.

BROTHERS IN GRAY

Miles was older, bigger and stronger and was quick to get the better of Wil Covington. As the younger man pulled himself out of the water coughing and sputtering he started to swing at Miles but checked himself when he found Corporal Gilbert standing in front of him with a wry grin on his face.

"Sorry, Corporal," he smiled, "I thought you was Miles."

"I see," nodded Gilbert. I don't suppose the two of you could grow up just long enough to get to the other side could you?"

"Sure...if that's what you want."

"I'd find it most pleasin'."

"I just grew up," said Wil standing up as tall as he could manage.

"I never did," noted Miles. "Probably never will, but I reckon I can contain myself till we cross."

"Awfully considerate of you," said the Corporal. "Shall we continue across?"

All of them rejoined the march across the ford. Within minutes they had put most of the river's width behind them. Only ten or twelve yards remained to the Maryland shore. For the most part, the mood of those in the column was relaxed and jovial: talking was constant. It seemed like the cavalry was always present as individual troopers rode up and down both sides of the column. Horses were highstepping through the water while their riders tried to impress lowly infantrymen with their skills in the saddle. As if on cue regimental bands on both sides of the river began playing a lively rendition of "Maryland, My Maryland!" All along the column those who could sing, as well as those who couldn't took up the song so that its words could be plainly heard on both sides of the Potomac.

To one cavalryman the entire spectacle was nothing short of beautiful. The evening sun caught the bright colors of the rebel battle flags so that they seemed to stand out above all else. This along with the sounds of the various bands thrilled the heart of this particular trooper, and the gold reflection from the waters of the Potomac seemed to convey a Divine message, as though this venture beyond the Confederacy was blessed by God Himself. So far as omens were concerned, this one appeared to be most favorable.

Levi was first out of the river. As soon as his footing was secure he reached back, extending his hand to help first Wil, then Miles out of the water. All along the line of march on the Maryland side, Wil could see hundreds of men who had fallen out to rest or dry their tattered clothing. He spotted several soldiers leaving a cluster of rocks just to the left of the column, perhaps thirty yards from the river's edge. Quickly he motioned to Miles and Levi, and stepped out of the column toward the rocks.

The regimental band passed, but another soon took its place as the three men spread their gear out on the rocks and started to put their socks and boots back on. Levi yawned and stretched his arms overhead then glanced to his right. "Hey, Wil," he said as he tapped Covington's shoulder. "Did you see them two boys watching us from the shore upriver?"

"Yeah. What about 'em?"

"Lookie yonder."

Wil turned to his right leaning slightly forward so he could see around Levi. Approaching them were two young boys. One was perhaps fourteen, the other no more than twelve. Within a minute or two both had reached the rocks and found themselves staring into the faces of three Confederate soldiers.

"Howdy, Boys!" Miles was his usual affable self. "Word is we're lookin' for recruits, but I'm afraid y'all might be a tad too young. You got older brothers?"

The younger one shook his head, his eyes wide with amazement as they took in the spectacle of an army passing through on the narrow dirt road which led from the river.

The other boy replied verbally. "I do," he explained. "but he ain't likely to be joinin' with you fellers. He's in the Yankee army."

"Humph!" grunted Miles. "I reckon we shouldn't

hold that against you." He paused and peered closely at the boy as if studying his potential as a soldier. "Nah," he gestured at last. "The war'll be over before you're old enough. Which side do you favor anyway?"

"Can't say I have much of an opinion one way or the other."

"A fence-sitter," chuckled Turner. "What's your name, boy? You've got a name don't ya?"

"Zach Smith."

"How you do, Zach? This here's Wil Covington. That's his sidekick Levi Henry, and you can call me Miles."

"What's your friend's name?" asked Wil.

"Bobbie."

"Is he some sort of mute or has the cat got his tongue?"

"Reckon he's pretty amazed."

"Reckon so!" laughed Miles. "How 'bout you, Zach? Has the sight of this magnificent army impressed you?"

"Magnificent?" An incredulous smile spread across the boy's face. "That's not exactly what I've been thinking."

"Oh? And just what have you been thinkin'?"

"Well...both good and bad I suppose."

"Let's hear the bad first."

"All right," nodded Zach. "I reckon y'all are about the dirtiest men I've ever seen. You're a most ragged lean lookin' bunch. You remind me of what a hungry pack of wolves might look like."

"Imagine that," chuckled Wil as he stared at the hole in the sole of his left boot. "Ol' Zach here thinks we look like a ragged bunch of wolves. Where did he ever come up with an idea like that?"

Zachory moved to position himself on a rock just across from Wil. "Reckon I've been watchin' Yankees too much. They've all got uniforms. They always seem to look good. They march in compact formations like they're all thinkin' the same thought at the same time. They don't spread out like you boys do, and they sure don't make as much noise as y'all do. Listen for yourselves. Don't it sound like you're headin' for a Saturday night social?"

"That's because we're free, boy," interjected Miles. "Our government doesn't control us the way yours controls you. I reckon we're about the freest people to ever walk this green earth."

"Not him", Zach gestured toward Levi.

"Excuse me," said the young black man. "I've been free since the moment I drew my first breath."

"Oh." Zach smiled a little sheepishly. "I figured you was a slave."

"Reckon you figured wrong." Levi seemed a little miffed.

"Don't be mad at him," urged Wil. "It's an easy mistake to make. Anyway, he's just a kid."

"I suppose." Levi's frown slowly faded.

"All right, boy," interrupted Miles. "You've told us the bad. What about the good?"

"The good?" Zachory paused a moment to ponder his answer. "There's somethin' about you fellas. I don't quite know how to describe it. You've got a dash about you the Northerners just don't have. I can tell by the way your cavalry rides. They remind me of circus riders. I can tell by the way you're all the time cussin' and talkin'."

"Like I said," noted Miles. "We're free men."

By this time, the three soldiers had put their shoes back on. Gathering their muskets and gear they rose to resume the march. Wil and Levi bade farewell to the two young Marylanders and rejoined the column. Miles lingered a moment longer, pausing to tousle the younger boy's hair while he looked the other in the eye. "I hope I don't ever have to kill your brother, Zach. I truly do. Like I said before, I think this war will be over long before you're old enough to get caught up in it. But just in case I might be wrong, lemme give you a word of advice; Don't get caught up in it, you hear?"

"Reckon, I'll have to cross that bridge when I get to it." replied the lad.

"Reckon so." Miles stepped down from the rocks

and hurried to catch up with the others. "So long boys," he called back over his shoulder.

Frederick, Maryland was the immediate goal for the army, and there was still a half day's march in front of them when they went into camp for the night. Foot weary infantrymen gathered about their fires and swapped yarns under a clear star-filled sky. Speculation as to their prospects abounded. Miles stepped to the fire and poured himself a cup of coffee then returned to his place on the cool ground. He glanced over at Wil who was lying on his back staring up at the stars with his hands cradling his head. "So how does it feel to be spending your first night on foreign soil?" he asked.

"Not all that different than Virginia," came the reply.

"How abut you, Ivory?" Miles turned his attention to the teamster who was seated close to the light of the fire working on repairing a harness for one of his mules. "You ever been this far north before?"

"No, suh," returned Ivory as he lowered the harness to his lap and stared across the fire at Miles. "Can't say that I have."

"You think fortune'll smile on us?"

"Don't think I ought to be pretendin' I know what the Lawd has in mind, Massa Turner."

"How about you, Corporal?" Miles was determined to get a conversation going.

"Hard to say," Gilbert removed the pipe he was smoking from his mouth then used his free hand to scratch his head. "Seems to me Marse Robert's takin' a long shot this time, but if it works out we might be able to bring this war to a close."

"If it don't work we could find ourselves in a heap of trouble," remarked Wil to no one in particular.

"He's bankin' on us pickin' up lots of recruits up here," noted the Corporal. "So far I've seen a lot of folks gawkin' at us, but I don't see too many of 'em fallin' all over each other to join up with us."

"It's cause of the way we look," said Miles. "To

these Maryland folks we must seem like a horde of dirty scarecrows."

"Don't mean we can't fight," argued Wil.

"We know that...maybe they do too," said Gilbert. "But I don't think that's the problem. I doubt if anybody questions our ability to fight. I'm inclined to think that our government itself is the cause for hesitation."

"How so?" Wil offered the question..

"When Marylanders look at us they're seein' what the Confederate government put together out of virtually nothing. What do they see? Thousands of us have no shoes. Our uniforms are in tatters. To look at us is to see a government which commands precious little in the way of resources. I'm sure there's a bunch of folks here in Maryland who think we can't be sustained in the field."

"They might be right," said Miles.

"I don't understand," interjected Wil. "Maryland is a sister state. It seems to me they'd be eager to stand by us."

"Perhaps," nodded the Corporal. "Yet many of them might be wondering where we were when push came to shove last year. The Maryland assembly met in Annapolis to vote on the ordinances of secession. Most folks up here think the secessionists would have carried the day, but Lincoln made sure they didn't. He sent troops to break up the legislature and arrest anyone who expressed sympathy for the South. The Confederacy was powerless to stop Lincoln. He even suspended habeas corpus."

"What does that mean?" wondered Levi.

"It means they can arrest someone and just lock him away. No charges ever have to be filed. They can leave people in jail. Anyone suspected of being a Confederate sympathizer ends up behind bars. Has the Confederacy been able to stop this practice? The answer seems rather obvious to me. The future of the Confederacy is a question mark. If I was a Marylander, even one with southern leanings, I'd be inclined to watch and see before I did anythin' which might get me killed or locked up. I think that's the real reason we're seein' so few recruits up here."

"You're probably right, Corporal," said Wil. "But I also feel there is another reason, even more simple than yours. I just feel a bunch of these people are probably Yankees. They're no more interested in joinin' us than we are them."

"That's true as well," nodded Gilbert. "In any event these are matters for the generals and politicians to ponder. We've another march in front of us tomorrow and we'd be well advised to get some sleep."

By mid-afternoon of the following day, the 7th of September, the army was entering Frederick, a strategically located town in north-central Maryland. From here Lee could readily move in any direction. To the west lay Hagerstown, the National Turnpike and Ohio. Directly north waited Pennsylvania less than a day's march away. A two-day march to the east would put the army in Baltimore. Directly to the south the residents of Washington City had serious questions as to their security.

Unbeknownst to the Rebel infantrymen trudging wearily through the streets of Frederick, was the presence of an inspector general of the Union army. This officer was able to conceal himself from Southern eyes and took a tally of the Rebels as they passed his place of hiding. In the written report which he was later to submit, he estimated their numbers at no more than sixty thousand. He also pointed out the presence of at least three thousand negro soldiers in Lee's army. They were integrated among the white troops and they were armed and attired just like their white counterparts. He concluded that black soldiers were an integral part of the Confederate army - the Rebel horde, as he put it - which he found interesting in light of the public rhetoric emanating from Richmond mocking the idea of allowing Blacks to serve in the army.

On balance most of Lee's soldiers found Frederick to be a pleasant interlude when compared to the events which came before and after the four days spent in the town. Most of the people were friendly though a trifle reserved. As Wil had remarked, many of them were indeed Union sympathizers. Some waved American flags at their southern guests. There was some jeering and taunting but there were no incidents of a serious nature.

On the morning of the 8th, Wil and Levi received permission to leave camp and go into the town itself. Wil had saved most of his meager pay and hoped to purchase a pair of shoes to replace those he was wearing. Their regiment was camped about a half-mile from the outskirts of Frederick so the walk into town didn't take long at all. They passed several farms and encountered quite a number of civilians who had gathered to gawk at the Rebels. Just shy of the town they came across a man operating a small hand-press which squeezed the juice from apples. A fair number of soldiers were there watching as he took whole apples and produced cup after cup of fresh cider. His political thoughts he kept to himself but he was certainly warm and friendly to these soldiers of the Confederacy. Cup after cup of cider did he pour and handed them out to all who cared to partake. Some of the men offered to pay for their cider but the farmer wouldn't hear of it. Wil and Levi were quick to add their hands to those which were eagerly outstretched for cups of cool Maryland cider.

"Lord, is that ever good!" remarked Levi after downing the last sip from his cup.

"Sure is," agreed Wil. "I've tasted a lot of good cider in my time. This ranks with the best." He drained the last few drops from the cup and savored their taste for several moments before handing the cup back to the farmer. He thought about asking for seconds but decided against it. Several more infantrymen had assembled and all of them seemed to be salivating at the prospect of tasting the results of this farmer's efforts. "You ready?" he glanced over at Levi.

"Sure," came the reply.

With no further ado, the two of them resumed their trek into town. As they entered Frederick for the second time they were struck once again by the obvious prosperity enjoyed by the people of Maryland. The streets of the town were clean and well maintained, though the presence of so many gray-clad soldiers milling about created a mood bordering on uncertainty and confusion. The townspeople themselves had mixed reactions to the Southerners. Some were obviously sympathetic to the Confederacy and were openly warm to the Rebel soldiers. Others were frankly hostile and made it a point to display American flags from their doors and windows. Many revealed no opinion about the war but found themselves quite curious about the newcomers, so they simply stared at the southern scarecrows they had read so much about.

Wil and Levi were walking along one of the main streets searching for a cobbler when they nearly collided with a brigadier general who was coming out of a small book shop. It was E. P. Alexander, chief of artillery in Longstreet's corps. Startled by the near collision he dropped the item he had just purchased - a copy of the May, 1862 issue of Harpers magazine and a book titled *Father Tom and the Pope*. He did, however, hold on to a small box which he quickly cradled in both arms.

The two Shenandoah boys bent quickly to retrieve the fallen items, taking pains to wipe the road dirt from their respective covers before handing them back to the general: "We're sorry, suh." offered Wil. "We didn't mean to bump into ya."

"Well now don't you be worryin' about it." Alexander gave them an affable smile. "I should have looked before I walked out of the door. In any event the book and magazine won't break," he paused and glanced into the box still cradled in his left arm. "If these had broken I'd be out fourteen cents."

The only reply from the two boys was the inquisitive expression on their faces.

"Dishes," explained Alexander. "I visited a potter earlier this morning. Fascinating fellow...a true artist," he handed the book and magazine to Levi then reached into the box, pulling out one of the little bowls for the two soldiers to inspect. "I thought I'd add to my mess kit," he said. "And the price was excellent. Fourteen cents for three of these."

"Looks like right fine pottery," said Wil.

"Yes indeed," nodded the general. "But if you're of a mind to buy some for yourself I'd recommend payin' in silver if you have it."

"Why's that?" There was just the slightest indication of alarm in Wil's voice.

General Alexander chuckled and glanced around as though he preferred not to have too many people hear what he had to say. "I can't understand why," he said. "But it seems some of these folks are a bit reluctant to accept Confederate money. The potter for instance; I gave him a one- dollar Confederate bill. I should have received eighty-six cents as my change. Look what he gave me." He reached into a pocket on his tunic and withdrew half of a one-dollar Maryland bank note. "He cut the bill with a pair of scissors and gave me half. He added twenty-five cents in silver to this. He was searchin' for more coins but I told him to keep the rest. In any event, if you're plannin' a purchase I'd suggest coin."

"Thank you, suh. As a matter of fact, I was hoping to find a cobbler. Me and Levi could both use a pair of shoes."

"A cobbler..." Alexander scratched his chin and thought for a moment. "It seems to me I saw a sign for a cobbler's shop." He turned and pointed down the street, "Another block in that direction then left on that side street. I think you'll find it on the right side of the street."

"Thank you, General. We'll head that way."

Alexander gave them a nod and a smile and took back his reading material from Levi. "You boys enjoy your stay in town, hear? And remember...coins!"

Here the three of them exchanged salutes and parted company. Wil and Levi followed the general's directions and moved off down the street. "Wil," said Levi. "You got any coins?"

"Not a one. How about you?"

" I think I've got forty or fifty cents."

"I know I've got money," said Wil. "But it's

Confederate. I saved five dollars from the last time we got paid."

"You think we can use it?"

"General Alexander used his paper money. I see no reason why we can't".

Just then they turned the corner and at once spotted the cobbler's store about half way down the block where Alexander said it would be.

The shoemaker was an older man, perhaps in his late sixties. He was bald save for a wispy bank of white hair which connected his ears by way of the back of his head. "Not again." he groaned as the boys walked through the door.

"Good mornin'," greeted Wil as they entered and removed their hats.

"Don't tell me," said the old man. "You're lookin' for boots. I don't see why," he added as he glanced down at their feet. "Looks like you're both wearin' shoes to me. The last twenty of you graybacks I've seen have all been barefoot."

Wil turned half-around and lifted one foot to reveal the large hole in the sole of his shoe.

"All right put your foot down for God's sake! I can see! May be old but I ain't blind yet. What kind of money you got?"

"Confederate."

"And you expect me to take it?"

"We was hopin'."

"Do I have a choice?"

The boys exchanged glances and the somewhat helpless look in their faces told the old man all he needed to know. "Okay, okay," he sighed in an exasperated tone. "I reckon I can take care of two more. Ironic as hell ain't it? This is the busiest day I've ever had and I may not be able to spend a dime of it!"

"If we win you'll sing a different tune."

"That's one big if from where I'm standing. You're expecting me to take the money of a government which can't even put shoes on the feet of its soldiers."

"Well, suh," replied Wil. "If I remember my history right, the 2nd Continental Congress had problems of a similar sort. Those people endured their deprivations and they prevailed."

"So they did," muttered the cobbler. "You sound like you had yourself some book learnin'."

"Some," nodded Wil.

"You know your sizes?"

"Yessuh."

"Write 'em down for me and I'll see what I can find back in my storeroom."

A short while later both boys had been fitted with new ankle-high boots. "That should take care of you for awhile," the old man sighed as he returned to his counter. "Depending on how much marching you boys do. I'm chargin' you a buck and a half for each pair. Comes to three dollars."

"I'll take care of both pairs," said Wil as he handed three Confederate bills to the cobbler. Can I ask you something?"

"Sure," the shoemaker reached across his counter to take the money.

"If you really think our money's no good, why do you accept it?"

"Maybe I'm just plain feelin' sorry for ya. Maybe I'm secretly a Confederate sympathizer. Then again maybe I'm not. Maybe I know folks who can take all this Rebel money down to Virginia and buy goods I can use in my business. Maybe I'll just hold on to this money. If you lose, there might come a day when these Rebel dollars are worth something to collectors. Maybe I've got lots of reasons. Maybe I have none."

"But you still helped us...and you helped those who came earlier."

"You might think I'm helping you. I'll deny it."

"Why?"

"I should think the answer to that is obvious. The Union army will be along sooner or later and your army will probably move off. Federal authorities don't think highly of Marylanders who speak out for the South. Those kind of people end up in jail and there they'll stay till the war's over. I have no desire to join them. If I'm questioned about doing business with Rebels I'll simply say I was forced to. I only sold you boots so you wouldn't kill me. That's the story I'll tell."

"Everything you said is based on one assumption," argued Wil. "That we'll leave if the Yankees show up."

"Correct," nodded the cobbler. "And that's the assumption I'm sticking with until I see otherwise."

"You'll see," said Wil. "The Confederacy will be around a lot longer than anybody thinks."

"Time will tell," the cobbler shrugged his shoulders. "Meanwhile you boys can at least say you've got new shoes. Now you'd best be movin' along. I don't want anyone to think I may have enjoyed this conversation."

"Very well," nodded Wil. "But we do want to thank you for the boots."

"Consider yourself welcome...now be off with you."

As the two walked back to camp, it was Levi who first verbalized his thoughts about the encounter. "Seems like that feller was awful fearful about speakin' his mind," he observed.

"Seems that way," agreed Wil. "General Lee wants recruits from this territory but I've got to wonder if we'll get any."

It was late afternoon by the time Wil and Levi returned to the camp of the 5th Virginia. They put up with some good- natured ribbing about their new boots, but some of the comments were not of a humorous nature. Two men insisted it wasn't fitting for a Black to be wearing brand new shoes while so many white men were still barefoot. Wil pointed out that he and Levi had both paid for their acquisitions with their own money. Whether some disagreed with the propriety of Levi buying himself shoes was of no consequence as far as Wil was concerned. The shoes rightfully belonged to Levi and on his feet they would stay. It seemed as though the affair might come to blows, but then a sergeant intervened; defusing the situation before a punch was thrown.

Moving on to their own tents, both boys deposited their other purchases, then set about to locate their comrades. Miles Turner passed them with scarcely a hello.

"Hey, Miles!" chided Wil. "Don't you say hi to your friends anymore?"

A frown seemed to have Mile's entire face in its grip as he turned to speak. "Howdy, boys," he said sadly. "Didn't mean to ignore ya."

"Lemme guess," grinned Levi. "That Tiger fella...right?"

"Yep," nodded Turner. "That boy, Armelin. He done cleaned me out again."

"Maybe you ought not to play cards with him," suggested Wil. "Maybe you could hold on to your money a wee bit longer."

"Maybe," snorted Miles as he turned and walked away.

C'mon, Wil," beckoned Levi. "Let's find Ivory. He might have some food we can snitch."

"Good idea!"

They found the teamster-sometime cook seated on a small stool next to his wagon. He was peeling potatos but it wasn't spuds which caught Wil's eyes. The expression on Ivory's face was awfully glum, as though his spirit was mired in a deep sense of foreboding.

"Afternoon, Ivory," greeted Levi. "You want some help?"

"Who's offerin'?" Ivory arched one eyebrow as he glared back at them.

"Reckon we both are," replied Wil.

"Fine and dandy!" sighed the cook. "Reach up into my wagon. You'll find a couple more stools, some buckets and knives. There's another bushel of potatos yonder by that tree. Bring it on over and get started. I got one hell of a stew brewin' for tonight."

Within minutes the boys were seated on either side of Ivory and potato peels were flying everywhere.

"What's wrong, Ivory?" asked Wil as he tossed a

freshly peeled potato into the bucket.

"What makes you think anything's wrong?"

"You got that somber look on your face. The one that usually spells bad news."

"Bad news..." mused Ivory. "That pretty much says it. Ain't you boys heard?"

"Heard what? We've been horsin' around in town all day."

"Then I take it you boys ain't heard what happened to Stonewall."

"Jackson?" There was genuine alarm in Levi's voice.

"Is he hurt?"

"Sho' nuff," nodded the cook.

"What happened?" Wil dropped the potato he'd just started peeling and stared intently into Ivory's face.

"I can't believe you boys don't know! I thought the whole army knew!"

"C'mon, Ivory! Stop teasin' us!" demanded Levi.

"You just keep your britches on, boy! If you give me half a chance I'll be tellin' ya all about it!"

"Go ahead," urged Wil impatiently.

"All right," nodded Ivory. "It seems like some of the local folks took a shinin' to Stonewall. Said they was sympathetic to our cause they did, but I gotta wonder 'bout that. I think they was really Yankee saboteurs, that's what I think!"

"Did they shoot him in the back?"

"Gracious no!" laughed Ivory. "That'd be much too obvious!"

"So what did they do?"

"Gave him a new horse."

"A new horse?" Wil sat back but didn't take his gaze away from Ivory's face. "If all they did was to give Stonewall a horse how do you figure they're Yankee saboteurs?"

"How? I'll tell you how! That old horse done threw Stonewall right to the ground! First time he mounted! The first damn time!"

"How bad is he hurt?"

"Don't know. I heard he might be paralyzed. They got him in an ambulance right now!"

"Good Lord!" breathed Levi. "That means Lee and Jackson are both down!"

"Sure does!" huffed Ivory.

"Maybe so," agreed Wil. "But that thing with Jackson sounds like an accident to me. I don't think those people were Yankees."

"You go on ahead and think what you want. Ain't nobody gonna convince me otherwise. Those folks knew what kind of horse they was givin' to Stonewall. They planned it that way, and they did it 'cause they's Yankees!" Ivory brandished his potato knife in Wil's face to drive his point home.

"Well," muttered Wil. "We'll just have to believe he's gonna be all right. A couple of prayers and a little faith could work wonders!"

"We might need a lot of prayers," said Ivory. "Seems like we just got into Maryland but there's an awful lot of things goin' haywire. I got a bad feelin' about all this."

"Why? What else has happened?" wondered Wil.

"Well, if you boys didn't know 'bout Stonewall I reckon you probably don't know the first thing 'bout Hood or A.P. Hill."

"Are they hurt too?"

"Hurt? Nah... 'cept maybe their pride. Both of 'em is under arrest."

"Arrest?" gasped Levi. "C'mon, Ivory! You must be jokin'!"

"No suh! May the Lord be my witness! It's the gospel truth!"

"How?" asked Will.

"Well lemme see now," Ivory paused and wiped sweat from his brow with his left forearm. "Hood's problems go back to the battle we just won down in Manassas. Seems like the Texans captured some ambulance wagons," he paused again and glanced directly at

Levi. "Them Texans is a wild bunch," he noted. "I've been sayin' that all along."

Levi couldn't recall hearing Ivory ever say much at all about those Texans, but he enjoyed the old man's stories far too much to mention that. "You're right," he said. "The Yankees can sure tell you how wild they are! What happened with General Hood?"

"Oh! Well it seems like General Evans, that's Shanks Evans, wanted some of them wagons. Hood wouldn't give 'em up to save his life! Longstreet was gonna send him on back to Culpeper for a trial but Marse Robert stepped in. He's keepin' Hood with us, but the po' man is under arrest."

"What about A.P. Hill?"

"Oh, yeah! Now that's a problem between Hill and Jackson. Those two ain't exactly fond of each other. Seems like on the march up here there was a problem with the light division keepin' up. You know how Ol' Jack likes to march. There's got to be special rest periods at special times. Hill wasn't payin' attention to all that. Stonewall stepped in and halted one of his brigades. General Hill found out and done lost his temper. The way I heard it the two of them was nose to nose. Hill said he'd give up his sword, told Stonewall he wasn't fit to be a general! I swear it's true! That's just the way I heard it! Ol' Jack arrested him then and there!"

The old black man fell silent at this point and his audience were too shocked by what they'd heard to say much of anything. For several minutes the three of them sat there by the wagon wordlessly peeling potatos. After awhile Ivory yawned wearily and stretched his powerful arms overhead. "You boys see why I'm so worried?" he asked. "Four of our best generals are either injured or under arrest. Most of us look like death warmed over. What kind of picture do we make for these Maryland folks?"

"Well..." Wil paused to collect his thoughts. "Maybe we won't impress too many folks, with our looks, but at least we're here. I mean we're in Maryland now, not

Virginia. We moved the war out of Virginia, didn't we?
That should mean somethin' to somebody."

"Don't know," mused Ivory. "I just got a bad feelin'
'bout us bein' here." He shook his shiny bald head and
reached for another potato.

*   *   *   *   *   *   *   *   *

That same day was a busy one at Lee's headquarters. First on the agenda of Robert E. Lee was the issuance
of a formal proclamation to the people of Maryland, a
document prepared at the suggestion of President Davis.
In it the people of the Confederacy proclaimed their
affections for the people of Maryland, pointing out the
social and cultural ties which bound them together, and
urging the Marylanders to rise up and throw off the yoke
of foreign oppression.

Once the proclamation was written, Lee turned to
the tactical considerations which confronted his rag-tag
army now that they were encamped some thirty miles
north of the Union capital. In keeping with his initial
strategy he would soon be moving his troops to the
westward side of the Catoctin Mountains as a prelude for
a thrust to the Susquehanna River in Pennsylvania. Success in such a venture would depend heavily on secure
lines of supply. To this end the Shenandoah Valley was
critical. Any Federal presence in the lower valley would
have to be neutralized. In response to Lee's crossing of the
Potomac the Federals had already evacuated Winchester
but they had chosen not to evacuate either Martinsburg or
Harper's Ferry. With this in mind, Lee summoned several
of his officers to help decide on a course of action.

With Jackson and Longstreet on hand, the meeting got underway, though tactics and strategy took second
place in the conversation, at least during the initial stages.
All three of these men were nursing injuries, all as a result
of accidents. Not surprisingly these injuries dominated
the first few minutes of the council.

"It's good to see you walking," said Lee to Jackson.

"You gave us quite a fright yesterday."

Stonewall's lips creased in the faintest of smiles. "It was rather a bad spill," he admitted. "But it seems my pride suffered more damage than my back. I've always prided myself on being at least an adequate horseman. It appears I still have much to learn."

"And your back?" quizzed Lee. "The doctors feared the possibility of a spinal injury."

"I know," Stonewall allowed a grim chuckle to escape. "They kept me confined to that confounded ambulance all through the day. I guess the good Lord was looking out for me. My back was bruised and is still somewhat sore but there was no other damage to the spine. I have full freedom of movement and sensation throughout my legs."

"I can't tell you how relieved I am to see that," said Lee. "I can only hope that my wrists will mend quickly."

"What does the physician say?" asked Longstreet.

"Gwathmey tells me I can remove the splint from this one within two days." replied Lee holding up the wrist which had merely been sprained. "I understand you crossed the river wearing a carpet slipper yesterday."

"I'm afraid so," Longstreet smiled a little sheepishly. "A raw blister on my heel made it quite painful to wear a boot. It's much better today."

"Good," nodded Lee. "We all seem to be on the mend."

This remark elicited a quick laugh from Longstreet. "What a sight the three of us make!" he grinned. "The Northern press has all but deified us! The mention of our names stirs panic among the populace of Washington City, and here we sit consoling one another over our various injuries!"

"It is somewhat incongruous," admitted Stonewall. "Especially when you consider that none of our difficulties are connected to combat."

"It would seem a bit more manly if we were discussing wounds rather than injuries," said Lee with a chuckle. "All the same, I didn't summon the two of you so we could all feel sorry for one another. I have a number of ideas I wish to discuss with you regarding our present efforts."

"Might we soon be seeing action?" pondered Jackson.

"Perhaps," nodded Lee. "Though the possibility depends much on General McClellan. Quite frankly, many of my designs for this campaign are predicated on his reluctance to move quickly. I rather hope he doesn't surprise us."

"What exactly do you have in mind?" asked Longstreet.

"I intend to divide the army again."

"I see." A look of concern passed across Longstreet's face. He crossed one arm across his broad chest and with his other hand he began tugging at the whiskers of his beard. "To what purpose?"

"We can make no move in the direction of Pennsylvania without securing our line of supply. Both Martinsburg and Harpers Ferry are garrisoned by Union troops. These must be neutralized if we are to expect any possibility of success. A substantial force must be detached from this army to capture both towns."

"Unwise," said Longstreet at once. "A division of strength like this in the enemy's own back yard could easily work against us. I think you should reconsider your options."

"I disagree," argued Stonewall. "I see it as a bold maneuver. It certainly worked against Pope. I see no reason why it wouldn't work against McClellan." Turning to address Lee he continued, "I'd be happy to undertake this mission. It's been some months since last I was in the valley. My friends there no doubt believe I've forgotten them."

"You won't be going there for the purpose of making social calls," noted Lee.

"Understood, General. What exactly do you have in mind?"

"The capture of Harper's Ferry. I believe the town can very easily become a trap for its garrison." Here he paused and turned to Colonel Taylor, his chief of staff, and said, "Walter, would you get the map we were using earlier this morning?"

"Certainly, General," replied Taylor as he stepped to the rear of the tent and rummaged through a satchel which was sitting on the floor by the back wall. "Here it is," he said as he unfolded the map and placed it on the small table between the three officers.

"Harper's Ferry is dominated by heights on three sides," explained Lee as he drew the attention of the others to the map. "On this side of the Shenandoah is Loudoun Heights. Across the Potomac stands Maryland Heights. Just to the west is Bolivar. I suggest a convergence on those three heights. If it is successful the garrison at Harper's Ferry will find itself trapped with little recourse save surrender."

"What about Martinsburg?"

"It should be the first target. General Jackson, you will be in overall charge of this phase of the operation. Take your three divisions through Boonsboro then on to Williamsport. Cross the river back into Virginia and descend upon Martinsburg. You must either capture the garrison there or drive it eastward toward Harper's Ferry. I want you to end up on top of Bolivar Heights."

Jackson nodded his understanding.

"You will find General McLaws on Maryland Heights with two divisions. General Walker's division of two brigades will be assigned the task of securing Loudoun Heights.

Again, a nod was Jackson's only reply.

"Whereupon the town should fall into your hands," said Lee. "Assuming all goes according to plan.

"Which rarely happens." Longstreet's tone did little to conceal his misgivings.

Lee pretended not to notice this tone and turned to give the burly Georgian his instructions. "I want you to take your corps west to Boonsboro. Wait there until the ferry is taken. From that point we should be able to reunite the army and move north through Hagerstown into

Pennsylvania."

"As you wish," assented Longstreet.

"I will formalize this into a written order," continued Lee. "Today is the 9th. I expect all units to be ready
to march tomorrow. I would think the convergence on
Harper's Ferry would be accomplished by the 12th. Are
there questions?"

"Not so much a question," said Longstreet. "More
of a reflection."

"Please speak your mind," urged Lee.

"It seems to me this entire operation is predicated
on McClellan's old habits. If he behaves as you expect...that
is if he moves slowly and demonstrates a reluctance to
engage us the plan should work. What happens if he
doesn't behave according to your expectations? If McClellan shows up and we're spread out across two states we
could have serious problems."

"Very serious," nodded Lee. "Believe me I haven't
fully discounted the possibility of his moving with speed.
It would be quite unlike general McClellan to move
quickly, but it's certainly possible. I planned to have D. H.
Hill support your march to Boonsboro. Perhaps such
support would be most effective if Hill were to remain
astride one of these hills. Here," he tapped his forefinger
on the map indicating South Mountain as the position to
be held. "From here he'll be able to conduct a sturdy
defense against the Federals even if they appear in
strength."

"That will certainly lessen the danger," agreed
Longstreet. "Yet I still have my misgivings. It seems to me
we're taking one very long shot."

"You're right," said Lee. "But it seems to me we
have no choice but to take long shots if we are to nurture
any hope of prevailing in this struggle. I'm not blind to the
risks, Peter, but I feel that our overall situation demands
that we take risks."

"As you wish, sir," Longstreet demurred. "I, for
one, will be saying a lot of prayers over the next three
days."

"You won't be alone," added Lee.

Here the meeting adjourned. Both Jackson and Longstreet returned to their commands. Lee turned his attention to the dictation of Special Orders 191. When finished, the order contained highly detailed specifications for the division of strength and deployment which was to take place over the next three days. Copies were made and distributed not only to the corps commanders, but also to those divisional commanders whose units had specific assignments. Both Longstreet and Jackson were aware of the danger of allowing that order to fall into the wrong hands. The former quickly memorized the order then tore it up and chewed the pieces into something totally unrecognizable. Jackson however decided on a different approach. Realizing that D.H. Hill would be detached from his command he made yet another copy of the order and sent it to Hill's headquarters. A short while later another copy arrived at Hill's headquarters courtesy of R.E. Lee. One of Hill's staff officers saw this as an opportunity to snatch a souvenir. Since General Hill already had a copy of the order from Jackson, the staff officer simply kept the second copy for himself, going so far as to use it for a wrapper for the cigars in his pocket. Suffice it to say that Robert E. Lee was totally unaware of the casual use to which so vital a piece of paper had been put.

Lee did take the precaution of verbally briefing each officer involved in the operation, a choice which brought him to the tent of General Walker, a Missourian whose two brigade division would be assigned the task of occupying Loudoun Heights on the south bank of the Potomac River just below Point of Rocks. New to the Army of Northern Virginia, Walker was not familiar with Lee's manner, so the commanding general made an extra effort to explain the operation down to its finest details.

With his hands still in splints Lee pointed to the strategic places on the map. "This is the overall objective," explained Lee pointing to the location of Harrisburg, Pennsylvania. "I intend to sever the Pennsylvania railroad where it crosses the Susquehanna River. That will be the third link between the East and West which we'll either destroy or hold."

"I see," nodded Walker. "What about the first two?"

"The first is the Monocacy Aqueduct on the C&O Canal. You are to destroy it enroute to Point of Rocks."

"Understood. And the second?"

"The B&O rail crossing at Harper's Ferry. Hopefully it will be in our hands by the 12th."

"That should make it substantially more difficult for Lincoln to move troops from the West to reinforce McClellan."

"Exactly," nodded Lee. "They would be forced to move troops by way of the Great Lakes, a decidedly slower route, I can assure you."

"Which does buy us time," agreed Walker. "How do you plan to use it?"

"Hard to say. Philadelphia would be an option. So would Baltimore. The capture of Washington City would loom as a distinct possibility."

"We could bring the war to an end."

"Exactly my intention, but it all hinges on our reaching the Susquehanna."

"I must admit, general, you do not plan on a small scale. The design is ....sweeping? I can't think of a more appropriate word."

"Yet I detect doubt in your voice and the expression on your face does little to conceal the questions circulating in your mind."

Walker wasn't sure how to respond to this comment so for several seconds there was silence in his tent broken only by the buzzing of flies as they zipped through the still air.

It was Lee himself who supplied the question which Walker was pondering. "You doubtless regard it hazardous to leave McClellan practically on my line of communication, and to march into the heart of the enemy's country?"

"It does seem to be an inordinate risk," said Walker.

"Are you acquainted with General McClellan?"

"I know him, but in truth I've seen little of him since the Mexican War."

"He is an able general," observed Lee, pausing to glance outside, "But a very cautious one. His enemies among his own people think him too much so. His army is in a very demoralized and chaotic condition and will not be prepared for offensive operations for three or four weeks." He paused again and swatted at a fly which approached too closely. "In any event, he won't believe his army is ready even if it is. Before that time I hope to be on the Susquehanna."

"Well, sir," Walker smiled and shook his head in amazement. "I was told you were a bold and decisive officer. To be honest my first thought was to doubt what I'd heard. Suffice it to say you've dispelled my doubts. This is a bold plan...perhaps too bold. I can but assure you I'll do all in my power to insure its success."

"Of that I have no doubt." Unable to shake hands, Lee reached up and tipped his hat by way of farewell then departed for the next briefing.

Perhaps the most grievous error committed by Lee during this campaign could be identified within the final words spoken to General Walker. If he truly believed his own assessment of McClellan's army he was very much mistaken. In truth, the physical condition of his own army was far more chaotic than that of McClellan's. Also the morale of the Federal troops had improved dramatically since the return of "Little Mac." Both Pope and McDowell were gone, much to the relief of the junior officers, not to mention the rank and file. In point of fact the Army of the Potomac, eagerly anticipating action, was already on the move.

"On your feet! We're movin' out!" Corporal Gilbert's voice had less than an agreeable tone to it.

Wil opened his eyes and sat up almost as if by reflex. His thin bedroll fell away from his body and he yawned and stretched his arms overhead. He rubbed the sleep from his eyes and glanced up at the Corporal. "Why we leavin' so early? Sun's hardly up yet."

"Orders. Anyway it ain't your job to worry about why we do things, boy. You're here to obey orders...same as me."

"Whatever you say, Corporal." Wil grumbled as he rose slowly to his feet.

It was a crisp morning with just a hint of frost on the grass. The air was cool and it was easy for the soldiers to see the vapors from their own breathing, even though fall was still a good month distant.

In a matter of minutes they had packed their gear and had fallen into a column. Quickly they joined other units in a line of march, one of several long gray columns which snaked slowly west toward the low-lying mountain ranges which seemed a stone's throw from Frederick. Thus did their all too brief respite come to an end. What lay before them was anybody's guess. At the moment however few of them were wondering about the future. Most were content to be able to lift one foot and return it to the ground in front of the other. Considering the circumstances, little more could be asked of them.

*   *   *   *   *   *   *   *   *

It wasn't long before the same ground which had recently been home to the Army of Northern Virginia was serving the same purpose for the Army of the Potomac. Federal troops marched into Frederick to a wildly warm welcome. It seemed like American flags were everywhere. People leaned from windows and doors and cheered the Federal troops with boundless enthusiasm. Homemade pies and cakes were thrust upon the soldiers by the town's citizenry, along with a wide variety of fruits and breads. To the thousands of Union soldiers on the receiving end of such bounty, life couldn't have been much better. To them, Frederick, Maryland was suddenly a land of milk and honey. Most were determined to enjoy it as long as possible. The treatment they were receiving in central

BROTHERS IN GRAY

Maryland was quite unlike the cold stares and open hostility heaped upon them by civilians on the south bank of the Potomac.

For General McClellan, life was about to become decidedly easier. On Saturday morning the 13th of September two soldiers from the 27th Indiana, a Federal infantry regiment occupying ground recently vacated by their southern counterparts were reclining on the grass taking a welcome break from the rigors of the march. Private B. W. Mitchell and Sergeant J. M. Bloss were having a conversation sharing their impressions of Frederick. They spoke of the friendly people and excellent food, the lovely ladies. Having just commented on the quality of an apple pie handed to him by one of those ladies, Mitchell glanced away and noticed a rather long white envelope lying some distance away in the grass. It appeared to be rather well stuffed. "Look there," he pointed. "Looks like someone dropped their pay. I'll bet you there's a wad of bills in there thick enough to choke a horse."

"You think?" Sergeant Bloss craned his neck and peered at the white object on the ground.

"Fetch it and see. If there's money in there we can split it."

"What if it's Rebel money?"

"Then we've got ourselves some souvenirs. Go fetch it."

Mitchell did as he had been bade and couldn't hide the look of disappointment on his face when he rejoined Bloss. "Not even a dime," he complained. "Federal or otherwise. Nothin' but these cigars...looks like three of 'em." He withdrew the contents which were wrapped in a single piece of white paper.

"Oh well," sighed Bloss in resignation. "At least we'll get a good smoke out of it." He began fumbling through his pockets in search of a match.

"What's this?" Mitchell seemed a little exasperated. He had unwrapped the cigars and his attention was drawn immediately to the paper which had held them.

"What's what?" Bloss still hadn't found a match.

"This." Mitchell turned the paper around and showed it to Bloss.

"Headquarters, Army of Northern Virginia, Special Orders 191," Bloss read the heading out loud. The two men quickly exchanged glances. "Lemme see that," said the Sergeant as he took the paper from Mitchell's hand and studied it more closely. There he found detailed directions for the disposition of the Rebel Army. The names of R. E. Lee and his assistant Adjutant General, R. H. Chilton were at the bottom of the page.

What do you make of it?" asked Mitchell.

"Looks pretty official."

"Might be a fake."

"Might be, but I don't think it's our decision to make. Let's find the Captain. He'll know what to do."

"Can we smoke the cigars first?"

"I think maybe we better fetch 'em along with us."

Special order 191 soon found itself in the hands of the Captain of Company E, 27th Indiana. From there it went quickly to regimental headquarters, and from there to Division Headquarters. Before long it was resting comfortably in the hands of George McClellan, who found this stroke of good fortune difficult to believe.

"This has got to be a trick!" he exclaimed as he handed the paper to a staff officer. "No one could be so careless as to allow an order like that to fall so easily into his opponent's hands."

"It's genuine," said the staff officer at once.

"How's that?"

"The order is genuine, or at least Chilton's signature is. I've known him for a long time. That is his signature and his handwriting."

"It could still be a trick...something Lee brewed up to confuse us."

"If so it seems a rather elaborate ruse. Would he have gone to such detail just to trick us? He's even instructed his regiments to carry axes in the ordnance wagons to keep the campsites furbished. I believe this order is real, general. In my estimation, Lee has just committed a fatal mistake."

"He sure has," McClellan took the order back and read through it one more time. "He's got his army divided into more pieces than I care to count!" He moved to the flap of his tent and stepped into the clear brisk September air. Before him lay the ridges and hills of the Catoctin Mountains. "Once we cross these hills," he observed, "We'll be closer to the two halves of his army than either half is to the other. If we descend upon Boonsboro at once we can crush the better part of Lee's army segment by segment before he even knows it." He paused for a moment and took a deep breath, relishing the scent of the many wood fires burning in the Union Camps. He turned to a Brigadier standing near by and boldly declared, "Here is a paper with which if I cannot whip Bobby Lee I will be willing to go home! Gentlemen, we march at once! With any luck and the grace of God, this war will be over in a matter of days." Orders began to go out at once and staff officers were soon scurrying in all directions. This meant one thing to the many thousands gathered about those camp fires. They would soon see action.

McClellan's spirits soared. For days he had been under the most extreme pressure. His own Commander-in-Chief, Abraham Lincoln, made no secret of the mistrust he held toward "Little Mac." It seemed most of the hierarchy within the Federal government was howling for his head, a sentiment most frequently echoed in the press. He had been summoned by Lincoln in a time of severe crisis then burdened with the twin challenges revolving around the defense of the capital and the expulsion of Lee from Federal territory. His task was made none the easier by those who frequently gave voice to their doubts about his ability. Now however it appeared he could put them all in their places. Lee's errant special order had done much to create his present euphoria to be sure, but it wasn't the only factor. The reception afforded the Army of the Potomac by the people of Frederick was grand to say the least. This in itself had all but dispelled the gloom he'd been feeling as his army inched toward Frederick at a rate of six miles per day.

The hour was approaching noon when McClellan's officers began dashing off to their commands. As for the general himself he quickly retired to his headquarters to compose a telegraph message to President Lincoln. The elation which coursed through his veins could be readily seen in the words he penned for his president: "I have the whole rebel force in front of me, but am confident, and no time shall be lost. I have a difficult task to perform, but with God's blessing will accomplish it. I think Lee has made a gross mistake and that he will be severely punished for it. The army is in motion as rapidly as possible. I hope for a great success if the plans of the rebels remain unchanged. We have possession of Catoctin. I have all the plans of the rebels, and will catch them in their own trap if my men are equal to the emergency. I now feel I can count on them as of old...My respects to Mrs. Lincoln. Received most enthusiastically by the ladies. Will send you trophies." McClellan signed his message and paused to reread it with a smile of immense satisfaction planted firmly on his face. He failed to notice the civilian outside of his headquarters who casually mounted his horse and trotted off in a southerly direction.

This message to Lincoln and another to General Halleck gave the distinct impression that the army was moving with speed to demolish the Army of Northern Virginia. Sadly for the Federals this was not to be the case. The same ghosts which haunted McClellan during the Peninsula campaign came back to annoy him again. For some reason he was never able to accept his own numerical superiority in comparison to Lee. He was convinced the Rebels numbered more than 120,000 men. Whereas he could only deploy 88,000. Lee in fact had barely 50,000 effectives with which to do battle and these were now widely scattered across Maryland and Virginia.

The 5th Virginia was nearly across the narrow valley which separates the Catoctin range from South Mountain when Wil turned his right ankle and hobbled to

the side of the road with a painful sprain. Levi left the
column to stand by his friend as the rest of the company
passed.

"What did you do to yourself?" demanded Miles as
he approached.

"I guess I wasn't watchin' the road careful enough.
Reckon I sprained it." Wil had removed the boot from his
injured foot and was tightly squeezing the ankle with both
hands.

"Reckon so," continued Miles. "Didn't you just
spend a whole lot of money on those fancy boots? Now
look at you! Your feet ain't used to 'em boy! You should've
kept your old shoes. You would've been better off."

"Maybe. Maybe not," groaned Wil.

"No maybe's about it, boy. You done wasted your
money. you'd best be on your feet soon or you won't be
catchin' up to the likes of us!"

"I will. Count on it. You have any idea where we're
goin'?"

"Nobody seems to know for sure. You know how
tight-lipped Jackson can be. Some of the boys think we're
goin' to bag us some Yankees at Harper's Ferry. Some
think we're headin' for Pennsylvania. Reckon we won't
really know till we get wherever we're goin'. Anyway, I'm
movin' on. Levi, don't let him sit too long, hear?"

"Yessuh," nodded Levi. "I'll have him up in no
time."

Miles turned and rejoined the column and was
soon lost in the throng of graybacks filing west. By the
time Wil was able to regain his feet the main column had
long since passed.   Only stragglers remained on the
road but these were present in considerable numbers.
As they neared the base of South Mountain Wil glanced
up toward its crest, squinting his eyes against the bright
autumn sun.

"Ain't lookin forward to climbin' that," he complained. "How high you think it is?"

"Thousand feet or so," replied Levi. "Maybe twelve
hundred. Shouldn't be that bad. Looks like this road goes

straight through that gap up there. We'll be fine. You can lean on me when you have to. We'll just take it slow."

They had climbed nearly half of South Mountain's eastern face when they noticed a flurry of activity above them where the road cut through the mountain's crest. At least two batteries of guns had been unlimbered while regiments of infantry were coming back through the gap to take up defensive positions along the crest and down among the boulders of the mountain itself.

"Can't say that I like the looks of this," noted Wil.

"Don't look like we're gonna be catchin' up with our people anytime soon," agreed Levi.

Together they turned around and glanced back over the valley. Far in the distance they spied columns of Union infantry descending the western slopes of the Catoctins, moving out into the valley toward South Mountain. They were too far away to see the blue of their uniforms but the sun's reflection from tens of thousands of bayonets made for a dazzling and truly frightening sight.

"Offhand I'd say we're in trouble," remarked Wil with a sardonic tone in his voice.

"Could be," nodded Levi. "Don't you think we oughta keep movin'? I think I'd feel a sight safer if we was up there with the rest of our folks. It's already feelin' awful damn lonely down in these parts."

"Agreed. Let's go." Wil quickly forgot about the pain in his ankle and resumed the upwards hike. Before long they were nearing the crest but here they ceased their climb and left the road, moving off to take positions in the rocks with the other stragglers and at least two regiments from D. H. Hill's division. From so lofty a vantage they had a breathtaking view of the entire valley, but the sight which greeted their eyes caused their hearts to sink. Three long columns of blue clad infantry were snaking their way across the valley. Seventy- thousand Union soldiers were moving toward South Mountain, their silver bayonets still gleaming brightly in the afternoon sun. "Oh, my God!" hissed Wil as the severity of their predicament became increasingly apparent.

Wil and Levi weren't the only ones whose sentiments were expressed in prayerful fashion. Standing atop South Mountain at Turner's Gap was General D. H. Hill - Harvey Hill to those who knew him best. Lee had given him the task of holding the mountain against a Union advance. To accomplish this task he had one division of infantry consisting of five brigades along with a motley assortment of stragglers from the morning's march. With this force he faced four corps of Union infantry with a fifth on the way. There were twelve divisions to his one, thirty-two brigades to his five. Looking back on it in later years Hill recalled the sight quite vividly and remarked on how much it reminded him of certain phrases in scripture. Specifically he said that "the Hebrew poet whose idea of the awe-inspiring is expressed by the phrase 'terrible as an army with banners,' (doubtless) had his view from the top of a mountain." He described the sight as "a grand and glorious spectacle," saying that it was impossible to look upon it without admiration. At the same time, as he recalled it, he had never before in his life experienced a sensation of such intense loneliness. To. D. H. Hill "it seemed as though we were deserted by all the world and the rest of mankind." Quickly he sent word to Lee saying he could do little more than irritate the force which would soon be assailing his position.

George McClellan was anything but lonely. He was enjoying the high water mark of his command. Sitting atop his horse, Dan Webster, McClellan became the focus of attention to the many thousands who were filing past him toward South Mountain. Union soldiers cheered him until they lost their voices. Hundreds of men gathered around their general, adulation plainly visible on their faces. In a scene which probably would have seemed chaotic to an outsider the throng of men pressed itself unrelentingly upon the young Napoleon. Those closest to him reached out to hug the legs of his horse or stroke the animal's head and mane. One Massachusetts veteran was of the impression that an intermission had been called in the war so that a huge reception could be held to honor the army's commander. Acutely aware of the many thousands of eyes fixed upon himself McClellan played the situation for maximum results. Sitting erect in the saddle, shoulders squared, chest thrust forward, he raised one arm and pointed it straight at the crest of South Mountain. The message in this simple action was impossible to miss: there waits the enemy! Let's not keep him waiting! Every time he raised his arm men would shout and cheer then surge like a wave of blue toward the thin gray line waiting nervously along the crest of South Mountain.

When Robert E. Lee heard of the fight just getting underway on the eastern slopes of South Mountain his first reaction was one of puzzlement. McClellan had apparently moved with uncharacteristic haste and Lee found himself wondering why. Fortunately he didn't have to labor long on an answer. The solution to this riddle arrived shortly in the hands of a courier from Jeb Stuart. It seemed the civilian who had ridden with such haste from McClellan's headquarters was in fact a Southern sympathizer. Having seen the fate of Special Orders 191, he had ridden at once to inform Stuart, who in turn dispatched a rider to alert General Lee.

"That explains it," Lee muttered beneath his breath after reading Stuart's message.

"Sir?" The question came from one of his staff officers, Captain Venable.

"This message from General Stuart...it explains why McClellan is moving so quickly against us."

"How so?"

"It seems Special Orders 191 has fallen into the wrong hands... McClellan's to be exact."

"I don't see how that could be possible."

"Nor I, yet it seems to be true. The civilian who relayed this news to Stuart described McClellan as beside himself with joy."

"I shouldn't wonder." There was a touch of despair in Venable's voice.

"He knows that we've divided our army. Appar-

ently he has decided to isolate and defeat one of our
segments before concentrating on the second."

"Second? General, in all due respect, this army is
not divided in two. As we speak there are five distinct
fragments scattered from South Mountain to Harper's
Ferry to Hagerstown."

"True enough," admitted Lee in a tone which
betrayed no emotion. "Let's hope General McClellan does
not learn of how totally fragmented we are. If he does we'll
be facing indescribable peril."

"How do you plan to respond to this change in
circumstances?"

"Send word to Longstreet at once. Have him leave
Hagerstown at first light and march with all possible speed
to the support of General Hill at Turner's Gap. If South
Mountain falls..." Lee left the sentence unfinished, but the
implications in his words were perfectly clear to Captain
Venable.

"I'll see to it at once, Sir," came the reply.

"Remember," advised Lee. "They are to march
with all possible speed!"

South Mountain quite suddenly became a vital
piece of geography to the Confederate States of America.
If D. H. Hill and his badly outnumbered troops could
hang on long enough the Army of Northern Virginia
might have a chance to escape the destruction McClellan
had designed. As for the mountain itself, at first glance it
seemed an ideal defensive position. It ranged in height up
to 1300 feet with steep slopes all along its eastern face.
There were two main gaps: Turner Gap, the northern-
most notch through which ran the old National Road, and
Crampton's Gap, six miles to the South and directly east
of McLaws' position on Maryland heights. Unfortunately,
from the Confederate point of view, was the existence of
several minor passes all along the mountain's length.
Simply put, there were too many avenues over the mountain and D. H. Hill would soon find it impossible to plug
them all.

Already the lead elements of the three Federal

columns were coming within range of the Confederate artillery posted atop the mountain. Skirmish lines were formed and moved forward to ferret out the Rebel sharp-shooters near the base of the mountain. The battle had begun.

The sun was close to the horizon by the time Wil and Levi were able to bring their muskets to bear. The Union advance had ascended nearly a third of the mountain in some places but the day was fast waning and it didn't appear the Rebels could be driven off before night-fall. By dark it was over. The Union army, dug in along the base of South Mountain, waited for morning when the full weight of their ponderous numbers could be thrown against the crest.

Satisfied that the attack was over Wil sighed audibly and leaned back against a rock. "You got any ammo left?"

"Half-dozen rounds or so," replied Levi.

"I've got maybe ten. One of us should go up and fetch some."

"Reckon that'll have to be me seein' how you're the one with the bad ankle," smiled Levi.

"Not necessarily. How about we flip for it?"

"How about you just sit tight," countered the black man. "I'll go up. I'll see if I can scrape up some rations while I'm up there."

He was back within the hour with a canvas bag full of minie balls and several pieces of cold corn bread.

"That's all we got to eat?" wondered Wil.

"That and some hardtack."

"How much ammo?"

"Forty rounds apiece."

"Won't last long tomorrow."

"Agreed. Maybe we should relocate closer to the top."

"Nah. This'll work. We'll get out before they press us too hard."

"Maybe so," nodded Levi, "but I don't think it's goin' to make a lot of difference. The whole Yankee army is out there, Wil. I heard someone say we've only got five brigades to hold 'em off."

"Five brigades? Are you kiddin'? I hate to say this, old friend, but we don't stand a snowball's chance in hell of holdin' this mountain with five brigades. Does Lee know what's out there? They'll brush us off like a bunch of fleas tomorrow! You mark my words!"

"I'd rather not. I'd rather hope Marse Robert knows what we're up against. Maybe help'll get here before it gets too hot."

"Maybe," Wil bit off a chunk of hardtack and chewed it with obvious deliberation.

Levi spread his bedroll out on the cool damp ground and settled in for the night. "Sleepin' ain't gonna be easy," he noted. "Considerin' what's in store for us in the mornin'."

"You sure said that right," agreed Wil. "I wish I hadn't sprained my ankle. We'd be safe and warm with our own regiment."

"Can't cry over spilt milk," said Levi as he closed his eyes and waited for sleep to come.

Dawn of the 14th of September was marked by a distinct chill in the air. Two stale cold biscuits remained to Wil and Levi. These and a couple of gulps of water were all they had for breakfast. In truth they wouldn't have had time to eat it even if there had been more food. The Federal effort to wrest control of South Mountain from Rebel hands began shortly after first light.

From the outset it was a hopeless fight from the Southern perspective. The Confederates were desperately outnumbered. With so vast an advantage in numbers McClellan easily overlapped both ends of the Rebel line and started toward the crest. Wil and Levi continued firing their muskets until the scarcity of ammunition made itself felt, forcing them to limit their shots, taking advantage of only the best opportunities. About an hour before noon they were joined by five riflemen who had worked their way down from the crest to take cover among the rocks. They brought more ammunition and some encouraging news. Longstreet had been alerted to the danger by General Lee and even now was hard on the march to relieve the beleaguered defenders of South Mountain. Help was only hours away...if they could just hold on.

Longstreet had received Lee's orders the night before and understood at once how precarious was the situation in which the Army of Northern Virginia found itself. However he differed with Lee as to the best solution. He didn't think it wise to conduct a forced march of fifteen miles to be followed by a pitched battle. His reply to Lee argued that the march itself would leave his men exhausted and in no shape to fight. He suggested that South Mountain be abandoned and that he and D. H. Hill unite near a town called Sharpsburg about midway between the two positions. There they could safely await the rest of the army presently occupied at Harper's Ferry. Or if the need arose they could readily cross the Potomac back into Virginia. Lee did not agree with him and allowed his orders to stand. Later that night Longstreet sent a note to Lee repeating his objections but to this he received no reply. At dawn his lean, hungry veterans rose from the ground and began their march for South Mountain.

Hard and fast did these men march. Whatever complaints they had about food or rest were put aside and they moved toward the mountain with a grim sense of purpose. So fast did they march that by noon they were close enough to hear the battle which had already been in progress for several hours. Knowing how desperately their numbers were needed, they summoned reserves of energy few thought they had. Even faster did they now push themselves. By mid-afternoon they were ascending the western face of the mountain itself.

Here waited R. E. Lee mounted on Traveller despite the awkward encumbrance of wearing splints on both hands. He was off to the side of the road perhaps a hundred yards from the mountain's crest. He had been watching as Longstreet's troops filed past him into Turner's Gap where they were quickly deployed both on the right and left. Before long the Texans approached. They spied

Lee at once and began clamoring for their divisional commander, "Hood!" they shouted by the dozens. "Hood!" For two weeks General Hood had remained under arrest as a result of his altercation with General Evans over the Union ambulances captured by the former at Second Manassas. "Give us Hood!" The demand was echoed up and down the ranks.

Lee was hardly in a position at this point to refuse their request. He raised his hat to the dust covered soldiers from the Lone Star State and shouted his reply. "You shall have him, gentlemen!"

At the tail end of this column rode Hood, a decidedly despondent expression locked firmly on his bearded face. Lee beckoned to him as soon as he came within view and the Texan nudged his mount at once to Lee's side. "General," Lee addressed himself to the Texan. "Here I am just on the eve of entering battle, and with one of my best officers under arrest. If you will merely say that you regret this occurrence I will release you and restore you to the command of your division."

For a moment or two Hood pondered this offer. Should he express regret over the fact that his men had captured Union ambulances at Manassas? On it's face the offer seemed like a relatively painless way to lay the whole matter to rest, yet Hood found himself reluctant to go along with it. "To do so would be inconsistent with my true feelings on the matter," he said softly.

Frustrated by this rejection, Lee gave him one more chance by repeating the offer but again Hood declined. "Well," sighed Lee wearily, "I will suspend your arrest till the impending battle is decided."

Hood replied to this with a beaming smile and a smart salute. Whereupon he wheeled his horse around dug his spurs into the animals flanks and rode swiftly to join his division where he was greeted by raucous cheering and shouting.

In truth Longstreet arrived on South Mountain just in time to blunt an overwhelming Federal victory. D. H. Hill had spread his five brigades out so thinly they were unable to resist any forceful punch. Both ends of this line had been flanked by Union forces and several minor passes to the north and south had been pierced by the Federals as well. One brigade commander, Samuel Garland, was mortally wounded and died soon thereafter, causing his soldiers to break in confusion.

The role of Longstreet's corps in this situation was much like that of the Dutch boy who tried to save his people by putting his finger in the hole of the dike. On South Mountain however there were simply too many holes and not enough fingers. Longstreet launched counterattacks on both sides of Turner's Gap and at least brought temporary stability to those sectors of the line. Despite these mild successes it was clear to Lee that the Confederate position atop South Mountain had become untenable, and still there was no word from the rest of his army which by now had surrounded Harper's Ferry. As the sun began to inch toward the western horizon, Lee began to consider his options, which by now were decidedly few in number.

All that afternoon Wil and Levi held fast to their position in the rocks well shy of the mountain's crest. Of the five men who had joined them two had been killed and a third sustained a flesh wound to his right shoulder. As evening approached it appeared they would soon be forced to yield their craggy vantage point lest they be captured. Wil had just squeezed off a shot then turned to see if he could spy a more secure position closer to the crest. Safe haven he could not find, but he did notice a small cluster of fellow Confederates in the rocks well to his left. "Levi, lookee there," he nudged his companion and pointed toward those soldiers. "Ain't that the general we bumped into back in Frederick?"

Levi peered in that direction, studied the man for a moment or two and nodded his head. "You're talkin' about the one who was comin' out of the bookstore, right?"

"Yeah. That's him isn't it?"

"Sure is...it's Alexander, E. P. Alexander."

"If he's here that means Longstreet is too! We held

~175~

em! We held em!"

"Don't be gettin' all excited," growled one of the three surviving riflemen who had joined them earlier. "Longstreet won't change the fact that the whole Yankee army is out there. Keep shootin' boy!"

"Wonder why he came down so far from the crest," said Wil. "Seems to me he oughta be settin' up cannons up there behind us."

Actually Alexander had been sent by Lee himself to assess the situation on the eastern face. With eight hand-picked volunteers he had worked his way down the mountain until he had drawn roughly even with Wil and Levi's position.

"Here they come again!" Wil heard the voice from somewhere to his right. "They're sendin' us bucktails this time!"

All eyes went immediately to front. A Pennsylvania regiment was advancing on them in skirmish formation. They were known as the Bucktails because each soldier wore one dangling from his cap.

"Let's drop a few of 'em!" someone cried and the mountainside rang out with the renewed rattle of musketry.

Wil glanced over in Alexander's direction and gasped in surprise. The general was firing muskets at the Pennsylvanians as fast as his eight comrades could furnish him with loaded weapons. Wil watched mesmerized, his eyes darting from Alexander to his targets among the Bucktails.

"I'll be damned," he said moments later. "He got one! I saw him fall."

"You'd best be gettin' a couple," argued Levi as he quickly reloaded his musket. "Or they'll be gettin' us!"

Wil returned his attention at once to the task at hand and did not look over again until the Pennsylvanians had been driven off and were retiring toward the base of the mountain. By this time General Alexander was gone. He and the eight men who accompanied him had returned to the crest where they sought Lee and delivered their report.

The respite was short-lived. Within minutes Union troops were assailing the mountain in force. The tactical situation for the Rebels grew worse by the hour despite Longstreet's timely intervention. Casualties were mounting as position after position was overrun by the encroaching blue tide. At one point Levi spotted a group of at least fifty Confederate soldiers being led away as prisoners. With mounting desperation this portion of Lee's army fought tenaciously to hold that mountain until nightfall, praying that darkness would put an end to the whole affair.

The sun had already disappeared beyond the mountain when one of the men who had been fighting alongside Wil decided the time had come to abandon those rocks in favor of higher ground. Moments later all three of them were gone. Wil and Levi exchanged glances each reading the other's thoughts.

"Are you thinkin' we should be followin' them?" asked Wil.

"I was thinkin' it would make sense to do that," admitted Levi.

"I agree. Let's get out of here."

Grabbing their gear they moved quickly away from those rocks and began climbing. Union sharpshooters spotted them at once and opened fire. Bullets tore bark from trees and bounced noisily from the rocks all around them but they didn't slow their pace. They neared the crest and all three of their comrades slithered across to safety. Just then the intensity of the Union barrage increased substantially forcing Wil and Levi to ground. Both of them hugged the dirt for dear life as Union bullets smashed all around them. Only a few yards remained between themselves and the main Confederate line, but this tiny stretch of real estate would prove the most treacherous of all. Both men crouched low to the ground, waiting for the fire to slacken so they could make the final lunge to safety. At last their opportunity came as the level of fire died down for just the briefest of moments.

"Go!" urged Wil as he shoved Levi forward. The black man darted for the crudely built ramparts behind which Hill's men were positioned. Wil was right on his heels. From below Union soldiers opened up on them at once. Splinters from the wooden fortifications were flying as were chips of stone from the nearby rocks. Levi breached the line first but not until a northern minie ball had torn a sizeable chunk of flesh from his left shoulder. Wil planted one foot on a piece of rail and pushed off hoping to land unscathed behind those friendly earthworks. It was not to be. He howled in pain as a bullet ripped through his right hip imbedding itself in the bone. He dropped his musket and toppled face forward to the ground. Writhing in pain he groaned aloud and groped at the wound with one hand.

"I'm hit, Levi! I'm hit bad!"

Ignoring his own wound Levi hoisted Wil up from the ground and with the help of another soldier carried him back some twenty yards from the line.

"Thank ya kindly," said Levi.

"Don't mention it," nodded the man as he turned back to the action.

Levi turned his attention at once to his stricken comrade. Pulling out his knife he cut away a section from his trouser's leg and fashioned a primitive compress to stem the flow of blood. "Didn't hit nothin' vital," he explained as he applied gentle pressure to the wound. "Looks like it stuck in the bone."

"It is," Wil hissed through clenched teeth. "God it hurts!"

"You hold on! hear me? I'll get you out of this!" He began looking around him searching for the hospital tents. "Them doctors must be set up somewhere!" In the failing light he couldn't locate anything resembling a surgeon's tent. His efforts were further hindered by the general state of confusion on top of the mountain itself.

"They're turned Rodes!" someone shouted. Indeed they had. Rodes' brigade had held the extreme left of the Confederate position but the Federals overlapped and flanked their thinly held line. These Rebels had to abandon their position or risk being taken from the rear. The air was filled with the frantic shouting of officers as they juggled units in a frenzied attempt to blunt the new Union thrust from the northern end of the mountain.

"Gotta find a doctor," muttered Levi as his eyes scanned the terrain on the western slopes of the mountain.

"You're hit too," observed Wil still clenching his teeth.

"Just a flesh wound...I'll be fine. We gotta get you to a surgeon. You got yourself a bullet in that bone. It ain't gonna fall out by itself." Just then he spotted an officer and called out, "Captain! I need to get this man to a doctor! Can you point me in the right direction?"

The Captain eyed him carefully then shifted his gaze to Wil lying prone on the ground. He incorrectly assumed that Levi was the slave of the wounded soldier beside whom he knelt. "Down there," he pointed in a southeasterly direction. "About a half mile. You can't see 'em from here but the tents are set up between those two hills yonder."

"Thank you, suh. I'll get him down there as quick as I'm able."

"Do so. You're master's a brave lad, and we need all the brave men we can get."

"Yes suh, I know, suh."

The officer continued on his way and Levi hoisted Wil to his feet. "Put your arm around my shoulder," he instructed. "I'll take the weight for your right side."

Wil nodded and followed the black man's instructions.

"I'm sorry," he gasped moments later as they started for the surgeons.

"For what? Gettin' shot? Don't seem like you could have done much about that."

"No...no, not that. I mean that Captain...what he said."

"Don't pay him no mind, Wil. I'm a Darkie. What's he supposed to think?"

BROTHERS IN GRAY

"I'm still sorry."

"Don't say no more about it. Use what strength you got to help me get you out of here."

The going was necessarily slow and it was well past dark before they reached the hastily erected medical facilities. They found the tents full to overflowing and Wil was obliged to lie on the ground outside to wait his turn. Levi helped him stretch out next to a man who was sitting with his arms wrapped about his upraised knees. The fellow had sustained a head wound and had a bloody bandage wrapped carelessly about his head.

"Long time no see," said the man.

Wil peered up into his face but in the darkness he couldn't recognize him. "Do I know you?"

"We've met. How bad you hit?"

"I took one in the hip bone. Don't reckon it's fatal but it hurts somethin' awful! Who are you?"

"You ain't got much of a memory, boy. Name's Vaughn...Lemuel Vaughn."

Wil and Levi both responded with blank looks.

"Still don't remember? Maybe I got the wrong two. Seems like I met a couple of boys, one white, one black, last month at the Yankee supply depot in Manassas. If memory serves me we shared a can of lobster and a swig or two of German wine."

"I remember now," Levi nodded and grinned, his white teeth a stark contrast to the darkness.

"Me too," said Wil, but the words came out as a groan.

"Wish I had some of that wine now," sighed Vaughn.

"I wouldn't mind the lobster," added Wil through clenched teeth.

"I think I'd settle for a piece of cornbread at this point," said Levi.

"How you been since Manassas?" asked Wil.

"Pretty fair till now. Shrapnel tore my head open just after sundown. How about you?"

"I lost a couple of teeth at Manassas. Otherwise I got no cause to complain."

~180~

"How about you?" Vaughn turned toward Levi.

"Same as him I reckon," came the reply. "'Cept I still got all my teeth."

"Looks to me like you got hit too."

"Just tore some skin off my arm. I'm okay."

"Sit down here," instructed Vaughn. "My boys gave me some extra rags in case my head started bleedin' again. I'll patch you up some while we're waitin'."

"Why thank you, Private Vaughn," Levi sat down and presented his arm. "I'm obliged to ya."

"Ain't no problem by me," Vaughn grinned and pulled out a fistful of rags from within his tunic.

Wil had little more to say. He was slowly reaching the threshold of endurance so far as pain was concerned so he lay back and stared at the vast array of bright stars so clearly visible in the mountain sky. He tried not to hear the groans and cries of wounded men all around him. He began to wonder if he'd ever see home again.

*   *   *   *   *   *   *   *   *

For Robert E. Lee the night was no less anxious. A brief council with Longstreet and D. H. Hill merely verified what he already knew in his heart. Turner's Gap could not be held past daylight. Longstreet's arrival earlier that afternoon had merely forestalled the inevitable. Union troops had established themselves in strength on top of the mountain in far too many places.

"If we are here when the sun comes up we'll face certain defeat," observed Longstreet.

"Most likely," nodded Lee solemnly. "And if we're defeated here on this mountain..." he let his voice trail away.

"Annihilation," General Hill supplied the word Lee had been unwilling to utter. "At least for this portion of the army."

"Obviously we can't stay," said Lee in a tone which betrayed none of the disappointment he felt inside. All of his plans had gone for naught. The bridge over the

BROTHERS IN GRAY

Susquehanna wouldn't see a single Rebel, at least not this year. Baltimore, Washington, Philadelphia...all could breath a sigh of relief. Any threat to them had all but evaporated on top of South Mountain. The people of Maryland, the same people Lee had hoped to liberate, would remain under their "foreign yoke."

"The most recent reports I've received have us outnumbered by at least four to one." he noted. "The retreat must start immediately and be executed with stealth and speed."

"Where do you want us to go?" asked Longstreet.

"We'll do what you said we should have done last night. Concentrate at Sharpsburg. There's a ford across the Potomac at that location. It's not the best ford on the river but it'll have to do. I guess it's time we headed back to Virginia."

"So it seems," concurred Longstreet. "We have a lot of wounded, General. Many have yet to receive any attention. We don't have adequate transportation for them up here on the mountain. Trying to remove them could jeopardize the whole force."

"I know," sighed Lee. "I am loathe to leave anyone behind but in a situation such as this we really have no choice. We will have to entrust their well being to General McClellan. He is a man of honor. I know he'll do the right thing by them."

"Let's hope," remarked Longstreet. "In the meantime it's imperative that we get this thing underway."

"Do so." ordered Lee.

The two officers departed leaving Lee alone still studying his topographical maps by the dim light of a lantern. It was the rest of his army which now concerned him. Jackson and Walker were already in Virginia. At least they were in no immediate danger but it was now doubtful that they could take Harper's Ferry. Mclaws, however, faced perils he was probably not even aware of. He occupied Maryland Heights outside of Harper's Ferry but South Mountain was directly in his rear. He too would need to cross the river at the earliest possible moment. Lee proceeded to dictate a dispatch to General Mclaws which read as follows: "The day has gone against us and this army will go by Sharpsburg and cross the river. It is necessary for you to abandon your position tonight." The message continued with Lee's expression of understanding that Mclaws would not be able to cross by way of the ferry bridge since it was still in Federal hands. He instructed him to cross somewhere upstream but shy of Shepherdstown, which was just across the Potomac from Sharpsburg. That particular ford would be fully occupied by the troops of Longstreet and D. H. Hill.

The evacuation of South Mountain itself was already underway. Hill's troops were the first to leave and those of Longstreet were close on their heels. Aside from these two officers and General Mclaws no one knew of Lee's intention to continue the retreat all the way back to Virginia. Most of the men were under the impression they were marching in search of more suitable ground on which to confront McClellan.

Soon after the withdrawal started, a dispatch arrived which made the movement that much more imperative. Crampton's Gap, which was six miles south of Lee's position at Turner's Gap, had fallen to Franklin's Corps of Union infantry. Bluecoats were pouring through it unchecked. This sudden turn of events raised two possibilities, neither of them pleasant. The first centered on Mclaws. He and his command at Maryland Heights were in mortal danger as they were fully exposed to an attack from the rear by Franklin's forces. The second possibility was even more dire. Franklin's men were now closer to Sharpsburg than Lee. They were in a position to prevent any concentration of the widely scattered Confederate army. Indeed, Lee now faced the thoroughly dismal prospect of being cut off from the rest of his army and annihilated. New orders were issued and these held a frightenly urgent tone. The march must be hard and fast. Stop for nothing or no one. Survival of the army was now very much at stake.

As men and horses rushed hurriedly past them Wil

and his wounded companions could readily sense that something had gone terribly wrong. They may not have been privy to the fine details but they could certainly see that someone in command was in a definite hurry to get off that mountain darkness be damned.

One nurse volunteered to remain with the more seriously wounded at their particular aid station. Those who were still ambulatory would have to fend for themselves. Many were destined to fall into Union hands.

"Help me up!" insisted Wil. "We're gettin' outta here!"

Both Lemuel and Levi assisted him to his feet. "Just where in the hell do you think you're goin' with that hip?" demanded Vaughn.

"Don't know but I don't intend to end up a prisoner. I've heard enough about Yankee prison camps to know I don't want to see one."

"There's no way you can keep up."

"Will you help us? Please?"

"I'll do what I can," sighed Vaughn. "C'mon, we'd best not waste any more time jawin'.'"

Levi propped his companion up on the left while Vaughn did the same on the right. Down the mountain they moved as fast as the difficult circumstances would allow. All the while Wil kept his teeth tightly clenched and did his best not to cry out as one spasm of pain after another ripped through his side. By the time they reached the bottom of the mountain most of the army was well past them and all three men were virtually exhausted.

"This ain't gonna work," complained Vaughn. "The Yanks will be on us by mornin'. All three of us will end up prisoners."

"Don't leave me," these words came out as a gasp from Wil's throat. "Please don't! I'd rather die out here than in one of them camps!"

"You just hold your tongue a minute while I figure somethin' out, boy!" Vaughn's tone was sharp, but it didn't sound like he had any intention of leaving. "We can't follow the army. The Yanks will take us sure. We got one chance and that's to follow the base of the mountain north. If we can get past the Yankee positions they might overlook the likes of us when they start chasin' our boys."

"It's worth a try," agreed Levi with a nod. "You game, Wil?"

"Let's go!" Another gasp confirmed Wil's quick assent.

Turning north they left the macadamized surface of the National Road and disappeared into the trees.

As the night progressed Robert E. Lee became more combative than ever. Those around him were reminded of a cornered wolf or wounded bear, and most thought it best to keep their distance. That Lee was angry there can be no doubt, but most of his anger was directed toward himself. In retrospect, he was thinking it had been a mistake to divide his army into so many fragments. Now the army entrusted to him by the Confederate government was exposed to piecemeal destruction. He felt frustrated and helpless and in truth he yearned for an opportunity to pitch into the blue tide which threatened to sweep his men into the Potomac. It was late that night when a chance for redemption presented itself.

It came by way of a dispatch from Stonewall Jackson. Taking it from the courier Lee read it quickly searching for a ray of hope in the midst of so desperate a circumstance. He found it in these words from Stonewall: "Through God's blessing the advance which commenced this evening has been successful thus far, and I look to Him for complete success tomorrow...Your dispatch respecting the movements of the enemy and the importance of concentration has been received."

Already wheels were turning in the mind of Robert E. Lee. If Harper's Ferry were to fall on the morrow could this whole situation be turned around? If Jackson were victorious he could then join Lee north of the river. Once reunited the Army of Northern Virginia could turn on its assailants and deliver a stinging blow. Lee turned to study his maps. A march of only twelve miles lay between Harper's Ferry and Sharpsburg. It could be done. Orders were sent out by couriers at once. The essence of these new instructions was simply this: If we win the race for Sharpsburg, we stand and fight.

The race for Sharpsburg would not likely be won by the boys in blue. Much of the fault for this could be laid to the lack of accurate intelligence. Better put it might be ascribed to McClellan's age old habit of overestimating the strength of his opponents at every encounter. In this regard he remained true to form during the Sharpsburg campaign. He had marched from Frederick toward South Mountain convinced that Lee commanded nearly 100,000 men when in fact the old gray Fox had fewer than 40,000 all totaled. The stiff initial resistance offered by D. H. Hill on the mountain served only to convince McClellan that he faced a foe with vast superiority in numbers. In reality, if he had attacked the mountain with all his strength Hill's diminutive command might easily have been overwhelmed well before the arrival of Longstreet.

A similar situation ensued at Crampton's Gap where General Franklin's corps broke through the Rebel resistance to threaten Mclaws on Maryland Heights. Once through the gap his infantry bumped into another position of graybacks - a total of six brigades hastily deployed by Mclaws to defend his rear. Night was fast coming and Franklin decided to content himself with achieving at least one of his assigned objectives. He had cut Mclaws off from the rest of the Rebel army. He saw no need to press the issue any further and ordered his troops to bed down for the night. Thus was lost a splendid opportunity to both relieve the Federal garrison at Harper's Ferry and trap half of the Confederate army north of the Potomac.

* * * * * * * * *

"Gotta rest!" stammered Wil as the trio emerged from a stand of trees in the moonlight.

"Can't see why," said Lemuel Vaughn. "Me and Levi here are doing all the work."

Wil cast him a challenging look which caused the

older man to chuckle. "Just jokin', boy. Don't get all riled. Go ahead and lay yourself down a spell. I think we got some time. We should be a mile or so north of the Yankees."

Gratefully, Wil dropped to one knee, and with Levi's help reclined on to his back. With a deep sigh, he stared up at the clear moonlit sky and wondered again if he'd ever see home.

Vaughn took off on his own, but returned a few minutes later. "Dawn ain't far off," he said to Levi. "How's he doin?"

"Bleedin's stopped but that bullet's buried in his hip bone."

"Let's get him up. I think I found a place to hide you two."

"Hide us?" There was a trace of alarm in Levi's voice.

"Yep. My conscience is botherin' me. I got a gut feelin' Lee's gonna need every musket he can scrounge up. I need to get back with my boys."

"What about us?"

"I spotted a good size rock formation 'bout midway up the mountain. I'll help ya up to it. Then I'm afraid we'll have to part company. I'm gonna catch up with the army."

Levi wasn't too sure he liked Vaughn's idea of help but by the same token he could understand the other soldier's desire to return to his unit. Lee was obviously in a jam. Every musket would indeed be vital.

They pulled Wil up from the ground, braced him between themselves and started moving again. It took them nearly forty-five minutes to reach the rocks Vaughn had mentioned. By this time a pale pinkish glow was inching its way up over the eastern face of the mountain. Once there they placed Wil in a prone position on the ground while Vaughn went scrambling like a lizard through the rocks looking for a suitable hiding place. He was back in something less than ten minutes.

"C'mon," he beckoned. "I found a cave...sort of a cave."

"What do you mean, sort of?" stammered Wil in a voice which seemed decidedly weaker to Levi.

"It's a crack between two rocks." came the reply. "It goes back a good ways. No one's gonna find you in there."

"What about Wil?" pressed Levi. "He's got to have a doctor soon."

"I'm sorry, boy. I really am. I don't have all the answers. He said he didn't want to end up a prisoner. I've helped him avoid that. As for the rest...I'm afraid that's gonna be up to you, but that shouldn't worry him too damn much. You seem like a right capable fella to me even if you are black."

"Lem..." Wil opened his eyes gazed toward Vaughn.

"I hear ya, boy."

"Thanks...I appreciate this. Someday I'll repay the favor."

"I hope I don't ever need a favor like this." Vaughn smiled warmly. "Meanwhile let's get you into that cave. I want to be gone 'fore there's too much light."

A short while later Wil found himself on his back again. This time the ground was cold and damp. It was so dark he could barely see but he could hear the soft sounds of water trickling down through the rocks. The cave, if it could be styled as such, was so narrow in some places there was only room for one man to pass at a time, and with bellies and buttocks scraping rock at that.

"Told ya it was a good hiding place," boasted Vaughn. "You'll both be safe in here."

"Looks that way," agreed Levi. "What about you?"

"I spotted a horse in that pasture down at the bottom of the mountain. I imagine it must belong to the farmer in that house on the next ridge. I didn't see no houses closer. Anyway I reckon I'm gonna borrow that horse for a spell. I think I can outrun the Yankees. I ought to be back with the army by early afternoon."

"You take care of yourself, hear?" This from Wil whose voice was barely audible.

"I'll do that," said Vaughn. "You boys should stay

in here till the Yankees are gone from this mountain. Then see if you can find a friendly local to get Wil some medical help."

"I'll be taking care of that as soon as it's safe," said Levi.

"Well...I'll be goin'. I hope you boys make it."

"You too," returned Levi. He then followed Vaughn to the entrance of the cave and watched as the older man descended the mountain. He continued to watch as Vaughn crept stealthily to the split rail fence which ran the length of a broad, hilly pasture. Over the fence went Vaughn and straight for the horse he intended to borrow. The animal paid him no mind at first but as he drew nearer the horse shied away. Vaughn obviously knew his way around horses however for he was able to quickly sooth the startled animal, approach it and mount. Moments later he was at a full gallop and leapt the fence as if it weren't even there. Levi watched as horse and rider raced south for a couple of hundred yards then turned sharply west. Then he topped a rise and disappeared down the far side. "Good luck," whispered Levi as he withdrew into the cave.

"That you, Levi?"

"I'm back."

"Lemuel get out okay?"

"Sure did. He shoulda been cavalry. The man can definitely ride."

"Good," nodded Wil.

"How you feelin'?"

"Weak...thirsty."

"There's a spring in here someplace. I can hear it. You rest easy while I find it and fill the canteens."

"I don't figure I'll be goin' anywhere anytime soon."

Levi was back within minutes. With one hand he propped up Wil's head while offering the canteen with the other. Wil drank greedily, savoring each gulp as if it might be his last.

"Oh that's good!" he gasped. "It's so cold!"

"Sure is," agreed Levi. "Cold and clear just like

God intended water to be."

"I feel better already."

"Good! I need to look at that wound. Can you roll on your good side?"

"No problem," replied Will but he grunted loudly from the effort and its accompanying pain.

The sun had risen above South Mountain by this time and rays of light penetrated the cave through a variety of gaps and holes. Levi helped his lifelong friend slither on the ground until he lay beneath one of those gaps, giving the black man a good opportunity to study the hole in Wil's hip. "Don't look good," he said after several moments had passed. Needs to be cleaned pretty thorough. Looks like infection might be settin' in."

"Can you do anything?"

"Maybe. I found some right thick moss growin' on the rocks where the water's tricklin' through. Ma used to tell me certain kinds of moss were good at fightin' this sort of thing. Rest easy a spell while I fetch some. If nothin' else we can give the wound a good cleanin'.'"

As Levi set about his work action of a different sort was brewing in the hills just west of Crampton's Gap. General Franklin had arrayed his Federal infantry in a long line of battle and was preparing to go forward against Mclaws and Maryland Heights. Earlier he had listened to the fierce cannonade being delivered from those heights down into Harper's Ferry. Hoping he wasn't too late he was now determined to rescue the garrison at the Ferry before Mclaws could make further use of those guns.

Just then a wild cheer sang out from the Rebel lines. The boys in butternut were obviously happy about something. As throngs of Federals stared curiously at the enemy lines the cheer seemed to grow in fervor. This curiosity finally got the better of one northern infantryman. He leapt up atop a stone wall in easy range of the Rebel muskets: "What the hell are you fellows cheering for?" he demanded with a brashness anyone would admire.

"Because Harper's Ferry is gone up, God damn you!"

Came the immediate reply from someone on the Confederate side.

"I thought that was it," the northerner said glumly as he jumped back down.

Franklin immediately put his plans for assault on hold. If the Ferry had indeed been captured it would mean his men would have to storm the same artillery they'd been listening to all morning. Caution dictated against such a move and he elected instead to stand in place until the situation was further clarified.

As for Harper's Ferry it had indeed "gone up" as the unidentified Rebel soldier had so succinctly put it. Though the timing had not gone according to plan Jackson had been able to ring the Ferry with guns just as Lee had designed. One hour of intense artillery fire on the morning of the 15th was all that was required to force the garrison's capitulation. None escaped save two regiments of cavalry who had managed to slip away during the hours of darkness before the deadly barrage began. In all there were over 12,500 prisoners to be processed. These included all those who had come in earlier from Martinsburg. The bounty also included over 13,000 muskets and 73 cannon, not to mention a stash of quartermaster stores so large that several wagon trains would be needed to haul it away.

In penning a quick letter to his wife, Stonewall Jackson had mentioned his belief that, "Our Heavenly Father blesses us exceedingly." According to a northern reporter who was present at the surrender, Jackson and those he led were in dire need of all the blessings the Heavenly Father could ever bestow. In truth, his reaction to the sight of the fabled Stonewall wasn't unlike that of the northern civilian who survived one of the train wrecks outside of Manassas, the one who had inspired such mirth in Jackson's men when he cried, "Oh my God, lay me down!"

Believing he now had one of the better stories of the war the reporter described his impressions of the motley crew which had so easily brought the garrison of Harper's

Ferry to its knees. His description of Jackson himself is especially worthy of note:

> "He was dressed in coarsest kind of homespun, seedy and dirty at that; wore an old hat which any northern beggar would consider an insult to have offered him, and in general appearance was in no respect to be distinguished from the mongrel, bare footed crew who followed his fortunes. I had heard much of the decayed appearance of the rebel soldiers, but such a looking crowd! Ireland in her worst straits could present no parallel and yet they glory in their shame."

Well, no one ever claimed the fighting men of the South were pretty. It was not to win fashion contests that they took up arms in the first place. As for Jackson, seedy and dirty though he was, perhaps we should pay closer attention to the remarks made by one of his prisoners. "Boys, he isn't much for looks," he had said after getting a closer look at Jackson, "but if we'd had him we wouldn't have been caught in this trap." Who could have said it any better than that?

As they gathered their prisoners and reaped the bounty of Harper's Ferry, the mood among Jackson's troops was jubilant to say the least, but Jackson would not allow giddiness to distract him from the work still to be done. Lee was hard-pressed by McClellan, this much he knew, but since he was still unaware of the lost copy of Special Orders 191, he professed surprise at the Union Commander's new found audacity. "I thought I knew McClellan," he said to a staff officer, "but this movement of his puzzles me."

Puzzled or not he had no intention of waxing idle in Harper's Ferry while Lee and Longstreet were literally in a race for survival. By late afternoon Stonewall Jackson along with five of his six infantry divisions were on the march for Sharpsburg, Maryland and a reunion with their comrades. Earlier, he had sent a courier to Lee with the following dispatch:

Through God's blessing, Harper's Ferry and its garrison are to be surrendered. As Hill's troops have borne the heaviest part of the engagement, he shall be left in command until the prisoners, and public property shall be disposed of, unless you direct otherwise. The other forces can move off this evening so soon as they get their rations.

It was around noon when this message was delivered to General Lee. Longstreet's troops were already moving into their positions just north of the town of Sharpsburg. "This is indeed good news," said the Old Gray Fox as he breathed a silent prayer of thanks. "Let it be announced to the troops."

As Lee was receiving word of Harper's Ferry, Levi Henry was standing just outside the cave which had afforded sanctuary to himself and Wil Covington all morning. He was studying the National Road as he had done periodically since Lemuel Vaughn had taken his leave. What he saw gave him cause to both worry and hope. Silently he disappeared inside the cave and moved to the side of his stricken companion. "Wil?" he gently nudged the white man's shoulder. "You awake?"

"Uh-huh," came the barely audible reply.

"How ya feelin'?"

"Weak...wish to God I hadn't stopped that minie ball."

"Reckon a lotta folks are wishin' the same thing after yesterday."

"I reckon. You know what time it is?"

"I figure noon, maybe half past."

"Is it safe to leave?"

"Don't know. Looks like the last of their infantry is gone but they've got cavalry patrols fannin' out to round up stragglers."

"Like us."

"No doubt."

"What do you think we should do?"

"We got to get you to a doctor, not just any doctor,

a friendly one. Problem is, if we go out there now we're liable to be spotted by one of them patrols."

"So we're stayin' right here."

"Looks that way. At least till dark."

Wil nodded his agreement with Levi's assessment of their situation, though his spirits fell considerably. "I'm gettin' pretty hungry," he said. "We got any rations left?"

"A few biscuits...some hardtack."

"Don't sound like nothin' to write home about."

"It'll have to do, old friend. Maybe I could bag us a rabbit or somethin', but we sure can't be lightin' no fires."

"I miss Ivory."

"Me too. That old boy can sure make a pittance seem like a feast." Levi reached into his pouch and pulled out two cold, stale biscuits handing one to Levi while taking a small bite from the other, a bit which he chewed for as long as possible.

*   *   *   *   *   *   *   *   *

The spirits of a wounded Wil Covington may have been sinking, but the same could hardly be said of George McClellan. Elated by his triumph on South Mountain, he was in hot pursuit of the retreating Confederates. In keeping with his tendency to exaggerate, his dispatches to superiors fairly glowed with enthusiasm based on his perception of his supposedly striking victory on the mountain. To General Halleck back in Washington he conveyed "perfectly reliable" information that the Rebels were fleeing in a thorough panic toward Shepherdstown and that "Lee last night stated publicly that he must admit they had been shockingly whipped."

General Winfield Scott, the hero of the Mexican War, was now at West Point. He too received a message from McClellan in which the young Napoleon announced a "signal victory" over the Confederates, and boasted of having soundly trounced R. E. Lee.

Return messages from these men and others including President Lincoln, expressed universal support and appreciation for General McClellan and the men he led. All of these replies were filled with hope that the Rebels could be brought to bay and destroyed before they could escape Maryland. McClellan had no intention of disappointing them.

By early afternoon his army was passing through the town of Boonsboro, Maryland. Their reception by the people of this little town was no less enthusiastic than the one they received in Frederick. They thought this a good omen. Frederick had been followed by a great victory at South Mountain. Would Boonsboro be followed by an even greater victory? Their appetite had been whetted, and these foot soldiers of the Army of the Potomac found themselves eagerly scanning the southern horizon for any sign of the fleeing enemy.

Some five miles to the southeast of Boonsboro they found what they were looking for. Their commander and his staff crested a ridgeline which overlooked a shallow valley perhaps a mile in width. On the opposite side of this valley stood a lower ridge of hills and knolls. Here waited the Rebels. Lots of them. Artillery was already in place and as soon as the gunners spied the knot of horsemen wearing blue uniforms they opened fire. Shells began to burst around McClellan's entourage. Horses reared back and neighed in fearful panic. McClellan himself ordered his men to disperse and move back out of range while he sought cover in a position where he could conduct a detailed study of the terrain. Using his spy glasses he began to sweep the valley from one end to the other. The first important geographic feature he found was a muddy brown creek which wound its way in a southeasterly direction to join the Potomac. "What's that creek called?" he asked of a nearby staff officer.

The fellow glanced out toward the creek first then turned his attention to the maps he had spread out on the ground. "Antietam Creek," he announced after a brief perusal.

"Antietam," repeated McClellan softly as he continued to scan the opposite ridge. "I see some rooftops and spires just beyond that ridge." he said. "Would that be Sharpsburg?"

"Yes, General, that's Sharpsburg."

"And the Potomac," Mcclellan lowered his glasses. "How much farther is the Potomac river?"

"A mile, sir. Maybe a mile and a half."

A smile crept slowly across McClellan's face as he turned to watch his army moving into position all along the ridge. "I think we've got him!" he declared firmly.

* * * * * * *

None of this was known to the two Shenandoah farm boys secluded in the rocks of the northern reaches of South Mountain. Shadows were lengthening as the afternoon waned and Levi's most recent foray outside the cave found no evidence of Federal patrols.

"I didn't see any Yankees," he explained as he returned to Wil's side. "That don't mean they're not out there, but they ain't around here. I figure we've got two hours of daylight left. Maybe we could take a chance and leave now while we can still see where we're goin'."

"I'm game," said Wil in a weak voice.

Levi quickly gathered their gear, including the lone Enfield musket, then helped Wil slowly to his feet.

"Can't put much weight on it," groaned Wil. "Hurts too damn much!"

"You got to try, Wil, I don't think I can carry you."

"Can you brace me for a minute? feels like my head's full of cobwebs."

"I got ya. Get your bearin's straight and we'll be out of here in no time."

Within a short while they were. With Levi supporting Wil's injured side the two of them emerged from the cave and paused to decide their next move.

"The air out here sure tastes cleaner," noted Wil as he drew a deep breath.

"Yep," agreed Levi. "C'mon, we're gonna climb to the top of this mountain. Then we'll follow the crestline north for a spell. There's bound to be a farm somewhere on the opposite slope."

"I sure hope so," grunted Wil. "Don't know how long I can hold out."

Up the mountain they moved, stumbling frequently, sometimes falling face forward to the ground. For the most part they kept to the cover of trees, rarely exposing themselves to any unfriendly eyes which might be lurking about. The going was tortuously slow and darkness had enveloped them by the time they reached the mountain's crest.

"Gotta rest!" gasped Wil. "It's hurtin' worse than ever!"

"All right, Lay down here...get your breath back." Levi helped his comrade to the ground then collapsed himself. The struggle to reach the top of the mountain had drained much of his own strength. "We're gonna make it, Wil," he gasped between breaths. "I know we're gonna make it."

*   *   *   *   *   *   *

As the sun was drifting slowly out of sight and the two Rebel stragglers were making their way up that mountain George McClellan was fast losing any chance he had of crushing the Army of Northern Virginia and bagging Robert E. Lee. Perhaps if he had known how few men Lee had at Sharpsburg on the afternoon of the 15th he might have attacked with all of his available strength and put an end to the struggle. Perhaps.

Here again the young Napoleon, reverted to character. He had estimated Lee's losses on South Mountain to be somewhere in the vicinity of 15,000 men. Nevertheless he was convinced that Lee still had over 100,000 men at his disposal. Reality was substantially different than McClellan's perceptions. In point of fact Lee had lost about 2,600 men on the mountain - roughly equivalent to the losses he inflicted on the Federals. Regarding the men Lee was able to field at Sharpsburg on the 15th, the disparity between McClellan's wild guesses and the true situation was even more pronounced. Lee had only the troops of D. H. Hill and Longstreet to face the Army of the

Potomac. These numbered barely 18,000. Any one of McClellan's corps probably outnumbered the entire Confederate force which was deployed at Sharpsburg. True, Jackson was on his way and his arrival would bring their strength up to 26,000. The odds would still be more than three to one in favor of the Federals. When all those involved in the reduction of Harper's Ferry were finally reunited with the rest of the army north of the Potomac, Lee would still have barely 40,000 men at his disposal, and these were heavily worn by the constant marching and poor diet they had endured over the last three weeks. To all this McClellan was apparently blind, deluded no doubt by his own wildly inflated projections of his opponent's strength. Having robbed himself of clear vision, McClellan also denied his own soldiers the very real opportunity to end the war on the banks of Antietam creek.

Instead of immediate action McClellan opted to conduct a meticulous study of the terrain as a basis on which to form a proper plan of battle. He believed his hesitation to be vindicated by the results of his initial study. Lee had chosen his ground well. His troops occupied high ground overlooking the shallow valley which lay between the two armies. Both ends of his line were anchored along the shores of the Potomac, his position basically ran across the mouth of a four mile bend in that river. Using his glasses McClellan swept the line from left to right. About a mile above the town of Sharpsburg he spied a small white building, a church as it turned out, a place of worship for those who adhered to the Dunker faith, a people who rejected war and would soon see ample evidence to justify their beliefs. Further to the right was a field of corn some forty acres in all, lush green in color and standing tall in the afternoon sun. "A good position," thought McClellan, "but his back is to the river and he has but one ford available to him."

Evening was fast approaching. His men had marched hard and fast. Better it would be to wait for the morrow when his men were fully rested and properly fed. "Get the fires burning," he instructed a courier. "I want every man to have a good hot meal. We'll finish this thing tomorrow."

*   *   *   *   *   *   *

All through the night Wil and Levi continued their northward trek along the crest of the mountain. They had no way of knowing how much ground they were actually covering as their course wound about a host of trees and 'ocks. It wasn't long before Levi found himself half-carrying his wounded friend who could no longer put weight on his injured hip. There was still an hour remaining until dawn when both men collapsed from sheer exhaustion.

The first hints of the new sun were just beginning to appear in the eastern sky when Levi sat up and shook the sleep from his groggy head. He opened his canteen and took a long drink of the sweet spring water from the cave. Propping Wil's head with one hand he offered the canteen to his friend who drank greedily.

"It'll be light soon," said Levi. "We can start headin' down the eastern slope, maybe find ourselves a farm."

"I smell smoke," whispered Wil.

"Me too," concurred Levi after sniffing the air. "Someone's up early. They got their stoves goin'."

"Could be a Yankee cookfire," Wil's voice was weaker than ever.

"Not likely. Not out here. I think it's comin' from a farmhouse."

Levi hauled Wil up on his one good leg, braced him with an arm around his waist and started north again. Not long after sun-up he stopped and gazed out over the valley. He spotted a wispy column of smoke drifting skyward from a hollow perhaps a mile away as the crow flies. Unfortunately, he and Wil couldn't fly and the overland route was perhaps two or three times as long. Then he spied a path which wound in a northerly direction near the base of the mountain. The path intersected another trail, much wider than the first and running perpendicular to it. His eyes followed the course of the second trail until it disappeared through another small gap in the mountain.

"I ain't feelin' so good," stammered Wil. "Feelin' awful warm all over."

Levi raised a hard to touch the white man's neck and found it quite warm to the touch. Fever was taking hold of Wil Covington and Levi quickly realized time was running out. "Stay with me, Wil!" he urged. "We're close to help...do you hear me? We're close!"

Wil's response was only a nod and a feeble one at that. Down the slope they moved with Levi half- carrying half- dragging his wounded companion. They reached the narrow path Levi had spotted from the ridge and again turned north. Before long they came to the inter-section of the wider trail which ran to the west, but they were forced to stop again because Levi was very nearly exhausted and Wil was close to losing consciousness.

"I'm not gonna make it, Levi," Wil's fever-racked voice was barely audible. "Think I'm finished... I'm dyin'."

"No!" Levi fairly shouted the word. "Ain't no way I'm gonna let you die! You hear me? You and me are gonna make it back to the Shenandoah come hell or high water! We got farms waitin' for us, Wil! There's still a lot of plantin' and harvestin' in front of you and me! Don't you even think about dyin!"

From Wil there was no reply. He had finally lost consciousness.

"Goddamn!" cursed the black man. "There's got to be help somewhere!"

Just then a sound came to his ears which chilled the blood in his veins. It was a loud neigh from a horse still well to the west. "Yankee cavalry," Levi gave words to his first thought. Quickly he hauled Wil up to a sitting position and lifted the unconscious man up over his right shoulder. He started north at once along the narrow path and disappeared into the woods. He failed to notice Wil's kepi which fell from his head in the middle of the intersection of the two trails. Nor did he remember to grab his musket which lay on the trail only paces from Wil's cap.

As it turned out Levi's first thought upon hearing the horse was correct. The horse was one of ten each supporting a Union cavalryman, a patrol crossing the mountain from the western slopes. They were still some ten minutes away which gave the two Rebels at least a slight head start.

Levi moved along the little path as fast as his two tired legs could carry him. Wil didn't feel particularly heavy at first but as the minutes passed he began to feel the weight of the burden on his shoulder. His pace slackened considerably and his breath quickened. A thin sheen of perspiration appeared on his face as he began to sweat. Still he kept moving.

"Hold up!" The northern sergeant signalled to the rest of his patrol as the riders approached the convergence of the two trails. "Is that a musket on the ground?" He stood in his stirrups and peered over the head of his mount. "Ferguson," he gestured to one of his companions. "Get up there and check."

The other fellow dismounted without making any reply and moved on foot to retrieve the suspected weapon. "Sure is!" he called moments later. "Confederate issue!" he added after picking up and examining the musket. "Somethin' else," he noted as he glanced down at the leaf-covered ground. He reached down and snatched up Wil's kepi. "Rebel cap, Sarge! 'Pears there might be another straggler hereabout."

"Can you tell which way he went?"

"Nope. Too many leaves on the ground. No tracks, no bloodstain. Just the cap and musket.

The sergeant and the rest of the patrol moved at once to join their comrade. After a quick examination of the available evidence the sergeant made a decision. "Ferguson, take two men and follow this path north. Jones, you take two and move south. I'll push ahead with the others. All of you follow the path for fifteen minutes. If you don't come up with anything then swing east and

BROTHERS IN GRAY

link back up with us."

"Will do," Ferguson pointed at two men, mounted his horse and moved north into the woods.

The smell of wood smoke was heavy in Levi's nostrils and he could easily make out the sound of chickens in a henhouse. There was a farm up ahead and it didn't seem like it could be all that far. Levi summoned his last reserve of strength and quickened his pace. The path snaked through the woods for another fifty yards then suddenly he found himself in the open. Not twenty yards away stood a two story wooden-frame house at the base of a steep hill. On either end of this house rose brick chimneys. On the porch stood an elderly woman who was busily engaged snapping green beans. Beyond the house was a sizeable pasture in which several dairy cows were grazing contentedly. Between Levi and the house and just to the left was a large vegetable garden. Here stood a tall man with long white hair and a flowing beard of the same color. The man had been chopping weeds with a hoe, pausing occasionally to pick up a ripe squash or two.

Then Levi appeared as if from nowhere, the unconscious form of Wil Covington hanging across his right shoulder like a sack of potatoes. The black man paused but a second to take in the surroundings then he made a beeline for the porch. "Help me!" He called. "Help me, please!"

The woman on the porch rose at once to her feet, an expression of fright etched on her face as her eyes darted from the approaching black man to her husband who moved quickly to place himself between his home and these intruders.

"Stop right there, boy!" There was a decidedly authoritative tone to his voice Levi found difficult to ignore. He stopped in his tracks, still ten yards from the porch.

"Please, mister, I'm beggin' you...he's been hit bad and needs help. I think there might be Yankees behind us. Please help."

"What makes you think I'm not a Yankee?"

Levi fumbled for words but found none as his heart sank.

"Why would you want to save that rebel?" pressed the farmer. "If he dies you'll be free, will you not?"

To this Levi could reply readily. "Mister, I'm just as free as you are. Ain't never been a slave in my life! Me and Wil joined up with Stonewall together. Will you help us?"

Seconds ticked by with no noise whatsoever. The woman on the porch was nervously wringing her hands in the folds of her long apron. Levi thought he saw movement at one of the windows. The lace curtains parted. There was a face...no two. Then came the neigh of horses on the path he had just left.

"Please, mister!" Levi's eyes took on a look of sheer desperation as he pleaded one more time."He's the closest thing to a brother I've ever had. Don't let them take us! I can't run anymore! They're on horses! They'd take me down in a heartbeat!"

For a moment the old man said nothing as he continued to appraise the black Rebel soldier who stood before him with a wounded comrade on his shoulder. There was a sincerity about Levi which appealed to him, and the boy's fear was certainly genuine. He could hear hoofbeats now, and little time remained for him to dwell on his decision.

"Get inside the house," he instructed. Then he turned and addressed himself to the woman. "Mother, you know where to take them."

"Are you sure, Zebedee?" She asked quickly.

"We will trust to God that this is the right thing. Take them down and be quick!"

She immediately turned and opened the door as Levi climbed the porch in two quick bounds. She opened the door and ushered him inside. "Emily," she addressed herself to a girl of perhaps seventeen years. "Father says to take them down. Hurry!"

The young girl nodded and beckoned to Levi to follow her. Levi cast a quick glance at the black girl who stood to one side. Hers had been the other face he thought he'd seen in the window. There was no time to exchange greetings. He quickly followed the white girl through another door then down a flight of wooden stairs to a cellar with a hardwood plank floor.

After ushering the black soldier inside the elderly woman returned at once to her seat on the porch and grabbed her bowl of green beans. She took a deep breath to calm herself and noticed that her husband was already back in the garden chopping weeds. Then the first of the Federal horsemen emerged from the woods followed quickly by two more. One of them had his carbine cradled in one arm as his eyes took in every detail of the little farm. Maryland was a state with divided sympathies so these soldiers took precautions every time they approached the civilian populace no matter how close to Pennsylvania they happened to be.

"Good mornin', folks," it was Ferguson who spoke as he tipped his hat to the woman on the porch.

"Good morning, soldier," the reply came from the old man who shouldered his hoe and stepped out of the garden toward the riders in blue. "What brings you out here?"

"Lookin for Rebs, stragglers, from that battle up on the mountain."

"We heard it," nodded the farmer. "The sounds of it rattled our windows, but you're the first soldiers we've seen. Are there Rebels coming?"

"Not like you're thinking. We booted 'em off the mountain and sent 'em running for Virginia. We're looking for the ones who couldn't keep up, the ones that scattered into the countryside. We found a musket and cap about ten minutes from here. Are you sure you haven't seen or heard anything out of the ordinary?"

He chuckled and flashed a friendly smile. "To be honest, Private, seeing the three of you come riding out of those woods is probably the most unusual thing we've seen in months."

"Maybe years," quipped one of the riders.

"Maybe!" The old man joined in the soldier's mirth.

"We figure he's on foot," continued Ferguson along a more serious vein. "He dropped his musket, but he may have other weapons. Have you a gun or something with which to protect yourself?"

"A gun? No, I'm afraid not. You see, son, we're Quakers. We do not believe in war or violence. We own no guns...but there is an axe or two in the barn and a pitchfork."

"Fergie," said the third rider, "We're wastin' our time. There ain't no rebel here. If there was he'd most likely die of boredom. The sarge is probably waitin' for us. We'd best be ridin'."

"Would you like something to eat?" ventured the farmer. "It's not often we get to chat with guests."

"No...well...maybe," replied Ferguson. "We had breakfast, but if you have any potatoes and onions out of your garden we wouldn't mind taking a few with us."

"We've got plenty!" The old man beamed. "Hold on a minute and I'll fetch some." He started toward the garden "It's been a good year," he called back over his shoulder. "We've a handsome harvest to put up!"

As all of this was transpiring Levi was led across the basement toward the rear wall of the house. The young white girl stopped at the wall and reached down to roll aside a thick throw rug which covered a trap door. She opened and started down another set of stairs. Levi peered after her and spied a small lamp burning at the base of the stairs.

"Come on!" she beckoned with a clear sense of urgency in her voice.

"Right behind ya," said Levi as he cautiously descended the stairs.

"This way," directed the girl after he reached the earthen floor.

The lamp was dim and it took Levi a second or two to adjust his eyes to the lack of light. He saw the girl move a tapestry aside at the rear wall and open yet another door.

"In here," she gestured. He entered at once.

He found himself standing inside another dimly lit room perhaps twelve feet square. Bunk beds lined three of the walls. To his left sat four negroes staring at him fearfully from the lower bed of one of those bunks.

"Lay him over here."

Levi placed Wil on the lower bunk along the right wall, and did his best to make him comfortable.

"How long has he been unconscious?" asked the girl.

"Twenty minutes or so."

"He's burning up with fever."

"Wound's been festerin' for a couple of days." he explained. "I did my best to keep it clean but there's still a bullet in his hip."

"I'll fetch my father," she said. "He'll know what to do."

"Be careful!" warned Levi. "Them Yankees might still be out there."

"I'm not stupid," she replied simply and stepped quickly from the room.

This left Levi alone in the company of four fellow Blacks, a middle aged man, a younger woman and two children. "Good mornin'," he said, since he really wasn't sure what else to say, especially since all four of them seemed unable to take their eyes from the pistol which Levi wore around his waist. "You got nothin' to fear from me. I'm serious, folks, just rest easy. Reckon we're hidin' same as you."

"Not exactly," the man spoke for the first time.

"Is this place what I think it is?" asked Levi.

"We're slaves," said the man. "At least we were. We're headin' for Canada."

"Underground railroad," mused Levi softly. "Wil ain't never gonna believe this."

"Who's Wil?" the woman spoke.

"Him," Levi pointed at the unconscious form on the bunk.

"Are you his slave?"

"Everybody seems to think so but I'm not, never was."

"How is it you're wearing that uniform? Carryin' that gun?"

"I'm in the Rebel army. Me and Wil grew up together in the Shenandoah. He joined up and I went with him. I got the pistol off of a Yankee officer at the battle we had near Manassas a few weeks back."

"You was in a battle?" The older of the two children spoke, a boy of perhaps ten years. His eyes were as wide as could be as he gazed across the room.

"Hush, child!" The man cuffed the boy on the ear.

"Slaves," mused Levi with a nod.

"No longer."

"Where from?"

"North Carolina. Not far from Wilmington."

"Why'd you run?"

"Massah got hisself killed in Virginia...place called Seven Pines. Things ain't goin' too good for his widow these days. Says she might lose the plantation. She was talkin' 'bout sellin' us. Reckon the thought of bein' sold to different places didn't sound too good to us. We're a family. We plan to stay that way."

"I can understand that," Levi sighed deeply.

"You ain't never been a slave?"

"No suh. His Pa freed my father and mother before either of us was born. Gave my father about forty acres of his own land. We've been workin' it since."

"You're awful damn lucky. You know that?"

"I ain't blind and believe me I thank God for my freedom every day of my life."

"Few more weeks, we'll be in Canada. We'll never be no one's slaves again."

"I hope you make it...all of you."

"You ain't gonna turn us in? You're in their army after all."

"He ain't fightin' for slavery," he pointed at Wil, "and I sure as hell ain't. We're defendin' Virginia and our homes... that's all."

Just then they all looked up as the door opened and the old man entered, followed quickly by his wife and daughter.

"You folks comfortable?" he addressed himself to the family of escaped slaves.

"Yessuh...we're fine right now. A little spooked though. We wasn't expectin' Rebel soldiers for company."

"I don't think you'll have cause to worry about these two. A few days more and we'll have clothes, money and supplies for you. You'll be starting the next leg of your journey north."

"We're grateful, Mr. Havelin, more grateful than words can say. Someday we'll repay you for all this."

"Nonsense," smiled the Quaker farmer. "Live your lives in peace and be true to the Lord. That's all the thanks I've ever asked for."

"We'll do just that," nodded the former slave.

"Well now," the farmer turned his attention to Levi. "My name's Zebedee Havelin," he offered his right hand which Levi quickly accepted. "This here is my wife, Barbara, and my daughter, Emily."

"Pleased," said Levi as he tipped his floppy hat to the ladies. "Can you tell me, was it Yankees comin' behind me?"

"It was."

For a moment Levi was afraid to ask the next question but Zebedee Havelin sensed his concern and eased it at once. "The soldiers are gone," he said. "I rather doubt they'll return."

"Thank God." The words came from Levi in the single breath of a genuine sigh of relief.

"Emily tells me the boy's in a bad way. May I look at him?"

"Of course!" Levi stepped aside. "He needs a doctor pretty quick. There's a bullet in the bone of his right hip."

"So she says." The old man knelt by the side of the bunk. "Mother, would you bring the lamp close?"

Barbara Havelin stood close to her husband and

held the oil lamp, adjusting the wick to increase the brightness.

"Closer," he repeated. "Mine are the eyes of an old man."

She bent slightly and held the lamp close to Wil's side.

"Much better," The old man pulled Wil's worn bloodstained trousers away from the wound and studied it closely.

"Is there a doctor close by?" asked Levi.

"No," came the quick reply.

"None? There must be a doctor somewhere!"

"I'm afraid not," Havelin used the palm of his left hand to check the temperature on Wil's forehead, then the back of his neck and his shoulder. "The boy is quite ill," he announced at last.

"I've been sayin' that!" exclaimed Levi, unable to contain his frustration. "That's why we got to find us a doctor!"

"Mother," Havelin's voice lacked emotion. "Fetch my instruments please."

"Instruments? What instruments?" Levi demanded.

"You must calm yourself, my son," explained Havelin. "The bullet has shattered his hip. I intend to extract it. In this effort I will need your help. Gangrene has not yet set in. He is fortunate in that respect, but the wound is still badly infected."

"Wait a minute," demanded Levi glancing back at the slave family as if seeking support. "What do you know about removin' bullets?"

"I've dabbled in this sort of thing."

"Dabbled? Please don't take this as disrespectful, suh, but he needs a doctor, not a dabbler!"

Havelin fixed his steel gray eyes on the anxious face of the young black man who stood before him. "How old are you, boy?"

"Nineteen."

"I am sixty-seven. I was born in the last century out

in the mountains of this state when they were still thought of as frontier. We learned to do what had to be done, regardless of how difficult it may have seemed. There is no doctor for this boy, nor the time to bring one here. He has one chance and I am that chance whether you approve or not. I'll not tolerate more impudence on your part. When the time comes I will need your help. Otherwise you will lose the person you claim as brother. Do you understand?"

Levi nodded reluctantly, but he still wasn't satisfied. "Were you a soldier? Indian fighter?"

"Quaker," came the immediate reply.

"What is that?" he wondered aloud. No one had ever told him anything of Quakers, nor had he read anything about them.

"A Quaker. I am a Quaker, as are my family. You know nothing of Quakers? It is a religion. Our faith rejects war. The members of this family take no sides in this or any other conflict. Do you believe in the Lord, boy?"

"Yessuh. We go to an Episcopalian church back home."

Just then the conversation was interrupted by the return of Barbara Havelin. In her arms was a small oblong wooden box as well as another oil lamp. "There's a kettle of water on the stove," she explained. "It should come to a boil in ten to fifteen minutes."

"Very good," nodded Zebedee, who then turned to his daughter. "Emily, go upstairs; make sure there is plenty of wood in the stove. I want you to fetch a bucket of water from the well. Bring it here along with several towels. When the kettle on the stove is boiling vigorously bring it here as well."

"Yes, father," she moved at once to do his bidding.

"Mother, we will need the whiskey as well."

"I'll be right back," She nodded.

Havelin then addressed himself to the black man who was leading his family out of slavery. "Will you help us?" he asked.

"Can't say I'm fond of the idea of helpin' no Reb," came the reply. "But I reckon if this boy thinks high enough of 'em to go through all this, I'll lend a hand. What do you want me to do?"

"Hold his feet. If he regains consciousness he must not be allowed to move."

"Reckon I can do that much."

"And you...what did you say your name was?"

"Levi Henry."

"Yes...well, Levi, I expect you to restrain his arms and upper body."

"I will," agreed Levi.

Moments later Emily returned with a bucket of cold well water and several towels.

"Place them over there," instructed her father pointing toward the unused bunk.

Her mother was right behind her carrying the kettle of boiling hot water and a bottle containing nearly a pint of whiskey.

"Daughter, leave us."

"But, father..."

"Do not question me, child. Go!"

Making no attempt to mask her frustration Emily turned and stomped quickly out of the secret room which had been temporary quarters for hundreds of runaway slaves over the years.

"Mother, cut the boy's uniform away from the wound. Cleanse the area with hot water."

She nodded and immediately set about to follow his instructions. As she worked on the wound Zebedee Havelin removed a sharp probe instrument and prepared it by dipping it in a small quantity of whiskey which he had poured into a little bowl. "The wound is as clean as I can get it right now," explained Barbara. "You will have to cut away some of the infection."

"First the bullet." The old farmer knelt on the earth floor beside Wil after his wife had moved aside. "Please restrain his legs and arms now," he said. "I'm going to start."

BROTHERS IN GRAY

Both black men took their positions and gripped Wil's limbs in strong hands. The old man bent low and began to probe for the minie ball in the Rebel lad's hip. For several minutes he continued the search but then to his dismay and the shock of all those present Wil regained consciousness.

"Ugh! Oh God, No!" he cried, then loosed a howling scream as he became aware of the searing pain in his hip. The echoes of his scream reverberated off the walls of the earthen cellar, causing the black woman to grab both her children and clutch them close.

Havelin quickly removed the probe and sat back on his haunches, watching helpless as Wil twisted and turned in the grip of the two Blacks. "Knock him out!" he ordered. "He must be unconscious or I can't do this! Knock him out!"

Levi raised his right fist. "Sorry, old friend, but it's for your own good!" Down he swung striking Wil directly in the face, knocking him out instantly.

"Good!" Havelin nodded and wiped sweat from his forehead. "I found the bullet," he explained as he put the probe back into its box and snatched up a clasping instrument with which to grip the ball and remove it. "I'll need but five minutes more, he said as he bent low over Wil's unconscious form.

True to his word he sat back with a deep sigh and examined the minie ball he had just wrenched from Wil's hip. "Thank God it stayed in one piece," he observed. "There are no loose fragments to search for."

"Will he live?" It was Levi who advanced the question.

"If we can break this fever and prevent further infection I believe he will."

"Shall I take over, dear?" Barbara Havelin stepped to the old man's side.

"Please," he nodded. "Clean it thoroughly. You should probably douse it with a little whiskey to kill the remaining infection." He rose slowly to his feet and braced himself against the top bunk.

"Shall I close the wound also?"

"Yes, please." He nodded wearily.

"Where did you two learn all this?" wondered Levi.

Zebedee Havelin fixed his wise aged eyes on the young black man in Confederate garb. "Hundreds have passed through this room," he explained. "Not all of them have been as healthy or injury-free as the family you see here today." No further explanation was requested or offered.

The moments which followed were somewhat hectic as the old man summoned his daughter and instructed her to soak the towels in the well water, wring them out thoroughly, and place them over Wil's face, chest and arms to reduce the fever which raged through his body. All the while Mrs. Havelin continued her ministrations, cleaning the wound thoroughly before stitching it up with sewing thread. As she finished she stole a glance in Levi's direction. "When was the last time you boys ate?" she asked.

"We each had a biscuit yesterday," he replied. "Can't remember when we last had a full meal!"

"I see," she nodded sympathetically and rose to her feet. "I'm going to make a fresh pot of chicken soup. I'll bring a bowl or two down as soon as it's ready."

"We're much obliged, mam,...both of us are."

"We would do the same for any boy in this condition, regardless of the color of his uniform."

"Reckon you would," he returned. "You folks...well... you're right good people."

"Thank you, soldier," she turned and left the room.

"He'll be on his back for awhile," said the elder Havelin. "That bullet fractured his hip. Full recovery will take time."

"May we stay here?"

"We'll discuss that later," the old man picked up his little box of surgical instruments and left the damp, dark underground room.

This left only Emily, Wil, and the Blacks. Levi glanced across at the runaway slave who had finally loosed his hold on Wil's legs. "What's your name?" he asked.

"Peter. Down home they called me Old Pete.

"That a fact?" Levi flashed a grin. "We got us a general that a lot of folks call 'Old Pete', General Longstreet."

"Do tell? Reckon you can now say you know two Old Pete's."

"Seems like it. Anyway, I'm much obliged to ya."

"Weren't no problem." He left Wil's feet and walked slowly back to rejoin his family on the opposite bunk.

*   *   *   *   *   *   *

As Wil Covington lay unconscious in the secret underground room of the Havelin home. General Mc-Clellan was studying the Confederate defenses on the west side of Antietam Creek. He had arisen early and gone out to an observation post on a hill which was just beyond the range of the Rebel guns and which afforded him an excellent panoramic view of the entire area. He had the assistance of powerful telescopes which had been strapped to the side of stakes which in turn had been driven deeply into the ground. However these proved to be of little use during the early morning hours as the low-lying mist was simply too thick and easily masked most of what he hoped to see.

By mid-morning the sun had burned the mist away allowing the Union Commander to conduct a detailed study of his opponent's defenses. He found these changed from the day before, mostly in the placement of artillery. These changes he noted and with the latest information on hand he proceeded to devise a meticulously detailed plan of attack. Three stone bridges spanned Antietam creek in the vicinity of Sharpsburg and they formed the foundation on which McClellan planned his destruction of the Army of Northern Virginia. The lower bridge was literally a stone's throw away from Lee's right. The middle bridge was in less dangerous territory, but anyone crossing it would face an uphill sprint straight into the heart of the Rebel line. Well to McClellan's right the uppermost bridge crossed the creek where the enemy's guns could not reach them. This span became the heart of McClellan's plan.

His design for Lee's downfall was essentially this. Three corps of infantry - half of the Union army - would cross the upper bridge, turn south and hurl themselves upon Lee's left flank. Hooker, Mansfield and Sumner were chosen for the job. Simultaneously Porter was to cross the middle bridge and attempt to force the center of the enemy line while Burnside did the same against Lee's right. This last officer was also instructed to seize the town of Sharpsburg as well as the Shepherdstown ford, thus closing the trap on the fabled Lee and his battered warriors.

Noon had come and gone on the 16th of September by the time McClellan had finalized his plans. He decided the day was too far gone to attempt battle so the attack was scheduled for the next morning at first light. The remainder of the day was spent in shuffling his troops, getting everybody into position for the battle some thought might be the last of the war. Long range artillery and occasional exchanges of musketry from the pickets of either side provided the only action on the 16th. By and large the men of both sides settled down to await the inevitable.

On the afternoon of the 15th, when McClellan arrived on the ridge overlooking Antietam creek he might easily have destroyed the Rebels if he had gone immediately into action. He reasoned, perhaps rightly, that the day was too far gone and his men too worn from the long and arduous march from South Mountain. On the 16th however he could find no such excuses. Once again he held back and forfeited an incredible opportunity to bring Robert E. Lee to grief. The bulk of the Southern forces involved in the capture of Harper's Ferry had not yet arrived. Lee still had fewer than 18,000 men with which to face the entire Army of the Potomac, hardly one-fifth of the Union strength. If McClellan had found his nerve and gone forward as planned, Lee might have been over-whelmed swiftly. Convinced that he faced over 100,000 Rebels, McClellan continued to hesitate. This delay more than any other factor, foiled McClellan's designs before they were ever put in motion.

*　　*　　*　　*　　*　　*　　*

Three days later Wil woke for the first time since Levi had knocked him cold as Havelin was removing the Union bullet. He didn't open his eyes nor did he make any noise at first. When first he awoke he became aware that he was being held, but by whom? His first thought centered on Levi, but this idea he quickly dismissed. They were the arms of a woman which cradled his head. He breathed deep and inhaled her soft scent. The side of his head rested against her breast. This was an altogether new sensation to the young Virginian and he found he rather liked it. Who was she? He remembered being wounded. Was this a field hospital? Was she a nurse or perhaps an angel sent from Heaven? It occurred to him that he might still be sleeping and the delightful sensations he was experiencing were all part of a dream. Then he became aware of the dull ache in his side and he knew he wasn't dreaming.

The wounded Rebel soldier in her arms groaned and Emily realized he was at last rejoining the world of the living. She blushed slightly when she realized just how close she'd been holding him, slowly and gently she lowered his head to her lap and with her left hand she brushed his hair back from his forehead.

His eyes opened. He found himself blinking to get used to the light, though the underground room had but one lamp burning and this provided dim light at best. Directly above him was the upper bunk which blocked his vision. Shifting his eyes slightly he could see a wall. Was it brick? There was a table, a lamp, another bunk. Then his eyes drifted back and up into the face of the woman in whose arms he still reclined. Hers was truly the face of an angel and the sight of her caused the breath to catch in his throat. "Wh... Where am I?" His voice was so weak he could scarcely recognize it himself.

"Safe," she whispered with a smile so lovely it melted his heart.

"Where?"

"Our home. The closest town is Thurmont."

"Thurmont?"

"Maryland."

"Maryland," he repeated the word in a whisper. "I remember now." He tried to shift his position then shouted out loud as a sharp pain ripped through his side.

"No,No!" She gripped him more tightly. "You must lie still! The bullet broke your hip. My father says it will be a long time before you'll have full use of it again."

"Your father?"

"He saved your life....I guess we all did."

All of this was rather much for a man who had been unconscious for three days. Each of her answers simply generated more questions. A few minutes passed with neither of them speaking. At last Wil glanced up at the face of this angel and posed yet another question. "Who are you, I mean...What's your name?"

"Emily," There was that smile again, that thoroughly disarming smile. "Emily Havelin."

"My name's Wil."

"I know. Levi told us."

"Levi? Where is he?"

"I think he's upstairs with Naomi," she looked down into his eyes and all she saw were more questions. He started to ask another but she hushed him with one finger over his mouth. "Rest now," she said. "You've been through a terrible ordeal. We thought we might lose you. Are you hungry?"

He nodded his head. "Famished," he replied.

"I'll go fetch something for you to eat," She wiggled away from him supporting his head with one arm and laying it gently on the bunk as she rose. "Rest," she instructed. "I'll be back in a little while."

Wil watched her leave and at once he felt her absence. He didn't really know who she was. She had given him a name, Emily. He knew that much. Her scent and touch became familiar to him within minutes of awakening. Little else did he know save this: the moment she passed from view he knew he missed her.

Several minutes passed and another figure appeared in the doorway. Though it wasn't Emily, Wil recognized the person at once. Levi Henry had come to see him.

"You're a sight for sore eyes," said Wil, who managed a weak smile for his friend.

"Welcome back!" Levi returned the smile. "I thought maybe you were plannin' on sleepin' forever."

"That girl...Emily...she told me I was out for three days."

"Yep, seemed like three weeks to me. I figured you might be a goner but Mr. Havelin swore you'd pull through."

"Is he the one who pulled the bullet out?"

"He sure is. Did a right smart job of it too. He's a strange one, that old bird! Seems to know an awful lot 'bout doctorin' but he won't say   nothin' 'bout where he learned it."

"Don't seem like it makes all that much difference, Levi. Point is he knew what had to be done and he did it. Will he come down here? I'd like to thank him myself."

"I imagine he will. Right now there's somethin' else I need to tell ya. This place...this room...it's part of the underground railroad."

"What? Really?"

"I ain't lyin'. There was a family of slaves here when we came in. One of 'em helped me hold you down while the old man pulled the minie ball out of your hip."

"In this room?"

"Sho'nuff."

"Where are they now?"

"Gone. Long gone by now. These folks...the Havelins that is...they supplied them with new clothes and food and sent 'em on their way. They must be halfway to New York by now. Man's name was `Old Pete!' He held your legs down while the old man pulled the bullet out."

"Seems like I'm indebted to a lot of folks."

"Me most of all, I'll have you know!" Levi flashed a mischievous grin."You passed out on the trail. I carried you the better part of a mile and there was a Yankee patrol close on our heels."

"Thanks, Levi," Wil managed another weak smile.

"Don't mention it. I expect the same from you if I ever go down."

"Count on it."

"You comfortable? Anything I can get you?"

"Nah. I think Emily went for food. I'll be okay."

"I'll be gettin' back upstairs now."

"Levi, wait a minute. Who's Naomi?"

"How's that?"

"Naomi. Emily said you were upstairs with some-one named Naomi. Who is that?"

"Oh...just someone I met. She's a slave, at least she was. She ran away from her owners in Georgia. Managed to get this far on her own, but then she decided to stay put. She's been here ever since!"

"You like her?"

"I reckon."

"How old is she?"

"Sixteen as near as she can figure, and just as sweet as apple pie!"

"Do tell?"

"You'd best be believin' it! Now do like Emily said and rest! I'll check in on ya later."

Wil thought about resting, not that his hip would allow any other choice, but Emily soon returned with a tray of food from which emanated the most delightful aromas.

"Mother says I shouldn't stuff you, but it seems to me you'll need to eat a lot to regain your strength."

"How can I eat? I can't even sit up."

She placed the tray on the bunk between Wil and the wall. Then she sat down, lifted his head and shoulders and scooted down so he could rest on her lap. "Where there's a will there's a way!"

With Emily's help Wil managed to eat a rather copious meal - his first in recent memory. "So much food!" he muttered as he savored a mouthful of moist chicken breast. "Reminds me of home before the war."

"Is there someone waiting for you there? A girl I mean."

"A girl?" Wil was a bit taken aback by her rather direct approach. She didn't seem to be the least bit shy or reserved. "No...not really."

"Sarah?"

He looked up at her with an inquisitive expression on his face.

"Yes, Sarah. When you were sick with fever you cried out for her several times."

"I did?"

"In your delirium, yes."

"She's not a girl...at least not like you're thinkin'. Sarah is Levi's mother, but she's sort of my mother as well. My real mother died givin' me birth. Sarah nursed me and helped raise me."

"Oh..." She paused to gather her thoughts. "I'm sorry ... about your mother I mean. Are you angry with me? I didn't really mean to pry."

"How could anyone ever by angry with you?" he chuckled and nearly choked on a mouthful of potatoes and onions. "All you'd need to do is smile and they'd melt," he added after regaining his breath.

Her only reply was the same melting smile he'd just described.

"Emily," he continued, "do you know what's happened with our army?"

"No, I pay no attention to armies."

"You don't?" Once again he shifted his head to gaze up into her eyes. "Whose side are you on?"

"Do I have to be on a side?"

"There's a war going on."

"I don't believe in war. We're Quakers, Wil. To participate in war would violate our faith. We've taken no one's side. Personally I think the whole thing is a tragic, tragic mistake."

"I guess I can understand that," he said, but as he studied her honey- blond hair and soft blue eyes her political and religious beliefs were the farthest things from his mind. "Haven't you heard any news? Surely you must see newspapers."

"We don't get many visitors out here. My father usually takes the buggy into Thurmont every ten days or so. I imagine he'll pick up newspapers on his next trip. You'll just have to wait until then for news of your army."

Both of them fell quiet after that. The only noise was Wil chewing up the last of his meal. No question but that he found her something of a mystery. She was probably the most beautiful girl he'd ever seen and her outward somewhat aggressive demeanor certainly did not suggest a strict religious upbringing. Yet the mere mention of war seemed to have the most profound impact on her.

"Wil," she spoke at last. "Why are you fighting in this war?" As she spoke her fingers gently traced the contours of the damaged cheekbone he'd suffered at Second Manassas.

"For my home," he replied without the slightest hesitation. "For Virginia. For Southern independence. For the same reasons Americans rebelled against British rule."

"Do you support slavery?"

"How can you even ask me that?" There was an incredulous tone in his voice. "Haven't you talked with Levi?"

"Some. He seems pretty taken with Naomi. They're together most of the time."

"Then you must know my father freed his parents and gave them their farm."

"He mentioned something like that."

"We were born weeks apart. We grew up together."

"Yes, but you still haven't answered my question. Are you fighting to preserve slavery?"

"No... No I am not. I'll be honest with you, I don't really have that strong an opinion on it one way or the other. I would never own another human being, but that's just me."

"I think it's evil."

"It may be, but that's not the reason I joined to fight."

"We've been part of the underground railroad for years."

"That's what Levi told me. He said there was a slave family here when he brought me in."

"There was. They were here for over a week. They were very sweet people. I pray God will stay with them."

"So do I. Do many come through here?"

"Many," she nodded.

"And you've always helped them?"

"Always."

"Doesn't that make you something of a rebel yourself?"

"I hadn't thought of it that way," she replied.

"You've been challenging the authority for years by your own admission. I'm challenging it by becoming a soldier and fighting for the independence of my state. So in some ways we are alike, though I'll admit we differ as to the reasons for doing the things we do."

"And the methods," she insisted. "Like I said before we are pacifists by nature. We've never taken up arms against anyone."

"I respect that, though I would argue there are circumstances when the taking up of arms becomes inevitable."

"To you maybe, not to me."

*   *   *   *   *   *   *

Five more days passed before Zebedee Havelin made his next trip to town. Rather than Thurmont, which was closer to home, he chose Frederick as his destination, which necessitated his being gone overnight.

Wil continued to gain strength and the wound in his hip showed no sign of infection. Unfortunately the hipbone itself would not mend quickly and he continued to be bedridden. Levi's shoulder wound had been tended to also and was healing quite rapidly. Fortunately it had not been infected nearly as badly as Wil's. Both of the Virginians had become quite taken with the young ladies they had encountered in their Catoctin sanctuary and they paid little attention to time as the days sped by.

Upon his return the elder Havelin was greeted with joy by his wife, daughter, and Naomi, who can best be described here as his benefactor. He brought home supplies that were typical of a family preparing for winter, but he also brought clothing, lots of it. Much of it would go to slaves who would be passing through on their way north. Some of it, however, had been acquired with specific people in mind, namely the two Rebel soldiers in his home. Their uniforms and vestiges of their military connection were taken and hidden away. Both of them now looked like the typical farm boys they were before the war, except one had a broken hip. This was important because it meant they no longer had to be hidden in the secret underground room. They were brought upstairs and given a spare room in which to reside while they recovered - a room which was blessed with ample sunlight all through the day.

Old man Havelin brought something else with him from Frederick, something he withheld until the two boys were attired in civilian garb and brought up from their dark and damp hiding place. Newspapers, a whole stack of them, were presented to the two to satisfy their curiosity about the fate of their army. There were papers from Baltimore, Washington, Philadelphia and Frederick it-self. "There's been a terrible battle" he said with a grim expression as he handed the stack of papers to Wil. "It took place on the 17th, the day after you arrived here. The two armies fought along Antietam creek near a town called Sharpsburg, right on the Potomac itself. Some are calling it the bloodiest single day of the war."

Wil took a paper and handed another to Levi. The broken hip made it difficult to sit so Wil had to remain prone in the bed. Fortunately the room was filled with light and warmth from the early autumn sun which eased the pain in his hip and made it easy to read. The entire Havelin family along with Naomi gathered in the room to watch while the two boys digested the news of this horrific battle.

"Seems like they mauled us pretty bad," observed Levi after scanning the headlines and a couple of paragraphs of an article from a Baltimore paper.

"Where did you learn to read?" asked the old man.

"His Pa taught me." Levi gestured toward Wil and returned to the article.

"This just doesn't make any sense," mumbled Wil who was reading a Philadelphia paper. "They make it sound like Lee was driven pellmell across the river, like we was routed or somethin'!"

"Perhaps that's what happened," said Mrs. Havelin.

"I don't think so," argued Wil. "Not Lee, not our army."

"How can you be so sure?"

"I just know. No Yankee army could have driven those boys into the river! As God is my witness this paper ain't printin' the truth!"

"Wil," Levi interrupted, "Look at these casualty estimates." He showed his paper to Wil and pointed to the figures.

"Now I'm sure they're lyin'!" huffed Covington. "We barely had that number when we crossed into Maryland! If that article is true there is no more Army of Northern Virginia. McClellan can walk straight to Richmond!"

"It shore don't seem likely," Levi shook his head.

"Lookee here!" Wil pointed excitedly at another article. "McClellan claims we lost 15,000 men on South Mountain! That's where me and Levi got wounded. I can tell you for a fact we never even had 15,000 men at South Mountain! McClellan has no idea what he's talkin' about!" He paused and read further. "Look at this! Now I know he's nuts! McClellan says Lee had over 100,000 at Antietam! That's absurd! I may not be a general but I've got an eye for numbers! We barely had 40,000 when we came into Maryland! Does he think another 60,000 soldiers just popped out of thin air?"

"Maybe the Rebels got more soldiers from Virginia," ventured Emily.

"Not likely," Wil shook his head in rather determined fashion. "The numbers just aren't there."

"Perhaps the boy is right," Old man Havelin chimed in. "From what I've read about McClellan he does seem to have a tendency to exaggerate his opponent's strength."

"You can say that again!" Wil nodded emphatically.

"Wil...Wil look at this!" Levi pointed to another article three pages deeper into the newspaper. "Says here Stonewall captured Harper's Ferry and took the whole garrison prisoner!"

"It does? Lemme see!"

"Well," said Mr. Havelin. "I can see there's much the two of you need to catch up on. We'll leave you in peace and check on you later."

For the next thirty minutes neither Wil nor Levi spoke as they lost themselves in the vast array of articles about South Mountain and Antietam. Each was lost in his concerns for friends and comrades. Was Miles still alive? Ivory? Gilbert? What about Reilly and his men, Armelin, the tiger from Louisiana, or Vaughn?

Levi tossed his newspaper on the bed and stepped to the window, staring out at the hills which were already showing the bright yellows and reds of autumn. "Gonna be an early winter this year," he muttered absently.

"How much of this stuff do you think is accurate?"

wondered Wil.

"Hard to say," came the reply. "Seems like the Yankees would want to put the best possible face on it no matter what happened. You know what I mean?"

"Makes sense," agreed Wil. "100,000 men! If Lee had had 100,000 men we'd be sittin' in Washington City right about now!"

"Most likely," sighed Levi. "Reckon we oughta face one thing, Wil. We're not gonna know what really happened till we get home, and we ain't gonna be gettin' home till you can walk again. That's gonna be awhile."

Another week passed and the signs of Autumn were hard to miss. Green was no longer the predominant color on the hillsides, replaced by a kaleidoscope of color - reds, oranges and yellows mostly. The days were still relatively warm but the nights were decidedly chilly.

"I don't remember it getting this cold so early in the season," observed Wil one night as he huddled beneath a pile of blankets.

"Old man Havelin said we could share the firewood so long as I help cut it," said Levi. "Reckon I'll start cuttin' tomorrow."

"I'd help if I could."

"Don't worry about it. I'm goin' soft just sittin' around here. I could use the work. From what I've read we're still south of the Mason-Dixon line, but not by much. Pennsylvania's only a few miles north of here. Reckon that's why it's so cold compared to home."

"Strange ain't it?" mused Wil. "I figure a hundred miles, maybe a little more, between us and home. It's amazing what that little bit of miles means in the differences of climate."

"I'll take the Shenandoah anytime," Levi smiled as the image of his farm and parents came to mind. "Hey, Wil," he glanced over at his bedridden companion."You think our folks have given us up for dead?"

"Don't know," Wil's brow furrowed as he contemplated this possibility. "Reckon we're probably listed as missing. If we was to write to our folks you think old man

Havelin could get the letters across the lines?"

"Won't hurt to ask," Levi's mood brightened considerably at the prospect of sending a letter to his parents. "At least then they'd know we wasn't dead."

In this regard they approached Zebedee Havelin later that same evening and were delighted by his response. He did indeed have contacts who would be willing to smuggle letters into Virginia. He couldn't guarantee delivery to the right address, but he could get them across the river. However, the prospect of return mail would be remote at best. He provided both young men with writing materials and reminded them not to write anything on the envelope or stationary which could possibly reveal their hiding place.

By the middle of October the hillsides were absolutely ablaze in color and the temperature continued to drop. The old Quaker farmer departed for Frederick again, this time bearing a letter to Tom Covington and another to Moses and Sarah Henry. Prior to his departure he had fashioned a crude crutch for Wil from a stout length of hickory, allowing the wounded Rebel to move about on his injured hip for the first time since the minie ball had been removed. For Wil, it was as though he was experiencing some sort of liberation. He began to move about quite freely. First he confined himself to the house itself, and the thumping of his crutch on the hardwood floors became a familiar sound. Then as he acquired more strength and confidence he ventured outside and began to wander around the farm, though he rarely wandered too far from the house. For the first time he felt alive again. Muscles which had atrophied during the long weeks of inactivity found tone and purpose once again. Emily was with him every day, always with her boundless warmth, offering encouragement and support as he grew stronger by the day.

It was early afternoon in late October. Wil and Emily were sitting together on the front porch. Levi and Naomi had just returned from a hike to the top of the hill which rose behind the Havelin home. Before coming in they stopped in the garden and busied themselves picking the last of the squash and pumpkins. There was a stiff breeze that day which whistled sharply through the trees shaking thousands of leaves from their lofty perches, scattering them across the landscape with carefree ease.

"Will you go back to the war?" Emily as usual was quite direct with her thoughts.

"I don't know," replied Wil after pondering the question for a moment or two, "I reckon so, if my hip will heal enough to let me move again."

"I was afraid you'd say that," she took her eyes from him and stared out into the woods.

"You've got somethin' else in mind?" he probed.

"It's not proper for me to say," again she glanced away.

"But you're thinkin' it," he pressed. "You're thinkin' you don't want me to go."

"Suppose I am?" she huffed. "Does it make any difference to you?"

"Sure does!" he grinned. "Even if I go that don't mean I can't come back someday. The war won't last forever. Sooner or later one side or the other will win. Then I'll be able to come back for you."

"If you're not dead." She stared straight at him.

"Well...yeah...I guess so."

Several minutes passed during which neither of them spoke. Both were staring down the long dirt lane which led to the road which led in turn toward Thurmont or Frederick, depending on which fork you wanted to take. Zebedee Havelin was due back that afternoon and they'd been watching for his buggy to appear around the bend.

"Wil," she nudged him on the shoulder to get his attention.

"Yes?" he turned and their eyes met.

"Did you just propose to me? I mean...Do you want me to wait for you?"

Wil blushed beet red and found himself fumbling for the right words. "I...I don't know...I mean Yes! I mean...I guess I did, didn't I?"

"It sounded that way to me," she suggested.

"Well," he tried to think but the image of her face and those soft blue eyes filled his mind. "Well," he repeated. "I suppose I did say something like that. Anyway...um...will you?"

"Yes!" Her answer burst from her mouth and she leaned over to kiss him. Their lips met and that one moment seemed to freeze in time. It was not the first time they had kissed - in truth they had managed to steal a number of kisses over the last two weeks - but this one was special. Perhaps it was due to their open admission of love or his awkward attempt at a marriage proposal. Perhaps it was the way she parted her lips as she had never done before, or perhaps the way her mouth clung to his long after they should have broken. "I want a proper wedding!" she insisted after finally pulling away. "Since I'm the baby of the family all of my brothers and sisters will want to be there!" She was the youngest of seven. Two had died before seeing their tenth birthday. The others were grown with families of their own.

"I suppose we'll be able to manage that," The thought of so many future in-laws boggled his mind at first.

"And flowers," she continued. "Lots of flowers."

"Guaranteed," he grinned.

She smiled in obvious pleasure and leaned over to kiss him again when she spied her father's buggy coming around the bend in the lane. "Father!" she gasped as she sat back in her rocking chair and straightened her dress and apron.

Wil glanced quickly in that direction. "Sho'nuff" he nodded, "Looks like he's movin' right along too." He reached for his crutch and pulled himself to his feet with a groan. "I wonder if there's been another battle."

"I hope not," she whispered, "too many people have already died."

Old man Havelin didn't slow the buggy down until he was about to draw abreast of the porch. His aged face was flushed with excitement and his long white hair was in wild disarray as he jerked the reins back and brought the horse to an abrupt halt. "Lincoln has freed the slaves!" he cried excitedly. "I brought all the papers! He's freed the slaves! Emily, where is your mother?"

"Inside, father."

"Fetch her at once!" He took his eyes from his daughter and gazed at the two Blacks approaching from the garden each carrying a basket laden with squash and pumpkins. "Naomi! Did you hear me? You're free! You're all free!"

Naomi could scarcely believe her ears. Several months had passed since she slipped away from the plantation near Milledgville, Georgia. Not an easy night had she enjoyed since. Always she was glancing over her shoulder wondering if the next sound or the next face would be that of a lawman determined to send her back into bondage. Only since Levi's arrival had she started to feel secure. The moments they shared together made her feel alive and even more important, protected. The words from Zebedee Havelin were like music to her ears. Could it be true? Was she now truly free? Were those she left behind now free as well? She felt as though a huge weight was being lifted from her shoulders. Her heart began to pound inside her breast and she wanted to cry out for joy.

All was excitement and curiosity on the front porch of the Havelin home as questions came from every throat. As Wil and Levi exchanged glances each could read the questions and misgivings in the others eyes.

"No more questions!" The old man's voice fairly boomed across the yard. "All the talk in Frederick is about this Emancipation." he continued. "Let us all go inside and read for ourselves. Emily, take the buggy over to the barn and tend to the horse."

"Yes, father."

"I'll help," Wil quickly volunteered.

"We'll be inside waiting for you. Mother, is supper to be served anytime soon? I believe I'm quite famished."

"Within the hour, dear. There's a ham in the oven,

but I need more firewood."

"I'll bring a couple of armloads," said Levi.

"Very good." The old man offered an approving nod.

Within thirty minutes all were gathered inside, their eyes glued to the many newspaper stories about Lincoln's Emancipation Proclamation. Dinner was soon served but it was impossible to gather around a table. Too many other things were on their minds. Barbara Havelin simply made the food available and allowed people to serve themselves, all save Zebedee, whose plate she fixed in meticulous fashion.

For poor Naomi this was a trying time. She had never learned to read and found those moments horribly frustrating. The Havelins had tried to teach her but the going was slow. She had learned a few words, but not yet enough to handle a newspaper. Levi read some of it out loud but his preference was to read silently to himself and ponder each sentence as it passed before his eyes. Naomi could only wait, her impatience growing by the minute.

Wil Covington was first to break the silence. "This doesn't free a single slave," he pronounced.

"What?" Naomi's eyes widened in fear. "What did you say?"

"I'm sorry," Wil looked over at her. "I don't say this to hurt you, and I wouldn't wish slavery on you or anybody else, but this document does nothing for you or any other slave."

"Those are rash words, boy," said the old man. "Are you and I reading the same document?"

"Yessuh, we are, though perhaps we're readin' it from different perspectives."

"Would you kindly explain yours?" pressed Havelin.

"Gladly," came the reply. "What country does Mr. Lincoln lead?"

"The United States of course."

"That's my first point. I may be young, Mr. Havelin, and I may not be as wise and educated as yourself, but I can see what's right in front of my face. It is not an

Emancipation. It's an ultimatum. It does not apply to the United States, where he does have the authority to act. It doesn't even apply to those parts of the Confederacy presently under Union occupation. It's meant to apply only in those parts of the Confederacy which are still resisting Federal rule 100 days from now, or from whenever he wrote this. So I say again: it does not free a single slave. It's designed to have authority only in those places where Mr. Lincoln has no authority."

"The president does not accept that you people are out of the Union," countered Havelin. "Rebels you may be, but outside of the Union you are not, at least according to President Lincoln. Therefore his authority applies to everyone in the United States, including those places still not conquered."

"He can think that if he wants," argued Wil, "I reckon all of you can. But the fact remains we have left the Union. We are a separate country, the Confederate States of America. Mr. Lincoln's proclamations and orders do not apply to us. He has freed no slaves."

"Well," admitted Havelin. "I suppose we hold differing views on the matter."

Sensing an advantage or suddenly feeling a confidence he had rarely known Wil decided to press his case further. "Consider this: does this document free the slaves of Maryland?"

"It doesn't seem to."

"Kentucky? Missouri? Delaware?"

"Apparently not."

"What about those parts of the Confederacy which the Federals occupy? Northeastern Virginia, for instance, or Southern Louisiana?"

"It doesn't seem to apply."

"I think Maybe Wil's got a point," Levi looked up from his paper for the first time. "Yankees down in Louisiana is puttin' escaped slaves in this big camp. Word we get is that they're dyin' by the hundreds."

"It's true," nodded Wil, "they're also usin' slaves on the sugar and cotton plantations they've captured."

"I hadn't heard that."

"Course not! These papers are the same ones that said we had 100,000 men at Antietam! The point, suh, is this: Wherever Mr. Lincoln could have freed slaves he didn't. That's a fact."

"So it seems," said Havelin.

"That ain't all," Levi also felt more emboldened than he had in quite some time. "Mr. Lincoln makes it pretty clear that it ain't abolition he's seekin', it's an end to our rebellion. Look at this!" he paused and pointed rather forcefully at a particular paragraph in one of the articles. "He says his goal is still voluntary colonization. He wants us black folks to go somewhere else!" He paused again and looked directly at Naomi whose face did little to mask the confusion swirling around inside of her. "Would you want that? Would you want freedom with a boat ticket to some place else? Africa maybe?"

At the mention of Africa, Naomi turned and met Levi's eyes. "I don't even know where Africa is," she whispered. "I'm an American. That's what I want to be...an American, Levi. I won't go back to bein' anyone's slave."

"Yeah, well I ain't goin' nowhere either! Africa or anyplace else! Been free all my life and I got me a farm to go home to!"

"The more I read this the more it smells," said Wil. "It smells like politics. This is all a political game. It's a smokescreen to divert people's attention from the real reasons we left the Union."

"That may be," nodded Havelin, "but if it is I predict it will prove most effective. Lincoln is no fool. He has tried to place the United States on a moral high ground. What European country will recognize your country now?"

Wil's spirits sank as he saw the truth in the old man's words.

"And without recognition from the British or French, I predict your chances for success in this struggle are remote at best."

To this Wil could find no reply.

"Naomi," Levi was looking at still another section of the proclamation. "Your master, does he support the Confederacy? Is he in our army?"

She glanced over at him with an inquisitive look. "He wears a uniform. He's a captain or somethin' like that, but he's not in the regular army. He calls it something else...a state something or other."

"Militia," offered Wil.

"Yes...militia... that's it."

"According to this, at least as I read it, if he were to declare his loyalty for the Union and renounce the Confederacy by the first of next year he could still claim you as a slave. In other words you could be sent back to him, assuming he would switch sides."

"I don't think he'll do that," she said calmly, but inside she found herself deeply troubled at the prospect. What if he did? "I'll kill myself first," she looked away and stared out the window.

"Maybe you should move farther north," suggested Emily. "In Canada you'd be safe no matter what your master does."

"Do you want me to leave?"

"No, of course not. I love having you here. I just want you to be safe and it scares me to hear you talk about killing yourself."

Naomi looked back at Levi. "I want to stay here," she declared.

"I found something I find worrisome," Barbara Havelin spoke for the first time. "This clause," She paused and tapped the newspaper, "as it reads it would seem to invite the slaves in the Rebel areas to rise up and slay their masters. That will only lead to more violence, more death."

"It's total war, that's all it is," said Wil. "Lincoln's usin' every weapon he can think of."

"And this one will ultimately prove effective, mark my words," said Havelin, but his tone seemed devoid of any satisfaction with his own words. "Whether it frees slaves or not."

Shortly thereafter the discussion drew to a close. The feelings of those present ran through a gamut of conflicting emotions. The two rebel soldiers felt both confusion and resentment. The elder Havelins were both ambivalent about this proclamation of Lincoln's. They felt joy that a step was finally being taken to abolish a system they abhorred, yet they wondered if it would truly accomplish this goal, since the abolition of slavery seemed to be secondary to Lincoln's true goal - the salvation of the Union. They were also apprehensive over the possibility of horrific violence if slaves resorted to uprisings against slave-holders. As for Naomi, she felt no safer than she had prior to this news. Moreover she couldn't escape the feeling that she and her people were being used, that they were merely tools in a much larger game. Her mind was full of questions for which there didn't seem to be any answers. Wordlessly she rose and left the room. Pausing at the front door she retrieved her woolen shawl from a hook on the wall and wrapped it tightly about her shoulders. Then she stepped out to the porch and walked to the rail. With a heavy sigh she leaned against a verticle support and stared out into the night.

"What are you thinkin'?" Levi had approached her from behind and put one arm around her shoulder.

She looked up into his broad, handsome face. "I don't know," she sighed, "lots of things...just wonderin' where all of this is gonna take us."

"Hmmm," he nodded as he pulled her closer. "Chilly tonight. We can see our breath."

"I know," she smiled, glancing up at the vast array of stars which filled the night sky. "Look up there, Levi. They're so close we could almost touch 'em."

"It's a beautiful night," he agreed with a smile.

"Will I ever be free?" She asked in a suddenly somber tone.

"I think so," he affirmed. "You want my gut feelin?"

"Uh-huh."

"I think slavery's days are numbered no matter

who wins this war. Too many things are changin' too fast for slavery to survive. You'll see. Mark my words."

"I'll do that," she nudged his ribs with an elbow.

For several minutes they stood there in silence, awe-struck by the celestial dance taking place over their heads.

"Will you keep fightin' for the South?" She asked at last.

"As long as I'm able."

"Despite President Lincoln's paper?"

"I'm a Virginian," he replied calmly.

"I had a feelin' you'd say somethin' like that."

"What about you? You think you might like Virginia?"

She shifted in his arms to face him. "Just what does that mean?"

"It means I'd like to come back here someday, come back and bring you home...my home...our home."

"Are you serious?"

"Sho'nuff."

"You want me to be your wife?"

"Yep. Someday you'll be free. Someday this war will be over. If I live through it, I want you to be my wife. Will you?"

"That's a lot of ifs, Levi," she laid her head against his chest and wrapped her arms around his back. "If the Lord's willin', I reckon I am too."

This reply brought a smile to Levi's lips. Holding her tightly against his chest he glanced once more at the dazzling stars and mouthed a silent prayer.

*   *   *   *   *   *   *

December came and with it the howling cold of winter. Wil's hip had improved to the point at which he could walk without a crutch. He and Levi had even begun to talk of making their way back home so that they might rejoin the army of Northern Virginia which they knew to be dug in south of the Rappahannock River. Other ties had grown however, and both boys felt a certain reluc-tance to part company with the two girls who had come into their lives, the escaped slave and the Quaker. Accordingly they postponed their decision and kept thinking of reasons not to start their journey south.

Christmas was fast approaching and snow covered the hills of north-central Maryland. One afternoon Wil helped Levi cut and split a substantial pile of wood before sundown. It was the first physically demanding challenge he'd faced during his prolonged recovery from the shattered hip. Though he pronounced himself satisfied with his ability to wield an axe and carry wood, tell-tale signs from his hip told him he may have overdone it and there would be a price to be paid that very night.

Not long after dark the aching pain in his hip had reached a bone grinding crescendo. The exercise combined with the frigid, damp weather left him groaning out loud and threatened to immobilize him completely. It was Barbara Havelin who came to his rescue. She and Levi helped him up to his bed which Emily had piled high with quilts and coverlets. As they made him comfortable Mrs. Havelin turned to leave. "I'll be back shortly," she said in departing, "and I think I know just the thing for you."

Shortly turned out to be about twenty minutes. In her hands was a small rectangular object which was wrapped in a thick towel. Wil eyed the object curiously and quickly posed his question. "What is that?"

"A brick."

"A brick?"

"Exactly. It's been sitting on top of the wood stove for the last quarter hour. It's quite hot." She reached the side of the bed and put the shrouded brick down at once. "Roll over on your good side." She instructed.

Wil was hardly in a position to argue. Besides, he could already see the logic in what she had in mind. He rolled over on his left side and pulled the covers away. Barbara Havelin proceeded to lay the towel-encased brick directly on the injured hip. The effect was instant as heat radiated at once through his bones. "Oh, yes!" he sighed and a smile appeared on his face as the pain disappeared in a wave of warmth. "Praise the Lord," he whispered, "that feels so good, so very good..."

"Should that become too hot put a thin blanket underneath it."

"I will," he said, "but right now I can't imagine it being too hot."

"Good," she smiled. "I'll go put another one on the stove. We'll get you back on your feet by morning."

Indeed they did, but by mid-afternoon the old man had returned from a brief saunter to Thurmont. As usual, he brought newspapers and this time there was word of another major battle: Fredericksburg. To the Quaker family, this news brought only sorrow for it meant the deaths and maiming of thousands of young Americans in Blue and Gray. To Wil and Levy the news was promising. Even the northern newspapers found it difficult to mask the one-sided nature of Lee's victory at Fredericksburg, and the two Virginia farm boys found ample criticism of the Federal commander, General Burnside.

However, the news of this victory also aroused some measure of guilt in the two Rebel soldiers. Both were of the opinion that they belonged with their comrades in the field, that they shouldn't be enjoying the comforts of this warm Maryland home while their friends were enduring the harsh winter in flimsy tents. When they announced their decision to leave they were besieged by protests from every quarter but they held firm in their decision. Nevertheless it was Zebedee Havelin, ever the ruler of his own house, who had the final word. "You will share Christmas with us," he declared in a tone which allowed no room for arguments, "then I will arrange to help you back into Virginia."

Three days after Christmas, the two southern soldiers bid farewells to the Havelins and their home. In their rush to leave it was difficult for Wil and Levi to find time alone with the young women who had stolen their hearts. When they found time to be alone, tears were shed and promises made, but everybody knew the war itself would have the final word on any promise shared among these young people as 1863 approached and winter took an even harsher grip on a divided land.

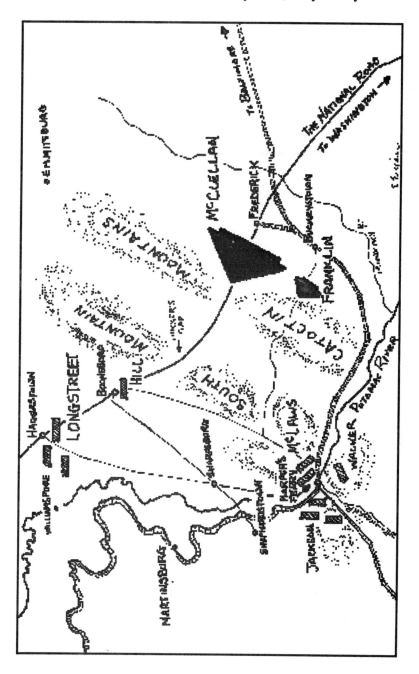

~ Chapter Five ~
The Telling of Sharpsburg

"**H**ey, Boys!" Corporal Gilbert thrust his head into the bulky white tent which housed a half-dozen Confederate soldiers. "Look what the wind blew in!" He opened the tent flap and stood to one side as Wil Covington and Levi Henry stepped in.

"Wil!" Miles Turner was grinning from ear to ear, "Levi! You good-for-nuthin' polecat! I done gave both you boys up for dead! Where you been?"

"Maryland," replied Wil, who returned Mile's grin as his eyes scanned the familiar faces in the tent. "I got hit at South Mountain. Levi saved my life, him and another fella name of Vaughn. I've been recuperatin' the last couple of months in a farmhouse northwest of Frederick. Some real grand folks took care of us."

"Whose side they on?"

"Side? Nobody's I guess. They're Quakers. They try not to get involved in wars, but I guess we involved them a little bit."

"I guess so!" Miles was obviously pleased to see them again. "How bad you hurt?" he gestured toward the crutch which Wil still used to keep the weight off of his right hip.

"It was pretty bad for awhile. I took a minie ball in the hip. The old man...Zebedee, the one who owned the farm...he's the one who pulled the bullet from my hip, but the bone was all busted up. It took me a spell to get back on both feet again. I can walk, just not as straight nor as fast as before."

"Hell, boy!" Miles broke out into a laugh. "If memory serves me you couldn't walk all that straight or fast before you got shot! Last time I saw you was when you fell off the road and sprained your ankle. You remember that?"

"Sure do," Wil glanced away a little sheepishly, thinking he had a fair idea as to what was coming next.

"Now just how do you fall off of a perfectly good road, can you tell me that?"

"Don't know, Miles, just lucky I guess."

"Lucky? Must not have been too lucky cause it

stuck you on South Mountain."

"And got his hip all shot to pieces," added Levi.

"No matter," Miles groaned as he pulled himself to his feet. "Point is you're both alive, you both look half- way healthy and you're back with us! Welcome home, boys! Now you can freeze like the rest of us!" He hugged both of them in turn. "Shore did miss you boys. Did I tell you I'm the last? I'm the only one left out of the gang from Suffolk that signed up outside Richmond. Been feelin' awful lonely around here."

"He ain't been the same since Sharpsburg," noted Gilbert.

"Yeah, but I'm feelin' better now! You boys hungry? I hope not cause there ain't much to offer ya."

Actually, they were both hungry, though famished might be a better word for it. With the help of old man Havelin, they had managed to secure a ride across the frigid waters of the Potomac River in a small rowboat. They had crossed into Virginia just below Point of Rocks. From there they made their way to Leesburg covering much of the ground on foot at a pace which was slow to say the least. Once in Leesburg they were able to meet with men who rode under the command of John Singleton Mosby, the "Gray Ghost." With the help of Mosby's rangers they moved by horseback and wagon across the mountains into the Shenandoah Valley near Winchester. Here they struck South getting close to Harrisonburg before re-crossing the mountains to link up with the Army of Northern Virginia.

Aside from the welcome given to them by their comrades, there was little else about their return which could be described as warm. In point of fact they were freezing. Neither Wil nor Levi had uniforms or parts thereof, though Levi still had the revolver he'd taken from the Union officer at Second Manassas. The tent which housed their friends did shield them to some degree from the winds, but this didn't change the bone-chilling cold of the air itself. Blankets were offered to both men and before long they looked just like their comrades with rags wrapped around their heads and hands, blankets draped over their shoulders and clutched tightly about their throats. More blankets were dropped on the frozen ground and on these the newly returned soldiers tried to make themselves comfortable.

Through most of the night they swapped tales. Levi and Wil were asked to recount their adventures several times before their friends tired of hearing the story. Since Fredericksburg had been the most recent battle, the two boys were treated to a host of stories about this confrontation between Burnside and Lee, a clash which the Southerners won handily. From the outside their tent might have seemed like a steam bath, what with all the frosty vapors visible each time someone exhaled or laughed. Thus did they spend their first night back with the army.

The next day brought something of a warming trend in that the temperature actually rose to 10 degrees above the freezing mark. Wil and Levi reported to the quartermaster to procure new uniforms and weapons. Whereupon they sought out Lemuel Vaughn, both to insure themselves that he had survived the fighting in Maryland and Fredericksburg, and to thank him again for his efforts in helping them avoid capture after South Mountain. They found him alive and well and spent close to an hour with him recounting their adventures since the three parted company back in September. Then they moved on to look for more familiar faces.

Wil's hip wasn't bothering him too badly and he found himself able to walk without the help of a crutch and with only a slight limp. This did much to buoy his spirits as they moved from one camp to another. By mid-afternoon they were wandering back to their own regiment and spied Miles trying his hand at still another game of poker with Armelin, the Louisiana "Tiger."

"Armelin!" cried Wil. "How do?"

The Louisianan glanced up at Wil and a wide smile appeared on his face as he recognized Wil and Levi. "Howdy, boys! Long time no see! In fact, I didn't think to ever see the two of you again. Someone told me you bought it on South Mountain."

"Almost," replied Levi, "but not quite."

"Glad to see it," Armelin nodded enthusiastically, "Care to join the game?"

"Nope," returned Wil with a chuckle, "unlike some people we know there's a limit to our ability to lose money."

"We ain't playin' for money no more," Armelin glanced over at Miles with a mischievous grin."I done cleaned him out long ago. As of now he owes me his salary for the next... What is it? Year? Thirteen months?"

"Seven months," said Miles glumly.

"Only seven? Maybe we ought to start playin' for money again."

"Then again, maybe not," replied Turner.

Wil and Levi joined the other two but not their game of cards. After awhile the conversation began to orient toward the recent battles and Wil suddenly realized they had heard nothing thus far about the battle in Maryland at Antietam.

"Hey, Miles," he said, "Can you tell us what happened at Antietam?"

Turner closed the hand he was holding and laid these cards face down on the cold barren ground.

"Where?" He asked.

"Antietam...you know the battle where y'all were pinned against the Potomac."

"You mean Sharpsburg," said Miles calmly.

"Sharpsburg," repeated Wil with a nod, "the Yankees call it Antietam. What happened? All we know is what we read in northern newspapers. They claim it a victory. You wouldn't believe the stuff we read...outrageous claims. Can you set us straight?"

A somber expression took hold of Turner's face, creating a change as distinct as that which might be experienced when a thick cloud passes in front of the sun. "Sharpsburg," he mused, "I reckon I could tell you what happened with me at Sharpsburg. That's where I ended up as the last of the Suffolk boys. But somethin' tells me that's not what you're hankerin' to hear. You want to know what happened. That right?"

"More or less. We've only heard one version, the one that says we lost."

"We didn't lose, boy," said Armelin, "I can guarantee you that."

"Listen," Miles glanced over at Wil, "if you're lookin' to hear about Sharpsburg I think I know who you should be listenin' to." He paused and rose to his feet, stretching his hands high overhead and yawning loudly. "You comin', Tiger?"

"Hell Yeah!" Linscombe reached down, retrieved his cards and carefully put the deck away. "If Ivory's gonna tell Sharpsburg again, I don't want to miss it."

"Ivory?" Levi's face broke out into a wide smile, "He's still alive?"

"Shore is!" grinned Miles. "That ol' boy is indestructible! Did you know he got away from the Yankees?"

"Got away?" Quizzed Wil, "We didn't even know he was captured."

"He wasn't! That's the point! C'mon, let's go find Ivory. He can tell you all about it himself."

"Let's do it!" Levi jumped to his feet and offered an arm to help Wil up.

Within twenty minutes they located Ivory. The heavyset bald slave from South Carolina was busy replacing a shorn buckle on a harness for one of the mules of his team.

"Hey, Ivory!" called Miles, "Look what the wind blew in!"

Ivory turned and at once he spied Wil and Levi. "Lawd have mercy!" he exclaimed as his eyes lit up with joy. "I never thought to see the two of you again! I figured you was either dead or off in some Yankee prison camp! Welcome home boys! By God, welcome home!" He dropped the harness and took both boys in his burly arms at the same time, squeezing the breath out of them with a fierce bear hug.

"Hold on, Ivory!" laughed Levi as he struggled to

breathe. "You'd best loosen your grip a little or we'll both be pushin' up daisies!"

Ivory let them go at once and stepped back a pace. "Lemme look at ya," he demanded, "Y'all look awful damn good! Well fed! Who's been cookin' for ya?"

"Some folks up in Maryland," said Wil.

"Well they did a right smart job," smiled the black man. "You boys got more meat on your bones than most of the steers I been cuttin' up."

"We came to hear about Sharpsburg," explained Wil.

"Oh...Sharpsburg," Ivory's expression changed at once. Where joy had danced in his eyes there was now both sadness and something else. Was it pride? "A mean fight that one," he said with a nod of his head, "and now you want to hear about it, eh?"

"Miles said you were the one to talk to."

"Did he now?" Ivory glanced over at Turner.

"Hell, Ivory," said Miles, "ain't nobody in camp can tell Sharpsburg like you! Who else would I send them to?"

Ivory shifted his attention back to the two soldiers who had just rejoined their army. "You boys got some time?" he asked.

"Seems like we got the rest of the afternoon free."

"Do tell? Gather round the fire yonder and make yourselves comfortable. This might take awhile. Sharpsburg was one of the longest days this army has ever had and we left a lot of good boys up there...a lot of 'em."

"Miles says you got away from the Yankees," said Levi, "Can you tell us about that first?"

"I suppose I can," the older black man snatched up a heavy pot and some cooking utensils, and as he prepared to start a batch of soup he continued talking. "Did y'all hear anythin' about Harper's Ferry?"

"The only thing we know about the whole campaign after South Mountain is what we read in northern newspapers," explained Wil, "and a lot of what we read didn't make much sense. According to McClellan we lost more men on South Mountain than we ever had there in the first place."

"That a fact?" Ivory glanced over at Wil, all the while continuing his preparation for the soup.

"Sho'nuff," nodded Levi. "He also said we had over one hundred thousand men at Antietam."

"Sharpsburg, boy, Sharpsburg," corrected Ivory, "the Yankees call it Antietam; not us."

"Sorry," Levi grinned sheepishly.

"A hundred thousand, eh?" chuckled Ivory. "Reckon that'll give you an idea of how we fought at Sharpsburg. The most we ever had at any one time was about forty thousand, if that."

"We knew that," offered Wil. "That's what we told the folks who took care of us."

"Good!" grunted Ivory. "Set them folks straight. Now, about Harper's Ferry, Stonewall captured the place with its whole garrison, except some of the cavalry. They got out before the surrender."

"Kinda like Forrest at Fort Donelson," commented Wil.

"'Bout like that," agreed Ivory. "But the ones that got out, they was the ones I had to run from."

"What happened?"

"Well now, it's kinda complicated. Marse Robert had us spread all over creation. When you boys started feelin' the heat up on that mountain Marse Robert called for General Longstreet for help. Longstreet was in Hagerstown and that's where I was along with most of the wagons in the army. We started east straight away and I reckon we was due north of Harper's Ferry when those Yankee cavalrymen hit us. I'm tellin' ya, it was all I could do to keep my wits about me! Bullets was flyin'. Teamsters was gettin' shot. Mules were goin' down. Don't know when I've ever been so scared!"

"How'd you get away?" pressed Levi.

"By the Grace of God! I swear it! I got every bit of speed out of them mules, I'll warrant you that! We lost forty-three wagons to the bluecoats but the rest of us got away. Wasn't a pretty picture...sure wasn't!" By this time

Ivory had cut up some old dried potatoes and a generous portion of beef from a recently slaughtered steer. All of this he threw into the soup as well as a canvas sack full of dried black-eyed peas. To this concoction he added salt, pepper, and a special mixture of spices. "That oughta get it started," he nodded approvingly and stepped back from the fire, reaching down to his woodpile to add an armful of quartered logs to the flames. "We gonna eat fine tonight!" he observed with a grin. "Now where were we?"

"Sharpsburg," said Miles.

"Oh yeah! Well now...when it looked like we couldn't hold that mountain any longer Marse Robert put us on the march again. We didn't know where we was goin', but most folks figured we was headin' for Virginia. Then we heard 'bout Harper's Ferry and we knew Stonewall and his boys would be joinin' us pretty quick and we kinda figured General Lee wouldn't be inclined to leave Maryland without at least takin' a swipe at the Federals. I'm tellin' you, if there's a bolder man in either army than Robert E. Lee, I ain't met him yet and neither have you. Lemme see now, who did I hear say that?" He paused and scratched the back of his thick neck. "Alexander!" He exclaimed. "General Alexander...two months back I heard him say, `audacity, thy name is Lee'."

"What's audacity?" asked a young soldier who had just joined the gathering by the fire.

"Boldness, boy," smiled Ivory, "Sheer boldness!"

"What's goin' on over there?" The question was shouted by a sergeant standing by a cluster of tents about twenty yards away.

"Ivory's tellin' Sharpsburg!" Miles turned and hollered the reply.

"Tell him to hold on! I got me some new boys in camp. They'll want to hear this!"

"Bring em on!" Beamed Ivory with a wide grin. "Reckon I need to stir the soup some anyway," he said to those already gathered.

Several minutes later four newcomers became part of the ever-growing audience. They weren't the only ones.

From behind Wil came a familiar voice, "Hey, boy did you decide to take a vacation for three months?"

Wil turned around and found himself looking directly into the face of Seth Reilly of the Stonewall Brigade. The scar from the saber slash he'd suffered at Second Manassas was still quite visible on Reilly's face, but his smile had lost none of its warmth.

"Professor!" Greeted Wil, "Glad to see you're still here, and by the way, we weren't on vacation. I got hit at South Mountain."

"I heard. Good to see you made it back. You remember Ox?" Reilly gestured at the big man on his left.

"Who could ever forget Ox?" laughed Levi.

"And Corporal Simmons," Reilly nodded toward the man on his right.

"Good to see all of you again," said Wil.

"We heard Ivory was tellin' Sharpsburg," explained Reilly. "I don't much care for readin' about it but whenever Ivory tells it I like to be on hand. He can tell a story like nobody I've ever seen."

"He can at that," agreed Wil, "Me and Levi don't really know what happened there. Reckon we're about to find out."

"You're in for a treat," confirmed Reilly.

By this time more than twenty soldiers were gathered around the fire and someone had rolled a right good sized stump over for Ivory to stand on. He climbed up and looked out over his highly attentive audience. "Where was I?" he pondered while running one hand across the smooth expanse of his head.

"You was tellin' us how bold Marse Robert is," offered a soldier from the opposite side of the fire.

"Oh, yes," nodded Ivory, "Marse Robert decided not to retreat across the Potomac, but to stand and fight. We marched to the town of Sharpsburg so close to the river you could smell the water. There's a wide deep creek runs through that territory. A creek they call Antietam. Marse Robert had our boys dig in on the west side of that creek. We didn't have long to wait, I tell you that! 'Fore the afternoon was out the Yanks was right on us. You know somethin'? If they had hit us that first afternoon they mighta done us in. We didn't even have twenty-thousand men at that point and I hear tell the Yankees might have outnumbered us by four to one!"

"How come they didn't charge?" asked one of the soldiers.

"Lord only knows. Maybe it was the time of day. It was pretty late in the afternoon and they probably figured they couldn't get much done'fore dark. Anyway, if Wil over there is right, they thought we had over one-hundred-thousand men at Sharpsburg. Ain't that right, Wil?"

"That's what we read in their papers."

"We figured they'd come for sho' next day but they didn't. They shot cannons at us and we did the same at them, but nobody came at us so we just kept waitin'."

"Were y'all dug in all along that creek?" asked Wil.

"No, suh, not at all, 'cept for the far right side of our line. They were right on the water practically. The rest of the line angled away from the creek by a considerable distance, and behind us was the river...remember that."

Wil nodded and formed a mental image of the terrain and the two respective lines of battle.

"All of us was tense that night. The field hospitals was all set up. All the wagons and animals was down by the river. Seemed like nobody could sleep. Everyone knew they'd hit us the next day. That would've been the 17th of September. We were all wonderin' who would still be alive when the sun went down on the 17th."

Ivory paused a moment and stepped down from his stump to stir the soup again, adding a couple of pieces of wood to the fire before climbing back up to resume his story.

"Sharpsburg was a strange battle," he continued, "Seems like it wasn't one battle at all but three separate battles one after another. They went after our left first, then the middle, and finally the right. I'll tell ya somethin', them Yankees thought they had us. Thought they was gonna push us right into that ol' river. Reckon we showed 'em different."

"Reckon we did!" echoed a soldier from somewhere in the circle.

"We all knew they'd hit us on the left first," explained Ivory. "Hood and his Texans were out there alone the first night. Stonewall showed up from Harper's Ferry the next day and Marse Robert sent him out to take over on the left. That's where I was when the sun came up on the 17th. Lemme tell ya what the place looked like first. Get a picture in your minds now, hear? There was a road comin' out of Sharpsburg headin' up toward Hagerstown. Maybe a mile or so north of the town there's a little church right next to the road. A Dunker church it was, not much to look at just a small white buildin', that's all. Just above the church was a big ol' corn field and there was woods on either side of the corn. The folks up there call 'em the West Wood and the East Wood. That's where Jackson was.

"Now the night befo' the fight got started General Hood went to see General Lee. He was askin' permission to pull his men back from the line so they could cook up some rations. His boys hadn't had but a half- ration of beef in three days. They was hungry and worn out and needed to eat real bad. General Lee didn't have no reserves to call on. There wouldn't be nobody to take Hood's place so Marse Robert sent him on up to Stonewall. Jackson said he'd spread his line even thinner so the Texans could eat. Hood and his boys pulled back to the Dunker churchyard and started up a bunch of cook fires. That's where I was. I saw General Hood but I didn't get no chance to talk to him or hear what he was sayin'. I was busy fryin' up dough and bacon for his boys." He paused here to gather his thoughts and after several moments had passed he resumed speaking.

"Seems like that night was the longest of my life. Hardly anyone slept. A lot of them boys knew they wouldn't be alive when the fight ended and they refused to spend their final hours sleepin'. Dawn finally came but it shore wasn't much to look at. The sky was everywhere gray and there was a heavy mist in the air - not quite rain mind you but definitely not dry. We heard the muskets first, thousands of 'em. Then the cannons - oh, God; were those cannons terrible to behold! The roar of them Yankee guns is somethin' I'll never forget! The ground shook under our feet and the air...the air was filled with the whistlin' of them shells. They crashed into the woods and the cornfield where Stonewall's boys were dug in. We were scared, I'm tellin' ya that! Every damn one of us, even the cooks like me! I musta said every prayer I knew a hundred times or better. But I tell you what, Stonewall's boys may have been scared but they didn't lose heart, and heart's one thing them boys got plenty of! They're the same boys who held off Pope's whole army back in August at Manasses and they knew they could do it again. Yessuh, they knew it!"

Despite the cool temperatures of that afternoon a thin sheen of sweat appeared on Ivory's face and head as he began to lose himself in his story, becoming more animated with every passing minute. "The sound of them big guns was fierce enough," he declared, "but the sound wasn't near as terrible as what those guns was doin' to our boys on the ground. I snuck up closer to see for myself and the sight done chilled the blood in my veins! Trees and soldiers was fallin' all over the place and the cornfield...Lemme tell you boys somethin', Hell couldn't be no worse than what was goin' on in that cornfield. You ask some of the boys what lived through it, they'll tell you true!"

"Well, what happened?" A young impatient voice sounded out somewhere on the fringe of the crowd, which was still getting bigger as more soldiers continued to drift in the direction of Ivory's cook fire.

"Well now, be patient, young fella," Ivory searched for the source of the question but could do no better than to address himself in a certain direction. "I'm gettin' there. Lemme see now," he paused to scratch his head and reflect a moment, "where was I?"

"The cornfield!" someone cried.

"Oh yeah! The cornfield! It was Hooker's whole

corps comin' at us straight down from the North. They was three, maybe four hundred yards off...Blue uniforms as far as you could see, thick as flies! And then they stopped. Up came their guns again. I think there was more'n thirty of 'em. They opened up on us and then another line of guns started firin' at us from our right, way up on the ridge across Antietam creek. They had us caught in a crossfire and it seemed like they was aimin' everything right at that cornfield! Pure Hell it was and I ain't stretchin' the truth a'tall! They mowed that corn down just as smooth as your faces when you take a razor across 'em! It was a horrible thing to watch, horrible! Corn stalks were flyin' everywhere! So were men and pieces of men! I cried right then, couldn't help it. I swear I didn't think anyone could live through the poundin' Jackson's boys were takin', and it broke my heart. I thought sure we'd be overrun."

"So did Hooker!" chortled Miles.

"Seems that way!" Ivory nodded vigorously and flashed a grin in Turner's direction.

"Then what happened?" Wil was impatient to hear more.

"Then they stopped shootin' their cannons and sent all that infantry at us again. Stonewall opened up with everything he had, and believe me he had a lot more than anybody expected. Yankees was fallin' all over the place, not one or two at a time mind you, they was goin' down by the dozens! Problem was there was too many of 'em and Jackson was spread too thin. He couldn't hold 'em and he knew it. Our boys finally broke and headed back toward that church I told you about, and I was runnin' in front of em! We reached the church and the Yankees was close on our heels, but they wasn't close enough. Guess who saved the day?"

"Hood!" someone cried.

"Sho'nuff!" grinned Ivory. "The Texans! I've been sayin' all along them Texans is a wild bunch, haven't I?" he glanced directly at Wil seeking an answer.

"Sure have!" Covington nodded. "More times

BROTHERS IN GRAY

than I can rightly recollect."

"They're wild all right!" continued Ivory.
"And Hooker's boys couldn't handle 'em. Out of the woods they came, chargin' them Yankees madder'n Hell! You would be too if someone interrupted the only meal you'd had in three days! Ain't that right? Anyway it was like someone done stuck a stick into a nest full of yellow jackets! They stormed out of the trees and ran to within point blank range of the bluecoats and let 'em have it! One good volley tore that Federal line to shreds! But Hood wasn't content to just stop the Yankees. He planned on driven' 'em and drive 'em they did! All the way back across the cornfield they ran, with Hood's boys chasin' 'em every inch of the way!

"I was proud of them boys I tell ya, proud! They was hollerin' and screamin'! Shoutin' and jeerin' at the Yanks! Darin' 'em to stand and fight! The Texans fought like lions they did! I remember seein' that one officer, the one they call 'Howdy'. He was magnificent at Sharpsburg, just magnificent!

"Anyway, Hooker's boys done stopped when they got to the far side of the cornfield and they formed ranks behind a line of guns. By this time the sun was well up and had burned off the clouds and mist. From where I was standin' I could see the sunlight gleamin' off the bayonets of both lines, Hooker's and Hood's, and I watched as they stood there and poured lead into each other's ranks, Hood knew he had to hold on and give Jackson time to reorganize, but he only had 2400 men and Hooker was out there with his whole corps and more on the way!

"As for Jackson, he had his work cut out for him. His boys had been chewed up pretty thorough, especially the officers. General Jones was down. Starke went down. Lawton was dead and all but two of his regimental commanders were killed or wounded. There was a colonel in charge of an entire division! Stonewall's I think. Let me tell you boys somethin'. That was just the first among many desperate moments in a long desperate day."

By this time the sun had edged awfully close to the

western horizon and a late afternoon winter wind began whipping through the camp. More logs were thrown into the fire and those present crowded closer to the flames to warm themselves. Those soldiers who had overcoats closed them tighter about their throats and pulled the collars up over their necks. Those without coats, and there were many, made do with blankets wrapped around their shoulders or simply endured the cold.

Within the breast of Wil Covington and that of Levi Henry a sense of pride was fast growing. Ivory had relayed but the first stages of the battle to them but this was enough for them to develop a firm grasp of what took place on that fateful day in September of 1862. Being themselves part of Jackson's "foot cavalry" they were thrilled to hear of how bravely their comrades had conducted themselves against incredible odds. At the same time they were saddened to hear about the deaths of so many of the boys with whom they had shared many a march.

"Soup's almost ready," said Ivory as he sipped from a ladle, "needs just a little more of this," he reached into his pocket and withdrew a small tin packed with spice. He shook it several times over the pot and quickly stirred the mixture into the soup. "Few more minutes," he repeated.

"You gonna keep on with the story?" someone asked.

"Sho'nuff," nodded Ivory, but he didn't step back to the stump. Instead he remained close by the fire and raised his voice a little.

"Hood wasn't too sure he could hold Hooker off for long but he did. Ol' Jeb and Jubal Early came into it from the left and we got some help from D. H. Hill on the right. In the end it wasn't Hood what fell back. It was Hooker. Them Yankees had been tryin' to drive us for two hours and they had done all they could do. Back they went over the same ground they charged over when the sun came up. We was all happy to see them boys run, but we didn't have no time to celebrate. There was another corps of Yankees movin' up to take their place."

"Whose was it?" Ivory couldn't see who asked the

BROTHERS IN GRAY

question.

"It was Mansfield," he replied. "We all recognized him. He had that long white hair just a flowin' down over his shoulders and a full beard too, just as white as snow. We saw him come up and we saw him go down. Someone in Hood's division got him. Shot him right in the belly while he was tryin' to climb over a rail fence. They carried him away and I don't know what happened to him, but I figure he musta died. I've seen a lot of stomach wounds and I ain't seen too many people walk away from 'em."

"Did they retreat?"

"No such luck," Ivory shook his head. "Someone else took over and sent 'em all straight at us. They swept through the cornfield and threw Hood back, even captured one stand of colors from the Texans, which didn't please them too much I'll guarantee you that! Them Yankees came stormin' through and for the second time that mornin' it looked like we might be overrun." He paused there to catch his breath and stir the soup.

"Don't stop there, Ivory! You're just gettin' to the good part!"

"Seems like someone's heard this story befo'," chuckled Ivory, who paused to clear his throat before he resumed the saga of Sharpsburg. "Earlier that mornin' when Stonewall was hard pressed he sent word to Marse Robert that he had to have reinforcements, so the General sent General Walker's division from way down on the right side of our line. North Carolina boys they were, two brigades of 'em! They didn't arrive in time to stop Hooker, Hood done took care of that, but they reached us just in time to stop Mansfield's boys cold in their tracks, just shy of the Dunker church same as Hooker! This time it was different though. These Yanks wouldn't pull back. They just stood there tradin' lead with Walker's boys, givin' as good as they got!

"Then a third corps of Federals showed up! This one under Sumner. They came out of the East Wood headin' straight for the church, except they was still in marchin' formation, movin' toward us three abreast, packed in close together real tight, and comin' right at us!

"Now I have to tell you this. I heard a few people complainin' that mornin' 'bout General McLaws. When the battle started he still hadn't arrived from Harper's Ferry, neither him nor General Anderson. I found out later they got to Sharpsburg about an hour after sunrise, but they didn't get right into the battle 'cause Mclaws couldn't find Marse Robert. When he finally did the General sent him to reinforce us by the Dunker church. He was reachin' us just about the same time Sumner was comin' out of the East Wood with the lead division of his corps. General Mclaws saw that Sumner's flank was wide open and he pitched right into it. I think you boys know well enough what happens when your flanks get exposed don't ya? Mclaws shattered that division! I heard later they shot down more than two thousand Yankees in less than fifteen minutes! Sent the rest of 'em scramblin' for the rear! Walker's North Carolinians joined the charge, so did Jubal Early's boys! They drove Mansfield's corps from the field and sent 'em all limpin' for safety, and that was it on the left. Three Federal corps came at us, three of em! We turned 'em all back, every damn one of 'em!"

"Amen!" someone shouted as Rebel yells began to echo skyward from the throats of those gathered around that fire.

"They sent more than thirty thousand men at that one position," continued Ivory who was finding the excitement of his listeners infectious, "and we stopped 'em cold and sent 'em packin'! That's not to say we didn't bend, mind you. We bent like reeds befo' a stiff wind but we never broke! No, suh! Never broke!"

"Tell 'em, Ivory! Tell 'em!"

"7000...that's what I heard. 7,000 casualties among them three federal corps!"

"We showed 'em!"

"So we did," nodded Ivory. "But we paid the price. After the Yankees retreated for the last time I was in the yard of the Dunker church helpin' with our wounded. Stonewall himself was there, sittin' his horse not five yards from where I was workin'. I remember it like it was yesterday. He sat in that saddle straight as an arrow, almost like a statue, 'cept no statue would be eatin' anything and Stonewall was nibblin' on a peach and starin' out over that cornfield. I heard him speak, but it didn't seem like he was talkin' to anyone in particular. God has been very kind to us this day,' he said, and I found myself noddin' my head and givin' thanks to the Lawd.

"Dr. McGuire was there and I heard him give our casualty report to Jackson. He said we'd lost about five thousand men ourselves and those of us who was left probably couldn't withstand another charge. Stonewall just shook his head and pointed out toward the Yankees a mile away. `Dr. McGuire.' he says, `they have done their worst.' Lemme tell you boys somethin'; he was right on the money!"

"Was that the end of the battle?" the question came from a face so young there wasn't even evidence of peach fuzz on its cheeks.

"No, young-un," Ivory shook his bald head and paused a moment to order his thoughts. "Remember what I told you earlier. Sharpsburg was like three different battles one piled after another from left to right. All I've told you about happened on the left."

"What happened in the center?"

"I'm gettin' to that. I was still in the churchyard when we hears gunfire breakin' out behind us from the center of the line. Then this captain yells out to me. `Ivory,' he calls, `can you handle a wagon full of ammo?'

"`Yessuh!' I calls back, `Reckon they ain't yet made the wagon I can't drive or the mules I can't handle!"

"`C'mon, boy!' he says to me, `Got a job for you!'

"I follow him around to the other side of the church and back to the road some fifty yards from where we'd been fightin'. There was the wagon and four mules.

"`You've got to get this ammo to General Hill pronto,' says the captain.

"`Yessuh!' I nods and salutes him. `Where's the driver?'

"`Yanks got him,' he answers. `Don't let 'em get you! Now off with ya, boy!'

"And off I went! I got them mules turned around and started down the road and I realized how strong a position Marse Robert chose for us. That road was the key to the whole thing. It was a hard-packed surface and it ran behind our positions the whole length of the line. It allowed the General to move troops and supplies from one end to the other real quick like!

"Anyway, I got this wagon movin' down the road at a right decent clip and I'm gettin' right close to General Hill's position - that's D. H. Hill, in case you new boys didn't know. Not A.P., he'll be along later - Shells were burstin' in the air and hittin' the ground on both sides of me. Bullets is hittin' that wagon and I'm just-a-prayin' like crazy!"

Ivory stopped for a moment to study the faces of his audience in the fading light. He found all eyes on him, even those which belonged to men who had heard this story three or four times. One thing was obvious: they were hanging on his every word. "'Fore I tell you what happened here," he continued, "lemme tell how Hill's boys were dug in. Now you got to listen careful, hear? Got to have the picture of this place in your minds so you can understand what happened up there."

Darkness was nearly upon them as he paused and added still more wood to an already blazing fire. "The center of our line was the only place that was entrenched along the whole position," he said noting with satisfaction that the soup was just approaching a boil. "The Federals had to cross from the eastern side of Antietam Creek then climb the ridge on our side. General Hill had his men dug in on the western side of the ridge long about a hundred yards back from the crest. There was a sunken lane which wound off the main road and ran across the western face of the ridge to link up with the Boonsboro road. The road was like a ready made trench with split rail fences on both sides. The boys took down the fence on the outer side and built themselves some right decent earthworks. That's where they were when I pulled the wagon off the road. There was fifteen or twenty sets of hands waitin' for me, slaves and soldiers alike. We were quick about unloadin', but not quick enough. We got maybe half of them munitions off before a Yankee shell hit that ol' wagon and done blew it into the next world! Three good men died right there and the whole sky lit up crazy-like from all those explosions. Those of us who could still stand grabbed what we could carry and headed for the sunken road.

"I got up pretty close to the front line myself and for the first time I could see how strong a position that was. When the Yankees crested the ridge they had another hundred yards 'fore they reached that sunken road. They'd be runnin' downhill and would be outlined against the sky every step of the way. Do y'all understand what I'm sayin'? Wouldn't be no background for them to blend into, no hills, no trees. They'd be perfect targets. On the face of it this should have been the strongest part of our line, but I'm afraid it didn't work out the way it was planned."

"You talkin' 'bout the Bloody lane?" asked a soldier.

"Sho' am," nodded Ivory.

"I've heard 'bout this before. People say it was a hell of a mess!"

"They wasn't lyin'," agreed Ivory. "It started when Mclaws pitched into Sumner's boys and mangled his lead division. The other two divisions came out of the woods opposite the far left of the sunken road. Right about then we had two divisions to hold that position, Hill's and Anderson's. Together they numbered maybe seven thousand men but Sumner was comin' at us with at least twelve thousand. Things started to go wrong real quick. General Anderson went down wounded real bad and his division just seemed to fall apart. There was no longer a division there, just a bunch of regiments all goin' their own way.

"That wasn't so bad. In time they'd have gotten reorganized, but they never got the time. The brigade at the far left of the line received an order to refuse its flank. The commander misunderstood the order. He thought he'd been told to pull out and that's what they did. It was a mistake, no question, but it turned out to be a fatal mistake for a whole lot of our boys. Yankees poured into the road and just started fillin' it with lead. We lost hundreds of our boys right there. It was like a nightmare. The wounded was cryin' out in pain. Bullets was flyin' everywhere. Officers was shoutin' orders but not too many folks was listenin'. Confusion was like a God that ruled over the whole sunken road. Our strongest position disappeared just like that," he snapped his fingers, "and those of us who hadn't been shot had only one thing on our minds and that was to get out of there alive. It ain't easy to admit this boys, but we ran like jack rabbits. That's how the sunken road came to be called Bloody lane.

"I was runnin' as fast as these old legs could carry me and all around me every one else was doin' the same. Up ahead of me I saw a boy go down with a minie ball in the heel of his left foot. He was an Alabama boy and a long way from home. I stopped and gave him a hand up. I tried to help him walk but we were way to slow so I stopped again and just threw that ol' boy right over my shoulder. Carried him like a sack of potatoes I did. Bullets was whizzin' past mah ears and kickin' up little plumes of dust when they hit ground. I thought sho' I'd get shot but I was wrong. Got that boy outta there without a scratch on me.

"I gotta hand it to General Hill though, he kept his head the whole time. Did y'all know he had three horses shot out from under him? Three of 'em! Anyhow he knew he had to stop us and stop us he did, most of us anyway. We was right on the edge of the town itself but that's all the farther we ran. General Hill got us formed into a line and he made everybody understand how crucial it was to hold on. This was a thin line, mind you, awful damn thin, and it was all that stood between Lee and disaster. If that line broke the whole army woulda been cut clean in two.

"Back up on the sunken road the Federals was formin' like they was gonna charge, and on they came.

BROTHERS IN GRAY

There wasn't enough of us to hold 'em and we all knew it. You could feel the desperation in the air. General Hill kept callin' for reinforcements but there wasn't any to be had. Jackson's boys had been fought out on the left and the right had already been stripped to plug the gaps on the left and center. I imagine General Lee must've been beside himself cause there was nothin' he could do.

"That's when Longstreet showed up. He was roundin' up every cannon he could lay his hands on to back up Hill's line. Sad to say we lost a bunch of 'em too. It was them damn Yankee cannons! They're bigger and they got better range. They was tearin' us up! I was makin' my way back up to the line after deliverin' that Alabama boy to the surgeons and I came upon our line of cannons. This was right about the same time they came under fire from them Union guns. All of a sudden caissons is explodin' all over the place. Horses is screamin' and kickin', and men were droppin' like flies. I saw two cannons get blown to bits one after the other.

"That's when I saw General Longstreet. He rode up on one battery where everybody was either dead or wounded. Old Pete was a sight I'll tell you that. He was still wearin' the same carpet slippers he wore when we first crossed the Potomac. He had his staff dismount and work those guns while he stood by holdin' their horses. I remember this like it was yesterday. The general was holdin' those horses with one hand and he had an unlit cigar in the other. He was givin' orders gesturin' with that cigar. Shells was burstin' here and there all around us, fragments flyin' everywhere! His officers would fire those guns and General Longstreet would correct the range and they'd fire again! It was somethin', I'm tellin' ya true! They got close to us, but we forced them back. Any of y'all got some water handy? I'm workin' up a powerful thirst."

Someone had a canteen and passed it to the front of the circle hence to Ivory, who proceeded to drink greedily. "Much better!" he breathed after taking his fill, "Now where was I?"

"Longstreet was directin' the fire of guns manned

by his staff officers," replied Wil.

"Oh Yeah! I decided if all those colonels and generals could be in there gettin' their hands dirty and dodgin' cannonballs the least I could do would be to lend a hand. So I grabs me a ramrod and went to work, and then the strangest thing happened!

"General Hill knew the Federals were massin' to charge us again, and he knew we didn't have the numbers to hold off so big an attack. So he figures the best way to stop them from attackin' us was to go after them first! Can you imagine? Anyway he starts askin' for volunteers to charge the Yankee line. I reckon you can figure what kind of response he got; nobody was too eager to go chargin' back up toward the Bloody Lane. Finally, one man stands up, bless his soul, and says he'd go if General Hill would lead the way. Well now I reckon ol' Hill recognized an opportunity when he saw one. He nods to that soldier, grabs a musket, let's loose a Rebel yell and takes off. A bunch of the boys, maybe two hundred in all, jumps up and follows him. They didn't get too far cause there was just too many of them Federals firin' a whole lot of lead. I think they was back in the line again within five minutes, 'cept the ones who got shot." He stopped speaking so as to catch his breath.

"Don't stop there, Ivory, what happened next?"

"Now you boys got to be patient. I'm talkin' every bit as fast as I can. What happened next? Well, right there in the center it all kinda ground to a halt."

"The Yankees didn't charge again?"

"Not there. If they had I mighta been tellin' a different story. I can't explain why they didn't charge. Lawd knows there was enough of 'em. I don't know what was goin' through their minds, but I do have my opinion about it."

"Well let's hear it!" Urged Levi a little impatiently.

"I think we played it like a good poker game. We bluffed 'em and they bought it. Lemme give you an example. In front of the guns Longstreet was workin' there was a regiment of North Carolinians. I think it was the 27th under a Colonel name of Cooke. Comin' at 'em was a division of Yankees. Cooke's boys was out of ammo and he kept callin' for it but there was none to be had. Longstreet tells him he had to hold and to wave the regiment's colors as long as there was a man alive to carry them. The Colonel answers that he'll hold that line, till ice forms where it never has before! And he did! Course Longstreet's staff was pourin' cannister into those Yankees every time they got close - I 'magine that's one reason they didn't take us.

"All across the center it was the same. Flags wavin' everywhere. Lots of bravado. The line wavered from time to time when the pressure grew too heavy, but it never snapped. Long about mid-afternoon the fight in the center just petered out. The Federals had massed a whole bunch of infantry along the sunken road but they didn't come. Reckon they was just as fought out as our boys."

At this point Ivory stopped talking and dipped a ladle into the soup. Raising it to his lips he took a tiny sip. "Oh yeah!" he smiled. "Yessuh! She's right where she oughta be! You boys hungry?"

Instantly he was confronted by a host of hands holding cups, bowls, mugs or whatever would hold soup. "Step close," he instructed, "I think I can stretch this pot far enough to give everybody a taste or two." One by one he filled their bowls. Each soldier waited his turn then stepped aside for the next man. By the time Ivory had served all those present, night had fallen and the sky was pitch black. Only a little of the soup remained and from this Ivory poured himself a bowl which he sat back to enjoy.

Aside from the winter winds whistling through nearby trees there was little noise. Grateful soldiers savored every spoonful of the hot soup. Those lucky enough to get strips of beef in their servings relished every bite. Some chewed the meat for so long their broth had grown cold before they dipped their spoons back in. In this fashion thirty-five minutes passed before Wil asked the one question on his mind, "Was that the end of the battle?"

The Telling of Sharpsburg

"No, suh," Ivory shook his head which appeared to be gleaming in the moonlight. "I done already told you there was three parts to Sharpsburg. You've only heard two." Ivory rose to his feet and stepped over to the woodpile. Here he was joined by two soldiers who helped him carry a bunch of logs back over to the fire. "Lemme get my pot out of the way," he said, "then we can build this fire up nice and proper. Keep these boys warm!"

Logs were piled high and soon there were great fingers of flame leaping skyward warming the limbs of those who were crowded in close.

"Now where were we?" Ivory had pulled his stump close to the fire and seated himself for the duration of the story.

"You just finished tellin' about the center," replied Wil.

"Oh yeah," nodded Ivory. "It died down along the center long about two o'clock in the afternoon, but we knew the battle wasn't over and a lot of folks was thinkin' the worst was yet to come. Right about then General Longstreet calls me over and hands me a message for General Lee. Now you might be wonderin' why Ol' Pete would use an ol' darkie like me 'stead of a regular courier. I'll tell you why. For one thing, I've been knowin' General Longstreet since the beginnin'. Many a supper I've cooked for him, and I'll say this: he's a fine man, that one, yessuh, a fine man! The second reason is pretty simple. There weren't no couriers around. In fact, in that section of the line there weren't too many of our boys still standin'. So he gives me the message and off I go to find General Lee.

"About a half-hour later I'm standin' in the main headquarters. I delivers the message to one of Marse Robert's staff people. I think it mighta been that Captain, the one who goes by the name of Venable! Anyway, he tells me not to go anywhere so there I am. I'm listenin' to all these officers talk so I was able to get an idea of what they was plannin'. Marse Robert had no more people to send to help anybody, and he knew we might not be able to

BROTHERS IN GRAY

stand the pressure if they came at us again. He figured the best way to stop such an attack was to hit them first, and since Jackson's end of the line was still the strongest he'd already sent word to Stonewall to prepare to go on the offense if they could find a weakness way out on our left. Headquarters seemed like a train depot on a busy afternoon. People comin' and goin' constantly. Seems like there was no let-up in the traffic. A little while after I got there in comes this artillery captain with a few of his boys, the only survivors from his battery. He was askin' for instructions. Marse Robert tells him straight away to head up to the left to support Jackson's attack. Now I gotta tell you this: you could scarcely tell whether these boys was white or black like me. They was covered with grime and blood from head to foot. One of them grimy boys speaks up and says, `General, are you going to send us in again?' It was the General's own son, Robert! His father didn't even recognize him till he spoke! That's the kind of day Sharpsburg was. Marse Robert looks at his boy and say, `Yes, my son, you must all do what you can to drive those people back.' So off goes this Captain and his cannoneers, headin' for Jackson but before long a courier from Stonewall shows up with bad news. It seems like General McClellan took pains to make sure his flank was anchored right proper-like against the Potomac. In other words there would be no attack against the Yankee right."

Here he paused once again, rubbing his hands, holding them close to the fire for warmth and glancing up to study the many faces gathered closely to hear the final episode in the telling of Sharpsburg. Most of those faces were those of white men and boys but several were just as black as Ivory's. No matter their race each of them was intent on hearing every word from the mouth of this slave from South Carolina.

"Now," he continued, "now I'm gonna tell you boys about Burnside's bridge and how Sharpsburg came to an end. General Lee looks straight at me. `Ivory,' he says, 'cause he knows me too. I done cooked a meal or two for Marse Robert. So he says, `Ivory, can I trust you to get a message over to General Toombs? He's holding off those people across the lower bridge on our right.' Well you know I could hardly turn down the General, so I stands at attention and nods my head. So he gives me the message, just words mind you, nothin' written down. Basically, I was to tell General Toombs to hold on at all costs and that there wasn't help to send from anywhere on the line. I gave the General my best salute and took off for the bridge." He stopped speaking and scratched his head a moment as he pondered his next words.

"Reckon I oughta give y'all some background on this 'fore I tell ya what happened," he said. "That ol' bridge is made outta stone, and it used three arches to cross Antietam Creek. This was the extreme right of our whole line and our weakest point. On the other side of the creek was General Ambrose Burnside. Y'all know him don't ya? He's the one we done licked couple of weeks back right here in Fredericksburg! Anyway, Burnside had over 14,000 Federal infantrymen on hand with orders to get across the creek and drive us to the Potomac. Now how about one of you new fellas tellin' me how many boys we had on our side of the bridge? Go ahead now. Gimme a guess. Don't be shy!"

"2,000," ventured one.

"Twice that," said another.

"Do tell?" Ivory's teeth flashed pearly white against the night as he broke out into a broad grin. "I reckon General Toombs woulda loved to see those numbers! No suh. I reckon you're just a wee bit off. It was General Robert Toombs who held our side of the bridge and all he had was a handful of South Carolinians."

"Now wait a minute, Ivory!" someone called out from well back in the crowd. "You know good and well it was Georgians what held that bridge!"

Ivory sat straight up as though he'd just heard the most grievous of insults. "Georgians?" he gasped. "Well I reckon there was a few Georgians there, but they never woulda held that bridge without my South Carolina boys!"

"Here we go again!" laughed Miles.

"C'mon now, Ivory," called another, "you know there wasn't but a company of South Carolinians at that bridge."

"That's cause a company was all that was needed," he huffed. "Y'all just sit quiet a spell and lemme straighten this out." He paused and looked directly at Wil and Levi. "General Toombs was in charge there. He had the 2nd Georgia, and the 20th and 50th. That one company from South Carolina was from Jenkin's brigade. Toombs had 'em posted in the trees along the ridge just above the bridge. Altogether he only had 550 men. 550 men against 14,000! Who's a gambler out there? What kinda odds we talkin' 'bout here?"

All eyes seemed to gravitate in the direction of Miles Turner who had the reputation of a gambler, albeit a not-too-successful gambler. "28-1" said Miles a little self-consciously.

"28-1!" Exclaimed Miles as he sat back and slapped his thigh for emphasis. "Can y'all imagine that? Can you picture it in your minds? 14,000 of them Federals and just a wee bit over 500 of our boys! Who do you think packed the most firepower on our side of the creek?"

"Your South Carolina boys!" cried someone from the right side of the crowd.

Ivory flashed a wide grin and jabbed his right fist in the fellow's direction. "You know it!" He returned gleefully.

Miles Turner leaned over and nudged Wil on the shoulder. "Ivory's got this thing for South Carolina," he said.

"I never would've noticed that," chuckled Wil in reply.

"Now lemme tell y'all 'bout ol' Burnside," continued Ivory. "He had orders to get his men across that creek and he started right about the time Hooker was hittin' us at the Dunker church. Sad to say for a lot of them Federal boys, he seemed obsessed with takin' that bridge. He even marched his troops up the road which ran alongside the creek until it reached the bridge. One regiment after another was exposed on that road and every one of them got tore up 'fore they even reached the bridge. This went on all mornin'. What Burnside didn't know was this Antietam creek ain't so deep after all. His men coulda splashed in anywhere along the line and crossed without even getting their armpits wet! That's a fact!

"I reckon it was a little bit after 1:00 p.m. when I delivered Marse Robert's message to General Toombs. I wanted to pay my respects to the Carolinians but there weren't no time. They were hard pressed...all of 'em, even the Georgians. All day long they'd been fightin' like supermen against terrible odds! 28-1! Can you imagine? Anyway, I'm just fixin' to leave and head back up to Stonewall's boys when a captain grabs me and sends me to bring ammo from a wagon parked well back from the ridge. I heads that way but then all of a sudden like the Yankees is across the bridge! Burnside finally wised up and sent two regiments stormin' straight down the hill onto the bridge instead of walkin' 'em up that road!"

He paused there and reached out for a small cup of what passed for coffee in the Confederate. army. Someone in the crowd had just poured it and passed it to him. After taking three quick sips he resumed his story. "It wasn't just the ones who stormed over the bridge," he explained. "The Yankees finally found themselves a ford well down from the bridge and put a sizeable force on our side of the creek. They were rolling up Toomb's right in a hurry and the General knew he'd best get his boys out of there or they'd be overrun. I was comin' up with a crate of cartridges when I saw 'em withdrawin' from the creek ridge. They wasn't routed mind you. None of 'em panicked. None of 'em ran. Looked to me like they was conductin' a good orderly retreat. I fell in with 'em and we ended up on the last ridge before the town of Sharpsburg itself. Longstreet was there along with about 2,000 men. Toombs added his 500 and together we prepared to face four Yankee divisions!"

"Did we hold?" This question came from a wide-eyed drummer boy who couldn't have been more than twelve years of age.

"Well, son, at first we didn't have to. The attack didn't come right away. We found out later from prisoners that Burnside's lead division, the one that got across, was just about out of ammo. So he pulled them back and plugged in a fresh one. All this took time so it was late in the afternoon before they finally charged us.

"Up they came and believe me there was a whole lot of 'em! We started givin' ground 'cause there was just too many of 'em. Right about then a captain grabs me by the arm and points me toward a wagon full of wounded men and orders me to get 'em out of there. I tell you what, it was gettin' awful hot right about then. Shells burstin' all over the place! The air was alive with the buzzin' of minie balls. They was flyin' like a swarm of yellow jackets! When that captain told me to get them wounded boys outta there, I was only too happy to oblige!

"I got down into Sharpsburg and what I saw scared me no end! The town was full of our boys, the wounded and the ones who were just too tired to take another step. That's when I saw panic for the first time. Yankee shells were rainin' on that poor little town. Wall's were explodin'! Roofs cavin' in! Men and women alike were screamin' for help and runnin' all over the place!

"From the town we could look up and see the ridge where Longstreet and Toombs was tryin' to hold on. Blue flags, that is to say Yankee flags, was poppin' up all along that ridge. All of us knew that if the Yankees broke through here the game was up! There was only a mile between the Federals and the Shepherdstown road. If they reached that road they could cut our whole army off from the only ford leadin' across the Potomac, our only route of escape. We was all holdin' our breath right about then, dodgin' Yankee shells and watchin' those blue flags movin' toward us from the ridge."

"What happened?" demanded the same drummer boy as Ivory sipped gingerly from his mug of coffee.

"Got to be patient, young-un," Ivory held up one

hand palm outward. "Got to be patient. I stayed in the town helpin' with the wounded for the rest of the battle. But I found out what happened later on by talkin' with some folks and listenin' to others. This is how it ended up. Marse Robert was standin' outside his field tent watchin' the battle when he looked to his right and spied a column of troops comin up from the Southeast. There was a caisson rollin' by on the way to the front line and General Lee calls out to the lieutenant in charge. `What troops are those?' he asks. This lieutenant starts to hand him a telescope, but Marse Robert held up his bandaged hand and tells him he can't use the lookin' glass. So the lieutenant uses it and when he lowered it he turned to Marse Robert and tells him those troops was flyin' the United States Flag. Now you boys listen careful-like, you hear? This was the most dangerous moment in the whole battle cause it looked like we was done for. Federals was already movin' into the eastern edge of the town and we was in deep trouble! There weren't but an hour of daylight left and our boys was clingin' to their lines with just their fingernails! Marse Robert spotted another column, this one comin' up from the Southwest. `What troops are those?' he asks again, and once more that lieutenant raises the glass. When he lowered it there was a smile on his face. He says to Lee, `They are flyin' the Virginia and Confederate flags.' No one knows what was goin' through Marse Robert's mind right then cause he was just as calm as a river's water on a still night. Now who do you suppose was at the head of that second column?"

"A.P. Hill!" shouted a soldier who was listening to this story for the third time.

"Sho'nuff!" replied Ivory with a slap of his knee. "And that's almost what General Lee said!"

"What did he say?" The drummer boy wanted every detail.

"Well, he just turns to that lieutenant and says, `It is A. P. Hill from Harpers Ferry.'"

"Was he in time?"

"Was he ever! Harper's Ferry was 17 miles away

and A. P. done left at 6:30 in the mornin' with five of his brigades, 5,000 men in all. I'm tellin' you those boys marched harder than they ever had before! A. P. was on his horse and he was proddin' the stragglers with the point of his saber. No time for rest! He drove them boys like a herd of cattle! All the day long they could hear the sounds of this battle driftin' in the air. Those boys pushed themselves beyond the limits of what they could endure! They started out with 5,000 men but 2,000 of 'em dropped from exhaustion before they ever reached Sharpsburg! When they came on the field A. P. saw right away how desperate our situation was. He only had 3,000 men still on their feet but he pitched straight into the Yankees! No time for rest! No time to deploy! Just charge! A. P. was in front of 'em all! He weren't wearin' no uniform. He had his battle shirt on. You know the one I mean! That ol' red shirt led them boys into the fight!"

He stopped for a moment and drained the rest of his coffee in one gulp, wiping his mouth with the forearm of his sleeve. The campfire seemed to dance in his eyes as Ivory himself became caught up in the final climatic moments of the telling.

"There weren't but 3,000 of 'em," he explained, "and they was chargin' into at least 12,000 Yankees! At least! Any of you boys ever been in a good fist fight! Y'all know it ain't the size of the fist that matters. It's the power behind the punch! That's what A. P.'s boys had...power! They tore into the left of the Yankee line and sent 'em scramblin' for their lives! Now a lot of his boys had on blue uniforms they took at Harper's Ferry. That confused the Yankees. Plus a lot of them Federal boys was brand new. They was in their first battle and A. P. made it the last battle for a bunch of 'em!

"On they came, just-a-yellin' somethin' fierce! They cleaned the Federals out of the eastern end of the town and the Yankees started to panic! Burnside's whole line came unhinged right there! The Federals was so close to reachin' the Shepherdstown road they could spit and almost hit it, but that was as close as they got! A. P. Hill's boys drove 'em back toward Antietam creek! Longstreet and Toombs joined in and they chased the Federals all the way back to that ridge where my South Carolina boys spent the mornin'!"

He paused here and took a deep breath, his face more animated than ever it had been. "That was it," he sighed. "The sun set and twilight settled over the land. It was an eerie sight, I'm tellin' ya true. There was this amber glow in the air. Some from the sunset I reckon. Some from all the fires burnin' in the fields. Seemed like smoke was everywhere. You couldn't breath without it stingin' your nostrils. I remember seein' General Longstreet in the town. He was on his way to deliver his report to General Lee and he stopped to help some folks put out the fire in their house. We was all numb inside. Most folks was too tired to even stand up. There were still hundreds of wounded from both sides on the field. They was huddled behind rocks or sittin' by fences. All through the evenin' you could hear 'em cryin' out for help or just groanin' in pain. Lawd, what a night that was. They kept me in town with the surgeons and it seems like I worked all night long, and still there was more wounded comin' in. I remember someone askin' Hood where his division of Texans was. He just said they was out in the field...dead.

"Word is that all the generals wanted to retreat cause we lost about a quarter of our army. Marse Robert didn't agree. The way he figured it, if McClellan wanted to fight again the next day, we'd oblige him. Lee ordered everybody to stay in place and cook rations. So stay we did.

"All night long we could hear the groans of the wounded out there between the lines. Both sides sent out parties to bring in the wounded boys, so you might say there was a truce of sorts between us.

"The sun came up the next mornin' and anybody who thought the whole thing was just a bad dream knew otherwise when he looked out over that battlefield. There was thousands of bodies lyin' out there. Thousands of 'em. We braced ourselves for McClellan to come again but he never did budge. I reckon we both just kinda fought each other to a standstill. They say it was the bloodiest single day in the history of America, and I reckon they say it true.

"There weren't no fightin' that second day. There was lots of truce parties from both sides out between the lines lookin' for anybody who was still alive. Wasn't hard to tell the dead ones. It was hot that day and their bodies was bloatin' somethin' awful under that blazin' sun. It was a day I'd just as soon forget.

"That evenin' Marse Robert decided to pull out and get us back into Virginia. Any of you who think this was an easy thing to do have got to be dreamin'! We had only that one ford to use and it was probably the most narrow ford on the whole river. We waited until after dark and we lit the campfires nice and bright. Volunteers stayed close to 'em and kept 'em burnin' all through the night. The rest of the army pulled out and started across.

"You have no idea how hard it was to pull off that retreat. There was only room for one wagon at a time to pass across the ford. It was pitch black out there on the river. Everyone was kinda holdin' their breath cause if one wagon broke down the ford would be blocked. If a team of mules strayed more than a couple of feet to the left or right we'd lose a wagon to deep water. It was a long night, I'll tell ya true!

"I didn't get my own wagon back straight away. They kept me in Sharpsburg to work with the wounded, so I was one of the last to leave. The passage over the Potomac took the whole night. General Walker's troops was the last to cross and I drove my wagon into the ford right behind them. There were ten wounded men in my wagon, some of 'em hurt mighty bad! The wagon was bumpin' and bouncin' and I'm sure those boys were feelin' the pain, but they held their tongues.

"The sun was up by this time so I could at least see where I was goin'. And then I saw him. It was General Lee himself sittin' his horse in the middle of the river just to the side of the ford. I heard later he'd been out there all night watchin' the army pass into Virginia. General Walker was there and he told Marse Robert that we were the last. I could see the General's face when he heard that. I could see the relief on his face and I could almost feel the tension leavin' his muscles. And I heard what he said to General Walker. He said, `Thank God,' that's all he said, just `Thank God.'

"I was next to pass him and when I caught his eye I doffed my hat and said, `God Bless you, General Lee. God keep you, suh.' This is somethin' I'll remember so long as I live. He looked at me and smiled, nodded his head and tipped his hat - you boys know how he does sometimes. Then he says to me, `May He keep you as well, my friend, and those you're carryin' home.'"

Here he stopped at last and with one burly hand on each knee he sat back and breathed deeply, still savoring the memory of his encounter with Robert E. Lee. No one spoke. For hours they had been hanging on his every word and now that he was finished it was almost as if they wanted the story to go on for hours more.

"Lemme tell y'all one more thing," he said after a minute or two and again all eyes were riveted on the slave from South Carolina. "Wil and Levi here ain't been with us for a spell. They been up in Maryland and they been readin' what the Yankees had to say 'bout Sharpsburg."

"Up there they call it Antietam," said Wil.

"Whatever they call it," countered Ivory. "Those papers been sayin' they whupped us. Not so. They didn't whup nobody. That fella McClellan had in mind to push us into the Potomac River. He failed. Every time they pushed us we stopped 'em cold and rolled 'em back. When you think 'bout how few we are and how many they had then you know which army is the best!"

"Amen, Ivory!" cried someone in the crowd, and his sentiments were echoed time and time again.

Ivory rose to his feet and stretched his muscular arms high overhead with a loud yawn. "Reckon you boys done wore me out!" he grinned. "Reckon it's time for ol' Ivory to be turnin' in. Yessuh, lots of work in front of me tomorrow. Y'all have yourselves a good night, hear? I'll see ya in the mornin'.'" With that he turned away and moments later he was gone, swallowed by the night.

One by one or in groups of two or three those who had thrilled to the telling of Sharpsburg parted company and drifted back toward their respective camps. One thing was apparent in the conversation between Wil and Levi as they moved off into the darkness. Both felt an incredible pride at being part of an army they believed was the finest on earth. Both were awed by the heroism their comrades displayed against incredible odds at Sharpsburg. At the same time they both felt a sense of relief that they had missed this, the most deadly of battles.

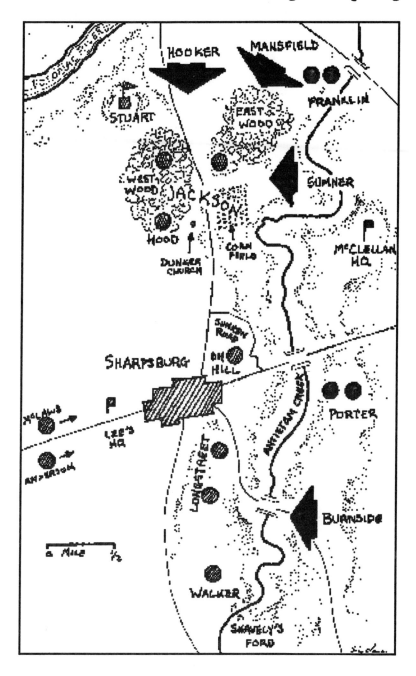

~ Chapter Six ~
Independence and a Chance Encounter.

Wil and Levi spent the month of March on furlough at home on their farms in the Shenandoah Valley. April brought the return of warm weather and it found the two boys back in the ranks of the 5th Virginia. Wil's hip had completely healed at last. He no longer required the use of a crutch, but he still experienced pain whenever the weather was cold or exceptionally wet. The two of them fought at Chancellorsville and were grief stricken by the death of Stonewall Jackson. June brought further cause for grief. Lemuel Vaughn, the same man who had helped save Wil's life on South Mountain, died of an illness while the army was in camp outside of Culpeper. With the loss of so many held so dear, both Wil and Levi were becoming hardened veterans. Farmboys no longer, they had truly become soldiers.

July of 1863 found the Confederates conducting their second invasion of the North, only to be stopped in three days of intense combat at Gettysburg in Pennsylvania. The rest of 1863 was reasonably quiet in Virginia aside from a series of tactical moves on Lee's part which forced the Army of the Potomac back from the Rapidan River all the way to the outskirts of Washington itself.

This was followed by several months of virtual stalemate in Northern Virginia which came to an abrupt end upon the appointment of Ulysses S. Grant as over-all commander of the Union war effort. He who had earned such a powerful reputation in the western theater crossed the Rapidan River in April of 1864. His object was not Richmond. Instead he placed the Army of Northern Virginia squarely in his sights and announced his intention to destroy that army.

The two forces clashed first in a densely wooded heavily overgrown region known as the Wilderness, lo-

cated a little to the west and south of Fredericksburg. Here
Grant learned what so many Union officers had already
been roughly taught: Lee would be no easy nut to crack.
In point of fact the Old Gray Fox defeated Grant in the
Wilderness more soundly than any General he had yet
encountered, stopping his center dead in its tracks then
crushing both his right and his left.

Both Wil and Levi came through the Wilderness
fighting unscathed but they were surprised by Grant's
next move. Rather than retreating as had all of his
predecessors, Grant simply refused to acknowledge his
defeat and moved to close with his opponent a second time
on different ground even deeper into Virginia. The battle
which followed was called Spotsylvania. With one spectacular breakthrough Grant very nearly broke Lee's army
in two, but the breach was quickly sealed and the attackers
finally thrown back.

Once again Grant shifted to his left and thrust
southward. For the third time Lee correctly guessed his
opponent's destination and with the advantage of an
interior line of march the Confederates reached the
North Anna River just in front of their adversaries in blue.
Here it was that Lee set a trap for Grant which would
ultimately prove the undoing not only of U. S. Grant but
also of the entire Union war effort. With its apex on the
river itself at a little known place called Ox Ford, Lee
positioned his forces in an inverted V. To confront the
Rebels, Grant was forced to divide his army into three
separate parts, all of them divided by the North Anna
River.

Lee himself fell seriously ill with an intestinal ailment which left him prone and sometimes delirious.
Despite his illness he could not let the opportunity pass
without at least trying to ensnare the Federals in the trap

he'd so carefully drawn. He dispatched General Hampton with a force of cavalry to probe the enemy's right flank for signs of any weakness. While this search progressed he also created a strike force of 10,000 men under the command of John B. Gordon of Georgia. Among these men were Seth Reilly, who had just received a promotion to the rank of lieutenant, and the handful of soldiers from the famed Stonewall Brigade who had managed to survive the destruction of that unit at Spotsylvania. Wil and Levi were not part of this strike-force. They were in the entrenchments on Lee's right under the command of General Ewell. Facing them were the men of Hancock's corps of Union infantry, the same corps which had earlier achieved such a remarkable but fruitless breakthrough at Spotsylvania. The two boys did not take part in Gordon's spectacular charge which destroyed the corps of Generals Wright and Warren driving the survivors into the North Anna itself. However they did contribute their efforts to the bloody repulse of Hancock's assault, which Grant had ordered in an attempt to force Lee to abort his attack on the Union left.

The Battle of Ox Ford ultimately proved to be Lee's most extraordinary victory. The Army of the Potomac was left in shambles reduced to a shadow of its once formidable strength. At day's end Phil Sheridan was dead and his Federal cavalry decimated. Upon hearing of Sheridan's death Ulysses Grant slipped into a state of shock and command of the army passed to General Meade who was able to extricate the remainder of this once proud force from the North Anna.

Lee wasn't about to let them escape. His personal physician had returned from Richmond with a treatment for the ailment which had sidelined the general. With his strength slowly returning, Lee prepared his army for the pursuit of the fleeing Federals. Gordon's men were allowed to rest for a spell but Ewell's troops, including Covington and Henry, were put on the march. Eventually, they would catch then bypass the Federals and interpose themselves between Grant's forces and those of Baldy Smith who had arrived at Port Royal on the Rappahannock river with 15,000 men to reinforce Grant. At a place called Wheatley's Farm Ewell and his men would do battle both with Smith and Grant before Lee arrived with the rest of the army to drive off the Federals. It was here that Levi was wounded. A northern bullet tore off a substantial chunk of flesh from his right cheek. Fortunately, the wound was superficial. Once it was cleaned and properly dressed he was able to return to duty.

Having been rebuffed at Wheatley Farm Grant swung about and started west: heading for Fredericksburg. Once again, his designs were to be thwarted by the Rebel chieftain until finally he found himself trapped against the Rappahannock with no choice but to seek terms for the surrender of his army. On the day of the surrender Wil and Levi were standing by the side of the road along with hundreds of their comrades watching intently as the Federal commander was escorted by Seth Reilly to the Shaner Farm, and the end of his military career.

Thus did the Army of the Potomac pass into history. Elsewhere however the war raged on and a beleaguered South struggled to maintain its independence. Lee well knew the South could not continue the present war of attrition. To hasten the war's end he invaded Maryland once again and drove straight for Washington D.C. Using a two-pronged assault he was able to seize the Federal capital in a single day's fighting. Wil and Levi participated in the charge which broke the last vestiges of Union resistance. It was here they witnessed the death of young Cody Wilder who carried the battle flag over the last enemy barricade. The boy was felled by a single bullet in the chest and collapsed dying into the arms of Seth Reilly.

Thus began the Confederate occupation of Washington whose principal resident, Abraham Lincoln, attempted to escape by ship down the Potomac river with the hope of establishing a temporary Federal capital in Baltimore. It was not to be. General Longstreet had earlier dispatched the well known partisan fighter, John Singleton Mosby, to the lower Potomac with seventy-five of the cannons captured by the Rebels at Ox Ford. Mr. Lincoln's flotilla of three ships was swiftly destroyed as it attempted to run the gauntlet of artillery on both sides of the river. The president himself ended up as Mosby's prisoner and was escorted at once to Richmond along with a host of Federal officer holders.

It was during the occupation of Washington that Levi Henry began to experience misgivings about his service for the Confederacy. Both he and Wil were awed by the city itself having never seen a town larger than Charlottesville or Winchester. They must have seemed like foreign guests as they gawked at the White House, Capitol and other Federal buildings. However, it wasn't the city itself which fueled the consternation in Levi's breast. Within the city's boundaries resided thousands of negroes many of them slaves escaped from their owners. These people were much concerned with the fate which might be awaiting them now that the Rebels held Washington. Levi, Ivory and most of the other Blacks in Gray were much besieged by these folks who demanded to know what was going to happen to them. Many had thought of fleeing into Maryland, but this was a questionable haven at best. Maryland may have remained in the Union but it was most definitely a slave state: Besides, the

BROTHERS IN GRAY

Confederate capture of Washington had been swift and most of the people who were able to escape had been part of the Federal government.

"I understand," nodded Wil as he stuffed his mouth with fresh cornbread, "didn't you tell 'em what our officers told us? General Lee says we didn't come here to serve as a slave posse. We're to leave 'em alone."

"I told 'em but they all seem so scared. They've had a taste of freedom, Wil. They don't want to go back into bondage. They want what I've had all my life....freedom."

"No doubt," said Wil as he washed the cornbread down with two gulps of water from his canteen.

"We been in this army for two years, you and me," said Levi. "I joined 'cause I wanted to defend our homes and Virginia. Those are causes I'm willin' to die for and I think I've proved that several times over."

"Agreed," replied Wil with a nod.

"But I can tell you one thing for certain. I want no part of puttin' people back into slavery. I'll head home 'fore I have anythin' to do with that."

"You want to know what I think?" posed Wil.

"Tell me."

"I don't think it's gonna make any difference who wins this war. I think slavery's days are numbered either way. Yankee armies have already destroyed most of the slave owner's property and took the slaves themselves. Slavery's finished. It's just a matter of time. Even our own government is talkin' about raisin' all-Black regiments. If they do that they'll have a hard time justifyin' the continuation of slavery."

"You've told me that before, and I've been thinkin' the same way for a long time, but you've got to understand how hard it is for me to look some of these folks in the eye and tell 'em that. They're scared and I don't blame 'em. If

INDEPENDENCE AND A CHANCE ENCOUNTER

I live through this I'm plannin' on marryin' Naomi and bringin' her home to Virginia. I want her to be safe and I want her to be free. We're gonna have kids and I don't want there to be a chance they could end up slaves. You understand what I'm tryin' to say?"

"Fully," nodded Wil, "and like I told ya, I think slavery's days are numbered. You just got to be patient."

"That's easy to say: You try bein' patient when you're surrounded by all those black folks with all those questions in their eyes."

"I know," said Wil with a weary sigh. "I know."

From this point the war drifted into a stalemate. General Halleck was able to gather 70,000 Union troops around him in the northern regions of central Maryland, but he made no move toward Washington. Elsewhere, the story was much the same except in Georgia where Sherman continued his offensive directed at Atlanta until that city finally ended up in Union hands.

All this time Jefferson Davis had been trying to persuade his "guest", Abraham Lincoln, to agree to a negotiated peace. Lincoln managed to learn of the fall of Atlanta and felt it would be more to his advantage if he did not cooperate. However, acting on Lee's advice, Davis replaced Hood with General Longstreet as commander of the Army of Tennessee. Longstreet promptly turned back Sherman's attempt to expand his sphere of control in Georgia and Lincoln's last hope proved forlorn.

Following Longstreet's victory, negotiations between Lincoln and Davis resumed. The talks got off to a rocky start with each side presenting demands deemed unreasonable by the other. Lincoln insisted on the abolition of slavery as a condition for ending the war and granting independence to the Confederate states. Davis at first balked at the idea but after consultation with R. E. Lee and Judah Benjamin, Secretary of State for the Confederacy, he returned to the talks with the following proposal: The South would abolish slavery if the North would pay war reparations equivalent to three times the monetary value of each slave to be freed. Davis also agreed to relinquish any claims on Missouri or Maryland but insisted on the dissolution of West Virginia as a state within the Union and the recognition of Kentucky's secession. There was still a little dickering to be done by both sides, but in the end an agreement was drawn up largely along the lines just described and the long and terrible war between the States came finally to an end.

As the Confederate States of America took their place among the nations of the world, celebrations by Blacks and Whites alike broke out all over the South. Both races were celebrating the independence of their new country, but the Blacks had an even greater reason to rejoice. The days of slavery were over. No more chains. No more whips. Freedom had come at last to a people who had so long yearned for its taste.

Having accomplished its goal of Southern Independence the Army of Northern Virginia withdrew from Maryland and went into camp in the hills just outside of Culpeper. Here, many of the units were mustered out of the service and allowed to go home. It was the 23rd of October, 1864. Two days had passed since the proclamation from President Davis which declared the 21st of October to be a National Day of Thanksgiving. While many of the soldiers in Lee's army were receiving discharges and heading home, Privates Covington and Henry were assigned to a special unit with orders to report to Richmond. Their homecoming would be delayed as they assisted in the processing of Union prisoners held in the Richmond area. Wil and Levi would not see their own discharges until the last of these prisoners was enroute to the United States.

The afternoon of the 23rd was gorgeous. There was a crispness in the air which had the feel of Autumn. The sky was a vivid shade of blue and the Blue Ridge mountains were ablaze with the colors of Fall. Wil and Levi were heading for the wagon which would carry them to the train depot in Charlottesville when they spied Lt. Seth Reilly along with those few who remained of the Stonewall Brigade. Reilly was saying good-bye to the men he had led through the war so Wil and Levi stopped to listen. When he finished speaking and bid farewell to each of his men the two boys from the Shenandoah stepped forward.

"Ox was right," said Wil, "You do have a way with words."

Reilly turned to gaze at the young man who had saved his life at the Second Battle of Manassas. "Howdy Wil," he smiled, "you boys headin' home?"

"Not just yet," answered Wil. "They gave us one more job. We're headin' for Richmond to help get all those prisoners back north."

"Ah," Reilly nodded his understanding, "don't count on seein' home for a few weeks."

"So we've been told," returned Wil. "How about you? Are you headin' for Williamsburg?"

"Sure am," Reilly smiled happily. "And I'm counting the minutes."

"I can believe that!" grinned Levi.

"Do you really think you'll be gettin' back into teachin' at that college?" pressed Wil.

"Hope to. Reckon there's no way of knowin' for sure but that's what I'd like to do."

"You think you could deal with havin' someone like me for a student?"

"I'd be right pleased to see you," nodded Reilly. "Is that what you're lookin' to do? I always kinda thought y'all were itchin' to get back to your farms."

"I am," said Levi casting a questioning gaze in Wil's direction, "and then I've got to make a trip up to Maryland."

Both Reilly and Levi were looking at Wil waiting to hear what he was going to say next.

"Well," he paused and scratched the stubble on his chin. "I reckon I'll be goin' home same as Levi. Reckon we'll both be makin' that trip up to Maryland."

"Why's that?" probed Reilly.

"You remember when we invaded Maryland back in '62? Remember how I got wounded at South Mountain? Me and Levi each met us a young lady while we were up there. Reckon they're gonna be our wives if they'll still have us."

"That so?" Reilly flashed a wide smile. "I remember you being wounded. You didn't get back to us until after Fredericksburg if I recall, but I don't remember anythin' about these young ladies you're talkin' about."

"I guess we didn't say much about 'em," said Wil shyly as his face flushed ever so slightly.

"No need to be shy, Wil." Reilly clasped both boys by the shoulders. "I'm real happy for all four of you. I hope everythin' works out."

"Thank you," stammered Wil, "but when we get back I ain't so sure I want to stay on the farm. I mean I plan to for a spell. Lord knows there's plenty of work to be done. But after awhile I think I'd like to be educated....I'd like to be like you," Wil blushed again and averted his eyes.

"You're not sure," corrected Reilly in a tone of voice better suited to a classroom.

"Pardon me?"

"If you're plannin' on attendin' the college you'll have to learn to speak the language correctly. You shouldn't use the word `ain't'. What you should have said is: I'm not so sure."

"Oh," Wil smiled a little sheepishly.

"To answer your original question one more time, I'd be right pleased to see you at the college. The South will sorely need educated citizens to help rebuild. We've a long and arduous road before us and we'll certainly need to work together. I'm sure there'll be a place for you at William and Mary."

"Watch for me," asserted Wil. "One day I'll show up there. Count on it."

Just then they heard the sounds of a heavy wagon approaching and they turned to see Ivory driving his favorite team of mules. Beside him sat Miles Turner. Ivory reined in the mules as he drew abreast of the three men standing by the side of the road.

"Hey, Ivory!" Wil grinned and reached up to slap the Black man's thigh. "How's it feel to be a free man?"

"Right fine, Massa Wil. It feels right fine."

"You're gonna have to get yourself a last name, Ivory," explained Levi. "You can't be just Ivory anymore. You gotta be Ivory somethin-or-other."

"Well now, young Levi, I suppose that's so," Ivory set the wagon's brake and relaxed his hold on the reins. "To tell you the truth I ain't given the matter much thought, but I reckon I'll come up with a name when the time's right."

"Did Miles con you into givin' him a ride down to Suffolk?" asked Wil.

Turner sat up straight and did his best to feign an indignant expression. "I'd never do such a thing!" he huffed. "Anyway we're not headin' for Suffolk."

"Oh?" Wil peered over toward the white soldier. "Where y'all goin'?"

"Nothin' left for me down in Suffolk," explained Miles. "Everyone I knew joined up when I did and every damn one of 'em got hisself killed. Reckon it's time for me to move on."

"Where to?" asked Reilly.

"Well...since the first day I met him this ol' boy's been singin' the praises of South Carolina... so that's where I'm headin'. Me and Ivory...well maybe we can buy us a farm or start some kind of business together."

"That true?" Levi looked up into Ivory's face.

"Reckon so," nodded the teamster. "I got me a tidy sum saved up. I reckon me and Massa Turner ought to be able to think up some kind of business or somethin'."

"Not until you stop callin' me Massa!" countered Miles with a playful jab into the black man's ribs.I've been tellin' you that for the last two years or better!"

"You sho' have," smiled Ivory, "but you know somethin'? I've been sayin' that to white folks since I learned to talk. Won't be easy to change but I'll work on it."

"I should hope so!" insisted Turner.

"With slavery gone the whole South's gonna be different." observed Wil.

"That it will," nodded Reilly, "there's changes afoot and we'll all have some adjustments to make. Let me say this: We stood together against the Yankees for the last three years and we endured everything they could throw at us. We suffered together. We sacrificed together. Now we've got to rebuild this devastated land and if we stay together we'll prevail just like we did in the war."

"I heard that!" nodded Levi with an approving nod. The four of them fell into a silence which seemed to hang awkwardly in the air for several moments. Each of them knew it was time to part but each was reluctant to say the last word.

"Ivory," said Wil, "you really think you want Miles for a business partner?"

"We get along all right. I think it might work."

"You'd better not let him handle the money. You know how he is."

"Now just you wait a cotton-pickin' minute!" snorted Miles. "You know I'm honest!"

"I know you gamble," grinned Wil.

"And you ain't real lucky with the cards," added Levi.

"Take my advice," said Reilly, "When you start makin' decent money don't let him anywhere near that fella you called 'Tiger.' What's his name?"

"Armelin," answered Wil.

"Keep him away from Armelin," Reilly reached up and shook Ivory's hand then Miles'. "Safe journey," he said, then he turned away and started for home.

Then it was Levi's turn. He too climbed up on the wagon to shake the hands of both men. "God speed to both of you," he said as he jumped down.

Wil followed and when he had said his farewell to the two Ivory released the brake and called out to his mules. The wagon started rolling and within a minute or two Ivory and Miles passed from view, both of them enroute to new lives in South Carolina. For the longest time, Wil and Levi stared after the wagon until at last Levi reminded his companion that Corporal Gilbert was waiting for them and there was still a job to be done in Richmond.

*   *   *   *   *   *   *

BROTHERS IN GRAY

The two of them were awed by Richmond. Never in their lives had they seen so large a city, except when they took part in the capture of Washington. That was different. In the process of capturing the Federal Capital they really didn't have much time to inspect the city itself and shortly after taking control of the city their unit was sent to Silver Spring, Maryland, there to await any move by the Federal forces being gathered in Howard County. Richmond presented an entirely different scenario. The capital of the Confederacy was bedeviled by shortages of every kind, but with the war over and the blockade finally lifted, it quickly took on the airs of a triumphant nation. Traffic on the James River was heavier than it ever had been as ships from both countries ferried Union prisoners back to the North. European ships laden with supplies of all types were now free to enter the Chesapeake Bay and the James River. As for the people themselves it was impossible to miss the joy on their faces. Everyone was celebrating victory and the long awaited end to a terrible war. The city's Black population had even more reason to smile. Slavery had ended. All of the South's people were now free. Surrounded by so much activity in the midst of a city which was rapidly taking on the appearance of a bustling international capital, it's no wonder that Levi Henry and Wil Covington felt just slightly out of place.

On the evening of their fifth day in Richmond the boys were able to get a few hours of leave so they each put together fishing poles and headed for the bank of the James intent on enjoying fresh fish for dinner. Since their arrival in Richmond they'd been processing on the average about a thousand Union prisoners per day. In some ways they found themselves envying their former foes because those men were all heading home, whereas these boys in Gray were still in uniform and still at work. Wil and Levi were able to console themselves with one thought. Every ship and train which left the city with prisoners bound for the United States brought the two Confederate soldiers that much closer to their own homes. As they walked the last few yards to the James, they knew their own discharge would soon be at hand.

"I've been meanin' to ask you about somethin',", said Levi as the two of them settled down on the riverbank.

"What's that?" Wil dropped his line into the water and watched as it was pulled downstream by the river's current.

"Last week, when we was up in Culpeper sayin' goodbye to all those folks we've been servin' with, you said somethin' 'bout goin' to school."

"I remember," said Wil as he tugged twice on the pole.

"How come you never told me about it? You and I....we're like brothers you know? I mean sometimes I know what you're thinkin' before you're even thinkin' it, but I didn't have an inklin' about this school thing. How come you didn't tell me?"

"Don't know. Reckon because I haven't really made up my mind yet. It seems like there's so much to do. Do you know what I mean? Naomi's waitin' for you. Emily's waitin' for me, at least I hope she is. We got weddin's in front of us. Both farms are damaged cause of this war. Our fathers are both gettin' old. They need us, no doubt about it. There's just so much to do it ain't right for me to be thinkin' about goin' off to school."

"But you're still thinkin' on it."

"Reckon I am. It's important, Levi. You want to know when I started thinkin' about it?"

"May as well."

"After South Mountain. When we were in the Havelin home. Actually it was the day the old man came back with all those newspapers tellin' about Lincoln's Emancipation Proclamation."

"I remember," nodded Levi.

"I started thinkin' about how easy it is for governments to manipulate people, especially if the people don't know enough to think for themselves."

"Hold on a minute," Levi interrupted Wil's train of thought, "I think I've got somethin'." Both boys watched his line bob about in the water.

"Give it a tug," urged Wil.

Levi pulled back on the pole setting his hook deep in the mouth of a fish, which dove at once bending the hickory pole almost to the water itself.

"Looks like he might be good size," noted Wil.

"Come to papa!" laughed Levi as he began pulling the line from the water.

Moments later there was a quick flash of silver as the fish leapt from the water in a vain attempt to break free. "Smallmouth!" Identified Levi as the two of them ducked to avoid the splash of the fish as it fell back into the river.

"Sure is!" Agreed Wil excitedly. "I'll bet he goes four pounds or better!"

"Nuff to feed you and me!" said Levi as he grasped the line close to the water and jerked the fish from the river, depositing it none too gingerly on the bank several yards behind them. "Might be closer to five," observed Levi as the bass flipped and flopped through the grass.

Their previous line of discussion was temporarily forgotten as the two of them set about cleaning the fish and getting a small fire going. "Wish we had some batter and cookin' oil," said Levi. "We could fry this boy up right proper."

"No matter," said Wil. "He'll be good enough over the open fire."

"Keep him up high," instructed the black man. "Don't want to dry him out now do we?" As the two of them sat back to watch their meal cook Levi returned to their original conversation. "Since you mentioned goin' to school the other day I've been thinkin' about it too."

"Where would you go? There ain't no schools for Blacks."

"Not now, but I'm thinkin' there will be and when a school for black folks opens up I'd like to be there. By the way, you said `ain't' again. Lieutenant Reilly said you ought not to do that."

"Can't help it," smiled Wil, "You know how it is tryin' to break old habits."

"I suppose," nodded Levi as he reached over to rotate the fish. "You interested in makin' a deal? Brother to Brother?"

"Deal? What do you have in mind?"

"Whenever you're ready to go off to school I'll help by takin' care of your farm for ya if you'll do the same for me when I'm ready."

"Deal," replied Wil after scarcely a moment's thought. "Someday you and me...we'll be the pride of the country."

*   *   *   *   *   *   *

Two days later late in the afternoon they watched impassively as the last of the Union prisoners boarded a train bound for Alexandria. The last car had barely passed from sight when the two of them received their discharge papers. Upon their receipt, both boys tossed their hats high in the air and howled with delight. "Let's go home!"

shouted Wil. "Two days and we're there!"

"Well now hold your horses a minute," urged Levi, "I've been thinkin' about somethin'."

"Now what?" Wil appeared slightly crestfallen at his companion's lack of enthusiasm for starting the trek home.

"When was the last time we went to church?"

"Church? Are you serious? We've been to services in camp on most Sundays."

"I'm not talkin' about camp services, I mean a church. A real one. An Episcopal church like the one we used to go to at home."

"I don't know," said Wil after pondering the question for several moments. "I guess maybe the last time we were home, and that's been a good while."

"Exactly, and think of all we got to be thankful for. The war's over. We won. Neither of us got killed. The South is free. The slaves are free. There's a whole new day in front of us. I think we ought to stay over for one more night. Tomorrow's Sunday and there's an Episcopal church not far from here. Let's pay our respects to the Lord first, then we can head home. We oughta be able to catch a ride up to Hanover Junction tomorrow and hop a train for the Valley."

It didn't take long for Wil to agree to this idea so the two of them returned to camp and prepared to spend their last night in Richmond.

*   *   *   *   *   *   *

St. Paul's Episcopal church seemed rather crowded Sunday morning as the two veterans made their way down the center aisle. They found seats not too far from the back of the church and sat down to await the opening of the service. The congregation of St. Paul's was biracial. Probably a third of those gathered that morning were Black. Most were seated near the back of the church but no few sat with white companions where they chose to sit. As they waited Levi leaned over toward Wil and whispered, "Wonder why it's so crowded? Ain't never seen so many people in a church before. They're linin' both walls."

"Don't know," whispered Wil in reply. "This is the biggest church I've ever seen, but it don't seem big enough to hold all those people. Is today a special Sunday?"

"Not that I know of."

Moments later the answer to their questions walked briskly through the door. Accompanied by his wife and several members of his family, Robert E. Lee made his way down the center aisle to a seat in a pew several rows back from the altar. He was wearing a full dress uniform and walked with an assurance which seemed almost regal. As he entered the church, all of the whispering and murmuring which had been going on ceased abruptly. People craned their necks to catch a glimpse of him and many of those seated by the center aisle found themselves consciously resisting the temptation to reach out and touch him as he passed. Soon, he and his family were seated and the organist began playing the opening hymn.

As the rector of St. Paul's began the service, Wil leaned over to Levi. "Did you know Marse Robert was gonna be here?" he whispered.

"Nope. I just knew this was an Episcopal church."

"This is the closest we've ever been to him. He walked right past us!"

"I know," Levi nodded as he motioned for Wil to be quiet.

The service continued until at last it came time for

communion. The rector approached the rail with chalice in hand accompanied by an acolyte who would assist while he administered communion. Several white people rose and made their way down to the front. TheBlacks stayed seated. By custom they were expected to wait until the last white person had left the rail before they moved up to receive communion.

Suddenly Levi rose to his feet. Turning toward the center aisle he looked down at Wil and said, "Excuse me."

Wil glanced up with a look of horror on his face. "What are you doing?" he hissed.

"Excuse me," repeated the young black veteran, who then stepped past his friend into the aisle. He turned toward the front of the church, took a deep breath and started for the communion rail. Several people gasped in shock and surprise at this brazen attempt to defy tradition. Levi reached the rail quickly and knelt down to wait for communion.

The entire congregation was stunned. Not a sound was to be heard anywhere in the church. Everyone seemed frozen in place as if time had simply stopped. The rector was openly embarrassed. He blushed beet red and appeared thoroughly befuddled. What was he to do?

Just then a lone figure rose from his seat, drawing to himself every eye in the church except those of the young black man who knelt at the communion rail. General Robert E. Lee made his way into the center aisle and without a moment's hesitation started toward the rail. No one knew what to expect. Some may have anticipated an act of violence against this upstart black soldier. Perhaps they thought the General would jerk the black man up by his collar and toss him out on his ear. If any were thinking such thoughts they were quickly disappointed. General Lee reached the rail and proceeded to kneel down right next to Levi.

Young Levi was slightly taken aback. This was something he hadn't anticipated. Just as Wil had kept certain thoughts to himself over the last two years so had Levi. From the moment he'd seen the Emancipation Proclamation he knew that slavery was doomed regardless of who won the war. From that point on, he began to worry about his people. What life was waiting for them after slavery? Would they be able to fend for themselves? Would they ever be regarded as equals? His participation in the capture of Washington served only to magnify his doubts and fears. When he and Wil arrived at the church that morning his mind was already made up. He was determined to do something that would make a statement....send a message. Now he found himself kneeling next to Robert E. Lee and this frightened him because he simply wasn't sure what to do next. Slowly he turned his head until his eyes met those of the General. In those eyes he saw no malice nor anger of any kind. Instead, he saw understanding, patience and kindness, characteristics he knew to be the signs of love. For a moment he felt overwhelmed but this sensation quickly gave way to one of pride mixed with humility. He averted his eyes and waited for communion.

Wil watched in amazement as his Commander walked up and knelt beside Levi. For several moments more all was still within St. Paul's as an uneasy silence continued to hold the congregation in its grip. Then a man and his wife seated several pews in front of Wil stood and started for the rail. Then other people on the opposite side of the church did likewise. Wil didn't hesitate another moment. He rose and started forward, joining the rest of the parishioners, both black and white, as they filed side by side to receive communion.

BROTHERS IN GRAY

Visibly relieved as the tension subsided the rector stepped forward and administered the communion host, first to General Lee then to the black man in the uniform of a Confederate private.

As the service ended Levi resisted the urge to bolt out of the church and waited until the General's party had exited before he turned to leave. He walked out of the church with Wil right at his side. They spotted the General at once standing perhaps ten yards from the door. He was surrounded by well-wishers and reporters but he broke free from this crowd and beckoned to Levi. As the black man approached General Lee held out his hand which Levi took with a firm grip.

It was Lee who spoke first. "I see by the buttons on your tunic that you're with the 5th Virginia. Is that so?"

"Yessuh," Levi felt slightly overwhelmed by Lee's presence but he kept his composure.

"The 5th is a fine regiment. Were you ever shot?"

"Yessuh, a couple of times. The first time was on South Mountain. Me and Wil here were both wounded."

"I'm glad to see that you've both recovered. The South has urgent need for young men like yourselves. There is much to rebuild."

"You can count on us to do our part, General. But suh, there's somethin' I'd like to ask of you."

"If it's within my power," nodded Lee.

"When I was young Wil's father taught me to read and told me about George Washington, about how he led Americans to freedom and defeated the British."

"I know the story," smiled the General.

"And how he became known as the Father of the Country," continued Levi.

"He's truly one of the greatest men Virginia has ever produced."

INDEPENDENCE AND A CHANCE ENCOUNTER

"Yessuh, but I think you've gone him a step better. I think you're gonna be known as the Father of this Country. You've led us to freedom from the Federals and I think one day we'll all be callin' you Mr. President."

"I don't know about all that," Lee appeared to blush slightly.

I do," pressed Levi, "and there's one thing I need to say, Marse Robert. I need to say it for all us black folks. We were there too, General. We stood side by side with the white folks through all the horrors of the last three years. We stood by you. When you're the one livin' in that ol' White House down by the James don't forget us, General. Please don't forget us." As Levi finished speaking he stood to attention and saluted the Commander of the Army of Northern Virginia. He looked straight into the General's eyes and what he saw there filled his heart with hope. Robert E. Lee would not forget.

Thus ends *Brothers in Gray*.

The Alternative History Trilogy concludes with *Gray Visions,* coming soon to your favorite bookstore.

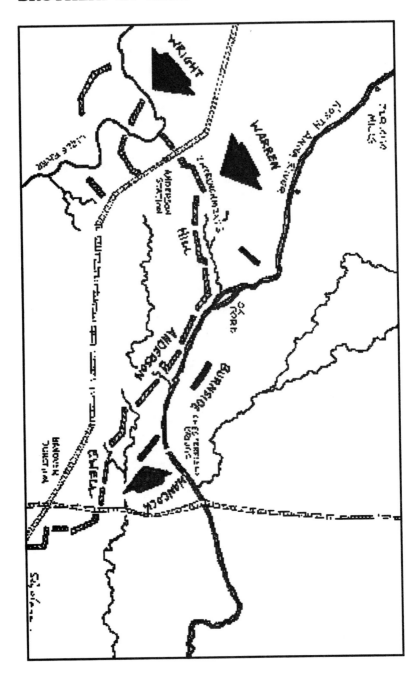

~ APPENDIX ~
AUTHOR'S NOTE

W hen first I took pen in hand to write *A Southern Yarn* it was not with the intention of writing a sequel, much less a trilogy. My goal at the time was to fashion a fast-paced martial adventure which would appeal to Civil War buffs like myself. I also wanted to create something unique, an alternative history as it were. Others have done this before but Gettysburg seemed to be the primary focus for typical "what-if" scenarios about this conflict. I looked elsewhere and my search led me to the North Anna River less than twenty miles from Richmond, Virginia.

There were several reasons for this choice. The confrontation between Lee and Grant at Ox Ford on the North Anna took place late in the war just after the Battle of Spotsylvania, at a point when many assumed a Union victory was just a matter of time. To my way of thinking the trap set by Lee for Grant on the North Anna was clear evidence of the former's superiority as a general. I saw Ox Ford as the last bona fide opportunity for Lee to reverse the outcome most people anticipated. So with *A Southern Yarn* I sprang the trap which was never sprung.

In the process of promoting this novel during the summers of 1991 and 1992 I frequently found myself in the midst of controversy. I am a Southerner (by choice as opposed to birth) and I'm quite proud of it. My love for the South and the Confederacy runs deep, as does my reverence for the Confederate battle flag. This does not make me a racist despite the images consistently projected by the establishment media.

I appeared on talk shows and news programs throughout the South as well as Ohio and Pennsylvania. Time and again I found myself defending the flag and the other symbols of our heritage. It seemed as though every city I visited had its own controversy simmering as I was passing through, New Orleans, Dallas, Atlanta, Houston, Richmond...the list goes on. From my perspective it certainly seemed as if someone was going to a lot of trouble to extinguish even the memory of the Confederacy and to stamp out any expression of a Southern identity.

I've met quite a few people over the last three years and many have asked when the next book would be out. Therefore I decided to write two more and expand the project into a trilogy, in this decision I confess to ulterior motives. The teaching of history is not being well served by the barrage of propaganda and invective oratory currently being directed at the South. Why did Americans go to war with one another in 1861? Today's rhetoric would have us believe it was all about slavery and racism. As a lifelong student of history I see this argument as a gross simplification which does nothing more than serve the interests of the conquering power. So I decided to write *Brothers in Gray*, to be followed by *Gray Visions*, to offer an alternative viewpoint as to the nature of that war.

On the face of it, the use of an alternative history as a means of seeking truth must seem strange. To justify my choice allow me to refer to an argument advanced by Shelby Foote in the Bibliographical Note to be found at the conclusion of the first volume of his *Civil War Narrative*. His words say it quite well. "...the novelist and the historian are seeking the same thing: the truth - not a different truth: the same truth - only they reach it, or try to reach it, by different routes."

I had several goals in mind in writing *Brothers in Gray*. One of these was to simply point out that Southerners of all races were divided over the war and its causes. True, many Southern Blacks opted to serve the Union, as did many Southern Whites. Just as true however is one unavoidable fact. The vast majority of the South's Black population supported the Confederacy and remained loyal to the Southern cause right up to Appomattox. Thousands served in the armed services of the Confederacy and no few gave their lives for the Stars and Bars. With *Brothers in Gray* I simply wanted to make visible a truth which time and politics have rendered invisible. The heritage of the South is one shared by all of her people no matter their race. To bury this heritage would be to sever us all from our past. What future do people have if they allow themselves to be cut off from their heritage?

As we were preparing this manuscript for the press the United States Senate, spurred by Senator Carol Moseley-Braun of Illinois, took time out from the governing of this nation to engage in an orgy of self-righteous rage directed -- where else -- at the South. Obviously the rest of the country has no blemishes when it comes to race relations.

We are told by Senator Moseley-Braun that there is no place in our society for the symbols so many of us hold dear. I respectfully disagree.

The struggle continues.

R.W.R.
~